A MATCH
in the
MAKING

Books by Jen Turano

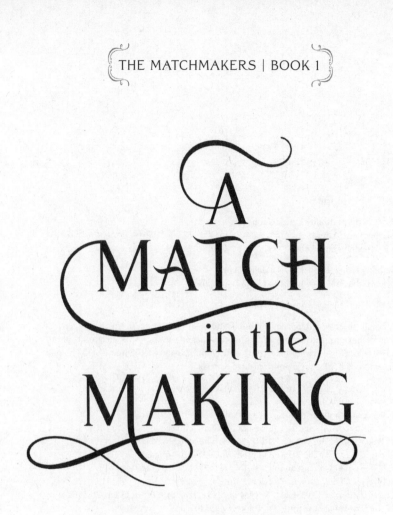

A MATCH in the MAKING

JEN TURANO

BETHANYHOUSE

a division of Baker Publishing Group
Minneapolis, Minnesota

Published by Bethany House Publishers
Minneapolis, Minnesota
www.bethanyhouse.com

Bethany House Publishers is a division of
Baker Publishing Group, Grand Rapids, Michigan

Printed in the United States of America

Library of Congress Cataloging-in-Publication Data
Names: Turano, Jen, author.
Title: A match in the making / Jen Turano.
Description: Minneapolis, Minnesota : Bethany House Publishers, a division
of Baker Publishing Group, [2023] | Series: The matchmakers ; 1
Identifiers: LCCN 2022035043 | ISBN 9780764240201 (paperback) | ISBN
    9780764241345 (casebound) | ISBN 9781493440658 (ebook)
Subjects: LCGFT: Romance fiction. | Novels.
Classification: LCC PS3620.U7455 M36 2023 | DDC 813/.6—dc23/eng/20220725
LC record available at https://lccn.loc.gov/2022035043

This is a work of fiction. Names, characters, incidents, and dialogues are products of the author's imagination and are not to be construed as real. Any resemblance to actual events or persons, living or dead, is entirely coincidental.

Scripture quotations are from the King James Version of the Bible.

Cover design by Kelly L. Howard
Cover model photography by Lee Avison / Trevillion Images

Author is represented by Natasha Kern Literary Agency.

Baker Publishing Group publications use paper produced from sustainable forestry practices and post-consumer waste whenever possible.

23 24 25 26 27 28 29   7 6 5 4 3 2 1

For Natasha Kern

My extraordinary literary agent,
who never hesitates to lend me her invaluable wisdom,
whether it be professional or personal.
It's been a privilege working with you all these years.

With much love,
Jen

One

⚜

One of the most curious discoveries Miss Gwendolyn Brinley had made during her brief sojourn as an unexpected and oh-so-reluctant assistant matchmaker was this—securing advantageous marriages amongst the socially elite was not for the faint of heart and, frankly, could be considered a blood sport.

She'd been in Newport a mere six days, and yet the events she'd attended leading up to this evening's official opening of the Season at Mrs. Astor's impressive Beechwood "cottage" had allowed her to observe underhanded tactics one didn't expect from young ladies of such illustrious social significance.

She'd witnessed an "accidental" punch spill at a pre-Season picnic, seen ladies edging other ladies out of their way with sharp elbows to the ribs, and then watched from the balcony of the esteemed Newport Casino as a lady took out an opponent she apparently saw as competition on the marriage mart by whacking a tennis ball directly at that opponent's head, which resulted in the young lady sporting a spectacular black eye a few hours later.

In retrospect, Gwendolyn's decision to accept a paid position for the summer to afford herself a respite from the drama that always surrounded her cousin, Catriona Zimmerman, whom she'd been a companion to for years, seemed ridiculous, given that she'd now landed in a most dramatic situation.

"Miss Brinley, would you be a dear and maneuver me and this dreadful chair to the other side of the ballroom?" Mrs. Parker, her employer, said, pulling Gwendolyn from her thoughts. "I'm having difficulties keeping track of our targets from this vantage point. If we want to succeed this summer, we must learn what the most eligible gentlemen desire in potential brides. I won't be able to point out the location of those gentlemen if I can't find them in the crush we're currently in."

Mrs. Parker's blue eyes began to gleam. "I'm determined to secure the best matches for the ladies I'm sponsoring this summer, Miss Elizabeth Ellsworth and Miss Hannah Howe. To accomplish that, we're going to have to throw ourselves whole-heartedly into reconnaissance work, which was delayed due to the unfortunate breaking of my leg."

"A leg that wouldn't have been broken if you hadn't entered a three-legged race," Gwendolyn said, taking hold of the handles on the back of Mrs. Parker's wheeled chair and pushing it slowly through the guests milling about the edges of Mrs. Astor's ballroom.

"In hindsight, the three-legged race was sheer foolishness on my part," Mrs. Parker admitted. "But how could I have refused to participate when my partner was Mr. Russell Damrosch? He's worth millions and is known to be searching for a wife. I'm quite convinced he'd be a perfect match for Miss Howe."

Gwendolyn stopped pushing the chair and leaned close to Mrs. Parker's ear. "Mr. Damrosch is the last gentleman you should consider for either of your young ladies. He's obviously a thoughtless man, what with how in his pursuit of winning the three-legged race he dragged you over the finish line after you stumbled and fell to the ground."

"I'm sure he didn't realize I'd fallen."

"It would have been difficult for him to miss, because one minute the two of you were galloping along and the next you were lying on the ground. It speaks volumes about his character, or lack thereof, that he was so determined to win two bottles of The Marsh and Benson from 1809, he didn't bother to notice the grievous injury he was causing you."

"You can't blame the man for being so earnest in his attempt to win the grand prize—1809 was an excellent year for Madeira."

"Considering Mr. Damrosch is a multimillionaire, he's capable of purchasing an endless supply of 1809 Madeira. He should have abandoned his desire to win the race the moment you fell."

Mrs. Parker bit her lip. "I suppose you have a point. It may be prudent to have you monitor his behavior to see if that inconsiderate nature you believe he possesses rears its ugly head again."

"It would be more prudent if you'd simply take him off your list of eligible bachelors. The last thing Miss Howe needs is to be shackled for life to an inconsiderate man."

"Miss Howe will be only too happy to overlook inconsideration if it means she'll have access to millions."

"That's a mercenary approach to marriage if there ever was one, and I haven't gotten the impression Miss Howe's a mercenary sort. I believe she may be interested in securing a love match over a profitable one."

Mrs. Parker waved that aside. "If she wanted a love match, she'd have convinced her mother to approach Miss Camilla Pierpont to sponsor her, not me."

"Miss Pierpont?"

Craning her neck, Mrs. Parker waved toward a beautiful lady with golden hair, dressed in the first state of fashion and surrounded by an entire brigade of gentlemen. "That's Camilla over there. She's a grand heiress, the only heiress, in fact, to the Hubert Pierpont fortune."

"And she's a matchmaker?"

"I know, she hardly fits the standard image of matchmakers, since we tend to be older matrons of society. Camilla's twenty-five, unmarried, and has allowed it to be known she intends to embrace her spinster state forever."

"It seems peculiar for a confirmed spinster to dabble in match-making."

"Indeed, but she's unusually successful with her matches, which makes her direct competition for me. I haven't heard a peep about a specific lady she may be sponsoring this Season, but even if she's decided to sit the summer out, she's surely sizing up the gentlemen surrounding her. It won't benefit us if she sets her sights on one of them for a match in the future. That means you need to get me settled and then get to the task I've given you this evening."

Mrs. Parker gestured to a spot next to the orchestra. "There's Mrs. Ryerson. You may deposit me beside her. I've been meaning to speak with her about her son, August. He's a quiet young man but may be a prime catch in the next few years because he's due to inherit a substantial fortune. He'll only be a catch, though, *if* he can learn to mingle more comfortably in society. I believe tonight is the night I'll present that concerning matter to his mother."

Gwendolyn opened her mouth, then swallowed the opinion she'd been about to broach. Mrs. Parker didn't appear to welcome unsolicited advice from a mere employee, but it was doubtful Mrs. Ryerson was going to enjoy listening to Mrs. Parker wax on about the deficiencies she saw in the lady's son. Pushing the chair into motion again, she kept to the edge of the ballroom floor as Mr. Nash, Mrs. Astor's cotillion leader, called out instructions to dancers weaving their way through a "German" known as the Hungarian.

She was forced to stop when she reached a gathering of young ladies dressed in lovely creations of soft-colored silk, the colors adding a festive atmosphere to an already splendid ballroom. Unfortunately, even though the ladies clearly saw they were blocking Gwendolyn's way, not one of them bothered to step aside to create a path for her. Instead, they continued chatting amongst themselves, acting quite as if Gwendolyn and Mrs. Parker were invisible.

Their lack of acknowledgment wasn't much of a surprise, because when she'd first arrived in Newport and accompanied Mrs. Parker to Mrs. Elbridge Gerry's pre-Season picnic, young ladies and their mothers had been only too keen to make Gwendolyn's acquaintance—until they learned she was in Mrs. Parker's employ. That information spread like wildfire, and after everyone realized she was not in Newport as competition, not one lady bothered to speak with her again.

At first, she'd been taken aback to find herself slighted, because she'd never experienced being labeled an outcast before. Truth be told, after spending the past several years traveling the world with Catriona, she'd grown accustomed to being well received by aristocrats, foreign leaders, and a variety of diplomats in whatever country they were visiting.

Granted, her reception in those far-off lands was directly connected to Catriona, who'd been a world-renowned opera singer before she'd fallen madly in love with Mr. Barnabas Zimmerman and left opera behind without a backward glance. Barnabas had been an industrial titan, and until his unexpected death after a short illness had showered Catriona with affection and love, leaving her despondent after he died, as well as a very wealthy widow.

When it became clear Catriona was becoming a shadow of her former self, Gwendolyn had taken matters into her own hands. She'd always considered herself an unconventional woman and, unlike most of her friends, had never longed to marry right out of the schoolroom and settle into wedded bliss. Because of that, she'd not hesitated to insist Catriona embark with her on a world tour, taking on the role of her cousin's companion—a position Catriona wholeheartedly approved of, because when she wasn't despondent, she knew full well she was capable of attracting trouble on a concerningly frequent basis.

Traveling the world had seen Catriona begin to heal from the devastation of losing her Barnabas, while Gwendolyn had been given the privilege of meeting fascinating people who genuinely seemed to enjoy spending time in her company.

But not once in her travels had she run across the blatant snobbery she was encountering in Newport. She'd been warned that Newport was one of the most pretentious summer retreats in the country, but not putting much stock in the warnings, she'd accepted Mrs. Parker's offer.

She'd believed summering in Newport as a paid companion would provide her with a much-needed rest from her travels, as well as a well-deserved reprieve from her cousin. Unfortunately, rest and relaxation seemed in short supply these days.

"Ladies, good heavens," Mrs. Parker barked, snapping Gwendolyn back to the situation at hand. "Have you failed to notice that Miss Brinley is trying to push me to the other side of the ballroom? She certainly can't be expected to plow through all of you, unless she doesn't mind taking out a few of your limbs, which I'm going to assume she *would* mind. You need to make a path for us—and quickly, if you please."

A chorus of apologies rang out before the young ladies glided out of the way, leaving Gwendolyn free to wheel Mrs. Parker across the floor. She maneuvered the wheeled chair into the spot directly beside Mrs. Ryerson, who didn't look overjoyed to be joined by the illustrious matchmaker. The lady's lips thinned before she began taking a marked interest in the orchestra—not that Mrs. Parker noticed, because she was squinting at something across the room.

"Ah, there he is," Mrs. Parker proclaimed. "And thank goodness, Miss Pierpont hasn't joined him yet. I'm not certain you're ready to go up against a matchmaker of her repute."

"I'm not up for going against *any* matchmaker, whether they're possessed of a wonderful repute or not. To remind you, yet again, I accepted a paid-companion position with you, not matchmaker."

"Assistant matchmaker, dear. You don't have the experience needed to be a true matchmaker."

"I'm not qualified to be an assistant matchmaker either. Frankly, I've been thinking I should do both of us a favor and bow out of your employ before I prove how unqualified I am. From what you've told me, you never fail with making splendid matches. I would hate to be responsible for your suffering a failure this Season."

"I have every confidence you'll rise magnificently to your assistant-matchmaking position," Mrs. Parker countered. "You, out of any of the candidates the agency sent me when my last companion left without notice, impressed me with your no-nonsense attitude and your air of competency. Add in the notion you were a paid companion of Catriona Zimmerman, a lady known for her temperamental nature when she was Catriona Sullivan, the opera singer, and I believe you'll find your summer as my assistant matchmaker downright successful."

"I beg to differ. I have no qualifications as a matchmaker and am doomed for failure. That will reflect poorly on you and is exactly why you should contact the employment agency again and have them send you actual matchmaker candidates."

Mrs. Parker waved Gwendolyn's declaration aside. "Matchmakers aren't a dime a dozen, Miss Brinley. I highly doubt the agency has any candidates qualified for the position I need fulfilled." She gestured across the ballroom. "With that out of the way, your first task awaits you underneath that chandelier—Mr. Walter Townsend."

A knot immediately developed in Gwendolyn's stomach before she settled a frown on Mrs. Parker. "Didn't you tell me Walter Townsend is considered *the* catch of the Season?"

"Indeed. And as such, it would be a true feather in my cap if we landed him for one of our young ladies." Mrs. Parker rubbed her hands together. "I adore my feathers, so off you go. And remember, I'm counting on you to not let me down."

Two

The knot in Gwendolyn's stomach increased when she turned her attention Walter Townsend's way and discovered him surrounded by a throng of young ladies doing their best to attract his attention.

Fans were being plied with languid grace, lashes were fluttering like a chorus of butterflies, and well-practiced smiles weren't wavering, each of those smiles settled firmly on *the* catch of the Season.

Gwendolyn swallowed and returned her attention to Mrs. Parker. "I don't believe now is an opportune moment to approach Mr. Townsend. He seems rather occupied."

"Of course he's occupied. He's the most in-demand gentleman of the Season, and for good reason. Not only has he been described as boyishly handsome—what with that floppy dark hair of his that is always falling over his forehead—he's in possession of one of the largest fortunes in the country. He's merely thirty-three years of age. Most gentlemen don't secure that type of wealth until they're much older."

Gwendolyn forced her attention back to Walter, who was bending his head close to Miss Elizabeth Ellsworth and smiling—

a good sign, considering Miss Ellsworth was one of Mrs. Parker's young ladies.

"I definitely shouldn't interrupt now. He seems to be engaged in conversation with Miss Ellsworth, and . . ." Gwendolyn winced. "Oh dear, another young lady has shouldered Elizabeth out of the way and taken her spot beside Mr. Townsend."

Mrs. Parker craned her neck, her eyes narrowed on the lady who'd displaced Miss Ellsworth. "Miss Tillie Wickham. Why am I not surprised? She's a brash young lady and was the one responsible for blackening Miss Cordelia Lowe's eye on the tennis court the other day. The very idea she just shoved our delightful Miss Ellsworth aside is not to be borne, which means you'll need to intervene."

"When discussing my new job requirements, you didn't mention anything about my being expected to do any intervening. Frankly, I'm beginning to feel rather weak in the knees at the mere thought of interrupting Miss Wickham, who is now giggling into her handkerchief and won't appreciate my disrupting her amusing time with Mr. Townsend."

"You're hardly the type of woman to suffer from weak knees, but I will apologize for constantly changing the requirements of your job. I've never had an assistant matchmaker before, so I'm making up job requirements as we go."

"That's hardly fair."

"No one ever claimed life is fair." Mrs. Parker nodded toward Walter again. "But the evening isn't getting any younger, and I know you're deliberately dawdling to avoid speaking with Mr. Townsend."

Gwendolyn crossed her arms over her chest. "Too right I am. Sending me after our biggest fish first isn't what I'd consider the best-laid plan. I should start with a smaller fish, perhaps Mr. E. J. Boettcher. If you'll recall, I met him at Mrs. Gerry's picnic, so he won't find it odd if I show up at his side and begin speaking with him."

"On the contrary, he'll find that curious indeed since he couldn't get away from you fast enough at the picnic."

Gwendolyn tucked a wayward strand of hair behind her ear. "I suppose that's a valid point, as well as good reason for you to remove Mr. E. J. Boettcher from your list of eligible gentlemen. It was not well done of him to seek out an introduction to me and then flee from my presence the second he learned I'm in your employ and not a new addition to the society set."

Mrs. Parker's forehead furrowed. "I must admit I've been reconsidering my decision to let people know you're in my employ. But in my defense, I had no idea at that time I was going to break my leg, leaving me no choice but to turn you into my assistant matchmaker."

"You did seem determined to let everyone know I was your paid companion right off the bat."

"At the time I thought it was prudent to do so."

"Because?"

Mrs. Parker frowned. "Have you not looked in a mirror lately? You're far too beautiful to ignore, what with that fiery hair and striking bone structure of yours, not to mention your green eyes. Gentlemen are drawn to women who look like you. I was concerned that, if everyone didn't know you were my companion, you'd draw attention away from Miss Ellsworth and Miss Howe."

She bit her lip. "I didn't realize society would give you what almost amounts to a cut direct. That's bound to make your new position a touch tricky to implement, but I say there's no time like the present to see if you can overcome society's lack of acknowledgment and attempt to obtain a short audience with Walter Townsend."

Gwendolyn blinked. "I thought I was only supposed to observe gentlemen this evening."

"That was before Tillie Wickham shoved our Elizabeth out of her way. You might as well, after your intervention, use the moment to your advantage and spend a few minutes probing Mr. Townsend's deepest thoughts."

"You definitely never mentioned anything about *probing*."

"Well, now I have, and with that, time's a wasting." Mrs. Parker gave a waggle of her fingers in Walter's direction. "Remember that enthusiasm is in order, and a smile wouldn't be remiss either. Gentlemen always find smiling ladies far more appealing than scowling ones."

Gwendolyn drew in a breath, slowly released it, and then summoned up a smile, one that left Mrs. Parker shaking her head.

"Good heavens, dear, I hope that's not the only smile at your disposal, because it's downright terrifying."

Gwendolyn pressed her lips together before she tried again, and Mrs. Parker responded with a wince—hardly an encouraging sign.

"Maybe you should forget the smiling," Mrs. Parker muttered.

"Agreed. Besides, since I doubt an intervention with Tillie Wickham is going to go well, it won't matter if I'm smiling or not. Given her questionable temperament, I'll be lucky to survive our encounter unscathed, although thank goodness she doesn't seem to have brought her tennis racquet with her tonight." With that Gwendolyn lifted her chin, sent a nod to Mrs. Parker, and began striding along the edges of the ballroom.

"This is the worst summer ever," she muttered, edging around a lady whose perfume wafted over Gwendolyn like a heavy cloud, the scent so cloying it was difficult to breathe. Sneezing soon commenced, and after blotting a now-runny nose with a handkerchief, Gwendolyn continued on her way, the thought returning that her summer was going to be nothing less than dreadful when the lady drenched in perfume called after her that one shouldn't attend balls when suffering from a summer cold, her comment leaving guests scrambling out of Gwendolyn's way.

Three

⚜

With guests giving her a wide berth, that circumstance aided when Gwendolyn continued sneezing, she'd made it halfway across the ballroom when her path was suddenly blocked as a willowy older lady dressed in the first state of fashion wandered to a stop in front of her.

"This is your chance, Adelaide," the lady began. "Many of the young ladies monopolizing Mr. Townsend's attention have now been claimed for the next waltz. Since your dance card remains woefully empty, it's the perfect opportunity for you to speak with him."

The young lady in question, apparently Adelaide, drifted into view, the sight of her taking Gwendolyn by such surprise that it took a great deal of effort to keep her mouth from dropping open.

Adelaide was swathed in the expected pale colors young ladies wore to evening events, but that was the only thing expected about the gown she'd chosen to wear to Mrs. Astor's ball.

Yards and yards of poufy fabric billowed around what might have been a slender frame, additional yards cascading over a bustle the size of which Gwendolyn had never seen before and hoped to never see again.

How Adelaide was capable of walking, let alone dancing, in such a bustle was beyond Gwendolyn, but she didn't linger on that puzzle long, not when her gaze settled on the high neckline of Adelaide's gown, or rather, the numerous frills wrapped around the young lady's neck.

"I have no idea why you believe Walter Townsend will be keen to become acquainted with me, Mother," Adelaide said. "No gentleman has longed to make my acquaintance over the numerous seasons I've been out. It's highly unlikely someone of Mr. Townsend's repute will view me any differently."

"You've attracted plenty of attention over the years," Adelaide's mother argued.

"Not the right kind of attention—and the gentlemen you browbeat into dancing with me don't count."

"I've never once browbeaten Charles Wetzel, and he dances with you all the time."

"That's because Charles is my cousin, and he only dances with me because he's more socially awkward than I am. If he at least takes to the floor with me, Aunt Petunia doesn't nag as much."

"My sister does know her way around a good nag."

"It runs in the family."

Gwendolyn grinned, finding herself hard-pressed to leave the amusing conversation she was blatantly eavesdropping on.

"Yes, well, Charles and nagging aside," Adelaide's mother continued, "you mustn't drag your feet with Mr. Townsend. He's in high demand this Season, what with how it's become known he's once again in the market for a wife."

"That's exactly why I'm hesitant to approach him," Adelaide said. "The crème of society is currently surrounding him, including Miss Elizabeth Ellsworth. She's recently been deemed by Ward McAllister as one of *the* diamonds of the first water out this summer. Diamonds are incredibly difficult for gentlemen to ignore, especially ones who have large dowries attached to their names."

"You have a large dowry."

"A large dowry is not going to allow me to compete for Mr. Townsend's affections with the likes of Miss Ellsworth pursuing him. No one has ever mistaken me for a diamond of anything."

"You'll always be a diamond to me, although . . ." Adelaide's mother tapped a finger against her chin. "Perhaps you're more on the lines of an emerald. Not quite as dazzling as a diamond, but rarer and far more precious."

Adelaide's eyes twinkled. "I love the sound of that, but society prefers their diamonds over any emerald out there, even an emerald that sports the distinguished Duveen surname."

The woman—Mrs. Duveen, apparently—blew out a breath. "I suppose you're right, but diamonds and emeralds aside, Mr. Townsend probably hasn't asked anyone to waltz because he doesn't want to offend the bevy of ladies surrounding him. This may be the only dance he's sitting out, which means it's the perfect opening for you to meet him. Mrs. Oelrichs is now standing beside him. As a dear friend of mine, she'll be only too happy to perform an introduction. That way you can't accuse me of browbeating him into speaking with you."

Adelaide squinted in the direction her mother was gazing. "Of course Mrs. Oelrichs will be happy to perform an introduction. She's with her niece, Miss Cordelia Lowe. Poor Cordelia is still sporting that black eye she received at the Newport Casino the other day. She, like most young ladies, doesn't show to advantage with a hideous-looking eye, but she'll look much more advantageous next to me."

"Why would you say that? You look very well turned out tonight."

"I heard two ladies whispering about me earlier, and they were in full agreement I look like a tiered cake."

Mrs. Duveen frowned. "If they were referring to your gown,

I spent a fortune on it and had it created with Mr. Townsend specifically in mind. His late wife, Vivian, was possessed of a voluptuous figure, which is why I asked Mr. Hayworth for a design that would give you the illusion of possessing curves. I'm hopeful one glance of you in that gown will leave Mr. Townsend completely besotted."

"Or in danger of tossing up his accounts," Adelaide countered, sweeping aside an inky strand of hair that had escaped its pins. "If you haven't noticed, my head now appears disproportional to the rest of my body, what with all these frills wrapped around my neck. That's hardly a look a gentleman is going to want to peruse for any length of time."

Mrs. Duveen bit her lip as her gaze traveled over her daughter. "I never considered the cake comparison before, but . . . you might have a point. The question that now must be asked is why you didn't balk at leaving the house dressed like that."

"You seemed rather enthusiastic about your latest scheme to make me appear more toothsome. I didn't want to dim that enthusiasm."

Mrs. Duveen laughed. "You are such a delight, my darling, but perhaps, in the future, if you feel you're looking like a course that's served at dinner, you should simply tell me." She blew out a breath. "I suppose we should make an early departure and try again at the Harper ball, where you won't be dressed like dessert."

"We're not going home," Adelaide argued. "You spent a fortune on this gown, and like it or not, this is the gown my maid stuffed me into tonight. It would be a disservice to her diligence if we abandoned ship now."

"Perhaps this particular ship was never meant to go out to sea," Mrs. Duveen muttered.

"Too right it wasn't." Adelaide shoved aside a frill that had made an escape from the other frills and was now brushing against her ear. "With that said, allow me to get this over with and seek out an audience with Mr. Townsend." She grinned. "If we're lucky, he will possess a great sense of humor and view my appearance in an amused light over an appalled one."

Mrs. Duveen gave a bit of a shudder. "Now that I see your resemblance to a cake, I'm betting on appalled over amused." She suddenly turned and set her sights on Gwendolyn. "What do you think?"

Gwendolyn winced. "I think I should apologize for listening in on your conversation."

Mrs. Duveen waved that aside, sending her diamond bracelets jangling. "No need to apologize, dear. It's close confines in here, and conversations are often overheard." She arched a brow. "So . . . amusing or appalling?"

After taking a second to consider Adelaide in all her frilly glory, Gwendolyn smiled. "Truth be told, it might be a great test of Mr. Townsend's character to see how he reacts to such a dress. Amusement would speak highly of him, while the other reaction would suggest he's not a man a lady would care to waste time on in the future."

Adelaide brushed aside another frill. "A thought-provoking response, and one that holds a great deal of merit." She dipped into a curtsy. "I'm Miss Adelaide Duveen, by the way, and this is my mother, Mrs. Stuart Duveen."

"It's a pleasure to meet you," Gwendolyn said, dipping into a curtsy as well. "I'm Miss Gwendolyn Brinley."

Mrs. Duveen took a step closer to her. "A Pierson Brinley from Boston is an old friend of mine. Dare I hope you're related to that darling gentleman?"

Gwendolyn smiled. "Pierson is my father."

"How wonderful," Mrs. Duveen exclaimed, her eyes twinkling. "I adore your father because he was responsible for introducing me to my dashing Stuart years ago. They attended Harvard together and became fast friends, which means you and I are practically family and means you simply must call me Phyllis."

"While that's very kind of you to offer, it wouldn't be proper for me to abandon formality. I'm not in Newport in a guest capacity but rather in Mrs. Parker's employ for the summer."

Phyllis's brows drew together. "Why in the world would you take on any type of position? You're a Brinley. Granted, your family name is a tad tarnished, what with Pierson falling in love with your delightful mother and then marrying her against your grandparents' wishes. But Pierson told my Stuart that though his family cast him out after he married Finella, he had access to a substantial trust and has a way with choosing shrewd investments. To this day, he uses my Stuart's bank to safeguard his fortune. According to Stuart, Pierson is one of the shrewdest and most successful investors in the country."

Gwendolyn had the sneaking suspicion her evening had just taken a turn for the complicated, which was saying something given the assignment Mrs. Parker expected her to see through to fruition.

"Mrs. Parker *does* know who you are, doesn't she?" Phyllis asked, pulling Gwendolyn straight back to the conversation at hand.

"Not exactly," Gwendolyn forced herself to admit.

"You didn't tell her you're a member of what Boston considers the Scandalous Brinleys?" Phyllis whispered.

"My family history didn't actually come up during the interview process."

Phyllis began waving a hand in front of her face. "How unfortunate, because Mrs. Parker is a stickler when it comes to whom she'll associate with. Granted, you're not her guest in Newport, but even so, I'm afraid your days in her employ may be numbered if she learns you're an heiress from a somewhat scandalous family, even though I know your family isn't actually scandalous."

She stopped waving and narrowed her eyes. "But again, why are you working for Mrs. Parker in the first place? I know full well your father would never cut off any of his children, considering what happened to him back in the day. May I assume you've taken up this post for Mrs. Parker as some type of lark, perhaps because of a wager lost amongst friends?"

"And how did you secure a position to begin with?" Adelaide asked before Gwendolyn could answer Phyllis's questions. "I would think Mrs. Parker needed to see references before she hired you."

"I have references, and before you ask, no, they weren't forged. I've been a paid companion to Catriona Zimmerman for years."

Phyllis blinked. "The former opera singer? Good heavens, child, what could you have been thinking, agreeing to work for that woman? I remember Catriona's reputation when she was singing at the Academy of Music. Rumor had it she was quite demanding."

"In the spirit of full disclosure, Catriona is my cousin from my mother's Sullivan side of the family, and yes, she's incredibly demanding. But when she fell into despair after her husband died, I decided the best remedy for her would be to travel the world. That decision, besides aiding my cousin with her despondency, also allowed me to pursue the unconventional life I've always been determined to embrace, one where I'm not bound by the restrictions placed on women of some means. By taking up a paid companion role to my cousin, I was given the freedom that would have escaped me if I'd done what's expected—marrying as soon as I graduated from the finishing school I attended."

"An unusual decision to be sure, but . . . ." Phyllis frowned. "Why leave her to take on a position with Mrs. Parker?"

Gwendolyn permitted herself the luxury of a sigh. "Ridiculous as this sounds, I accepted Mrs. Parker's offer of employment because I was in desperate need of a relaxing summer, one far away from my cousin's constant demands. Given the tasks

Mrs. Parker has doled out for me to complete this evening, it's become crystal clear my summer is not going to be filled with leisure time."

"Too right it's not," Phyllis said, reaching out and taking hold of Gwendolyn's hand. "Were you unaware that Newport is the least relaxing place in the world during the summer? Our social calendars are filled to the brim, and it's often difficult to fit in proper amounts of sleep."

"I'm now well aware of that. But in my defense, during our interview for a paid-companion position, Mrs. Parker told me I wouldn't be expected to attend many events with her. She said I would mostly be assisting her with correspondence, reading to her while she got ready for events, and perhaps accompanying her every so often out to lunch or to the beach. Unfortunately, after she broke her leg, she insisted I take up the role of assistant matchmaker. She now expects me to attend every social event available, which means my summer is destined to be anything other than tranquil."

Phyllis's eyes took on an unusual gleam. "You're an assistant matchmaker?"

Before Gwendolyn could do more than nod, Adelaide began shaking her head. "Absolutely not."

Phyllis batted innocent lashes Adelaide's way. "I'm sure I have no idea why you're suddenly looking disgruntled. I was merely asking a question."

"And you'll content yourself with that single question instead of pressing Miss Brinley to find a match for me. She's working for Mrs. Parker, who, believing I'm far too peculiar to ever marry, refused to sponsor me a few years back."

"Perhaps she's changed her mind about that," Phyllis argued. "You were, after all, only twenty . . . ah . . . something, and it's a known fact that some ladies, such as yourself, are merely late bloomers."

Adelaide rolled her eyes. "I have yet to do any blooming,

Mother, and even if I would get around to that, society will never find me anything other than odd."

Gwendolyn frowned. "Why does society find you odd?"

"Because I *am* odd," Adelaide said cheerfully as she smoothed down a frill obscuring her bosom. "But my peculiarity doesn't bother me. I'm perfectly comfortable with who I am—a blue-stocking at heart, who besides loving the written word has a great affection for cats."

"She has sixteen of them," Phyllis said.

"Twenty, Mother. You're forgetting about those kittens I found at Mrs. Gerry's picnic."

Phyllis blanched. "You never mentioned a thing about finding any kittens."

"Must have slipped my mind. But returning to Gwendolyn . . ." Adelaide quirked a brow Gwendolyn's way. "You don't mind if I call you Gwendolyn, do you?"

"While that's very kind of you to want to abandon formality, to point out the obvious, addressing me—a member of the help—by my first name isn't going to improve your reputation amongst the social set."

Adelaide waved that aside. "I'm dressed like a cake. Clearly, I'm not overly concerned with my reputation. But before Mother, who is currently pondering the kitten situation, launches into a lecture about my propensity for collecting cats, why don't you explain the tasks Mrs. Parker gave you tonight. I couldn't help but notice a trace of panic flickering through your eyes when you mentioned them."

"She wants me to speak with Mr. Townsend, or perhaps interrogate him would be a better way to put it."

Phyllis's brows drew together. "Has she lost her mind? There's no way the ladies surrounding Mr. Townsend will make way for you, a lady they've obviously already discovered is in Mrs. Parker's employ. Yes, they'd make way for Mrs. Parker, but her assistant matchmaker? I think not. That means you're doomed unless . . ." She tapped a finger against her chin before she nodded. "We'll have you and Adelaide approach him together."

The knot that had been lingering in Gwendolyn's stomach eased ever so slightly. "That's a generous offer, but I'll only accept if it's alright with Adelaide."

"Of course it's alright with me," Adelaide declared. "Do know, though, that there's a strong possibility the ladies gathered around Mr. Townsend will close ranks against us, but we can at least find comfort in the idea we'll be closed out together. Rejection is always better when one doesn't face it alone."

"A cheery thought," Phyllis murmured. "But you're not going to be rejected. Mrs. Oelrichs is still in Mr. Townsend's vicinity. She'll, again, be only too happy to introduce you, as well as Gwendolyn, to the gentleman."

"Perhaps she will at that, because presenting Mr. Townsend with a society failure, along with a newly minted assistant matchmaker, will certainly have Miss Cordelia Lowe, even with a black eye, showing to greater advantage than ever," Adelaide returned.

"That's the spirit, dear," Phyllis said as Adelaide surprised Gwendolyn by entwining her arm with hers.

After Phyllis told them she'd be waiting with bated breath for their return, Gwendolyn strolled with Adelaide into motion, a comfortable silence settling between them as they moved across the room—until Adelaide stopped ten feet from where Mr. Townsend still held court and released a sigh.

"Is something the matter?" Gwendolyn asked.

"I've just noticed that Miss Suzette Tilden is engaged in conversation with Mr. Townsend. She's been out two Seasons, and at the end of last Season, she stepped on the train of my evening gown, which sent me lurching forward, knocking Mrs. Newbold over. Unfortunately, given Mrs. Newbold's stout figure, it took four footmen to get her back on her feet." Adelaide shook her head. "Mrs. Newbold has yet to forgive me, even though I'm relatively convinced Miss Tilden stepped on my train on purpose."

"That's dreadful."

"As is Miss Tilden, who is known for pranks designed to make her look favorably and others—those who are odd like me—look clumsier than we actually are. Nevertheless, I suppose there's nothing to do but join Mr. Townsend's group even with Miss Tilden present since Mother is anxious for me to speak with him and you need to try to interrogate him—which, if nothing else, may amuse me. I've never seen a matchmaker in action before."

"Don't get your hopes up. I've not seen any action yet, and my attempts may turn into an unmitigated disaster."

"Something to look forward to for certain."

Exchanging grins, they made their way closer to Mr. Townsend, who took that moment to stop speaking with Miss Suzette Tilden and lift his head, his eyes widening ever so slightly when he caught sight of Gwendolyn. His gaze lingered on her, but then he blinked and switched his attention to Adelaide, which had his eyes widening even more. To his credit, he then settled a warm smile on Adelaide right as a lady squeezed her way closer to him, bumping into Suzette Tilden, who was holding a crystal glass brimming with red punch.

It came as no surprise when Suzette began lurching about, but what *was* a surprise was how Suzette's gaze suddenly sharpened on Adelaide, and to Gwendolyn's disbelief, she reversed course and began staggering toward them, wobbling about in an exaggerated fashion before she aimed her glass directly Adelaide's way.

As the contents of the glass began splashing about, disbelief, paired with a hefty dose of temper, had Gwendolyn stepping in front of Adelaide before she reached out and knocked the glass out of Suzette's hand.

As the sound of glass shattering against the marble floor reached her ears, Gwendolyn's gaze followed the trail of brightly colored punch splattered about, apprehension settling over her when she lifted her gaze and discovered that, while some of the punch had spilled on the floor, the majority of it was now drenching the front of what had been a pristine dinner jacket worn by none other than Mr. Walter Townsend himself.

Four

For the briefest of moments, Walter Townsend found himself frozen in place, having no idea how to react to a dousing by fruit punch at the hands of a lady who'd captured his attention the moment she'd stepped into Mrs. Astor's ballroom.

There he'd been, speaking about the weather to Miss Tillie Wickham, when he'd glanced up . . . and there she was, a vision dressed in ivory—and one of the most beautiful ladies he'd ever seen.

He'd been struck speechless at the sight of the exquisite redhead, feeling as if the air had been sucked out of the room, which left him feeling light-headed, an unusual circumstance for him. He'd only started breathing again when Tillie took hold of his arm, gave it a shake, and demanded to know if he'd suddenly taken ill.

He hadn't known how to answer, because he'd never experienced being unable to speak or breathe before. Thankfully, Mr. E. J. Boettcher joined them and asked Tillie if she'd heard about an upcoming storm. Just like that, Tillie abandoned her questioning to answer E. J., leaving Walter free to return his attention to a lady who'd, quite frankly, mesmerized him.

The longer he'd watched her, the more he'd begun to realize it wasn't merely her beauty that captured his notice, it was the way she held herself as she moved through the crowd, confidence in her every step. She also seemed oblivious to the admiring glances she'd drawn from every gentleman she passed, although, curiously enough, none of those gentlemen tried to speak with her.

The reason behind that was explained when, after Tillie's dance partner came to claim her, Walter asked E. J. to perform an introduction and learned the lady wasn't out in society but was in the employ of Mrs. Parker as a paid companion. E. J. then mentioned how unfortunate that circumstance was, given how beautiful the lady was, and then reminded Walter he had a responsibility to his family name and, as such, couldn't pursue a woman who wasn't suitable to take up the role of the next Mrs. Walter Townsend.

Regrettably, Walter knew E. J. was right, so he'd tried to ignore the beautiful redhead from that point forward, spending his evening speaking with a variety of other ladies but unable to keep from seeking her out every now and again. . . .

"You're dripping," Mrs. Oelrichs whispered, pulling him from his thoughts as she handed him a handkerchief, which he immediately used to dash away the punch dribbling from his chin right as the redhead responsible for the dribbling stepped his way, wincing as her green eyes traveled over him.

"Forgive me, Mr. Townsend," she began, handing him a handkerchief of her own. "It was not my intention to drench you in punch, some of which seems to be in your hair."

Before Walter could respond or attend to his apparently punch-drenched hair, Suzette Tilden stepped forward, her eyes blazing with temper.

"What were you thinking, Miss Brinley?" Suzette demanded. "I can only assume you've taken leave of your senses, because why else would you accost me in the midst of Mrs. Astor's grand ballroom?"

To Walter's surprise, Miss Brinley, apparently, beamed a smile as she moved Suzette's way, which was brave of her considering Suzette was bristling with animosity.

"My dear Miss Tilden," Miss Brinley began, "I would love to be able to offer you a sincere apology for knocking aside your drink, but since you and I both know what your true intentions were, I'm unable to beg your forgiveness. I will, however, encourage you to beg Miss Adelaide Duveen's pardon, seeing as how she was supposed to be the recipient of the contents of your glass."

Suzette seemed to swell on the spot. "How dare you suggest I had nefarious intentions. I assure you, I had nothing of the sort. As everyone here can attest, I stumbled. Punch has a habit of spilling when a lady loses her balance."

Miss Brinley inclined her head. "True, but I don't believe that was the case in this particular instance. It's been my observation that sabotage by "accidental" beverage spills is all the rage this Season. And before you argue the point, I suggest you tuck your indignation away, because I highly doubt you want me to voice my suspicions of what truly happened for everyone to hear."

Suzette's mouth gaped open for the briefest of seconds as additional temper flashed through her eyes. "You're forgetting your place, Miss Brinley. You've been afforded an invitation to this ball only because you're Mrs. Parker's companion. Mark my words, you may consider your position in jeopardy, because I intend on speaking about your unacceptable behavior to Mrs. Parker at my earliest convenience."

Miss Brinley gave a shrug of delicate shoulders. "I would expect nothing less. To set the record straight, though, I'm no longer a paid companion, having recently been promoted to Mrs. Parker's assistant matchmaker. With that said, you're probably right about my assistant-matchmaking position being in jeopardy. I'm sure you'll take great pleasure in my termination, since that will spare you additional encounters with me when you feel compelled to aim future beverages in the direction of other ladies you may wish to embarrass, or step on trailing trains that send ladies tumbling about society events."

Without bothering to wait for a response from Suzette, Miss Brinley returned her attention to Walter and grimaced as her eyes traveled the length of his dinner jacket.

"I truly am sorry about the state of your jacket, Mr. Townsend. You must allow me to assume the costs for having it laundered. But where are my manners? We have yet to be formally introduced."

She set her sights on Mrs. Oelrichs, who was standing still as a statue beside him. "I believe it may be too much to prevail upon you, Mrs. Oelrichs, to perform a proper introduction, what with how you seem to be in a state of shock. Besides, there's every chance you don't recall being introduced to me at Mrs. George Norman's picnic, even though Mrs. Parker did perform those introductions, before she broke her leg, but . . . no matter."

She turned back to Walter and dipped into a perfect curtsy. "I realize introducing myself to you is going to be beyond the pale, but I believe the whole beyond-the-pale business got tossed out the window the second the punch began to fly. I'm Miss Gwendolyn Brinley." She nodded to the young lady beside her. "This lovely lady is Miss Adelaide Duveen."

Miss Adelaide Duveen dipped into a curtsy as well, although she struggled to straighten, probably because the bustle she was wearing seemed to be pulling her straight to the ground. Walter stepped forward and took hold of Miss Duveen's arm, helping her regain her balance as the peculiar thought struck that the Astor ball was turning far more interesting than he ever imagined it could be.

"It's a pleasure to meet you, Miss Duveen," he said, earning a smile from Miss Duveen in the process.

"It's a pleasure to meet you as well, Mr. Townsend, although this is an odd way to meet anyone, what with all the dripping punch. With that said, and even though I know this will greatly disappoint my mother, I'll now bid you a hasty adieu since I'm sure you're anxious to get out of your clothes and into . . ."

Walter fought an unexpected laugh as Adelaide's eyes widened and the guests surrounding them began tittering behind gloved hands—the tittering due, no doubt, to Adelaide's suggesting he get out of his clothing. Before he could think of a single thing to distract her from her obvious discomfort—although given that her lips were now twitching in a suspicious manner, he had the feeling she was more amused by her faux pas than appalled—Gwendolyn gave Adelaide's arm a pat.

"I believe it may be best for the two of us to take our leave," Gwendolyn said. "But before I do that . . . " She turned to Walter and settled a smile on him that left his mind going curiously numb. "If I may beg just a moment more of your time, Mr. Townsend?"

He managed a nod, which had her smile widening.

"How gracious of you," she said. "This won't take long, but as has been mentioned, I am an assistant matchmaker, who is most likely soon to be a former assistant matchmaker. Before a termination happens though, I would like to at least attempt to fulfill one of the tasks Mrs. Parker assigned me this evening."

Walter's brows drew together. "I didn't know there was such a thing as matchmakers in society."

Gwendolyn winced. "I'm sure I've just made a bit of a blunder by broaching the matter in mixed company. Matchmaking is probably one of those matters approached with the utmost discretion. However, since I've just tossed out discretion, quite like the former contents of Miss Tilden's glass, allow me to make the most of my time here and get on with that task I mentioned."

"And this task has something to do with me?"

She took a step closer, allowing him a whiff of her perfume, which left his thoughts scattering, until he realized she was speaking.

". . . and the Four Hundred has become aware you've decided it's time to remarry, although allow me to extend my condolences on the loss of your wife before I say another word."

He tried to keep up with the conversation, but his senses were still reeling from the scent of perfume lingering in his nose, which made the simple task of listening somewhat difficult.

"From what I've been told," Gwendolyn continued, "society, at least as pertains to the ladies, is all aflutter about your long-awaited return. I'm sure you'll be pleased to learn you're considered *the* catch of the Season, which should see you enjoying great success in your rumored quest of finding a wife."

Walter's brow furrowed, because to say he was now involved in the most unusual conversation he'd ever held was an understatement. "That sounds as if I'm one of those prized trout fishermen are anxious to catch at the beginning of trout season."

"Oh, you're a prime trout for certain, Mr. Townsend," Gwendolyn said, her lips curving ever so slightly. "And because so many ladies are interested in *reeling you in*, Mrs. Parker wants me to learn what you're looking for in a wife."

"Because?"

"I probably shouldn't divulge all the matchmaking secrets in one fell swoop, so allow me to simply say she needs to discover the answer to that particular question," Gwendolyn returned, her green eyes twinkling. "I would consider it a great service before I find myself tossed out of Newport if you would tell me the key requirement you're looking for in the future Mrs. Townsend."

Walter gave himself a bit of a shake when he realized he was losing track of the conversation, and all because he couldn't seem to pull his attention from Gwendolyn's twinkling eyes.

"You want me to disclose what I'm looking for in a potential wife?" he finally asked, earning a beaming smile from Gwendolyn, one that left him feeling decidedly unbalanced, a feeling he'd never experienced in his life.

"If it wouldn't be too much of a bother."

Given that Gwendolyn was still smiling at him, Walter found himself nodding even though he never disclosed personal tidbits about himself.

Rubbing a hand over his face, he took a second to consider her request. Truth be told, over the five years that had passed since Vivian died giving birth to their twins, he'd never considered marrying again . . . until he'd come to the realization his children had turned unruly, that state increasing over the past few months.

Oscar, his eldest son at nine, had gotten expelled from his boarding school a mere month before term ended. The reason for the expulsion had been failing grades mixed with pranks that entailed flooding a shared bathroom, taking all the doors off the dormitory rooms, and causing a fire in the chemistry lab, although Oscar swore that had been an accident because he'd not realized how flammable oil was.

His twins, Priscilla and Samuel, at five years old, were in a stage that could only be described as monstrous, their demanding ways and constant tantrums responsible for a revolving door of governesses his mother, Ethel, and mother-in-law, Matilda, kept hiring and losing in quick succession.

Some of the twins' behavioral problems were due to the grandmothers indulging their every whim, but Walter had been hesitant to step in, because, for one, society gentlemen weren't expected to concern themselves with the day-to-day issues of their children, and for two, he knew his mother and mother-in-law overindulged the children to make up for their motherless state.

After learning about Oscar's expulsion though, and after

the twins were removed from a birthday party when Priscilla demanded the birthday girl fork over a doll she'd been given, and then launched into a fit of rage when the birthday girl's mother reprimanded her—which apparently caused Samuel to dump his piece of cake on that mother's lap—Walter had realized that drastic measures were needed to get his children in hand.

Marriage seemed the most logical option, because providing the children with a new mother would introduce a measure of stability in their lives, which would then restore order to his life. That right there was why he was in Newport, still dripping a bit of punch as he tried to puzzle out how he should phrase the answer to Gwendolyn's surprisingly blunt question.

"Is it a companion you're searching for, Mr. Townsend?" Gwendolyn prompted, dragging him from his thoughts.

"A . . . companion?" he repeated.

She wrinkled her nose. "Given the blank expression residing on your face, I'll assume a companion isn't your greatest concern, although there is something to be said about seeking an alliance with a lady who has similar interests. That helps the conversation flow, as well as allowing a shared enjoyment in whatever amusements you pursue." She arched a brow his way.

"Are you asking me what my hobbies may be?"

"Only if those hobbies have something to do with helping you secure a perfect match."

"I don't have many hobbies. My business interests consume most of my time."

Her eyes narrowed. "I was told you have three children."

"I do."

Her eyes narrowed another fraction. "Don't *they* consume much of your time?"

"Ah, well, like most society gentlemen, I leave the rearing of the children to the governesses, as well as to my mother and mother-in-law. However . . ." he hurried to continue when Gwendolyn's eyes suddenly flashed in a concerning fashion, "the children are the reason I've reentered society this Season."

Whispers immediately reached his ears as the crowd of ladies gathered around him began edging closer.

"Now we're getting somewhere," Gwendolyn said briskly, taking another step toward him, which lent him another whiff of her perfume, one that smelled like vanilla mixed with something he couldn't quite put his finger on.

"To narrow your response to where it'll be perfectly clear to everyone—how important of a role do the children play in your search for a wife?" Gwendolyn continued, pulling him directly from thoughts of vanilla.

"I suppose my children play the most important role, because I'm interested in securing an alliance with a lady who'd relish taking on the role of mother to them."

Whispers immediately sounded around him again as Gwendolyn inclined her head. "See? That wasn't so difficult, was it?" She leaned forward and lowered her voice. "I have the sneaking suspicion you'll soon be inundated with candidates longing to provide your children with a mother."

Before he could respond to that—not that he knew how he should respond except to perhaps thank her, not that he was certain a thank-you was in order when after glancing at the ladies surrounding him he noticed telling gleams in their eyes—Gwendolyn stepped back and nodded to the ladies at large.

"There you have it, ladies. Mr. Townsend is in search of a lady who longs to become a mother to his three no-doubt adorable children." She dipped into a curtsy. "You're welcome." With that, she straightened, sent him a smile that left his mind going numb again, moved to Miss Duveen's side, took hold of her arm, and together they began making their way through the crowd.

Giving himself a shake that resulted with his thoughts returning to order, Walter realized he'd just participated in the most curious conversation of his life, and one with a lady he found undeniably fascinating. Regrettably, given her lack of society status, she was not a lady he could afford to find fascinating, which meant he needed to put all thoughts of Miss Gwendolyn Brinley aside, no matter how much the lady intrigued him.

Five

―――――――❧―――――――

"I don't believe you've thoroughly considered our current situation, Mrs. Parker," Gwendolyn said as she stuffed a bathing costume into the woven bag she was packing. "In my humble opinion, your only option is to terminate my employment because you must be mindful of your reputation. To make our parting more palatable, I'll take it upon myself to arrange transportation on the Fall River Boat Line. I can organize that this morning while you're off to Bailey's Beach."

Mrs. Parker set aside the paper she was reading on a cozy chaise positioned by bay windows that sported a stunning view of the Atlantic. "Don't be ridiculous. I have no intention of sending you packing, and contrary to your belief, I *have* considered the matter at length. As I mentioned over breakfast, you've become an instant sensation in Newport. It wouldn't benefit me to terminate your employment now. In the spirit of full disclosure though, I was planning to give you the boot after Mrs. Oelrichs told me what transpired between you and Miss Suzette Tilden."

"I think people should act on their first impulse, and because your first thought was to fire me, allow me to pack my bags and get off to the docks."

Mrs. Parker narrowed her eyes. "Don't think I'm oblivious to the fact you want me to fire you so you won't feel as if you're shirking your commitment to me. I believe shirking goes against your nature, which does speak highly of you. Nevertheless, I'm not going to appease your desire for termination, because you've done something I've never been able to accomplish— you've shown a negative side to one of this Season's reigning diamonds, Suzette Tilden. That proves you have substantial worth, and it was only your first night out as my assistant."

"It wasn't a difficult feat to accomplish, what with how Suzette deliberately tried to embarrass Adelaide Duveen, most likely in an attempt to show herself to greater advantage."

"Well, quite, but you see, until last night Suzette was thought to be above reproach. After her punch debacle, and because she had the audacity to publicly engage in a verbal skirmish, her diamond status has been significantly diminished. Her misbehavior has permitted our very own Miss Ellsworth to shoot straight to the coveted spot of being considered *the* incomparable of the summer."

Mrs. Parker snatched up the fan she always kept at the ready and waved it in front of her face. "Besides accomplishing that unusual feat, by announcing yourself as my assistant matchmaker, society gentlemen have learned my closely guarded secret. I've been inundated with calling cards today—not from ladies, but from gentlemen, all of whom long to secure meetings with me to discuss their interest in Elizabeth."

Gwendolyn winced. "It was badly done of me to release the cat from the bag about your secret. In my defense, though, I was unaware matchmaking was such a hush-hush occupation."

Mrs. Parker stopped waving her fan. "Mothers, of course, know how to find us matchmakers, dear, but society gentlemen have always been kept in the dark about the matter."

"Why would keeping gentlemen in the dark be a preference?"

"Not allowing gentlemen to know there are matchmakers roaming about society allows us to use subtle manipulation to get clients' daughters the best possible gentlemen to the altar without those gentlemen realizing they've been manipulated."

Gwendolyn frowned. "I would think gentlemen would be avoiding you now, not seeking you out."

"That's what I thought, until I began receiving all those calling cards." Mrs. Parker's cheeks began to flush, which left her plying her fan again. "If I'd have known gentlemen would come courting me once they learned I'm a matchmaker, I'd have publicly declared my position years ago." She smiled. "I'm now going to be able to interview gentlemen here, in the comfort of my cottage, quite like a queen granting favors as she lounges on her throne."

Gwendolyn folded a towel into her bag, stilling when an interesting thought sprang to mind. "It seems to me you no longer have need of an assistant matchmaker, which means I can either remove myself from Newport or resume the position you originally hired me for—that being paid companion."

"You are tenacious, I'll give you that, but I have no intention of relieving you of your matchmaking duties."

"But the reason behind turning me into an assistant matchmaker was because you lacked mobility. Clearly, you won't need to be mobile to interview gentlemen here at Raven's Roost."

"But not every gentleman has paid a call on me, which is why we're preparing to head out to Bailey's Beach to speak with Mr. Clarence Higgenson. I've heard that gentleman has been asking questions about Miss Hannah Howe."

Gwendolyn stuffed another towel into the bag. "I was wondering if you'd forgotten you were representing Hannah, what with how often you've been speaking about Elizabeth Ellsworth this morning."

"Elizabeth is currently the darling of the Season, but that doesn't mean I'm not going to devote attention to Hannah, especially with Clarence Higgenson showing interest in her. He's the heir to the Higgenson shipping empire, is quite handsome, and would be a wonderful catch for Hannah—even though he's rumored to be fond of a questionable woman by the name of Mrs. Lanier. She traveled in society until she had the audacity to divorce Martin Lanier a few years ago because, well, he was a disreputable sort who drank to excess."

"Clarence would *not* be a wonderful catch for Hannah if he's in love with another woman and is only considering marrying an acceptable society lady to appease his family."

"I doubt that's why he's showing an interest in Hannah. She's a delightful young lady. Any gentleman would be fortunate to have her as a wife."

"But if Clarence is in love with this Mrs. Lanier, *Hannah* won't be fortunate in the least if she marries him. And before you insist he's not in love with Mrs. Lanier, if society is aware he spends time in her company, odds are he *is* in love with her and is merely trying to placate his family by considering other options. That circumstance is something I understand because my grandparents tried to coerce my father into abandoning his interest in my mother, who was not considered society-worthy, and turning that interest on an acceptable young lady, an option my father refused to entertain."

Mrs. Parker sat forward on the chaise. "Am I to understand your father was society?"

"Oh dear." Gwendolyn muttered before she suddenly found it difficult to resist a smile when she realized she'd been given an unexpected opportunity presented to her in the form of an unintentional slip, one that could result in her being released from a commitment she was ill-equipped to complete with any success, no matter that Mrs. Parker believed differently. "I must beg your pardon in advance for what I now feel compelled to disclose, even though doing so will most assuredly have you relieving me of my post."

"I'm not certain you should look so cheerful about the matter."

Gwendolyn pressed her lips together, earning her a rolling of the eyes from Mrs. Parker before her employer patted a spot beside her.

"You might as well make yourself comfortable as you go about disclosing everything. Believe me, I'm all ears."

Abandoning her bag, Gwendolyn settled herself beside Mrs. Parker, taking ten minutes to explain the particulars of her family, during which time Mrs. Parker's eyes widened, narrowed, widened again, then narrowed as Gwendolyn finished her tale.

"If I'm understanding correctly, you're an heiress?" was Mrs. Parker's first response.

"I thought you'd be more concerned that I'm a member of the Scandalous Brinleys."

Mrs. Parker pursed her lips. "That is disturbing, as is the idea your father fell in love with an Irish woman, but I'm more curious to learn why you'd take up a paid position when you have no need to earn a living."

"I told you, I needed a bit of a respite from my cousin."

"But you said she was paying you to be her companion as well."

"Catriona knows how difficult she can be. Paying me a salary allowed her to alleviate the guilt she felt when she behaved poorly, and it allowed me an opportunity to make my own way in the world, never having to touch the trust my father has set aside for me. Given that my cousin enjoyed lavishing bonuses on me, as well as picking up the tab when we visited the House of Worth in Paris, I was able to live a very comfortable life without relying on my father's support to do so."

"But young ladies from wealthy families always rely on their fathers to support them."

"I've always been a little different."

Mrs. Parker settled back against the chaise. "I won't argue

with you there, because there's little doubt you enjoy embracing a most unconventional attitude."

"Indeed, which is why it wasn't out of character for me to accept your offer of employment. With that said, this is where I assume we part ways."

An airy wave of a hand was Mrs. Parker's first reply to that. "You should assume nothing of the sort. I'm not getting rid of you. In fact, now that I think about it, I should have immediately realized you're from quality, albeit somewhat tarnished quality. Your manners are impeccable, except when you speak your mind, and you have an air of confidence one doesn't usually see in companions. That confidence will surely come in handy as we travel through the Season, procuring spectacular matches for our two ladies."

Disappointment was swift. "But if word gets out I'm one of the Scandalous Brinleys, I'll undoubtedly be snubbed more than I already am, which won't help you in the least. It truly will be in your best interest to fire me. No one will blink an eye about that, not after what happened last night."

"Another impressive attempt to wiggle out of your commitment, but I doubt anyone will learn about your family. As I mentioned, you've become a Newport sensation. We're going to capitalize on that, especially since there are a few gentlemen who haven't dropped off their calling cards. Besides Clarence Higgenson, Walter Townsend has not come to call. I have it on good authority he's expected at Bailey's Beach today as well, which suggests our seaside excursion will be very productive."

"Walter Townsend isn't going to want to speak with me, no matter if I've become a sensation or not. I did, after all, douse him with punch, and gentlemen usually prefer to stay far removed from ladies who have a propensity for dousing."

"Do you make a habit of saturating gentlemen with beverages?"

"Well, no, but he doesn't know that."

"You're reaching, Miss Brinley, and besides that, since you're concerned Clarence may harbor feelings for the scandalous Mrs. Lanier, I would think you'd relish the opportunity to seek him out. If you discover he holds Mrs. Lanier in great affection, I'll take it under advisement and will perhaps discourage his interest in Miss Howe."

Gwendolyn arched a brow. "Because you, under that formidable air you project to the world, are a romantic at heart, which is why you've set yourself up as a matchmaker?"

Mrs. Parker arched a brow right back at her. "Don't be absurd. I'm a businesswoman at heart. I set myself up as a matchmaker because Mr. Parker is miserly when it comes to jewelry." She sighed. "I enjoy diamonds, sapphires, rubies, and the like, but Mr. Parker decided years ago I had enough jewels to last me the rest of my days. I knew drastic measures were needed to appease my desire for jewelry and found the solution to my problem after I joined a cantankerous society matron by the name of Mrs. Andrew Stillwater for tea."

"Mrs. Stillwater knew something about the matchmaking business?"

"Knew about it? My dear, she was practically the one who invented it." Mrs. Parker picked a piece of lint from her light blue morning gown. "Frankly, I was reluctant to join Mrs. Stillwater for tea because she's a frightful sort, but during our tea, she shared with me her most delicious secret—she dabbled in matchmaking. She'd taken up that role because her husband wouldn't indulge her love of prime horseflesh. After realizing there were society mothers who would willingly provide Mrs. Stillwater with whatever horse her cantankerous heart desired if she could navigate advantageous unions for their daughters, she threw herself into making match after match, securing herself a stable that's the envy of devoted equestrians everywhere. After learning of her success, I decided to try my hand at matchmaking as well."

Gwendolyn tilted her head. "So Mrs. Stillwater received horses as payment and you receive jewels, but do any match-makers accept cash for matches made?"

"Good heavens no. That would be common, and society matrons are never common." Mrs. Parker checked the watch dangling from a chain on her wrist. "But time is getting away from us. The carriage will be here soon, and then we'll be off for the beach."

"Where you want me to have this tête-à-tête with Clarence Higgenson?"

"Exactly, and if you discover he doesn't hold Mrs. Lanier in great esteem, I then expect you to extol Hannah's many virtues to him."

"I'm not certain how you think I'm going to go about receiving an audience with Clarence—a gentleman I've seen at several events but have never met."

Mrs. Parker's eyes began to gleam in a most concerning fashion. "You'll be pleased to learn I've come up with a foolproof plan to guarantee you unrestricted time with him."

"A foolproof plan?"

"You're going to suffer a near drowning."

"I know how to swim."

Mrs. Parker shrugged. "No one knows that, and we'll use their lack of knowledge to our advantage. A gentleman can't ignore a drowning woman, and since Clarence spends most of his time in the water at Bailey's Beach, it's the best possible way to give you a reason to converse with him. All you need to do is position yourself close to him and begin thrashing about as if you're about to drown. You might want to duck underneath the water a time or two for good measure."

"I'm not feigning a drowning."

"How else will you get Clarence to admit he holds any affection for Mrs. Lanier unless he's distracted? That's not information a gentleman's going to blurt out. But his guard will be down after he carries you from the ocean, where, of course, you should simulate a grave coughing incident before you oh-so-delicately begin interrogating him about the divorcee."

Gwendolyn couldn't resist a snort. "Because that's exactly what a woman who almost suffers a drowning immediately does—launches into an interrogation. And before you argue that point, no, I'm not going to pretend I'm drowning, which means you need to put that idea straight out of your head."

The far-too-innocent smile Mrs. Parker sent her was hardly reassuring, but before Gwendolyn could respond to that, Mr. Hutton, Mrs. Parker's butler, stepped into the room.

"The carriage is out front, Mrs. Parker. Are you ready for me to assist you into your chair?"

"That would be most appreciated, Mr. Hutton."

After the butler helped Mrs. Parker to her feet and then assisted her into her wheeled chair, he began pushing her toward the door, stopping when she held up her hand and glanced back to Gwendolyn.

"Make certain you don't *conveniently* forget that bag containing your bathing costume," Mrs. Parker said. "Even if you're not keen to fake a drowning, you're still going to have to get into the water to attempt a conversation with Clarence."

Gwendolyn permitted herself a touch of a sigh as Mrs. Parker vanished from sight, because the lady was far too astute for her own good, given that the thought of purposefully leaving her bathing costume behind had certainly crossed her mind, since that would put to rest a feigned drowning episode once and for all.

Six

***

It was a disconcerting position for Walter to find himself in, and one that could only be described as an assault of the feminine persuasion.

Looking past Cordelia Lowe—who was still sporting a black eye from an unfortunate tennis accident he now suspected may have been a maiming on purpose at the hands of Miss Tillie Wickham, who was currently giggling into her handkerchief over a remark he'd made about the weather—he refused a sigh when he saw seven additional young ladies marching his way. An urge to flee to less feminine pastures settled over him because he would soon be encircled by a total of fourteen ladies, a concerning circumstance given that it wasn't much past noon yet.

Fourteen was an unprecedented number of ladies to speak with at one time, especially given that he'd brought his children for a relaxing day in the sun.

Relaxation didn't seem to be on his agenda for the foreseeable future, not when all the ladies who'd come to see him today had come bearing gifts for what many of them called his *sweet little lambs.*

Unfortunately, Oscar, at nine, didn't appreciate being addressed as a sweet little lamb, and it had sent him hightailing it down to the water with his toy sailboat under his arm, refusing to return to Walter's side for the expected introductions to ladies arriving late to Bailey's Beach.

If Oscar's unacceptable behavior wasn't bad enough, his twins, Priscilla and Samuel, were in trying states brought about by being presented with one extravagant present after another.

To say they'd behaved ungraciously was an understatement. Their increasingly dramatic moments reaffirmed his certainty that drastic measures were indeed going to be necessary to get them in hand.

As he'd watched his children's behavior go from concerning to downright deplorable, one thought kept springing to mind—it was entirely Miss Gwendolyn Brinley's fault he now found himself in such an unenviable situation.

If she'd not wrangled out his confession regarding one of the most pressing requirements he needed in a wife—that being a mother for his children—he wouldn't now find himself inundated with this level of attention, nor would his children find themselves the recipients of far too many gifts.

While he'd certainly thought only the evening before that Gwendolyn Brinley was the most fascinating woman he'd ever met, he'd now had a change of heart and decided she was more on the lines of vastly annoying.

How Gwendolyn had been able to wrangle out his confession was still confusing, because he, given the delicate nature of the business deals he brokered, was always careful with his words, but wrangle out a confession she'd certainly done. That regrettable circumstance was exactly why he kept finding himself waylaid by one eligible young miss after another.

"Begging your pardon, Mr. Townsend," Tillie Wickham said, interrupting his thoughts, "but I believe the pony Miss Tilden presented to your children has gotten loose. It appears to be eyeing Mrs. Elliott's hat, which, unfortunately, is on Mrs. Elliott's head."

Chancing a glance to where Tillie was gesturing, Walter discovered the pony, which now apparently belonged to his family, was indeed eyeing Mrs. Elliott's hat.

He refused a sigh. "If you'll excuse me, I need to attend to what could turn into a disturbing pony debacle."

"We'll help you," Tillie pronounced, earning nods from every lady gathered around him.

Walter inclined his head. "Thank you, but I wouldn't want the pony to turn its attention to your hats next. It may be best for me to deal with this situation alone since I'm currently without a hat, having misplaced it while attending to the needs of my daughter, who was in a slight state of distress."

Frances Bottleworth took a step closer to him. "Little Penelope does seem to have a set of lungs on her."

Before Walter could think of a suitable response to what was clearly an understatement, Elizabeth Ellsworth released a titter. "Forgive me, Miss Bottleworth, but Mr. Townsend's daughter's name is not Penelope. It's Paisley." She fluttered her lashes Walter's way. "Isn't that right, Mr. Townsend?"

Walter fought a wince. "Her name is actually Priscilla."

"Are you certain about that?" Elizabeth asked as her forehead took to puckering.

Walter rubbed a hand over his face. "Ah, well, yes, quite certain. She is my daughter, and I've been addressing her as Priscilla since the day she was born."

"I suppose you would know best what her name truly is," Elizabeth muttered as her cheeks turned a telling shade of pink, matching the pink spreading across Frances's face.

Feeling distinctly out of his element, Walter struggled for something to say to lessen Elizabeth's obvious embarrassment, but before he could summon a response, Tillie cleared her throat and caught his eye. "Don't let us keep you, Mr. Townsend. You have a pony to get in hand."

When all the ladies began nodding, Walter realized he'd just experienced the novelty of being dismissed. But unwilling to lose the opportunity to escape what was becoming an uncomfortable atmosphere, he inclined his head, turned on his heel, and strode away, whispers that seemed to center around the names of his two sons following in his wake.

Setting his sights on the wandering pony, he realized that, while he'd been distracted by the ladies, the creature had sidled closer to Mrs. Elliott and was now champing its pony-sized teeth as it eyed the elaborate hat on Mrs. Elliott's head.

Walter increased his pace, snagged hold of reins trailing in the sand, and gave the pony a tug. Regrettably, the tugging merely earned him a whinny before the pony lunged forward, almost pulling Walter off his feet.

"That's enough of that," Walter said as he dug in his heels, bringing the pony to an abrupt stop. "You're going to curb that nonsense if you expect to find a home with me at Sea Haven."

He wasn't exactly surprised when the pony released an argumentative type of snort.

"That's hardly an attitude that's going to convince me to keep you," Walter said, blowing out a breath as the ridiculousness of his situation struck him yet again.

When he'd left Sea Haven that morning, he'd been looking forward to a pleasant day at the beach, but his day was turning out to be anything but enjoyable.

Frankly, he'd known mere seconds after Suzette Tilden handed him the reins to the pony and told him it was a gift for the children that his day was about to take a turn for the concerning. That theory had been proven moments later when a full-blown war erupted between Priscilla and Samuel, brought about because Suzette had not considered that presenting one pony to three children was likely going to cause a ruckus.

It had undoubtedly been one of the most spectacular ruckuses Bailey's Beach had ever witnessed.

Priscilla immediately laid claim to the pony, which caused Samuel to launch into a screaming fit. His screams mingled with those from Priscilla, causing more than one guest at the beach to move their chairs far away from the tantrums Walter's two governesses had been unable to control.

Realizing an intervention was required, Walter had stepped in, a mistake if there ever was one, because Priscilla had taken a large bite out of his arm when he'd tried to pick her up, causing him to almost drop her.

It wasn't until his mother, Ethel, and his mother-in-law, Matilda, stepped in to stop the screaming by promising their grandchildren they'd run right out and purchase another pony, that the uproar came to an end, but Walter was not in accord with the means used to stop their theatrics—that being, unfortunately, bribery.

Bribery seemed to be a mainstay in his world these days, or perhaps it had been a part of his world ever since Vivian died but he simply hadn't taken note of it. He'd taken note of it now though, even understood the reason behind it. His mother and mother-in-law were determined to compensate for the children being without a mother, but that compensation exactly explained how it had come to be that his children had turned into complete and utter terrors.

"Good heavens, Mr. Townsend," Mrs. Elliott exclaimed, drawing his attention as she settled a beady eye on the pony. "Have a care with that beast. I just purchased this darling masterpiece on my head yesterday in the smartest little shop on Bellevue. I'd hate for it to be devoured before I've worn it a full day."

Walter gave a tug of the reins, which only caused the pony to turn its head and send him a look filled with disdain.

It was a look he'd been receiving from Oscar for over two

months now, and one he didn't appreciate since Oscar was still a child and certainly didn't have reason to be scornful of his father—contempt normally waiting to make an appearance until a boy gained a few more years on him.

"I beg your pardon, Mrs. Elliott," Walter said, shaking himself from his thoughts when he realized the pony was now champing at the bit in its quest to take a bite out of the lady's hat. He gave another tug, then another, having to use a bit of muscle to pull the pony away from a treat it was apparently determined to savor. "I don't believe the pony inflicted any damage to your hat, but if you notice that is not the case, I'll be more than happy to replace it for you."

Mrs. Elliott smiled. "What a charming offer, Mr. Townsend. But you've always been a charming gentleman." She glanced to the pony before she sent Walter a wink. "That's quite the gift Miss Tilden presented to your children. I've been dying to learn if it may have put Suzette in the running to become the second Mrs. Townsend. Granted, she did not show to advantage last night, what with the punch incident, but she's obviously trying to make amends for her serious lack of judgment. I imagine that pony has left you feeling in a more charitable state toward her."

Thankfully, Walter was spared a response—because anything he might say could very well lead to Mrs. Elliott getting the wrong impression—when the pony lunged for Mrs. Elliott's hat again. It was sheer luck he was able to rein the little monster in, and after bidding Mrs. Elliott a hasty good-bye, he began dragging the pony away, earning more than a few amused glances from his gentlemen friends, who seemed to find his situation highly entertaining.

None of them seemed inclined to assist him, undoubtedly due to the fact he was now, through no fault of his own, attracting far too much feminine attention, which was obviously taking attention away from the other gentlemen assembled at Bailey's Beach.

When the pony suddenly came to an abrupt halt and refused to budge, Walter swiped a hand over a forehead beaded with sweat and glanced around as he debated his options, which weren't many since he couldn't very well pick up a pony and cart it away.

As he debated, his gaze traveled over the bathing houses placed sporadically up and down Bailey's Beach, situated far enough from the shoreline that they weren't affected by high tide.

The bathing houses, owned by the prominent members of the Spouting Rock Beach Association, commonly referred to as Bailey's Beach Club, were surprisingly derelict in appearance. Constructed from bleached wooden shingles and weathered wood, they didn't afford Bailey's Beach the exclusive atmosphere one would expect in a beach community frequented by the very wealthy—although given that great store was placed on appearances in Newport, plans were probably already underway to erect new huts. Members of society would hardly care for the common folk to take note of the shoddy huts and question the extent of the wealth the members of Bailey's Beach possessed.

Not that it was an easy feat for non-members to gain access to the beach. They were kept from enjoying the exclusive attitude of this section of Newport by the long drive leading up to Bailey's Beach. The drive ended at a wrought-iron gate complete with watchmen who knew every carriage of every member of Bailey's Beach, and they didn't hesitate to stop carriages they didn't recognize, only allowing non-members into the hallowed midst of Bailey's if they were accompanied by a member.

Sweat dribbling down Walter's face recalled him to the situation at hand, and after giving the reins another fruitless tug, his gaze returned to the bathing huts. His attention was suddenly captured by the sight of a lady strolling out of one of them, the gusty wind blowing in from the sea snatching off the lady's wide-brimmed hat, revealing brilliant red hair that obscured the lady's face.

Even without seeing the lady's face, Walter knew she was none other than Miss Gwendolyn Brinley, the reason behind his current troubling situation, and a woman he was quite convinced had turned into the bane of his existence.

Seven

꧁

"See that lady over there?" Walter muttered to the pony, who merely turned its head and began eyeing another hat. "She's a menace and is exactly why you're now apparently a part of my family—not that you should be excited about that, because the Townsends are currently a train wreck in the making."

The pony released a whinny, which Walter hoped was a nicker of sympathy instead of a warning the beast was about to make a move. Taking a second to wrap the reins around his hand, Walter returned his attention to Gwendolyn, allowing himself a moment to consider her.

She was dressed for swimming in a black frock that reached her knees, trousers covering her legs, and black stockings covering her feet, but she wasn't wearing the shoes most ladies wore into the water. The lack of shoes didn't impede her progress as she ran down her hat, the sound of her laughter reaching him on the breeze as Daniel Mizner, an acquaintance of Walter's who always had some new financial venture in mind, snatched the hat out of the air and presented it to Gwendolyn with a flourish. He then sent Gwendolyn what was certainly an appreciative look—perfectly understandable because Gwendolyn, while being the bane of Walter's existence, was, without a doubt, an incredibly striking lady.

Walter continued watching as, after exchanging a brief word with Daniel, Gwendolyn pivoted on stockinged feet and headed across the sand, edging around a society matron sitting at a small table covered in linen and set formally with bone china and sterling-silver cutlery. Ignoring the scrutiny the matron was giving her, Gwendolyn stopped and looked over the guests assembled on the sand, her gaze suddenly locking with his.

After reminding himself that, while she may be beautiful, she was the reason behind his current situation, he narrowed his eyes on her before returning his attention to the pony, which was now contemplating Mrs. Van Rensselaer's hat. "We have to go, and you need to cooperate or I'm handing you back to Miss Tilden."

To his surprise, the pony tossed its head before it took a few steps forward. Not willing to miss the opportunity of having the little beast cooperate for a change, Walter strode into motion, his pace slowing when he realized the pony couldn't keep up. It took him far longer than he would have thought possible to reach Gwendolyn's side, but when he did, he found her watching him, her lips curved into a smile.

The smile only served to remind him that she was a trial of a woman if there ever was one. "A word, if you please, Miss Brinley?"

Her eyes twinkled. "Given the expression on your face, I have to believe you want more than *a* word, Mr. Townsend."

"Too right I do."

"I thought so," she returned, the amusement in her eyes increasing. "May I assume those words are the sort that may require some privacy, and if so, may I suggest we remove ourselves from the beach?" She nodded to something behind him. "We seem to be attracting attention from that crowd of young ladies over there, quite as if they're dithering about whether they should join you."

Walter glanced over his shoulder, resisted a sigh when all the young ladies waved back at him, sent them a wave in return, and then took a step closer to Gwendolyn. "Those ladies are undoubtedly dithering because I'm sure they're scared to death of you. It's not often one witnesses the dressing down of a society lady."

"Is that what you want to discuss with me—the inadvisability of taking a lady to task for her unacceptable behavior toward the delightful and seriously misunderstood Miss Adelaide Duveen?"

"Of course not. It's hardly my place to lecture you on what many saw as a serious departure from the rules of etiquette society has embraced for decades—not only a departure on your part, but also on Suzette's." He nodded to the pony, who was, unsurprisingly, eyeing another hat. "But speaking of Suzette, I want to talk to you about this ridiculous pony, and how it's your fault I'm now in possession of it."

She shot a glance to the pony. "I've never seen that pony in my life, so I fail to see how it's my fault it's now in your custody."

"My proprietorship of this contrary beast lies squarely at your feet because you somehow managed to worm out of me what I'm looking for in a potential wife. Because of that worming, ladies have flocked to Bailey's Beach in droves, all of them offering gifts for my children. Suzette, clearly wanting to make amends for her part in the events last night, went to the extreme length of hauling this pony here and presenting it to my children."

Gwendolyn's brows drew together. "Miss Tilden presented your *three* children with one pony?"

"Indeed. Given your expression, you understand the problem with that. And yes, this quarrelsome pony has already been responsible for some mayhem amongst my children, specifi-

cally with Priscilla and Samuel. I shudder to think what's going
to happen when we get around to naming the beast. Priscilla
insisted we name it Trixie, whereas Samuel believes it should
be named something more dignified, perhaps from one of his
favorite stories. I believe Excalibur was mentioned at one point,
although it's hard to say for certain, given all the crying."

"Trixie might be an odd name for a male."

Walter frowned. "I never thought to discern the beast's gen-
der." He ran a hand through hair that had to be standing on end
by this point, what with the trying nature of his morning. "It
might have been prudent to investigate that matter earlier, because Priscilla doesn't like boys. It would have spared everyone
the impressive fit my daughter launched moments after Suzette
handed over the reins."

"Suzette should have known better than to give you an animal. It shows a distinct lack of sensitivity. It's never a good
idea to gift something that needs to be watered and fed." She
tucked an errant strand of hair beneath her hat. "She might
have been better served to have given Adelaide Duveen the
pony to atone for her serious lack of judgment last night. It
would have allowed society to see that Suzette possesses at
least a semblance of contrition about what she tried to do to
poor Adelaide."

Walter's dismal mood suddenly lightened. "Is there a chance
Miss Duveen might be receptive to taking this pony off my
hands? I would happily give it to her on behalf of Suzette."

"I highly doubt Adelaide wants to be responsible for a quarrelsome pony, Mr. Townsend. With that said though, if someone
were to give you a cat, Adelaide is quite fond of those." Gwendolyn dusted her hands together. "Since we've now cleared up
what you wanted to speak with me about, I must return to a
task Mrs. Parker assigned me. She's asked me to speak with
Mr. Clarence Higgenson about his apparent interest in Miss
Hannah Howe, one of the ladies Mrs. Parker is sponsoring.

I, however, am not convinced his interest is aboveboard, not when there are rumors regarding his affection for . . ."

When Gwendolyn faltered, as if she realized she'd been divulging too much, Walter finished for her. "Mrs. Lanier?"

"Ah, so there is something to that rumor?" Gwendolyn tapped a finger against her chin. "I was afraid of that. If you'll excuse me, I need to run Mr. Higgenson down and have a heart-to-heart discussion with him."

"I haven't finished everything I wanted to say to you."

"What else could you possibly have to say? I've now been apprised of your annoyance with me for getting you to disclose that bit about you needing a mother for your children." She cocked her head to the side. "Were you, perhaps, expecting me to apologize? Because if that's the case, know I'm very sorry for questioning you last night. I hope you won't suffer undue distress from too many ladies trying to win your affections."

"I wasn't looking for an apology."

Her lips curved. "Wonderful, because if you ask me, you should be thanking me for my interference. You now have an entire delegation of ladies trying to win your favor."

"*Thank* you? I never wanted to have an entire delegation of ladies seeking my affections in the first place. In fact, being besieged by so many ladies is leaving me feeling all sorts of discombobulated, a circumstance that's unusual for me, to say the least."

Gwendolyn readjusted her hat. "Forgive me, Mr. Townsend, but I'm not certain I understand where you're going with this conversation. Allow me to cut to the chase. What exactly do you want from me?"

"I want you to fix my situation because you're the one who created the chaos closing in on me."

"How, pray tell, do you figure that?" she countered, crossing her arms over her chest. "You're the one who let it be known you're in need of a wife, and that knowledge was swirling around the upper crust long before I entered the scene. All I did was allow the young ladies to know what your main requirement is in a wife. Again, I'd think you'd want to thank me for helping society understand your needs, which should help you select the perfect wife in the end. That means there's no reason for you to insist I fix a situation that's actually to your benefit."

"Did you miss the part where I said I'm under siege?"

"It would have been difficult to miss that, seeing how dramatically you've stated your situation, but they're merely young ladies. Young ladies are relatively harmless."

"Except when those ladies are on a mission, which makes them—especially when traveling in packs—downright terrifying."

She gave a roll of her eyes. "From what I understand, you're a successful man of business, unafraid to face down your competitors. I would assume you're up for the task of setting aside any trepidation you may hold over being set upon by the feminine—"

She suddenly snapped her fingers, which had the pony, who'd been inching its way closer to a lady wearing daisies on her head—something Walter had neglected to notice—swinging its head around and settling an annoyed look on Gwendolyn.

"Stop that!" Gwendolyn demanded, giving another snap of her fingers when the pony turned its head again and began straining against the reins.

"I mean it." She moved to stand in front of the small monster and leaned down to lock gazes with it for a long second.

After releasing a resigned-sounding snort, the pony sat down on its haunches and turned his head toward the sea, apparently realizing he'd met his match in Gwendolyn Brinley.

Walter's lips twitched. "I hate to admit this since I'm beyond put out with you, but that was impressive. You have a very authoritative way about you, Miss Brinley, and I find myself wondering how you came to possess that trait."

"I'm the oldest of six. Being authoritative allowed me to survive the antics of my younger siblings."

"The oldest of six?" he repeated right before an intriguing thought sprang to mind, one that might allow him to abandon his decision to find a new wife, while getting his children in order at the same time.

"Is there a reason your eyes have begun to gleam in a manner I find somewhat unnerving?" Gwendolyn asked.

He took a step closer to her. "Indeed, but there's no need to be unnerved, Miss Brinley. I'm hopeful what I'm about to propose will strike you as a beneficial proposition, one that will be advantageous for both of us. I believe it will allow *you* to remove yourself from an assistant-matchmaker position I'm convinced you're not qualified to hold, while providing *me* with a solution to a situation that has taken on a life of its own, and not a life I was expecting."

Eight

A pesky ache immediately took up residence behind Gwendolyn's temple. Taking a moment to soothe it away, she considered Walter for a moment before blowing out a breath. "Forgive me if I misunderstood, but this proposal of yours . . . It doesn't involve a marriage, does it?"

Given the horror now lurking in Walter's eyes, she was evidently off the mark.

"Forgive *me*, Miss Brinley," he began as he took to rubbing his temple as well. "I fear drawing the undivided attention of determined ladies so early in the day has left me unusually clumsy with my words. I certainly didn't intend for you to take what I'm about to suggest as a marriage proposal, but . . ." He frowned. "You immediately assuming that's what I was going to propose has me wondering if gentlemen you're barely acquainted with make it a habit to broach marriage with you."

"Oddly enough, that has occurred several times in the past, but usually because I was mistaken for my cousin."

His lips curved. "I doubt that. I would think such misunderstandings have more to do with your propensity for creating chaos than mistaken identity."

Gwendolyn began rubbing her temple again. "I don't make a habit of introducing chaos into anyone's life."

"You've singlehandedly turned what should have been my straightforward quest to find a suitable bride into a complete circus."

"I did not. I merely encouraged you to reveal the characteristic you're searching for in a potential bride. If you're unaware, that's what we matchmakers are supposed to do."

"I can't claim to be an expert on matchmakers in general, but I imagine those in the matchmaking business take on . . ." He paused and tilted his head. "Do they call them clients?"

"Mrs. Parker refers to her charges as the ladies she's agreed to sponsor for a Season."

He gave a bob of his head. "Perfectly understandable, since the word *client* reeks of trade, something no society matron would care to participate in. But returning to the point I was trying to make—may I assume the main job of a matchmaker is to find the most beneficial marriage for the ladies they're sponsoring?"

"I would think that doesn't need confirmation."

He inclined his head. "Indeed. But may I also assume matchmakers find advantageous matches by ferreting out personal information pertaining to each bachelor in a most discreet fashion?"

"Discretion might come into play."

"Of course it does. It then stands to reason that after matchmakers ferret out pertinent information regarding potential suitors, they keep that information under wraps so their competition is left in the dark about what a certain gentleman is searching for in the wife department."

Irritation sent Gwendolyn's toe tapping against the sand as she swallowed the argument she longed to voice, knowing she couldn't contradict his reasoning because he wasn't exactly mistaken.

"You know I'm right," Walter said. "But to spare you the indignation of having to admit that—something I'm convinced wouldn't sit well with you, given your attitude—allow me to present an employment opportunity I wish to offer."

Her toe tapping came to an abrupt end. "What do you mean . . . my attitude?"

He smiled. "Considering I'm hoping you'll agree to come work for me, I don't think it's in my best interest to delve into that topic."

"Why would you want to hire a woman you believe possesses an attitude?"

"Because your type of attitude could very well provide me a way to avoid searching for a wife this Season."

Gwendolyn's eyes narrowed. "On my word, now I understand what you're getting at. You want me to become your children's governess."

"Indeed, and to entice you into accepting that position, I'm willing to extend you a very lucrative offer." Walter took a step closer to her. "It's the perfect solution for both of us. You, Miss Brinley, are clearly a competent woman, because you managed to win a stare down with the most contrary pony I've ever met. I have a feeling, what with how you're the eldest of six, you're very good at managing children."

"I *am* very good at managing children, but I have no interest in becoming a governess."

"Did you miss the part where I said it will be a lucrative offer?"

"That would have been difficult to miss. But even with such a tempting proposition, I won't be taking you up on it."

"Why not?"

"I already have a position. I'm an assistant matchmaker."

"But again, you're not very good at it."

"That's simply your opinion."

Walter frowned. "It's not opinion—it's fact. You broke a

significant matchmaking rule last night by allowing everyone at the Astor ball to learn I'm looking for a mother for my three motherless children."

"I'm not going to argue that I broke a matchmaking rule, or several, but that doesn't mean I'm not competent in my position . . . or that I won't get competent in the future. I'm still in the infant stages of matchmaking, and you mark my words, by the end of this Season I'll be one of the best matchmakers in Newport."

He cocked his head, but before he could voice the argument he clearly wanted to voice, an ear-splitting howl of rage rang out from across the beach, drawing Gwendolyn's attention. To her amazement, the wailing came from a pint-sized little girl garbed in an ivory bathing dress, her golden locks tied back from her rapidly reddening face with a pink bow. Glancing to the right of the little girl, Gwendolyn discovered a little boy with the same golden hair stomping up and down on a sandcastle that had clearly been painstakingly engineered by a diminutive architect who was now in a massive state of hysterics.

"Priscilla still seems to be in fine form," Walter muttered as he watched the little girl begin tossing fistfuls of sand at the little boy, who didn't stop his destruction but seemed to increase the momentum of his stomps, eliciting louder howls of rage from Priscilla.

Gwendolyn shaded her eyes with her hand, wincing when Priscilla hurled a sand pail at the little boy. "Those are *your* children?"

"Those are my twins—Priscilla and Samuel." Walter jerked his head toward two women dressed in white blouses and dark skirts, both of whom were watching the drama unfold in front of them without moving so much as a finger to intervene. "It appears Miss Wendell and Miss Putman are hesitant to act because . . ." He gestured to two well-dressed ladies standing a few feet away from the ruckus, both seemingly attempting to cajole the children to no effect.

"My mother, Ethel, along with my mother-in-law, Matilda, have once again attempted to intervene on their grandchildren's behalf, a circumstance that often leaves the governesses I employ reluctant to take control of any unpleasant situation."

"If you employ two governesses, why do you need me?"

He winced as Priscilla abandoned her sand throwing and launched herself at her brother. "Is that really a question that needs answering as we watch my children and their unbecoming antics, which again, the governesses are ignoring?"

"Probably not. But to reiterate, I have no interest in becoming a governess and . . ." Gwendolyn stopped talking when Priscilla took her brother to the ground and began pushing his face into the sand. "This is ridiculous." She stepped closer to Walter and gave him a nudge. "They're your children. Do something."

"Given the large chunk of my arm Priscilla took off earlier when she bit me, I'm convinced I'm not qualified to handle these types of parental situations. If I were to interfere with sibling rivalry, there's a good chance I'd make the situation worse."

She rolled her eyes. "She's a child, Mr. Townsend, although one who seems to enjoy the role of pint-sized dictator. However, since you apparently have no intention of interceding, and your mother, mother-in-law, and two governesses are seemingly oblivious to a sibling maelstrom . . . if you'll excuse me?" She readjusted her hat, stepped around the pony, and set her sights on the two children now screaming in such a manner that one would have thought they were in imminent danger of killing each other.

"I'll assist you just as soon as I get the pony on its feet," Walter called after her.

"Which means I'll have the situation well in hand before you arrive," she called back, increasing her pace when she realized Samuel had turned the tables on his sister and was now sitting on her and trying to bury her face with sand he was pouring from a pail.

Reaching the children a second later, and ignoring the incredulous looks from Walter's mother and mother-in-law, although the two governesses were now looking rather relieved, she leaned over and grabbed the pail from Samuel's hand—unsurprised when both children ceased their theatrics.

"That will be quite enough," she said, earning a gulp from Samuel, still sitting on his sister, but a narrowing of the eyes from Priscilla, who was swiping sand from her face.

"Who are you?" Samuel demanded.

"I'm Miss Gwendolyn Brinley, an acquaintance of your father, and you're Samuel and you're"—she settled her attention on Walter's daughter—"Priscilla. With introductions out of the way, I'd now like for the two of you to explain to me why you thought it was appropriate to engage in such unseemly shenanigans."

Priscilla's eyes narrowed another fraction. "What are shenani . . . goes?"

"Shenanigans. It means mischief, but not of the becoming sort. More on the lines of the kind that should see the two of you sent to your room for the rest of the day without your dinner."

"Grandmother Ethel and Grandmother Matilda would never let me go without dinner," Priscilla shot back, shifting under Samuel's weight.

"That may be true, but they should consider doing just that because young ladies should never comport themselves in such a disgraceful fashion when they're out and about, and . . ." Gwendolyn nodded to Samuel. "Young gentlemen in the making should never brawl with a girl."

Samuel's nose scrunched up. "She's my sister."

"She's still a girl, and as such, you will from this point forward refrain from engaging in fisticuffs with her."

"She bit me."

"Cuz you ruined my castle," Priscilla argued.

"Cuz you tore the tail off my new kite."

"Only after you—"

Gwendolyn held up her hand, cutting short what would have certainly been a long list of grievances the twins had enacted upon each other. "It doesn't matter what started your feud. What matters is that the two of you understand that feuding is not appropriate when you're out in public. It's actually never appropriate, but because I have numerous siblings, I know there are times when tempers get the best of people. So if the two of you want to descend into an unseemly brawl while you're in the privacy of your own home, have at it."

"You told me I should never brawl with a girl again," Samuel pointed out, which had Gwendolyn fighting a smile because, clearly, he was unusually astute for his age and . . . had just made an excellent point.

"How encouraging to learn you're a wonderful listener, Samuel. And yes, you should refrain from physical altercations with your sister."

Priscilla settled far-too-innocent eyes on Gwendolyn. "Does that mean if I hit him, he can't hit me back?"

Gwendolyn's lips twitched. "Technically, yes, but since young ladies are expected to always comport themselves with grace, you will from this point forward behave accordingly. No screaming, crying, or biting is permissible, nor will you punch your brother."

Priscilla's little lips thinned as Samuel rolled off her and she sat up. "What about stomping on sandcastles? You should tell Sam he can't do that if you're going to tell me I can't bite him."

"Stomping is expected when you're playing in the sand," Gwendolyn returned. "My siblings always demolished one another's creations, sometimes pretending they were monsters intent on wiping out a sandcastle town. The fun of it is then rebuilding the castles and clomping on them again."

"That doesn't sound like fun," Priscilla argued as she pushed herself to her feet. She then began shaking sand out of her dress, sending it all over Gwendolyn. After realizing what she was doing, instead of apologizing she sent Gwendolyn a smirk before she kicked sand toward her brother, pivoted on her little heel, snatched up a toy boat lying in the sand, and headed for the sea.

"Oh no you don't," Gwendolyn muttered as Samuel took off after his sister, Gwendolyn giving chase a second later.

It quickly became evident the twins were exceedingly fast. By the time Gwendolyn reached the water's edge, Priscilla had flung the sailboat into the waves, where it immediately swept out with the tide, which sent Samuel flinging himself at his sister.

In a whirlwind of small fists and screams that left Gwendolyn wincing again, the twins tumbled into the shallow surf, but before she could do more than take a step to intervene, a boy charged past her and hurled himself into the waves, calling over his shoulder that he'd rescue Samuel's boat.

Horror was swift when Gwendolyn took note of the ominous surf created by the storm gathering offshore.

"Come back!" she yelled as she tore off her hat and headed after the boy, who was most certainly Walter's eldest son, Oscar. As she battled waves crashing against her, and before she dove underneath a wave, she thought she heard Mrs. Parker shouting something but couldn't hear exactly what before she caught sight of a wave cresting in front of her. Taking a deep breath, she dove under the wave, praying she'd be able to get to Oscar before he was swept out to sea.

Nine

⊱

The glimmer of a pale leg caught Gwendolyn's attention. Changing direction, she swam underwater as fast as she could to what she hoped was Walter's son. Reaching out, she snagged hold of the leg, kicking upward until she broke the surface, only to be met by an indignant face belonging to the boy she'd been trying to save.

"Let go," he demanded before he began to struggle, kicking out with his other leg and catching her in the stomach.

She winced but didn't let go as she wrapped her other hand around his neck, flinching when he bit her. "Stop fighting me, and for heaven's sake, don't bite me again. That hurt."

"I don't need saving. But if you don't let go, we're both going to drown."

A wave took that moment to crash over them, separating her from Oscar and sending her tumbling head over heels through the water. Just as her head broke the surface, a hand grabbed hold of her right arm and another hand grabbed hold of her left. Without the use of either arm, she began to sink but was hauled to the surface a moment later by someone who seemed intent on drowning her.

After expelling a mouthful of saltwater, she discovered Walter staring back at her, Clarence Higgenson bobbing in the sea beside him.

"Don't fret, Miss Brinley. I've got you," Clarence shouted, giving her a tug toward him, which sent her underwater again and caused water to go up her nose before her head broke the surface again.

"I've got her," Walter countered.

"Neither of you need to get me," she managed to get out before she spotted another wave about to crest overtop of them. "Duck."

Unfortunately, as they ducked, neither gentleman released their hold on her, and finding herself suspended under the water the peculiar thought sprang to mind that she was in some odd version of tug-of-war, with one gentleman trying to swim with her to the left, while the other tried to swim to the right, which only resulted in them thrashing rather awkwardly about. By the time they kicked their way to the surface, she was almost out of air and not feeling charitable toward either gentleman.

"Let . . . go," she demanded.

"Try to relax, Miss Brinley," Clarence said, treading water beside her. "There's no reason to put on a brave face or feel embarrassed you almost drowned. It was quite brave of you to go after Walter's son when you're not a good swimmer, but you're impeding your rescue by talking so much."

"Who said I'm not a good swimmer?"

"Mrs. Parker, right before she shouted that I needed to save you from a most unpleasant drowning."

A watery snort was Gwendolyn's first response to that before she turned to Walter, whose hair was covering most of his eyes but not covering his mouth, which to her vast annoyance was curved into a grin.

"This is not amusing," she said, kicking her feet to remain afloat since the gentlemen were still holding fast to her arms.

"On the contrary, it's humor at its finest since you attempted to save Oscar, who's been swimming since he was three, who then fought you off, and then you found yourself in that same predicament."

She stopped kicking, promptly sank, and then spit out another mouthful of water when the gentlemen hauled her above the waterline again. "Where *is* Oscar?"

"No need to worry," Walter hastened to reassure her. "He swam past me as I was coming to your rescue and is already back on shore." His eyes, oddly enough, began twinkling. "And while this hardly seems to be the moment to engage in conversation, I have a burning question I must ask."

She blinked water out of her eyes. "You want to hold a conversation now, while we're being buoyed about on the waves?"

"I know it's hardly an ideal setting, but there are no ears to overhear what I'm about to ask you."

"Mr. Higgenson has ears."

Walter shot a glance to Clarence, who sent him a quirk of wet brows. "His ears aren't the ones I'm worried about."

Gwendolyn found herself sinking again, gave a kick of her legs, and then nodded. "Fine. Since it seems we're not going to head for shore until you ask your question, ask away."

"I knew underneath that intimidating demeanor of yours was a reasonable woman," Walter began.

"I'm only reasonable when I'm not in danger of drowning, so please, get on with it before I sink again."

It was less than amusing when Walter flashed her a smile. "You're very prickly at times, but that was a good point, so tell me this. Do you believe Mrs. Parker deliberately misled Clarence—and myself, in turn, but only because I heard her calling out to Clarence that you couldn't swim—or is there a remote possibility she really believed you were in danger of drowning?"

"You probably already know the answer to that."

"Hmm" was all Walter said as he pulled her up and over a wave, Clarence going with them because he seemed intent on keeping hold of her other arm. "Should I assume she did that because of some harebrained notion that revolves around her matchmaking efforts?"

"Forgive me for interrupting," Clarence said before Gwendolyn could respond, "but am I to understand that you, Miss Brinley, can swim and didn't need rescuing?"

Gwendolyn nodded right as she took note of another wave about to crash over them. "Wave."

Thankfully, both gentlemen had the presence of mind to finally release her, and not wanting to allow them another opportunity to unintentionally drown her, she darted off underwater. After riding a wave almost to the shoreline, she staggered to her feet, Walter joining her a second later. He took hold of her arm and steadied her before they moved through frothy surf swirling around their feet, Clarence materializing by her side before she made it to shore. He took hold of her other arm, quite as if he still wasn't convinced she wasn't in imminent danger of drowning.

Before she could shrug out of either gentleman's hold, a rousing burst of applause erupted from the beach. Lifting her head, she discovered a crowd of Bailey's Beach devotees cheering their departure from the water.

"Good show, Mr. Higgenson," Mr. Russell Damrosch called.

"Excellent you were present today, Mr. Townsend," another gentleman called.

"Is Miss Brinley alright?" Mrs. Parker shouted, catching Gwendolyn's attention as well as a narrowing of an eye, something Mrs. Parker responded to by sending Gwendolyn a cheeky wink.

"That woman is a menace," she muttered.

Clarence stopped walking. "You really weren't in danger of drowning, were you?"

"I was only in danger of drowning after you and Mr. Townsend got ahold of me, Mr. Higgenson."

"Please, call me Clarence. Formality seems somewhat absurd at this point."

"And you must call me Walter as well," Walter added.

She shoved a strand of dripping hair out of her eyes. "This is a very curious moment to be having this conversation, but fine. Since the two of you did almost drown me, I suppose it's ridiculous to continue with expected decorum. You may both call me Gwendolyn, but you may not, as in ever, try to rescue me from drowning again."

"But what if you're actually drowning?" Clarence asked.

"I'll take my chances."

"Perfectly understandable," Clarence said with a grin. "But since Walter and I seem to have been misled about the situation, would you like us to apprise the crowd still applauding us that we're not heroes?"

Gwendolyn returned the grin. "I would hate to deprive either of you of your accolades, because you did have the best of intentions, even if you'd been misled by Mrs. Parker." She leaned closer to Clarence. "However, because I'm willing to assume the unlikely role of damsel who was rescued from her distress to allow you your accolades, I *will* ask for something from you in return."

Wariness flickered through Clarence's eyes. "And that would be?"

"Don't start looking concerned," Gwendolyn said, shoving another strand of soggy hair out of her eyes. "I merely need fifteen minutes of your time, at which point we're going to have a dialogue about Miss Hannah Howe, whom, I understand, you're interested in becoming better acquainted with."

"I doubt it'll take an entire fifteen minutes for me to explain my interest in Miss Howe," Clarence countered. "We should be able to complete our discussion in five, which will then allow me to keep a scheduled appointment I have with a . . . ah . . . friend."

Gwendolyn arched a brow. "Mrs. Lanier, I presume?"

He blanched. "You know Mrs. Lanier?"

"Not personally, but rumors have reached me about the two of you, which is why I'll need fifteen minutes." She nodded to a boulder jutting out beside the famous Cliff Walk that wound its way along the ocean, lending walkers an unparalleled view of the sea. "We can repair over there after we dry off. It'll allow us privacy."

Trepidation replaced the wariness in Clarence's eyes. "We need privacy?"

"Indeed."

Walter cleared his throat. "Since I may need some privacy as well, I'll join you."

"Absolutely not. That would defeat the purpose of my having a *private* chat with Clarence," Gwendolyn argued.

Walter nodded to something in the distance. "Perhaps, but surely you're not so cruel as to deny me an excuse to avoid all that, especially when it's your fault I've been placed in such an unusual spot to begin with."

Turning, Gwendolyn discovered a gathering of at least twenty ladies, many of whom were gesturing for Walter to join them. She caught Walter's eye. "Don't be such a coward. They're merely young ladies who want to speak with you, which will then allow you to get to know them better and perhaps find a suitable candidate to become the next Mrs. Townsend."

"I daresay any gentleman would be hesitant to find himself confronted with that many ladies at one time."

She pulled a piece of seaweed from her sleeve. "You're going to have to pluck up your courage at some point if you want to survive the summer with your nerves intact. But you did try to save me from a drowning, even though I didn't need saving. I suppose, because of that, I could intercede a little on your behalf so you don't find yourself inundated with admirers while I speak with Clarence."

After telling Clarence she'd meet up with him directly, Gwendolyn headed across the beach, her sights on the ladies still aiming their attention Walter's way. Stopping when she was a few feet away from them, she summoned up a smile and directed it all around, her smile dimming when she noticed Tillie Wickham dividing her attention between Walter and an ocean now roiling with waves.

One look at the glint in Tillie's eyes was all Gwendolyn needed to know exactly what that lady was considering, and frankly, she wouldn't be surprised if a few of the other more adventurous ladies were considering the same thing.

"While I know it must be tempting for some of you to follow suit and fling yourself into the Atlantic, hoping for a dramatic rescue from whatever gentleman you've set your eye on," Gwendolyn began, earning startled looks, paired with quite a few guilty ones, "there's a storm brewing, which means the ocean is the last place any of you should try out a would-be drowning.

"Besides, I've already done that today, so you might want to think up something more original. And . . ." She turned and nodded Walter's way. "He'd never tell you this, because he's a gentleman and would never care to hurt any feelings, but you're overwhelming Mr. Townsend with your attention today. If you want to make a positive impression, I suggest you extend the man some breathing room and limit how many of you approach him at any given time."

"Why are you taking it upon yourself to tell us this?" Tillie demanded, crossing her arms over her chest. "Is it a ploy to get us to abandon our interest in Mr. Townsend so you can promote the two ladies everyone has recently learned Mrs. Parker is sponsoring—those being Miss Ellsworth and Miss Howe?"

Gwendolyn plucked a strand of seaweed from her cheek. "I doubt you're going to believe me, but my advice is not a ploy. It's merely a favor I'm doing for Mr. Townsend because he appears somewhat mortified by how his day is unfolding. Mortified is not a result I'm sure any of you were hoping to achieve, but far be it from me to try to lend any of you my counsel."

She sent a wave in Walter's direction. "Feel free to continue to monopolize his time, give his children gifts, and even try your hand at drowning. Although you may want to wait to flail in the ocean another day, since there's a good chance, if too many of you attempt that all at once, one of you may very well drown because there won't be enough available gentlemen to rescue you."

With that, Gwendolyn turned and began striding away, unsurprised when mutters immediately commenced. Blowing out a breath, she realized there was every chance ladies would now do their utmost best to make her stay in Newport as unpleasant as possible. And the unpleasantness was certain to increase once they realized she was determined to help Mrs. Parker make the most spectacular matches of the Season for Elizabeth and Hannah, if only to prove to Walter he was completely off the mark about her matchmaking skills, or lack thereof.

Ten

That Gwendolyn Brinley was an unusual woman wasn't up for debate, but even though Walter was convinced she was the bane of his existence, there was no denying he admired her competency. As a man of business, he valued competency, and while he didn't know what Gwendolyn had said to the ladies gathered at Bailey's Beach, he now found himself in the company of merely three women, all due to the intervention of a lady who'd sent him a wink in passing before she'd strolled past him on her way to have a tête-à-tête with Clarence Higgenson.

"I'm so grateful you didn't incur any injuries from your heroic saving of Miss Brinley," Tillie cooed as she sidled next to him. "What that woman was thinking, going after that child when she couldn't swim, well, I'm sure I have no idea. *I* certainly wouldn't be so foolish as to throw myself into the ocean, especially not when there's a storm rolling in and I'd be putting the lives of whatever gentlemen felt compelled to rescue me in jeopardy."

"My dear Miss Wickham, you know you're only saying that because Miss Brinley suggested none of us follow her lead and take to the ocean in the hopes someone would jump in after us," Cordelia Lowe said, settling eyes still ringed with shades of green and yellow on Tillie. "With that said, I would hope, if a child *were* drowning, all of us would do what was needed to save that child without a second's hesitation."

"But that boy wasn't even drowning," Tillie argued.

Cordelia gave a flutter of her lashes. "That *boy* is Mr. Townsend's son Oscar, and his other two children would be Priscilla and . . ." She shot a glance to Elizabeth Ellsworth. "Were we in agreement his other son is Stanley?"

"I believe the general consensus was Samuel," Elizabeth said, casting a warm smile Walter's way before she returned her attention to Tillie and Cordelia. "With that settled, may I suggest the two of you seek out a bit of shade because it seems as if there's an edge of contentiousness to the current conversation. I daresay the sweltering heat is responsible for that, but I'm afraid you're making Mr. Townsend uncomfortable."

"I believe you may be right, Miss Ellsworth," Cordelia agreed as she stepped closer to Walter. "Forgive us, Mr. Townsend. I certainly never meant to cause you any discomfort."

"There's no need to apologize, Miss Lowe," Walter began. "I assure you, I haven't taken offense."

"How gracious of you," Tillie said, edging closer to him, which resulted in her edging out Cordelia. "Allow me to redirect the conversation to something less contentious. While you've assured us you didn't suffer any repercussions from saving Miss Brinley, may I dare hope the same for Mr. Higgenson?"

Before Walter could respond, Cordelia wiggled between him and Tillie, craned her neck, and gestured to something in the distance. "It appears Mr. Higgenson is in fine form, considering he's now engaged in what appears to be an intense discussion with Miss Brinley."

Walter turned to where Cordelia was gesturing and discovered Gwendolyn and Clarence sitting in the shade of the boulder, their heads together and looking quite oblivious to anything around them.

Tillie sucked in a sharp breath. "On my word but I now find myself wondering if Miss Brinley's drowning was intentional, a ploy, if you will, conceived by Mrs. Parker to assure her assistant matchmaker received some unbridled attention from one of the most eligible bachelors of the Season."

"If it was," Cordelia said, "it was a very clever ploy on Mrs. Parker's part."

Tillie's jaw set. "That's hardly fair. I know for fact Mrs. Nelson, my sponsor this Season, will not appreciate learning about the underhanded tactics Mrs. Parker is using to give her charges an unfair advantage on the marriage mart."

Cordelia released a snort, causing Elizabeth to begin eyeing her quite like she'd lost her mind, as if snorting was taking matters too far, even though the conversation at large had taken on an unexpected and slightly contentious tone. "As if Mrs. Nelson didn't encourage you, Miss Wickham, to sabotage my prospects this Season by smashing a tennis ball into my face."

Tillie's eyes flashed with temper. "I didn't intentionally hit you, and I resent your suggesting otherwise. Perhaps you should strive to improve your tennis game. Because that, and that alone, was responsible for you taking a ball to the face."

"You know I'm a formidable player, just as you know you deliberately took that shot when I was distracted by a duck that unexpectedly flew across the court."

Not wanting to be swept up in a drama he never imagined he'd be a witness to between society ladies from two of the oldest upper-crust families in the country, Walter took a few experimental steps backward, pivoted on his heel, and when no one tried to stop him, strode off down the beach, moving at a pace just shy of a run. He made it a good fifty feet before he noticed Clarence charging across the sand and disappearing around a bathing hut a moment later.

Walter's gaze darted to Gwendolyn, who was calmly dusting sand from her bathing costume, quite as if the conversation she'd just shared with Clarence had not sent him dashing away from her.

Curiosity prodded him in her direction.

"What did you do to poor Clarence?" he asked when he reached her side.

She stopped dusting herself off and wrinkled her nose. "There's no need to take that tone with me, Walter. It's not as if I did anything dastardly to the man."

"He just raced across the beach as if a pack of wild animals was chasing him."

She bent over, plucked a seashell from the sand, looked it over, then tucked it into her pocket. "His rate of speed only goes to prove how anxious he was to rectify a grave mistake he made, one concerning Mrs. Lanier, or *darling Michele* as he prefers to call her."

"Oh no, you didn't . . . ?"

"Encourage him to find some gumption, profess his love to his darling Michele, and then ask her to forgive him for nonsensical behavior?" She nodded. "Oh yes I did, proving I, contrary to your opinion, am on my way to becoming a most excellent assistant matchmaker."

"Encouraging Clarence to abandon what's expected of him to pursue a forbidden love, given that society frowns on unions between gentlemen and divorced ladies, proves you have no business being a matchmaker, assistant or otherwise. If he doesn't come to his senses, he's guaranteed to bring scandal to the Higgenson family. It would have been more beneficial to him if you'd convinced him Miss Hannah Howe would make him an excellent wife."

"That wouldn't have been beneficial for him or Miss Howe, and especially not better for Mrs. Lanier, who, from what Clarence told me, adores him."

Walter raked a hand through his hair. "On the contrary, it would have been better for everyone involved."

"We'll have to agree to disagree on that, because Clarence, after a mere three minutes of my questioning him, blurted out he's hopelessly in love with Michele and cannot imagine a life without her."

He scratched his nose. "Perhaps, instead of an assistant matchmaker, you should consider a job with the Pinkertons. They'd probably relish the opportunity to hire a lady capable of getting a man to confess in under five minutes."

"It wasn't as if I was brutally interrogating the man until he folded. After he told me he thought he and Miss Howe would rub along nicely together, I merely told him that was complete rubbish, and that a gentleman should expect more out of marriage than simply being able to claim they married a woman of good social standing."

"But gentlemen of society don't marry ladies who've been divorced."

"Is that written in one of those society manuals?" Gwendolyn shot back, holding up a hand when he opened his mouth to reply. "Don't bother telling me if it is. I'll only be more disillusioned with society than I already am. But returning to what you see as a lack of competency on my part, my encouraging Clarence to seize the day and go after his love is exactly what matchmakers should do."

"Not if it ruins the reputation of someone in the process, that someone being Clarence."

She plucked another shell from the sand, considered it, then tossed it aside. "I would hope Clarence's reputation can survive something as trivial as marrying for love, because what you don't seem to be grasping is that being madly in love with a woman is not the type of love a gentleman ever forgets. Because I've decided to take my position as an assistant matchmaker seriously, prodded into that decision by you, I would have been doing Miss Howe and Clarence a grave disservice."

"I have no idea how I could have possibly goaded you into

taking your position seriously. I've been doing my best to dissuade you from your current occupation because I'm of the firm belief you're not qualified to be an assistant matchmaker."

She pinched the bridge of her nose. "You've been very clear about your opinions regarding my matchmaking skills, and I've taken your skepticism as a direct challenge, one I intend to win. I'm very competitive, you see."

"My skepticism was never meant to challenge you. It was meant to encourage you to abandon your current profession."

She dismissed that with a wave of a sand-encrusted hand. "You're only trying to get me to abandon matchmaking because you want me to take up the role of governess—something that's never going to happen."

"What if I offered you twice the salary Mrs. Parker is paying you?"

"You could offer me five times the salary I'm earning, and I'd still say no, because I'm now on my way to achieving imminent success with my matchmaking endeavors."

"That's an appalling business decision. You should consider your bottom line above all else."

Gwendolyn shrugged. "Perhaps, but it's my decision to make, horrible or otherwise. Besides, I'm committed to Mrs. Parker for the summer, and I'm a stickler for seeing my commitments through."

"You've also committed to securing an advantageous match for Hannah Howe, and yet you just sent a prime candidate into the arms of another woman."

"Hannah deserves better than to be shackled to a man who would never love her."

"I highly doubt Miss Howe believes she's going to marry for love. Most society ladies are content if they hold a small bit of affection for their husbands and hope those husbands return that sentiment."

"And that way of thinking has all the makings for a great

romance novel," Gwendolyn said with a roll of her eyes. "May I assume you and your late wife enjoyed one of those polite marriages where the phrase *madly in love* never passed either of your lips?"

It was becoming evident he'd somehow lost control of the conversation. "Vivian was perfectly content with the polite marriage we shared," he argued. "She wasn't expecting a love match and seemed happy with our life together because I gave her anything her heart desired."

"Unless her heart desired more than a courteous relationship with you."

"Vivian's objective when she made her debut was to marry a gentleman in her social circle. Her requirements in a husband were straightforward—she wanted to marry a gentleman who could provide her with a house on Fifth Avenue, a cottage in Newport, keep her dressed in style, and escort her every so often to her favorite society events."

"That seems more on the lines of a business arrangement than a marriage."

"Most unions within society are business arrangements."

Gwendolyn frowned. "Should I assume you'd be comfortable marrying a lady possessed of the same sentiments as your late wife?"

"Of course."

A pucker immediately developed between her brows. "You should consider setting your standards a little higher, Walter. There's nothing wrong with trying to find a lady you're going to want to do more than enjoy an amiable relationship with."

"I never said I'm opposed to developing a little, well, ah, affection for someone, but the problem lies in that I now have so many ladies seeking my attention, I doubt I'll be able to get to know any of them well enough to discern whether there's a . . ."

"Spark between you?" Gwendolyn finished for him when he faltered.

"I don't think I believe in sparks, but I suppose that's one way of putting it." He released a sigh. "And to point out the obvious—by encouraging Clarence to embrace his love for Mrs. Lanier, you've now taken an eligible bachelor off the marriage mart, which will undoubtedly have the young ladies who'd set their eye on him turning that eye my way. Should I now expect Miss Howe to join me as often as Miss Ellsworth does?"

Gwendolyn's nose wrinkled. "You're not a viable candidate for Miss Howe. She seems to be a lady with a romantic heart, and the last thing she would know how to handle is a man with a heart I'm beginning to believe is made of stone. Because of that problematic circumstance, there's no chance I'll ever encourage her to try to capture your attention. Which should leave you extending me your deepest appreciation, given you'll now have one less lady to contend with."

Eleven

It was a curious situation to find himself in—one where he'd just been delivered what could certainly be construed as an insult, which added a nice cherry to the top of a day that was turning into a debacle.

Not only had he been given a surprising glimpse into how ladies comported themselves when they relaxed the restrictive rules of etiquette they embraced from birth, he'd also just been told he possessed a heart made of stone.

Walter crossed his arms over his chest. "How did you conclude that? Most ladies find me an engaging and attentive conversationalist, something a man with a stone heart wouldn't bother to concern himself with."

"Forgive me if I'm about to injure your gentlemanly feelings yet again, but it's been my observation that you don't appear to enjoy the conversations you're engaging in."

He frowned. "What signs did you observe that led you to that conclusion?"

"I've often seen you sport the exact same expression currently residing on your face when you're speaking with ladies."

"I'm sure you're mistaken. I've made a point over the years

to carefully school my expressions when I'm conversing with the feminine set, even when it's difficult for any gentleman to enjoy the fabricated conversations we're expected to hold at society events."

He raked a hand through his hair. "Fashion and the weather are not exactly titillating topics, but I'll have you know I read at least twenty fashion magazines before I stepped foot in Newport so I'd be knowledgeable about the latest styles. I've also been perusing the paper over breakfast to be up-to-date on the predicted weather on any given day. Miss Ellsworth, one of *your* ladies, was most appreciative when I told her a storm was expected because she can now plan accordingly for the ball tonight."

"Miss Ellsworth is apparently easily impressed, but have you ever considered you may enjoy the company of ladies more if you were to branch out and speak about topics that interest you?"

"I highly doubt any lady would be interested in hearing me wax on about the plans I'm considering for some real estate I recently purchased."

"Last year, after questioning him about different qualities of wool, I spent two hours speaking with the Prince of Wales about sheep and what breed he thought my mother might enjoy adding to her flock."

Walter blinked. "You conversed with the Prince of Wales?"

"He's a most captivating individual and . . ."

Whatever else Gwendolyn had been about to say got lost when one of Priscilla's howls rent the air.

Gwendolyn winced. "That child has quite the set of lungs on her, and frankly, it's going to take a special lady to take on the role of mother to your children. You're going to need someone sensible, strong, and unquestionably possessed of a great sense of humor, because she'll have her work cut out for her getting your children in hand."

She tapped a finger against her chin. "Even though I'm representing Miss Ellsworth and Miss Howe, you might consider becoming better acquainted with Miss Adelaide Duveen. From what I've gathered, she's mature, sensible, and has a wonderful sense of humor, because she was certainly humoring her mother when she agreed to wear that atrocity marketed as an evening gown last night. She also didn't descend into a fit of the vapors after almost finding herself the victim of a rogue glass of punch. That right there suggests she's a woman possessed of a strong constitution and could probably handle your children with one hand tied behind her back."

"How *is* she with children?"

"Adelaide didn't specifically address that subject with me, but she adores cats. I would think a woman who loves cats probably enjoys children as well."

"She sounds charming, but I'm afraid Miss Duveen isn't a viable choice for me."

"Because she doesn't dress in the first state of fashion?"

"You do seem to relish insulting me, but no, her fashion sense has nothing to do with my reluctance. Her love of cats does." Walter bent over to pick up a shell that caught his eye, handing it to Gwendolyn after he straightened. "Cats make Oscar and Priscilla sneeze."

After glancing at the shell, Gwendolyn sent him a hint of a smile before depositing it in her pocket. "How unfortunate, because I found Adelaide to be a most delightful lady. She has quite the collection of cats, and I can't see her giving them up for a gentleman who possesses numerous deficiencies, even if you're rumored to have quite the fortune."

"I do not have deficiencies."

"Yet another topic we'll need to agree to disagree about, but . . ." Gwendolyn narrowed her eyes toward Priscilla, who was now wailing in earnest and shaking a finger at the pony Walter had left with a footman. "Your daughter is in serious need of a nap," she said, before she began marching in Priscilla's direction without another word.

Walter strode to catch up with her, ignoring the concerned looks his mother and mother-in-law sent him—looks due, no doubt, to the fact Gwendolyn was now standing directly in front of Priscilla, who was howling louder than ever.

His mouth went a little slack when Gwendolyn leaned over and hefted Priscilla into her arms. Priscilla immediately went stiff as a board and stopped howling, probably because no one had ever treated her in what she undoubtedly considered a roughshod manner.

"Every bather at Bailey's Beach has heard quite enough of your theatrics today, dear," Gwendolyn said. "In the interest of sparing them a cacophony of continued screaming, you are now going to repair home." She arched a brow toward his two governesses, who were watching her with wide eyes. "I suggest, once you get home, the two of you get her down for a much-needed nap."

"Don't need a nap," Priscilla grumbled.

"Given your less than pleasant temper, yes, you do, but what caused you to make such a ruckus this time?"

Priscilla began wiggling, her face scrunching when Gwendolyn didn't let her loose, merely readjusted her hold so that Priscilla couldn't wiggle at all.

Evidently realizing she'd been thwarted in her bid for freedom, at least for the moment, and probably because she did look tired, his daughter jerked her head toward the pony, who was sitting on its haunches, its eyes on his mother-in-law's hat. "It's a boy."

"And why would that discovery be worthy of a tantrum?"

"I wanted it to be a girl."

Gwendolyn gave Priscilla's shoulder a pat. "Well, he's not a girl, and no amount of wanting is going to change that."

She set her sights on Samuel and Oscar, who were both looking at her in disbelief, as if they couldn't believe she'd put an end to Priscilla's tantrum. "Boys, gather up the sand pails, shovels, and those two toy boats and bring them to your carriage."

"They'll do no such thing," Matilda Stokes, Walter's mother-in-law, countered. "We employ footmen to fetch and carry."

Gwendolyn leveled a look on Matilda that had his mother-in-law inching closer to his mother, Ethel. "In the interest of making certain your family doesn't find themselves banned from Bailey's Beach, Priscilla needs to go home sooner than later. Given the number of toys the children now find in their possession, handed to them from Walter's many admirers, it'll take your footmen numerous trips to retrieve all of them. Having two boys who are quite capable of carrying a few toys to a waiting carriage will be the best way to expedite your departure, something I assure you all the bathers will appreciate."

After sending the boys an arch of a brow, which had them scrambling to scoop up pails, shovels, and their toy boats, Gwendolyn turned and marched past Matilda, who was looking rather incredulous, as if she couldn't believe her order had been ignored, or perhaps his mother-in-law was merely looking that way because Priscilla was now laying her head against Gwendolyn's shoulder, her eyes closing as Gwendolyn strode away.

Because he was relatively certain Gwendolyn would send him one of her frightening looks if he arrived at the carriage empty-handed, Walter snatched up two dolls, one kite, and a few toy soldiers lying on a blanket and headed after her. He paused to tell the footman holding on to the pony he was going to have to walk the beast back to Sea Haven, an unenviable task if there ever was one, because his cottage was on the other end of Bellevue Avenue.

By the time he reached his carriage, Gwendolyn had settled Priscilla into it, wrapping his already sleeping daughter in her favorite blanket. Samuel was sitting beside Oscar on the seat opposite his twin, clutching his toy boat to his chest as he stared solemnly at Gwendolyn, who merely smiled at the look.

"Thank you for helping with the toys, Oscar," she said, straightening after she'd tucked a corner of Priscilla's blanket under her chin. "We haven't been introduced. I'm Miss Gwendolyn Brinley."

"Is Father going to make you our new mother?" Oscar asked.

Gwendolyn gave Oscar's knee a pat before she backed out of the carriage. "You don't need to worry about me marrying your father. I'm not in Newport looking for a husband, and even if I was, I wouldn't be a contender in your father's eyes. Truth be told, he approached me earlier to become your governess."

Samuel's eyes widened. "Priscilla isn't going to like that."

Gwendolyn's lips twitched. "I'm sure she wouldn't, but no need to fret. Your sister is going to soon have reason to exercise her lungs again. I'm not a governess—I'm a matchmaker."

"What's a matchmaker?" Samuel asked.

"I help young ladies find suitable husbands."

"Too bad you don't help gentlemen find suitable wives," Oscar said. "Father was having a time of it today, and I didn't get the feeling he was making much progress in his search to find us a mother."

"Father really *is* searching for a mother for us?" Samuel asked, his eyes growing wider than ever. "Priscilla told me that, but I thought she might have been fibbing."

"She wasn't," Oscar said. "I overheard the grandmothers discussing how Father's determined to marry again soon." Oscar glanced to Walter before he returned his gaze to Samuel. "They said he's returned to what I guess is called the marriage mart because he's annoyed with our behavior of late."

Walter frowned. "I wasn't aware you knew I was considering marrying again."

It came as little surprise when Oscar rolled his eyes. "I'm

not a baby, Father, and I'm very good at listening, something the grandmothers seem oblivious about. It wouldn't have been hard to figure that out on my own though. You haven't joined us in Newport in years, except to drop in to make certain we're still alive. You've also not attended society events, but you're doing that now."

Oscar nodded to Gwendolyn, who was lingering outside the carriage door. "You could spare him the bother of finding us a new mother if you'd take on that governess role."

"True," Gwendolyn agreed, "but I highly doubt you or your siblings would care to have me as your governess. I'm not easily thwarted, something I believe all of you often do to your current governesses. I also expect children to behave, and believe me, none of you would be happy with the means I'm willing to take to make certain good behavior is adopted daily."

Oscar's brows drew together. "We can behave if we want to, but I guess it's good you're a matchmaker and not a governess. You told Priscilla she should have to go without her dinner because she was naughty, but I wouldn't want my little sister to ever go hungry. You wouldn't have cared for what might have happened to you if you'd tried that."

"Oscar . . ." Walter said, drawing his son's attention. "You're being rude."

Oscar shrugged and turned his head, his attention settling on something out the window.

"I'm beginning to understand the reasoning behind your decision to marry again," Gwendolyn said as Walter stepped away from the carriage, knowing any further reprimand of Oscar was only going to have his son turning more belligerent.

"I'm afraid I may have made that decision a bit late, but hopefully I'll find success and the children can be returned to a somewhat normal state, or at least to where they're not behaving as if they're being raised by wolves."

Gwendolyn sent him a small smile. "Odd as you may find

this, I hope you find success with your plan to marry again. It's clear you don't appreciate my advice, but you should try to engage in some honest conversations with the young ladies who are certain to seek you out at the Harper ball later this evening. You may find yourself enjoying the evening more if you don't limit yourself to talk of the weather and latest fashions. More importantly, you might find a lady you're compatible with if you put some genuine effort into your conversations."

"The mere thought of being the recipient of feminine attention this evening leaves me hesitant to even attend the Harper ball," Walter admitted before he shot a look to Oscar, who was still staunchly ignoring him, before he returned his attention to Gwendolyn when an unexpected thought sprang to mind.

"You know, there may be a solution to dealing with all that feminine attention, a solution I just came to because of an interesting comment Oscar made."

Wariness immediately clouded Gwendolyn's eyes. "What interesting comment?"

"He said it's too bad you don't help gentlemen in the match-making department."

The wariness increased. "Don't even think about what I know has begun brewing in your mind."

Walter took a step closer to her. "But it's perfect, especially since it's your fault I'm being inundated with so many ladies interested in securing my affections."

"Mrs. Parker doesn't take on gentlemen to sponsor, only ladies. It's how matchmaking works," Gwendolyn said rather weakly.

"She might change her mind if I write her a large enough bank draft."

"She doesn't deal in anything so common as money."

He tapped a finger against his chin. "If memory serves me correctly, Mrs. Parker was drowning in diamonds last night, which suggests she enjoys accepting jewels for payment."

"She won't take you on as a client," Gwendolyn said, a clear touch of desperation now lacing her tone.

Walter allowed himself the luxury of a grin. "Ah, but you see, my dear Miss Brinley, I have a Tiffany & Company diamond bracelet locked away in my safe at Sea Haven that I would bet good money says otherwise."

Twelve

"I must say this Newport Season is turning out to be one of the most peculiar Seasons I've ever participated in," Adelaide Duveen said, gesturing with her glass of champagne toward a congregation of ladies who seemed to be deliberating whether or not they should approach Gwendolyn. "I've never been so highly amused over the antics of society, and the Harper ball is only the second ball of the season. I'm only sorry I missed the earlier events at Bailey's Beach. Winkie, one of my new cats, settled down on my lap for a snooze. I was then subjected to what I refer to as feline paralysis, unable to twitch so much as a muscle in fear I'd disturb the little darling."

"I'm delighted someone is finding this Season humorous, because that's not an emotion I'm experiencing," Gwendolyn said, presenting the young ladies considering her with her back in the hopes that would dissuade them from approaching her. "Truth be told, I'm feeling slightly sympathetic to Walter's plight because I'm feeling decidedly under siege."

"I'm sure that is overwhelming, but it can't be much of a surprise to you, given that it's not every day—or any day, for that matter—that a matchmaker of Mrs. Parker's esteem agrees to sponsor a gentleman."

"She only agreed because she's unable to resist the temptation of sparkly baubles from Tiffany & Company," Gwendolyn muttered.

"Tiffany baubles do come with a certain panache, but her agreement to take up Walter's case has caused tongues to wag, the wagging only increasing after word somehow got out that you're taking on the role of buffer for Walter, any young lady interested in securing his attention having to go through you instead of personally seeking him out."

"It's no mystery how word about my being Walter's custodian got out," Gwendolyn said, jerking her head to where Mrs. Parker was holding court, waving a hand that now sported a Tiffany diamond bracelet. "Mrs. Parker decided it would spare Walter the bother of having to direct young ladies my way if she made it be known there were now rules where Walter's concerned. Honestly, what that lady was thinking is beyond me, and don't even get me started on her going out of her way to cater to the man."

"I'm sure she was thinking a bracelet from Tiffany & Company would look marvelous on her wrist, as well as thinking she needed to accommodate Walter's every little whim because he presented her with that bracelet before an engagement was announced. That's an unusual happenstance for Mrs. Parker— you told me she never gets compensated until an engagement is finalized."

"She was certainly ecstatic about receiving the bracelet before any hard work had been accomplished, whereas I'm not thrilled in the least because I have a feeling Mrs. Parker is now going to expect me to be at Walter's beck and call until we find him a suitable match. I'm certainly not enamored with being expected to be a high-society shield for a gentleman I'm not exactly fond of."

"I don't imagine you are." Adelaide gave Gwendolyn's arm a pat. "But I don't think you'll need to worry about kowtowing to Walter's every demand. You're in charge of his social calendar—overwhelm him with mandatory attendance at social functions. If you do that, he'll have no time to do that beck-and-calling you're concerned about."

"Except I wouldn't put it past Walter to challenge me about the events I want him to attend. He seems to relish sparring with me."

"The two of you do seem to be at variance with each other."

"It's a strange circumstance, because I'm generally not at odds with gentlemen when first introduced. It typically takes me a good few weeks before I begin annoying them, or vice versa." She blew out a breath. "Nevertheless, since it's apparent I'm stuck with the unenviable job of finding Walter that perfect lady, I'm going to have to figure out how to get the ladies of society to cooperate with any scheduling I may attempt to do on Walter's behalf. I'm convinced that trying to manage these ladies is going to be fraught with difficulties, because they're bound to resort to underhanded tactics to steal more time with him, not to mention the shenanigans they're probably even now devising against me."

Adelaide readjusted the bodice of a gown that, while not nearly as hideous as the one she'd been wearing the night before, wasn't well tailored to her form. "If you're unaware of this, every lady out this Season is terrified of you, except for perhaps Tillie Wickham, because, well, it's Tillie. I don't think she's prone to fits of terror."

"Is it wrong there's a part of me that wants to include Tillie often in Walter's schedule simply out of spite, because I know she's not a lady he'll find appropriate?"

Adelaide soothed a hand down Gwendolyn's arm. "You know you won't do that because you told me you're determined to become a top-notch assistant matchmaker by the end of the summer. That means you'll need to find Walter his perfect match, which I have no doubt you'll achieve, even with you being under assault—and not simply from the feminine set."

Gwendolyn stilled. "What do you mean by that?"

"Have you not noticed how many gentlemen are watching your every move this evening?"

"I'm being watched by gentlemen?"

"Indeed," Adelaide said. "And while I wish I could say gentlemen are watching you because of that delicious gown you're wearing, I'm afraid that may not be the case, given the calculating gleam I've detected in more than one gentleman's eye."

"You've detected calculation?"

"I'm afraid so."

"That can't be good."

"I'm afraid not." Adelaide grinned. "On a positive note, at least you didn't take Walter up on that bet he offered about the likelihood of Mrs. Parker sponsoring him. If you had, not only would you now find yourself his buffer, you'd also be poorer."

"That's one way of looking at the situation." Gwendolyn caught Adelaide's eye. "Are you certain you won't reconsider your position about your cats? I still believe you could be exactly the lady Walter needs in his life, which would put a rapid end to my association with the man."

Adelaide's eyes twinkled. "Even though I'd love to assist you with your unwanted association, I wouldn't give up my cats for any gentleman. And while I know my mother, if she were to discover you're keen to see me take up the Mrs. Townsend title, would be thrilled to have you attempt that unlikely accomplishment, I don't believe Walter and I would suit each other. I have no interest in confining my conversations to fashion and the latest weather." She readjusted her bodice again. "Fashion has never interested me, and I loathe fittings so much that my mother merely takes my measurements and gets my gowns made without my involvement."

"Going for a fitting once in a blue moon might result in you having some gowns that complement your figure," Gwendolyn pointed out.

Adelaide shrugged. "True, but there are so many more delightful ways to spend my time, such as reading, wandering through bookstores, or attending to my many feline companions. Besides that, I'm not convinced better-fitting gowns would lend me a stylish air. I simply don't have the flair needed to look fashionable."

"Style is not difficult to obtain. It's merely an attitude and how you present yourself to the world."

"I don't have attitude either. At a ball last year I tried to use a fan in an attempt to look the part of a femme fatale instead of a bluestocking." She shook her head. "It was abject failure at its finest because I flipped my fan open while engaged in conversation with Mr. Daniel Mizner, hit him squarely in the nose with it, and watched in horror as his nose began to bleed. He then dashed away from me, trailing blood as he dashed. He's not spoken to me since."

Gwendolyn's lips twitched. "How unfortunate."

"Not really, because Daniel Mizner is rumored to be a fortune hunter. That most likely explains why he was engaged in conversation with me in the first place, and . . ." Adelaide's voice trailed away as her eyes narrowed on something behind Gwendolyn. "Don't look now, but Mr. E. J. Boettcher seems to be heading our way. Given that he was just in conference with a few other gentlemen who've been watching you, I believe he's been elected to approach you first."

"Approach me for what?"

"I think you're soon to find out. With that said, I'm going to casually saunter away, because Mr. Boettcher isn't overly fond of me either. It's a long story, one I'll explain later, but know that an unintentional kicking of his shins may have occurred."

After sending Gwendolyn a wink, Adelaide strolled away,

barely making her escape before E. J. appeared at Gwendolyn's side, smiling brightly as he took hold of her gloved hand and pressed a kiss to it.

"Miss Brinley, how delightful you look this evening," E. J. began. "I'm not certain you remember meeting me, but I'm . . ."

"Mr. Boettcher," Gwendolyn finished for him, which sent a touch of wariness flickering through E. J.'s eyes. "Of course I remember meeting you. We shared a lovely conversation at Mrs. Elbridge Gerry's pre-Season picnic—until you discovered I was in Mrs. Parker's employ. You then fled from me without another word."

E. J. winced and released her hand. "I suppose that was not well done of me."

"There's no supposing about it."

He winced again. "An excellent point. Allow me to make reparations for my blatant rudeness and extend you a most sincere apology. My hasty retreat was *not* well done of me, and I truly beg your pardon." He sent her a genuine smile. "I hope you'll forgive me, and if so, then hope you can spare me a few minutes of your time."

Gwendolyn resisted a sigh, checked her watch, and then returned her attention to E. J. "I have exactly two minutes I can spare now."

"Only two minutes?"

"I'm a very busy woman, Mr. Boettcher. It's two minutes or no minutes at all, and you've already used up five seconds of your time."

His smile dimmed ever so slightly. "With such a time constraint, I might as well just blurt this out. I'm interested in having you represent me in the matchmaking business this summer, and before you say no, understand that compensation has no ceiling."

"Oh . . . dear," Gwendolyn muttered as understanding regarding the calculation Adelaide had noticed residing in gentlemen's eyes finally registered.

"Not exactly the response I was hoping for."

She smiled. "I'm sure it wasn't, just as I'm sure you were hoping I would agree to your proposal, but I must respectfully decline."

"Why?"

Gwendolyn consulted her watch again. "Your two minutes are almost up, but I will spare another few seconds to tell you that I simply don't have time to manage another gentleman this Season. Walter Townsend is certain to be a full-time effort, and I have two ladies to look after as well. Besides all that, I don't get the impression you need assistance in the lady department. You seem perfectly capable of attracting attention of the feminine kind on your own."

His lips curved. "You've been observing me?"

"Don't look so smug. I'm an assistant matchmaker. One of my job requirements is to observe gentlemen. My observations of you, brief as they've been because it is only the start of the Season—although allow me to say that my limited time in Newport seems like months instead of mere days—have me convinced you have no need of a matchmaker."

"I do if I want to secure a match like you made for Clarence Higgenson."

Gwendolyn frowned. "I thought society was supposed to be appalled once word got out Clarence was going to abandon convention and declare his honorable intentions toward Mrs. Lanier."

"Word has already gotten out, and yes, most of society, at least the older set, *are* appalled, especially his family." E. J. leaned closer. "Have a care if you happen to encounter his mother, Mrs. Higgenson. She's a force to be reckoned with, and according to Clarence she's furious that some matchmaker convinced him to follow his heart."

"It didn't take much convincing."

"Doesn't matter," E. J. said with a shrug. "Clarence wouldn't have followed his heart if you'd not had a chat with him." He smiled. "That right there is why I want you to represent me this Season."

Gwendolyn's brows drew together. "Do you have a certain lady in mind who may not be considered top drawer enough in society's eyes?"

"Not at all, but I want a lady who can make me feel how Clarence feels. I ran across him tooling down Bellevue Avenue, and I've never seen a gentleman so ecstatic. He was radiating happiness, and all because you convinced him to set aside what society demands of him and ask the woman he adores to marry him." E. J. leaned closer. "Clarence told me he's already spoken to Mrs. Lanier and she didn't hesitate to accept his proposal of marriage."

"Good for Clarence."

"Quite, but returning to me. I want you to find me a lady I can love as much as Clarence loves Mrs. Lanier."

"You realize I had nothing to do with matching him and Mrs. Lanier, don't you? Clarence said they've known each other for years, and I've never even met the woman."

"A valid point, but you evidently realized Clarence loved her even before he admitted that love to you. That type of intuition is what I need to find me the lady of my dreams."

"Don't you have any friends who could point you in the direction of such a lady? They probably already have a young lady in mind if you disclose you're interested in a love match."

E. J.'s brow furrowed. "My sisters have told me I should direct my attention Miss Frances Bottleworth's way, but they're my sisters, so I haven't put much stock in their suggestion."

"Sisters are exactly whom you should pay attention to in the lady department. They, even more so than your friends, want to see you happy."

His gaze sharpened on her. "Are you saying I should seek Miss Bottleworth out?"

"I don't really know Miss Bottleworth, so I have no opinion about whether you should seek her out or not."

"But you'll speak with her after you take me on as . . . Will you be referring to me as a client?"

Tension settled at the base of Gwendolyn's neck. "I won't be referring to you as anything other than a casual acquaintance, because as I already mentioned, I don't have time to find you the perfect lady."

E. J. shot a glance across the room, his gaze lingering on Mrs. Parker, who was still holding court, smiling at the many ladies and gentlemen surrounding her. He returned his attention to Gwendolyn. "Perhaps I should take this matter up with Mrs. Parker. I imagine she's the one who decides whom she wants to take on in any given Season."

He glanced to Mrs. Parker again, a gleam settling in his eyes, something that had apprehension slithering up Gwendolyn's spine. "She seems to have a fondness for diamonds. Clarence mentioned to me, before he rushed off to spend time with Mrs. Lanier, that he was going to drop off a lovely diamond-and-sapphire ring at Mrs. Parker's residence because that's what she apparently expects when she makes a marvelous match."

"I'm sure Mrs. Parker now has enough jewelry to see her through the next few months," Gwendolyn said, wincing at the distinct trace of panic lacing her tone.

"My sisters always say a lady can never possess too much jewelry. I happen to have a collection of tiaras collecting dust in my safe that came to me from various relatives." He nodded toward Mrs. Parker. "She's not currently wearing a tiara, which suggests she may very well need one of those to add to her collection."

"She does not need a tiara" was all Gwendolyn got out of her mouth before E. J. sent her a bow paired with a grin and turned and strode away, Mrs. Parker in his sights.

"There is no possible way Mrs. Parker is going to be able to

refuse a tiara," she muttered right as Suzette Tilden materialized at her side, thrusting her dance card into Gwendolyn's
hand.

"I've been told I need to go through you to secure a dance
with Mr. Townsend," Suzette began. "He's finally arrived at
the ball, so if you'd be so kind as to write his name down for
the waltz that's to begin next, I'd be ever so grateful."

Elizabeth Ellsworth took that second to join Suzette, a scowl
marring her beautiful face. "On my word, Suzette, but I did
not appreciate you muscling your way in front of me to get to
Miss Brinley first." She rubbed her side. "I might very well sport
a bruise where your elbow dug into me. I highly doubt, once
Miss Brinley apprises Mr. Townsend of your dubious antics,
he'll be all that keen to waltz with you."

Suzette's nose shot into the air. "If you've forgotten, Elizabeth, I was the one who presented his adorable children with a
pony this afternoon. You presented them with kites. Not in the
same league, which means I should get Mr. Townsend's name
on my dance card for the next waltz."

"I doubt your pony is going to have Miss Brinley choosing you over Elizabeth, considering Mrs. Parker is sponsoring
Elizabeth this Season," Tillie Wickham said, edging in between
Suzette and Elizabeth before she turned an unexpected smile
on Gwendolyn. "And while it's not fair to the rest of us that
you're representing Elizabeth and Mr. Townsend at the same
time, it's certainly fair to say you're looking very well turned
out this evening."

The tension at the base of Gwendolyn's neck increased.

"You'll put Mr. Townsend's name down on my card for the
waltz?" Suzette pressed, drawing Gwendolyn back into what
certainly had the potential of turning into a complete and utter
disaster, especially since more ladies had joined them, all of
them clutching their dance cards.

She squared her shoulders. "Before I jot down His Highness's name on any of your cards, he and I need to engage in a bit of a conference regarding the evening."

Tillie's brows shot all the way into her hairline. "Forgive me, Miss Brinley, but I couldn't help but detect what seemed to be a hint of sarcasm in your tone when you referred to Mr. Townsend as His Highness."

Elizabeth nodded before Gwendolyn could respond. "Oh, there was definitely sarcasm." She settled a frown on Gwendolyn. "I'm not certain I understand the derision though. You should be honored Mr. Townsend broke with convention to have a matchmaker look after his best interests, and honored he wanted you and Mrs. Parker to represent him."

"Honored does not remotely explain my feelings toward Mr. Townsend," Gwendolyn returned. "Appalled would be a more apt description, because sorting out a gentleman's lady problems was not something I thought I'd ever be doing."

Elizabeth raised a hand to her throat. "Mr. Townsend considers us problems?"

Mutters immediately resounded amongst the young ladies, ones that were certainly going to be accompanied by a barrage of questions regarding Walter's thoughts, his dislikes, and most importantly, why he'd consider the ladies of society to be problems.

"That probably didn't come out the way I intended," Gwendolyn muttered. "I'm afraid I'm a little tired considering I almost drowned today, which may explain why I'm having difficulties expressing myself well this evening."

"You seemed perfectly capable of swimming your way to shore," Suzette pointed out.

"My swimming abilities come and go. But if you'll excuse me, I believe I should have my chat with Walter sooner than later."

Before she could make a much-needed escape, Tillie stepped closer, her eyes narrowed. "How interesting you're evidently annoyed to be representing Mr. Townsend and yet you're very free with addressing him by his given name."

Gwendolyn narrowed her eyes right back at Tillie. "I would consider guarding that sharp tongue of yours, Miss Wickham. It won't help you get Walter's name on your dance card this evening."

"I would think it's up to Mr. Townsend to decide the ladies he longs to take to the floor with," Tillie shot back.

Gwendolyn released a breath when the thought struck that dealing with ladies of the Four Hundred would try the patience of a saint. Summoning up a smile, she lifted her chin.

"Ladies, I feel we need to clear the air between us once and for all," she began, earning more than a few blinks of surprise in return. "If you're unaware, Walter decided to secure my assistance as a matchmaker because he wanted someone to manage his Season for him. It's at my discretion which ladies will get to spend time with him and when, which means all of you may want to consider tucking your surly attitudes away when you're in my company. I assure you, surliness will not see you achieving much success toward spending time with *the* catch of the Season."

Thirteen

"I never pegged you for a man who'd resort to bringing in a matchmaker to sort out your love life, Walter."

Walter pulled his attention from Gwendolyn, who'd been heading his way until she was waylaid by Hannah Howe and Cordelia Lowe, and settled it on Mr. Gideon Abbott, a friend he often sought out to discuss prospective investment ideas. "It was a desperate act, Gideon, necessitated by finding myself awash in feminine attention."

"Because one *so* often hears gentlemen complain about too much feminine notice, especially gentlemen searching for potential brides," Gideon said with a twitch of his lips.

Walter rubbed the back of his neck where tension had settled. "When you put it that way, my reasoning does sound somewhat suspect. However, after I found myself privy to a spat between two society ladies I've never heard exchange a cross word, I realized that ladies have thrust aside the decorum they set their teeth on—apparently done so because a good majority of them seem to want to acquire me this Season."

"Bet that makes you feel all warm and fuzzy inside."

"Not particularly, which is another reason I decided I needed a professional to regulate the complex situation I now find myself involved in. Getting Mrs. Parker's agreement to have Gwendolyn Brinley act as a go-between for me and the ladies was the smartest decision I've made in weeks."

Gideon brushed aside a strand of black hair that had escaped the tie fashioned at the back of his neck. "I would think your smartest decision of late would be deciding you want to marry again."

"I'm not certain that was a *wise* decision, more on the lines of a *necessary* one." Walter blew out a breath. "The children have become almost unmanageable of late, their increasing misbehavior aided by two grandmothers who seem to believe their grandchildren are going to suffer irreparable harm if their every whim isn't appeased."

"Perhaps you should look into hiring more effective governesses as opposed to the life-altering permanence of matrimony."

"I've hired effective governesses before. They never stay long because they have a habit of tussling with my mother and mother-in-law. Constant friction seems to be a breaking point with the staff."

Gideon shot a look to Gwendolyn, who was jotting something down in a notepad she'd whipped out of a fashionable reticule hanging from her wrist. "It's unfortunate you couldn't talk Miss Brinley into taking on a governess position. From what you've told me, she has a very managing way about her. I don't get the impression she'd be cowed by the grandmothers."

"Believe me, I tried. She wouldn't consider my offer. She's evidently a woman who takes her commitments seriously, and she committed her entire summer to Mrs. Parker. I'm not happy to admit this, but I find her determination to see her pledge to Mrs. Parker through to the end impressive. It, annoyingly enough, speaks well of her character."

"It does indeed," Gideon agreed. "I don't imagine you enjoyed her refusal of a position though. You're not one to frequently suffer losses."

"I didn't appreciate her refusal, but I don't think I've lost the battle between us, not when I had the foresight to have Mrs. Parker sponsor me. That brilliant move has left Gwendolyn in charge of my social itinerary. Given how ladies seem to be unusually intimidated by my matchmaker, I'll now be able to enjoy a less stressful summer."

"How does Gwendolyn feel about being responsible for your social docket?"

"She's less than exuberant, which means we're certain to have a few confrontations in the near future."

Gideon tilted his head. "Why do I get the distinct impression you're relishing the idea of battles with Gwendolyn?"

"I never said I was savoring the idea of exchanging barbs with her."

"Your face suggests otherwise."

A laugh escaped Walter. "You, my friend, have clearly been immersed in cloak-and-dagger missions for far too long. You're looking for intrigue when none exists. Gwendolyn is my matchmaker, nothing more."

Walter ignored the rather telling snort Gideon sent him and shot a look to where Gwendolyn was still talking with Miss Cordelia Lowe. Her toe was now tapping against the highly polished parquet floor, keeping time with the words erupting out of Cordelia's mouth.

To Walter's concern, Gwendolyn looked up, caught his gaze, narrowed her eyes, then returned her attention to Cordelia for a second before she inclined her head and began heading his way.

"Your matchmaker doesn't look happy," Gideon muttered. "Which means I'll bid you adieu for now."

"You don't want to meet her?"

"And have her begin interrogating me after she discovers I'm a bachelor? She's representing two young ladies this summer—I think not. I, unlike you, am not in the market for a wife."

With that, Gideon turned and moved through the crowd, leaving Walter alone to face what would probably be another contentious exchange with Gwendolyn, something he was becoming accustomed to.

"You're late," Gwendolyn said when she stopped in front of him, her green eyes flashing with temper.

Walter presented her with a bow. "How lovely to see you as well, Gwendolyn. As for why I was late, I was unavoidably delayed."

"The children giving you difficulties?"

"Nothing out of the ordinary."

"Then why are you late?"

"I needed a nap."

The sparks in Gwendolyn's eyes turned to flames. "A nap? You don't have time for that type of nonsense. You should have been here right at nine, because while you were napping, or waking up from that nap, I was being inundated with requests to fill your name on dance cards. Lacking prior consultation with you, I was hesitant to act on your behalf, but if I'd have known you were at your leisure, I'd have . . ."

"Put my name on Cordelia Lowe's dance card."

"I was thinking more on the lines of Tillie Wickham, but since Cordelia just had the audacity to try to wheedle unfettered access to your social schedule by offering me a hat, one she claims is in the first state of fashion, she might end up with your name on her dance card as well." Gwendolyn crossed her arms over her chest. "I don't believe I've ever been so insulted. But hat nonsense aside, we are faced with a gargantuan task, further complicated by an eight-week timeframe, of which one week is almost over. You're going to have to keep your napping to a minimum."

Walter shrugged that aside. "It's not imperative we acquire a suitable candidate this Season. The children have been running amok for years, so if we're unsuccessful here, we'll try during the New York Season."

Gwendolyn's face was suddenly wreathed in a far-too-innocent smile, which seemed incredibly un-Gwendolyn-like. "I'll be sure to keep that in mind."

"Why are you smiling?"

"Am I?"

"It's a bit disconcerting." He frowned as he rubbed his neck, where tension seemed to be rapidly increasing. "You're not planning to leave Mrs. Parker's employ in the near future, are you, hence the reason for the smiling?"

Her eyes sparkled. "I'll say this for you, Walter, you're quick on your feet, which may be a direct result of your being well rested from your nap. I wouldn't claim I'm leaving soon, because from where I'm standing, the end of the Newport Season seems decades away instead of weeks. But yes, that is when my terms of employment with Mrs. Parker will come to an end."

He tilted his head. "Are you leaving her employ because you've realized you're not cut out to be an assistant matchmaker?"

"Of course not. I'll merely have fulfilled the terms of my contract. However, if you had lingering doubts about my proficiency as a matchmaker, why did you give an expensive bracelet to Mrs. Parker to secure my assistance?"

"I knew you'd be capable of managing all the young ladies who've been clamoring for my attention because you're a very managing sort. With that said, I'm still not convinced you'll be the one to introduce me to my future wife, no matter how competently you manipulate my social calendar."

Her eyes went from sparkling to glittering in the span of a heartbeat. "And that type of abject negativity is why I'm going to prove to you I can do an outstanding job of securing the best matches for the two ladies and one gentleman—that being you—Mrs. Parker is sponsoring this Season."

Walter fought a smile. "You're beginning to sound somewhat disgruntled about the whole matchmaking business, which suggests you should have availed yourself of a nap as well before you came to the Harper ball. That might have left you in a more pleasant frame of mind."

Fourteen

It came as no surprise when Gwendolyn's lips thinned before she took hold of Walter's arm and propelled him through the ballroom, a militant look in her eyes, guests scattering out of their way as she marched him along. She then steered him down a hallway, then another, before he found himself on a terrace overlooking the ocean with an awe-inspiring view of the moon casting a glow over the waves.

On a normal evening, the view would have lent him a sense of serenity. But considering he was in the company of a lady bristling with animosity, there was nothing peaceful about his current situation.

"I take it you wanted to have a word with me in private?" he finally said after Gwendolyn presented him with her back and took to contemplating the night sky.

"I have more than a word to say to you, quite like you were more than loquacious with me this morning."

"Was that only this morning?"

Gwendolyn stopped perusing the sky. "Yes, and to refresh your memory, we only met last night."

Walter frowned. "Seems as if I've known you a lot longer."

"Mutual animosity might be to blame for that."

Walter choked back a laugh. "An excellent point. But to spare us another heated exchange if we delve into what's behind that animosity, why don't you explain why you whisked me out of a ball filled with promising candidates?"

"You suggested I should have availed myself of a nap at some point today. That indicated you haven't the slightest conception of what a lady is forced to go through during a Newport Season. Frankly, there simply isn't time in my day, or any society lady's day, to afford the luxury of a good rest."

"Perhaps overburdened ladies should schedule time to repose during the day. I find such an interlude restores my sense of humor."

"I've yet to notice a stellar sense of humor from you, rested or not."

"My gentlemen friends find me most amusing."

"How lovely, but their opinion hardly matters," Gwendolyn shot back. "To remind you, you're out this Season to impress ladies. I suggest you put that sense of humor to use with them rather than wasting it on your gentlemen friends. That might aid us in whittling down the list, because you won't want to further an acquaintance with anyone who doesn't appreciate that particular trait."

"I'll take that into consideration."

"See that you do. But to return to your suggestion regarding ladies and napping . . . Are you unaware that ladies are required to change their wardrobe seven to nine times a day throughout the Season?"

"Seven to nine times?" Walter repeated.

"Indeed, and not only do ladies change for every occasion—from morning gowns, to bathing costumes, to afternoon gowns, to driving ensembles, and the list goes on and on—Newport society ladies never wear the same garment twice. That's why I was forced to send a frantic telegram to my cousin, Catriona

Zimmerman, begging her to send me the numerous port-manteaus I left with her before I traveled to Newport."

"Why was your telegram frantic?"

Gwendolyn swatted away a bug flying around her head. "Because I didn't pack appropriately, being under the mistaken impression I was to be a paid companion, not an assistant matchmaker. Companions occasionally escort their employers to balls, but I stress the word *occasionally*. That's why I only packed three ballgowns to last me the entire summer, of which I've already worn two." She blew out a breath. "I'm hopeful Catriona, once she receives my telegram, will realize I'm in desperate straits. But even though I included the word *urgent* in the telegram, Catriona isn't a lady predisposed to rushing about, which means I have little faith she'll comply in a timely manner. That means I'll have to wear this gown again next weekend at the Twombly ball."

Walter's gaze traveled over Gwendolyn. "What's wrong with wearing that gown again? It's a very nice gown, and you look quite well in it."

Gwendolyn rolled her eyes. "You apparently missed the part where I said ladies never wear the same garment twice. Also, it's a travesty to call a gown from the House of Worth 'nice,' as well as to tell a lady wearing a Worth gown she looks 'quite well' in it."

"I used to tell Vivian she looked quite well before we attended many a society event, and she never seemed to take issue with that."

"Which certainly accounts for why the two of you enjoyed a marriage where you merely rubbed along nicely together."

"There's nothing wrong with that. It's simply how marriages are in society," Walter said before he frowned. "But if we could return to the subject of gowns from Worth, I distinctly recall Vivian racking up some hefty bills whenever she shopped there, and . . . ?" He arched a brow.

"You're now wondering how an assistant matchmaker could possibly afford a gown from Worth?"

"That thought did cross my mind."

She shrugged. "I'm not your quintessential paid companion or assistant matchmaker and we'll leave it at that."

"That explanation leaves me with more questions than answers."

"Too bad, because I'm not in the proper mood to humor you right now. With that now settled, allow me to turn the conversation to something more pressing, your apparent lack of finesse when it comes to extending compliments. Evidently you believe telling a woman she looks *quite well* or that her gown is *nice* is appropriate, which it's not. It won't do to have you insulting ladies simply because you're deficient when it comes to flattery."

"I'm not deficient, but besides that, I wasn't under the impression I was supposed to be going out of my way to flatter ladies this Season."

"You're in the market for a wife. Flattery is a must." She settled a stern eye on him. "We'll start by having you practice with me. Go ahead, give me your best attempt at flattery."

"Right now?"

She gave an airy wave of a gloved hand. "Now's as good a time as any."

"This is turning into far more work than I was expecting."

"Good thing you had a nap."

He blew out a breath, taking a moment to consider her, as well as consider what compliment he could voice that wouldn't cause her eyes to flash with irritation. The longer he considered her, the more he realized that Gwendolyn was looking far more than quite well that evening—in fact she was looking downright exquisite. Frankly, her appearance eclipsed that of any other lady he'd seen that evening, and even with her being overly annoying most of the time, he couldn't deny there was something about her that intrigued him.

He cleared his throat when he realized he might be gazing at Gwendolyn in a manner best described as stupefaction, which was quite an unusual state to find himself in. "You're looking enchanting tonight, Miss Brinley, and your gown is downright enticing." He caught her eye. "Better?"

A snort was hardly the response he was expecting.

"You can't go around society telling ladies they look enchanting and enticing. That lends you the attitude of a Casanova, something I get the distinct impression you're not. Honestly, Walter, that kind of talk will see you heading down an aisle to exchange vows before the sun rises."

"Perhaps I should stick with words similar to *nice* and *quite well* then."

"Those particular words won't serve you well either, but for now I suggest you don't stray into uncharted territory until we have an opportunity to practice appropriate compliments and flattery tactics when we're not in the midst of a social event. With that settled, it's time for you to get back to the ball. Were there any specific ladies you'd like to dance with this evening? I believe there are ten dances scheduled."

"I'll leave it up to your discretion what three ladies I should partner with this evening."

"To repeat myself, there are ten dances planned."

"I'm aware of that. I only care to participate in three."

She crossed her arms over her chest. "You can't limit your exposure to the ladies. You need to dance every dance."

"No, I need you to be incredibly selective about what ladies I spend time with." He couldn't quite hold back a smile. "If you want to find success as an assistant matchmaker, you'll rise to the occasion and select the most suitable ladies for me to dance with tonight."

Her lips thinned. "No."

"It's not up for debate." He leaned closer to her. "I already ran it past Mrs. Parker and she was perfectly agreeable that three dances were all I needed to dance tonight."

"Running to Mrs. Parker is hardly fair, but . . ." Her toe began tapping against the stone terrace. "Fine, three dances it'll be, because Mrs. Parker will only take to lecturing me if I balk, and I'm not feeling up to a lecture tonight."

She pursed her lips for a second before she nodded. "You'll dance the waltz with Miss Frances Bottleworth, the round with Miss Elizabeth Ellsworth, and then the final waltz of the night with Miss Cordelia Lowe, even though she annoyed me with the hat business. You'll then take whichever of those young ladies you enjoy the most into the midnight supper."

"I thought I'd sit with you at supper so we could go over my thoughts about the evening."

"You don't need to spend time with me, your matchmaker. You need to spend time with ladies you may consider marrying."

"But then I'll have to worry about complimenting them in an unacceptable manner. As you pointed out, that could lead me to meeting a lady who isn't well suited for me at the end of an aisle come morning."

"You're very annoying" was all she said before she turned on her heel and marched her way toward French doors that led to the ballroom.

Unable to resist a grin, Walter followed her into the Harper cottage and pulled her to a stop a few feet from the ballroom floor. "I understand why you'd want me to dance with Miss Elizabeth Ellsworth, because she's now considered the incomparable of the Season, and with Miss Cordelia Lowe because she seems to have handled the black-eye business remarkably well, even though she probably shouldn't have tried to bribe you, but why do you want me to dance with Miss Frances Bottleworth? She's not a lady who's tried to speak with me much so far."

"Which is exactly why I want you to dance with her. Well, that and Mr. E. J. Boettcher mentioned his sisters believe Miss Bottleworth would be a fine lady for him to pursue."

"If E. J. is considering pursuing her, why have me dance with her?"

"I have my reasons" was Gwendolyn's only response to that.

Walter lifted his head, perused the ballroom, and to his concern, spotted E. J. in conversation with Mrs. Parker. His gaze shot back to Gwendolyn. "E. J. wouldn't happen to be interested in having you and Mrs. Parker take him on this Season, would he?"

She settled a far-too-innocent smile on him. "I told him I didn't have time to take on the responsibility of matchmaker for him."

"Looks like he overruled your refusal since he's now in earnest conversation with Mrs. Parker." Walter rubbed a hand over his face. "I get the sneaking suspicion you expected he was going to do that and concluded he may soon be on your roster of people Mrs. Parker has agreed to sponsor. That suggests you want me to dance with Miss Bottleworth because you don't know anything about her. And if she turns out to be a pleasant lady, as well as a chatty one, you can then use what I tell you about her to decide if you should match her up with E. J., which would then move you along on your way to becoming a competent matchmaker."

"That nap really did wonders for your cognitive abilities."

"So much so I now realize you're using me in some type of reconnaissance mission."

She surprised him when she sent him a cheeky grin. "Guilty as charged. But before you turn all indignant, if you find Frances Bottleworth captivating while dancing with her, I'll abandon any idea I may have regarding her as a potential match for Mr. Boettcher—whom Mrs. Parker will assuredly take on to sponsor since he claims to have spare tiaras lying about."

"But . . ."

"Unfair?" she finished for him with an arch of a brow. "I suppose it is, but you may consider it payment for the unenviable job I now find myself responsible for—that being managing your schedule."

"I don't enjoy being used in one of your reconnaissance schemes."

"And I don't enjoy your going behind my back to get Mrs. Parker's agreement on matters such as how many dances you'll dance, or with whom you'll dine. Perhaps we'll need to come to an understanding of how our relationship is going to proceed. Until then, I'm off to inform Miss Bottleworth of her good fortune. Since the waltz is due to commence soon, I suggest you follow not long behind me to claim your first dance partner. And Walter . . . ?"

She settled another innocent smile on him. "Do try to get Miss Bottleworth to disclose as much as you can about herself. That will go far in helping me decide if she's a good match for you . . . or Mr. Boettcher—if as his sisters believe, she's better suited to him. If that's the case, I can see me scoring a second matchmaker win in the not-too-distant future."

Fifteen

"I believe another word with you is in order," Walter said, materializing beside Gwendolyn as she tucked the notepad she used to keep track of the tidbits she was amassing regarding society members into her reticule.

"Is this *a* word or is it going to be another diatribe?" she asked.

"A diatribe," Walter didn't hesitate to say. "You've somehow managed to remove yet another gentleman from the ranks of bachelors, leaving me besieged again." Walter gave a jerk of his head to where E. J. Boettcher was assisting Miss Frances Bottleworth out of a two-seater phaeton that had pulled to a stop in front of Trinity Church, the flirtatious grins they were exchanging speaking volumes.

Gwendolyn raised a hand to her throat. "Oh, would you look at them? They seem completely besotted with each other, even though they only realized they're obviously meant to be together last night at the Harper ball." Her lips curved into a smile. "And not that I want to come across as a braggart, but you can't deny I'm well on my way to achieving that status of exceptional assistant matchmaker. I highly doubt any matchmaker to date has been able to secure a match so quickly, or one that's destined to become one of the great love connections of the year." She caught Walter's eye. "You should be delighted you were instrumental in helping me get those two lovebirds together."

"Because of that conversation I told you I shared with Frances last night?"

"Exactly."

Walter began looking decidedly grouchy. "It hardly seems fair I played a part in matching a gentleman who hasn't put in nearly the amount of work I have on the marriage mart this Season. I don't want to come across as a surly sort, but if memory serves, you promised you weren't going to direct Frances Bottleworth in E. J.'s direction if I thought she might be a suitable candidate for me."

Gwendolyn took hold of Walter's arm and began walking with him toward Trinity Church, where parishioners were gathering by the front door, which was directly adjacent to a graveyard where many a late Newporter had been laid to rest. "You gave me no indication you were interested in continuing on with Frances, especially not after you decided to take Elizabeth Ellsworth in to dinner. If you'd been enthralled with Frances after your dance, I would have assumed you'd dine with her. Since that wasn't the case, I felt free to take the information I gathered from you and pair it with information I got from E. J. when he asked me to join him for dinner at the ball. After I combined all I learned, it was obvious they were a match made in heaven."

Walter's brows drew together. "I didn't realize you dined with E. J. last night, and am now feeling sufficiently slighted because you refused to dine with me."

"It wouldn't have been productive for you to dine with your matchmaker."

"And that train of thought didn't apply to E. J. as well?"

"Not when I didn't have the slightest idea what E. J. was searching for in a potential spouse except that he was interested in securing a match complete with affection."

She waved a hand toward where E. J. and Frances were now wandering arm in arm through the graveyard. "I'm now of the belief that matchmaking as a profession has far more worth than I once thought."

Walter stopped walking, turning his back on the white church sporting a classic steeple that rose in stark relief against the storm clouds gathering in the sky. "I can't argue with you about the merits of a good matchmaker since you've managed to convince most ladies to maintain their distance from me— except for the young ladies who were apparently focused on E. J. and didn't bother to find out I now come with rules. With that said, though, I'm more than bewildered over how you managed to set up the Boettcher-Bottleworth merger so quickly."

Her lips quirked. "Their surnames alone suggest they belong together. I mean, Boettcher and Bottleworth? That's just too precious for words."

"If you're going down that route, I'm surprised you haven't suggested I pay more attention to Suzette Tilden because Townsend and Tilden have the same alliteration."

She tapped a gloved finger against her chin. "You know, I never thought about that."

"And you're not going to consider it now," Walter countered. "After the enlightening conversation I had with Suzette last night, I'm convinced we wouldn't suit."

Gwendolyn frowned. "What conversation?"

"Did you not notice Suzette managed to position herself on the other side of me at dinner?"

"I was somewhat preoccupied with my conversation with E. J."

"A preoccupation that evidently left you oblivious to my plight during a meal that consisted of eleven courses."

"There's no need to get snippy, Walter. I'm sure you're capable of maneuvering your way through a dinner without my assistance. Besides, my engaging dinner conversation with E. J. yielded impressive results, as can be witnessed by the happy couple strolling around the churchyard this morning."

Walter pinched the bridge of his nose. "I'm still confused how you concluded you might have a love match between those two. What information could I have possibly disclosed that had you realizing that?"

"You told me Frances enjoyed bird watching. You also mentioned she'd recently purchased a bicycle and adores tooling around Newport on it to search for birds she's not had an opportunity to discover yet." She smiled. "E. J., with no prodding from me, told me his favorite pastime is bird watching, followed by a recent love of bicycling. Clearly, the two of them share more than a few common interests. All that was left for me to do was suggest they enjoy a dance together and mention how lovely it was to learn they shared a passion for birds."

"That was all it took for them to become smitten with each other?"

"There's no explaining true love. But do know, if you'd mentioned you enjoyed bird watching, I would have suggested you take Frances for a second turn around the floor."

"I don't have anything against birds, I merely don't like to trudge around looking for them."

"Which means you should have no issue with my not pushing Miss Bottleworth in your direction, unless, of course, you have a great love for bicycling."

"I've never been on a bicycle in my life."

"Then I'm sure you're now going to extend your best wishes to E. J. and Frances since, clearly, you don't have much in common with that lady." She tilted her head. "With that now settled, allow us to return to Suzette Tilden. It was surprisingly bold of her to have joined you and Elizabeth without an invitation."

"She didn't force her way into my company, if that's what you're thinking. She and her dinner partner, Mr. Thurman Chandler, merely sat down at the table Elizabeth and I were seated at, although I believe Suzette deliberately sought me out."

"I don't believe I've been introduced to a Thurman Chandler."

"He only just returned from a business trip, hence the reason he missed the Astor ball. His family is heavily invested with the East Indies Company, and truth be told, now that he's in Newport, there's every chance *he'll* become the catch of the Season."

Gwendolyn glanced at the small watch attached to the cuff of her sleeve, took Walter's arm, and hauled him into the cemetery and over to a stone bench. She took a seat, dug her notepad out of her reticule, flipped it open, retrieved a pencil from her bag, and arched a brow at Walter, who was looking more than bewildered as he sat down beside her. "Why might this Thurman Chandler become the catch of the Season?"

"You dragged me over here to ask me questions about Thurman?"

"Of course, but because the service is to start in less than thirty minutes, tell me the most important thing I need to know about him—which is why he could dethrone you as *the* eligible bachelor of the summer."

Walter shrugged. "Thurman possesses an impressive fortune and the ladies consider him to be quite a, well, dish. But why is any of that of interest to you?"

"Because I'm responsible for securing matches for Elizabeth Ellsworth and Hannah Howe. If it turns out Thurman truly is a dish, I'll need to consider presenting Elizabeth and Hannah to him."

Walter leaned forward on the bench. "I thought you had your eye on Elizabeth for *me*."

"Since you didn't have much to share with me pertaining to the time you spent dancing and dining with her, I got the impression you weren't interested."

"And that means you're going to steer her in another direction?"

Gwendolyn swallowed a sigh. "I'm merely investigating all options. Frankly, I'm not convinced Elizabeth is a good match for you. I didn't glean through the snippets you shared with me last night that she asked you much about the children."

"True, but she was very complimentary about my house on Fifth Avenue."

"Another reason to hesitate about her appropriateness. Her interest in your house suggests she's more intrigued by your wealth than she is by your children."

Walter brushed a piece of lint from his sleeve. "A worthy consideration. But if not Elizabeth, and definitely not Frances because you went and matched her up with E. J., who do you have in mind for me?"

Gwendolyn tapped the pencil against the notepad. "I'm not certain, but I took the liberty of asking Cordelia Lowe to join us in your pew today. She, out of all the ladies I've met thus far, seems to possess the best chance of handling your children. She didn't hide herself away from society after receiving that black eye, nor did she hesitate to engage in a public dispute with Tillie Wickham at Bailey's Beach.

"Tillie isn't a lady I imagine anyone wants to tangle with, given her questionable temperament. Cordelia also didn't blink an eye over trying to bribe me with a hat to secure more time with you, though I'm not convinced that's a mark in her favor." She jotted down a bit about Thurman Chandler and flipped to a blank page. "But if we could return to Suzette, what was said that left you knowing she's definitely not suitable for you?"

Walter inclined his head to a passing society matron who was watching them with blatant curiosity and then frowned.

"I didn't like what I learned after I tried to return the pony Suzette gave me."

"You tried to return the pony?"

"It's the most contrary beast I've ever had the misfortune of meeting."

"Contrary or not, you can't give it back. The children must consider it their pet by now."

Walter blew out a breath. "There's no need to fret about that, because Suzette refused to retake possession of the pony, not that it was actually hers to begin with."

Gwendolyn's eyes widened. "She gave you a pony that wasn't hers?"

"It wasn't stolen. It belonged to Thurman Chandler, who is apparently an old friend of Suzette's. He regretted purchasing the contrary beast and even tried to give it away, with no takers because it nipped every prospective owner. Thurman seemed delighted with Suzette last night for rectifying his pony problem, even though I'm now saddled with it and am not delighted by that in the least."

Gwendolyn riffled through the notebook and drew a line through Suzette's name. "Suzette is most assuredly not mother material. She seemingly never considered the pony might nip one of your children." She scratched her nose with the end of her pencil. "It also doesn't speak highly of Thurman that he wouldn't take the pony back, but perhaps he realized your children would become distraught if he retook ownership."

For some reason, Walter released a grunt.

"Why are you grunting at me?"

He narrowed an eye on her. "Because, if I'm not mistaken, we're once again talking about Thurman because you're still wondering if he'd be a good candidate for Elizabeth Ellsworth or Hannah Howe."

"Perhaps I am, but you must realize that the Season isn't all about you. I'm obligated to apply myself to the plight of the ladies Mrs. Parker is sponsoring as well. Besides that, Mrs. Parker has her eye on a diamond-studded choker she saw in the small Tiffany shop down by the Newport Casino. The only way she'll come into possession of that is if she, with my assistance of course, fulfills her promise to Hannah Howe's mother."

"She may have her eye on a diamond choker, but she accepted a diamond bracelet from me, handed over to her with the expectation you would make a concerted effort to find me a wife. You don't seem to be directing much attention my way, because you only have one viable option for me right now, that being Cordelia Lowe—although I'm not sure you've completely taken Elizabeth Ellsworth out of the running. Truth be told, I don't think you're putting much effort into finding a lady for me because you seem to be matching up everyone *except* me and thereby decreasing the number of eligible ladies for me to consider."

"You should think of that as a strategy I'm employing to remove ladies who aren't your match from your orbit, while also allowing poor Mrs. Parker to acquire jewelry her husband refuses to purchase for her." Gwendolyn gave a wave of her hand toward Mrs. Parker, who was sitting in her wheeled chair under a tree, a footman standing behind her waiting to wheel her into the church once the crowd thinned out. "She gets great pleasure from her jewelry collection. In fact, it took quite a bit of coercing from me to convince her the tiara delivered to her cottage from E. J. this morning was not appropriate to wear to church."

Walter pinched the bridge of his nose. "You're deliberately avoiding my accusation of not devoting enough time to my situation."

Gwendolyn let that settle for a moment before she bit her lip. "You may have a point."

"You're agreeing with me?"

She rolled her eyes. "There's no need to sound so incredulous.

I'm not a lady who believes I'm always right. In all truthfulness, my attention *has* been directed elsewhere. But since you've kindly pointed out my neglect, I'll make a concerted effort to focus on you for the entirety of this new week. You mark my words, we'll soon have a concise list of appropriate names for you, and then you can spend the next few weeks escorting those appropriate ladies about Newport. Hopefully, you'll discover a spark with one of them, and then I'll be able to close my notepad on your case and move on to another."

"I don't need a spark. I only need a lady who possesses a semblance of maternal instincts."

"And I respectfully disagree with that. Yes, maternal instincts will be necessary because you have children, but a spark . . . Well, that will allow you and a new wife to enjoy a marriage instead of merely endure it."

She reached into her reticule and pulled out a small calendar. "We need to pencil in a time where I can finally learn more about you: activities you enjoy, what your favorite foods are, what type of animals you like—ponies clearly not being at the top of your list—and if there are any specific ladies you've spoken with in Newport whom you'd like to speak with further." She ran a finger over her calendar. "It looks as if I'm supposed to accompany Mrs. Parker to Henri Bendel's emporium for shopping tomorrow, but I'm certain she'll be receptive to my meeting with you instead."

"I won't be in Newport tomorrow. I'll be back in the city."

She abandoned her calendar. "What do you mean, you'll be back in the city?"

"I only come to Newport on the weekends, or more specifically, Friday afternoon until late Sunday afternoon, because I have a business to run during the week."

"At no point have you mentioned that to me." She leaned forward. "The Newport Season is abbreviated as it is. If you expect me to find you an appropriate wife when you're only here on the weekends, you've taken leave of your senses because that's an impossible feat."

Walter quirked a brow. "You appear to be a woman who enjoys challenges. I'm certain if you embrace my situation as exactly that, you'll be able to rise to the occasion magnificently."

"Nice try, Walter, but there's no way I'm going to rise to this occasion, even with you throwing down what is obviously a gauntlet." She shook her head. "No, you, I'm afraid, are going to have to be the one to make concessions, starting with your promise you'll make arrangements that will allow you to be in Newport seven days a week beginning next weekend at the latest."

"I'm in the middle of acquiring new real estate. I don't have time to twiddle my thumbs during the week when there are so many intricate details still needing to be attended to."

"Don't you have managers who could take up some of your business load?"

"Of course, but I prefer to have a hand in every Townsend business deal I broker. That's why I need to return to the city, and why I won't be able to accommodate your demand that I clear my schedule for the summer."

Gwendolyn stuffed her notepad, pencil, and calendar into her reticule and got to her feet. "Then you're going to have to find yourself a new matchmaker, because even Mrs. Parker will agree that you've given us an impossible task."

She turned on her heel, paused, and looked back over her shoulder. "And before you remind me that Mrs. Parker already accepted a bracelet from Tiffany's as a token of good faith to sponsor you, know that I'll remind her you never mentioned you'd be absent from Newport most of the Season. She'll not like that, and will certainly believe you withheld that pertinent information on purpose.

"When I refuse to continue with your case, her annoyance over the matter will certainly increase when she realizes she'll either need to personally take up your case—which she'll know is going to be impossible to successfully complete—or return the Tiffany bracelet to you in a gesture of goodwill, a gesture she'll be less than gracious about making. I assure you, either of those options will not sit well with Mrs. Parker, who may seem like a dear, charming woman at times, but who is nothing of the sort."

Sixteen

***

Thirty-five minutes later, Walter found himself experiencing a bit of a novel situation as he sat in the enclosed Townsend family pew, waiting for a service delayed because Reverend Eberhard had decided to rework his sermon, trying to ignore the irritated glances being cast his way from more than a few members of the feminine persuasion.

It was no surprise Gwendolyn was annoyed with him, but it was unnerving how Mrs. Parker kept swiveling her head from where she sat on the main floor of the church to glare at him as he sat in his balcony pew.

Granted, he should have been expecting the glares because to say Mrs. Parker had been annoyed to learn he intended to head back to the city for the week was an understatement. She'd not hesitated to launch into a lecture of magnificent proportions, telling him in no uncertain terms he needed to rethink his priorities.

It had been a definite error in judgment to respond by telling her his work *was* his main priority and that *her* main priority was to whittle down potential candidates for him to review once he returned on Friday.

Being a society matron accustomed to getting her way, Mrs. Parker's only response had been to send him a look that could have seared the flesh from his face before she'd had her footman wheel her away without another word—something that had Gwendolyn sending him a most telling "I told you so" arch of a delicate brow.

Unfortunately, Gwendolyn and Mrs. Parker weren't the only ladies irritated with him. Added to that list were his mother, Ethel, and mother-in-law, Matilda, who'd descended into annoyed states as soon as he'd ushered Gwendolyn into the family pew.

"I have no idea why you invited that woman to sit with us," Ethel hissed in his ear, jerking her head in a less than subtle fashion toward Gwendolyn.

Thankfully, Gwendolyn was preoccupied with helping Priscilla tie a ribbon in a rag doll's hair and missed the jerking, and Ethel had at least had the presence of mind to lower her voice to vent her displeasure.

"Gwendolyn's my matchmaker," he returned quietly. "She needed to join me today so she can observe how Miss Cordelia Lowe interacts with the children, if Miss Lowe decides to show up, which seems doubtful since the service should have already begun but there's no sign of her."

Ethel waved that aside. "Your matchmaker took it upon herself to take away the candy Matilda and I gave to the children to ascertain they'll be well-behaved during the service. You know we rarely bring the children to church since they've been known to cause disruptions. That's why we decided a special treat was in order. However, your *matchmaker* absconded with those treats. She then had the audacity to say sugar has been known to cause excess excitability in children, which is complete nonsense. She didn't even consider the twins would be devastated to have their sweets snatched out of their tiny hands."

Walter glanced to where Gwendolyn was showing his daughter a better way to tie a bow before he returned his attention to his mother. "Priscilla hardly seems devastated."

"Which may very well be true, but your matchmaker then took it upon herself to tell the twins God expects them to behave while in His house, and not because they've been bribed with delicacies to do so. That undoubtedly frightened the children half to death—that theory proven by the continuous glances Priscilla and Samuel keep making to the ceiling, as if they expect God to send a lightning bolt directly at them if they happen to step out of line."

"I never heard Gwendolyn mention anything about any lightning bolts," Walter said.

"Oh, she didn't. That was simply an aside Oscar made. It might have been a joke, but I'm not certain because I rarely understand what the young set finds amusing these days."

"You know very well, Ethel, that Oscar wouldn't have mentioned the lightning bolt, even in jest, if that matchmaker hadn't warned the children about behaving," Matilda whispered, leaning across Ethel to meet Walter's gaze. "You mark my words, the twins will be plagued with nightmares for days." She sent a sad shake of her head toward Samuel, who didn't notice because he was absorbed with a bag stuffed with toys he'd insisted on bringing with him to church.

"I suppose it's a blessing Oscar decided he wanted to sit with his friend for services," Ethel said. "He might have been subjected to a lecture from the matchmaker if she realized he has a habit of telling jokes. I'm sure, given her dislike of candy, she doesn't enjoy those either." She leaned forward and peered over the balcony railing, directing her gaze to where Oscar was sitting beside Sherman Kenton in the Kenton family pew.

As if he could feel his grandmother's gaze, Oscar swiveled

around in the pew, sent Ethel a wave, then settled a scowl on Walter before he turned front and center again, presenting Walter with his back. It was a rather telling gesture and lent credence to the idea it was not only the feminine set who were put out with him on what should have been a serene Sunday morning at church.

"You might want to take Oscar aside after the service," Gwendolyn said, drawing his attention. "The look he just sent you suggests he's still offended you were unaware Sherman has been his best friend since the boys were five." She leaned forward. "You might also consider taking him fishing at your earliest convenience since you additionally learned that's a hobby Oscar enjoys."

Walter frowned. "You heard him reject my offer to go fishing right before we entered the church."

"He refused because you didn't know he enjoyed fishing in the first place, nor did you know that Sherman's father, Mr. Kenton, is the one who taught Oscar to fish. You were also less than proficient at hiding how incredulous you were to discover Oscar has plans to ride his bicycle over to Sherman's cottage after services because Mrs. Kenton invited him to lunch."

"I was incredulous because I had no idea Oscar knew how to ride a bicycle, or that he even owned one."

"Which is why, in my humble opinion, you may want to, as you're enjoying your yacht ride back to the city, take some time to reflect on how it came to be you know nothing about your elder son, including but not limited to his friends, his hobbies, and the real reason behind how he managed to fail all of his classes at that private preparatory school he was attending a mere month before classes dispersed for the summer. From what I've gathered about Oscar thus far, he's remarkably intelligent."

Walter shifted on the seat, the uncomfortable thought taking root that Gwendolyn had just voiced some valid points, and that she wasn't wrong in her assessment of his relationship with Oscar.

He *didn't* know his son, or the twins—something he'd never considered before because gentlemen of society weren't expected to take an interest in their children until any sons reached their majority and were brought into family businesses.

Walter cleared his throat, but before he could get a word out, his mother sat forward.

"That will be quite enough, Miss Brinley," Ethel said, her eyes flashing with temper. "While I understand you've suddenly found yourself in high demand, you're merely Mrs. Parker's assistant, and as such, you have no business reprimanding my son." Ethel lifted her chin. "Nevertheless, since you *are* working on his behalf, and he won't listen to me about abandoning this absurd matchmaking fiasco, keep in mind that your only duty is to present eligible young ladies to him—something I'm not convinced you're qualified to do, considering Miss Lowe was supposed to join us for the service, per your invitation, and yet she's nowhere to be seen."

Gwendolyn, to Walter's surprise, merely smiled and inclined her head. "I would be more than happy to relinquish my role as Walter's matchmaker, Mrs. Townsend. In fact, I was vehemently against Mrs. Parker's sponsoring him in the first place but was overruled. Because of that, I have no reservations speaking my mind to your son. If you find that offensive, by all means, encourage him to part ways with me. You'd be doing me a favor, especially since Mrs. Parker, even knowing Walter is not going to be here for most of the Season, is still insistent about sponsoring him."

With that, Gwendolyn sent him a rolling of the eyes, as if it were his fault his mother had taken to lecturing her, and returned her attention to Priscilla, who was now changing her doll's dress.

Ethel and Matilda wasted no time bending their heads

together, clearly discussing Gwendolyn, even though the enclosed pew wasn't that large, and Gwendolyn was certainly aware she was the topic of conversation.

Not that she seemed concerned about that considering her lips were curving the slightest bit, as if she'd decided her current situation was rather amusing.

In his opinion, an amused Gwendolyn was far less terrifying than an irritated one, although . . .

Before he could finish that thought, Gwendolyn rose to her feet. "Ah, there she is," she said before she opened the half door to the pew and moved down the aisle, clearly to intercept Miss Cordelia Lowe, who was hurrying through the church.

"I certainly hope Miss Lowe has a reasonable excuse for why she's so late," Ethel said. "If she hopes to become a part of this family, she'll need to remember her high standing in society, and what the expectations are with that standing—tardiness, of course, being unacceptable."

Priscilla suddenly abandoned her interest in her doll and turned a face that had trouble stamped all over it his way.

"How would this Miss Lowe become part of the family?" she demanded as Samuel stopped fussing with his bag of toys and scooted closer to his sister.

Walter refused a sigh and prayed he wasn't about to be thrust into a twin storm of epic proportions. "It's far too premature to claim anyone is joining our family, but do try to behave yourself when Miss Lowe joins us. She's a nice lady, and I imagine she'd love it if you'd allow her to help dress your doll."

"Miss Brinley's helping me."

"But Miss Lowe might enjoy helping you as well."

Priscilla's lips thinned. "No."

Before Walter could get a word out regarding the benefits of sharing, or including everyone in an activity, Gwendolyn was ushering Cordelia into the pew. Rising to his feet, he took hold of Cordelia's hand, placed a kiss on it, then helped get her settled on the pew next to him while Gwendolyn retook her seat next to Priscilla.

"I must beg your pardon for being unforgivably late," Cordelia said after Walter sat down beside her. "When I called for my carriage this morning, it was discovered it had a broken wheel."

"Do you think someone deliberately tampered with it, such as someone who might have been miffed you were joining Walter for Sunday services?" Gwendolyn asked, a frown marring her face. "If that's the case, I'll arrange a meeting with everyone out this Season, because we need to nip this type of business in the bud once and for all."

Cordelia blinked before her lips twitched. "While the mere mention of your calling a meeting would be enough to strike terror into anyone contemplating any shenanigans, I don't believe my broken wheel was a result of tampering. It probably resulted after my driver rolled over a hole." She smiled. "Besides that, I don't know a lady in society who'd know how to go about intentionally breaking a wheel. Nor can I imagine anyone with skullduggery on their minds enlisting the aid of a servant, because servants talk amongst the houses."

She turned her smile on Walter. "That's why you were inundated with gifts for the children at Bailey's Beach yesterday. Elizabeth Ellsworth was seen purchasing kites in town by a lady's maid to another family, and it didn't take long for word to travel. Not wanting to come up short, we ladies descended on the toy department in droves—except Suzette Tilden, of course. She managed to rustle up a pony, which is what I had to resort to rustling up today as well, after my broken wheel. I don't take Daisy out much, because she's slow as molasses, which is another reason I was late getting here."

Priscilla suddenly settled an angelic smile on Cordelia, one Walter wasn't buying for a moment.

"You have a girl pony?" Priscilla asked sweetly.

"I do," Cordelia returned with a smile of her own.

Priscilla got up and scooted herself in between Walter and Cordelia, placing her little hand on Cordelia's skirt. "And you don't take her out much?"

"I'm afraid I don't, because as I mentioned, she's not very fast."

Priscilla tilted her head. "I'm only five, and my grandmothers wouldn't allow me to ride a pony that's too fast."

"Would you like to come visit me sometime and ride Daisy?" Cordelia asked.

"It would be better if you just gave her to me."

A crease settled on Cordelia's forehead. "Gave her to you?"

Priscilla's smile turned more angelic than ever. "I would take very good care of her, and she'd have a friend because some other lady gave us a pony yesterday, but it's a boy pony and I wanted a girl."

Cordelia swallowed, then shot Gwendolyn a look that clearly begged for assistance. When Gwendolyn merely arched a brow in return, Cordelia blew out a breath and returned her attention to Priscilla, who looked quite like a cat who'd just discovered a bowl filled with cream. "I imagine Daisy might enjoy a new home that would see her receiving more attention, even though I'm rather attached to her."

Walter glanced to Ethel and Matilda and found them with their heads bent together as they riffled through a hymnal, apparently trying to find the hymn Mrs. Wailing, who'd been playing the piano nonstop as the service continued to be delayed, had launched into.

Realizing it was going to be up to him to handle yet another incident where one of his children was behaving badly—and before Priscilla tried to cajole Cordelia's pony cart along with her pony from her—he caught Cordelia's eye. "Forgive me, Miss Lowe, for I fear my daughter has abandoned any semblance of the manners she's been taught. You will certainly not relinquish your pony to Priscilla."

He settled his gaze on his daughter. "And you, Priscilla, will now extend Miss Lowe a sincere apology for trying to wheedle her pony away from her in the first place."

It was hardly an encouraging sign when storm clouds immediately began brewing in Priscilla's eyes.

Seventeen

⁂

Bracing himself for the havoc certain to come, Walter rose to his feet and moved to whisk Priscilla out of the church before she released the fury settled in her eyes, but she suddenly jumped up and scrambled past him, launching herself into Gwendolyn's lap.

Gwendolyn didn't miss a beat and simply pulled Priscilla close, handed her the rag doll, then whispered something to her that had Priscilla's little shoulders sagging for just a second before she lifted her head and turned to Cordelia.

"I'm very sorry for wanting your pony," Priscilla said, her tiny lips trembling before she buried her face in the folds of Gwendolyn's dress right as Reverend Eberhard finally appeared on the raised pulpit.

"What in the world did you say to her?" Walter asked as he retook his seat.

Priscilla peeped over at him before Gwendolyn could respond. "She told me to 'member what she said about God expecting me to behave in His house." She gave a rather theatrical shudder. "I don't want a lightning bolt to find me, so I'm going to stay right here in Miss Brinley's lap."

Suppressing a grin, Walter watched as Priscilla buried her

144

head against Gwendolyn again before he settled his attention on Reverend Eberhard, who had spread his arms wide as he gazed over his congregation.

"How wonderful to see so many pews filled this morning," Reverend Eberhard began. "Forgive me for the delayed start. I'm afraid it was unavoidable because I felt called to change the sermon I was going to preach today. My original intention was to speak on Proverbs 31:9, which reads, 'Open thy mouth, judge righteously, and plead the cause of the poor and needy.' However, I felt pulled to speak on a different Scripture passage. I will, however, say one thing about Proverbs 31:9. As most of you remember, I frequently feel compelled to remind all of you who repair to Newport for the summer, given the many financial blessings most of you have received, that it's your responsibility to look after those less fortunate."

Reverend Eberhard took a moment to gaze out at his congregation again, smiling and nodding to the gentlemen in the audience, Walter being one of them, along with Mr. Thurman Chandler, Mr. Russell Damrosch, and then Mr. Clarence Higgenson, who was sitting beside Mrs. Lanier in the Higgenson family pew, empty except for the two of them. The rest of the Higgensons were apparently unwilling to accept Clarence's decision to become engaged to a divorced woman.

Reverend Eberhard then returned to his notes, lifted his head, and smiled once again. "Let us begin the service today with prayer."

Saying a quick prayer of his own that his children wouldn't decide to take that particular moment to turn disruptive, he glanced to the twins and saw Gwendolyn showing Priscilla and Samuel how to fold their hands properly. The twins didn't release so much as a whisper of dissent while the opening prayer was said, although they both gave a rousing "Amen" at the end, which earned them a grin from Gwendolyn in return.

Silence settled over the congregation as Reverend Eberhard

opened the Bible lying on the lectern, consulted it for a moment, then lifted his head. "As I mentioned, I felt called to speak on a different topic today, and whenever I feel called to act, I know I'm being sent a message God wants me to deliver. Today I'm going to speak on James 3:16. For those of you who do not have your Bibles open, that verse says, 'For where envying and strife is, there is confusion and every evil work.'"

Reverend Eberhard stepped around the pulpit and folded his hands in front of him, his gaze once again traveling over the congregation but this time lingering, or so it seemed, on the ladies in attendance instead of the gentlemen.

"It came to my attention early this morning that there seems to be an issue with appropriate behavior this Season in Newport," he said. "From what I understand, more than a few of our own seem to have forgotten some of Christ's most important teachings, specifically the one revolving around His commandment that we are to love our neighbor.

"To be clear," Reverend Eberhard continued, "love does not entail abusing an opponent during a friendly sports game, nor does loving one's neighbor ever consist of peculiar incidents where beverages spill out of their respective containers and land on unwitting victims." He stepped behind the lectern again. "I've also been apprised that shoving has been witnessed at more than a few events, sharp elbows delivered to the ribs of unsuspecting ladies in an effort to jockey into a better position when eligible gentlemen are out and about."

He shook his head. "It is my belief this questionable behavior is a direct result of jealousy, as well as greed, brought about from a desire to obtain the most advantageous unions. Jealousy is a dangerous creature, my friends, and can burrow into our souls and turn us hateful and bitter, unable to experience the simple joys of life. From where I stand, it's evident that jealousy is turning friend against friend this Season, and life without friends is joyless indeed."

Reverend Eberhard consulted his notes again. "As you of marriageable age traverse through the Newport Season, I encourage you to abandon the custom of choosing a matrimonial partner based solely on the size of their fortune or status within society. Each of you should strive to secure marriages of love and affection, setting aside any temptation to marry simply because of the lure of materialistic possessions and higher rank amongst the socially elite."

"Oh dear," Ethel whispered, leaning closer to Walter. "I hope Reverend Eberhard didn't misunderstand the calling he heard today, because it's one thing to lecture the gentlemen in the congregation about giving to the poor, but it's another matter altogether to go after the ladies. Mothers will not take kindly to him questioning the behavior of their daughters."

"I'm sure he understood exactly what God wanted him to impart today," Gwendolyn whispered back. "And while I'm sure you're correct about the ladies being annoyed at being taken to task, it's a message many in attendance needed to hear. And who better to deliver a message about questionable behavior than a servant of the Lord?"

"If I may have everyone's attention again?" Reverend Eberhard said, raising his voice to be heard over all the murmuring and rapid waving of fans by ladies who, as Ethel had mentioned, were not taking kindly to the reverend's words.

As the church grew quiet, Reverend Eberhard paced around the pulpit. "To those of you who have participated in unbecoming antics, I say this—you must go forward with grace and love, refusing to give in to the temptation to set yourself apart from the crowd by disparaging anyone. Everyone is considered your neighbor, and God, again, expects you to love them."

As Reverend Eberhard returned to his notes, silence settled over the church until Samuel suddenly jumped to his feet as the bag he'd insisted on bringing with him began to move, right before a gray face complete with whiskers and a black nose appeared—a nose that unfortunately belonged to . . .

Before Walter could finish the thought, Rat, Samuel's oddly named guinea pig, scrambled from its hiding place, clawed its way up the skirt of Ethel's gown, landed on her shoulder, and sat there trembling for the briefest of seconds—until Ethel released a shriek right as Samuel tried to grab him.

It quickly became evident that Rat didn't want to be caught, because he launched himself into the air, landing on Matilda's hat. She immediately began shrieking as well while trying to knock the guinea pig from her hat with her hymnal.

"Don't hurt him," Samuel yelled, lunging for Rat but missing when the guinea pig scurried down Matilda's back, eliciting renewed shrieking from Matilda. Rat then jumped onto the railing of the pew and took off as fast as his little guinea pig legs could carry him.

"Rat!" Samuel yelled as he leapt over the short wall of the pew and began chasing after his runaway pet. "Rat!" he called again as Priscilla, followed by Gwendolyn, dashed out of the pew, running pell-mell after Samuel.

As Walter raced to catch up with them, he soon discovered Samuel's continuous yells of "Rat" were not the shrewdest thing for his son to yell in a room filled with sensitive ladies, because a chorus of shrill squeals began echoing around Trinity Church.

Pandemonium was swift as some ladies jumped up on the benches while others made a beeline for the door.

Unfortunately, with the aisle now crowded with ladies attempting to flee, Walter's forward progress turned into a crawl. Craning his neck, he wasn't surprised to see Samuel, upon finding the steps leading from the balcony blocked by ladies, squeeze his way to the railing, hoist his leg over it, and begin sliding his way to the first floor, Priscilla following suit a second later.

"Priscilla, no!" he called, his heart skipping a beat as his daughter flung herself over the railing.

"Stop right there, young lady," he heard Gwendolyn shout. But Priscilla either didn't hear her or was intentionally ignoring her, because a blink of an eye later, she was zooming down the railing on her stomach, squealing all the way to the bottom.

To Walter's astonishment, instead of fighting her way through the crowd, Gwendolyn hopped on the railing as well and slid—sitting straight up, with perfect posture to boot—to the bottom, leaping gracefully to the ground before she charged after Priscilla and Samuel.

As he edged his way through ladies still attempting to flee the building, although why they were continuing to do so was beyond him since Samuel was no longer yelling "Rat" every other second, probably because Rat had left the building and was surely on his way to find guinea pig freedom, Walter forced himself to begin composing a suitable response to deal with what was assuredly going to be the loss of Samuel's pet.

Pressing past five ladies blocking the door, he, along with Cordelia, who'd been dogging his heels, finally broke free of the crowd, Walter hesitating beside the graveyard as he looked around for his children.

"Priscilla's over by that tall tombstone," he told Cordelia, nodding to where his daughter was peering around a headstone. "You get her. I'll go after Samuel."

Running toward where the carriages were lined up, Walter rounded the corner of the church and stopped in his tracks when he saw a footman striding down the cobblestone walkway, wielding a broom, his sights on a small bundle of fur that seemed to be frozen in place, a guinea pig that, if it survived this ordeal, might need a name change.

"Put that broom away," Gwendolyn yelled right as Rat began moving again—unfortunately in the direction of the footman still clutching his broom.

Disaster was imminent when the footman apparently didn't hear Gwendolyn and drew the broom back, clearly intent on taking care of what he believed to be a rat once and for all. Before he could let the broom fly though, Gwendolyn rushed toward him, snatched the broom from his hands, tossed it aside, and then set her attention on Rat, who was now scrambling up the drive, his sights on a green pasture that bordered the church. Without a second's hesitation, she broke into a run, made a flying leap a moment later, and landed facedown in what looked to be a large mud puddle.

"Is he dead?" Samuel demanded, traipsing into the puddle and stopping beside Gwendolyn, who took that moment to roll over, get to her feet, and brandish what turned out to be Rat, looking the worse for wear—although he might not have been as mud drenched as Gwendolyn.

"He's fine, Samuel, but what say you let me hold him until we get the little darling home and returned to his cage?"

While Samuel beamed a gap-toothed smile at Gwendolyn, Ethel materialized by Walter's side. "I'll deny this if you tell Miss Brinley, but she certainly is uncommonly competent. I would have never imagined any lady had the ability to catch a rapidly retreating rodent with her bare hands, or that she would do so while under threat of being walloped with a broom."

"She does seem to be a remarkably capable woman," Walter agreed. "But since Rat has been thwarted from his bid for freedom, I should check on Miss Lowe. She was going after Priscilla in the graveyard."

Ethel peered over Walter's shoulder. "I believe she found her and . . . oh dear." She winced. "This isn't going to be good."

Refusing a sigh, Walter directed his attention to where his mother was gazing, finding Cordelia standing two feet away from Priscilla, holding what appeared to be the arm of Priscilla's rag doll in her hand. Given the outrage stamped on his daughter's face, it wasn't a stretch to assume Cordelia had tried to catch Priscilla by grabbing hold of her doll, parting his daughter's doll from her arm.

Striding into motion, Walter shuddered when Priscilla took a step backward, a telling sign if there ever was one—and something that usually preceded an attack of the kicking or biting sort.

Just as Priscilla lowered her head, a brilliant flash of lightning streaked across the sky, followed by a loud burst of thunder that had the ground trembling. A mere second later, Priscilla was in motion, flying his way as fast as her short legs could carry her. He barely had a second to open his arms to scoop her up, and then she was burrowing her head in the crook of his neck right as the heavens opened up.

A rusty-sounding laugh escaped him as Priscilla arched away from him and caught his eye, her eyes wide even as she blinked rain out of them.

"Miss Brinley wasn't jesting, was she, Papa?"

"About what, darling?"

She wrinkled her nose. "About God expecting me to behave in His house. I'm going to try awfully hard to behave from now on, because I think lightning hitting me might hurt."

Another laugh escaped him, and after pulling his daughter close, he lifted his head and found Cordelia waving his way.

"I'm going to accept a ride with Miss Wickham," Cordelia called before she spun on her heel and raced to where Miss Wickham was gesturing for her to get into a carriage, a groom already steering a pony cart down the drive, one pulled by a pony moving at a plodding rate, obviously the rarely taken out Daisy.

The thought struck that Cordelia may have beat a hasty retreat because she wasn't up for dealing with his contrary daughter and her one-armed doll, but he tucked that thought aside and headed for his carriage when it began raining harder than ever.

He couldn't help but smile when Priscilla tucked her face into the crook of his neck as he reached his carriage, where

Gwendolyn was already getting Samuel and his mother and mother-in-law settled in it. She turned and shoved a sopping strand of hair out of her face, her brows drawing together when she caught sight of him.

"You're smiling," she said.

"You seem surprised."

"Given the circumstances, yes, I am a little surprised, but . . ." Her lips curved. "You should do that more often. It suits you." With that, she turned and climbed into the carriage right as Oscar materialized by his side.

"She's right," Oscar said, holding Priscilla's rag doll and its missing arm.

"About what?" Walter asked.

"Smiling. You should do it more often." Sending him a genuine smile of his own, something Walter couldn't remember Oscar sending him in a very long time, his son scrambled into the carriage, leaving Walter with the distinct feeling he might have turned a corner with his children, and all because of Gwendolyn Brinley, who currently looked like the drowned guinea pig she was still holding, but who'd accomplished something most ladies would have been hard-pressed to do—rising to a most unusual circumstance, and rising magnificently to it at that.

Eighteen

"Miss Brinley, thank goodness you've decided to pay us a visit, even with it being unexpected," Ethel said as she rushed down the hallway of Sea Haven, Gwendolyn in her sights.

Gwendolyn handed her umbrella to the Townsend family butler, who'd said his name was Benson, and returned her attention to Ethel, who was looking quite unlike herself.

Ethel's hair was straggling out of her chignon, her sleeves were rolled up, and she appeared to have chocolate dribbled down the front of her morning gown.

Granted, Ethel had not been at her best three days before, after the deluge at the church, but any other time Gwendolyn had seen her, she'd been well put together—something that couldn't be said about her today.

"I sent a note an hour ago, telling you to expect me," Gwendolyn said when Ethel stopped in front of her. "Did you not receive it?"

Ethel fanned her face with her hand. "I probably did, but with the crisis I'm currently trying to manage, I haven't had a spare moment to check my notes or calling cards." She reached out, surprising Gwendolyn when she took hold of her arm. "Come with me. You will not believe what's happened now."

A blink of an eye later, Gwendolyn found herself being tugged through an entrance hall showcasing an ornate heart-styled staircase that led to the second floor, then down a hallway lined with paintings of seascapes. Many of the scenes depicted were from Newport, but she didn't have an opportunity to admire them, because Ethel picked up her pace and they were now moving so rapidly things were beginning to pass by in a blur.

Before she knew it, Gwendolyn found herself in the kitchen, the sight that met her eyes rendering her speechless.

Food displayed in various bone-china serving dishes was everywhere—stacked on the kitchen worktable, counters, spare chairs, and even in the three sinks the kitchen sported.

"What in the world?" she asked.

"I know—it's complete madness," Ethel said, gesturing around the room. "Meals started showing up this morning at seven, and they haven't stopped." She shook her head. "They're from some of the ladies out this Season. The only explanation I've arrived at is they've taken Reverend Eberhard's words to heart from Sunday's service and this is their peculiar way of loving thy neighbor, or more specifically, showing their affection for Walter."

Gwendolyn blinked. "An odd twist of Reverend Eberhard's words to be sure, and it's unfortunate he was unable to complete his sermon. I'm relatively convinced he would say that inundating a household with meals was not what he had in mind when he told the congregation to love one another. Frankly, he might need to consider revisiting the jealousy business since it appears the ladies are still in what can only be described as competitive states of mind."

"Tillie Wickham sent fourteen courses, Suzette Tilden sent eleven, and then the twelve other meals we've received thus far were all extravagant ten-course offerings." Ethel swiped a handkerchief over a forehead that was now perspiring. "Evidently realizing Walter wasn't impressed by sending the children presents, the ladies have apparently decided to change tactics and appeal to his stomach."

"It's often said the way to a gentleman's heart is through his stomach," Gwendolyn said, shaking her head. "I'll say one thing for the ladies though—they've mastered the art of stealth. I've spoken with many of them over the past few days at different society events, and not once did I hear a whisper about this latest plot to impress Walter. I have to wonder how it came to be they all decided to send meals, and also why they would send these meals today, when Walter is still in the city."

Ethel began fanning her face again. "I was informed by my lady's maid that Tillie Wickham is the one who first came up with this idea. She mentioned it within earshot of one of her footmen, who happens to be courting a scullery maid at Suzette Tilden's cottage. I imagine word traveled from there."

"But why now? Why not wait until this coming weekend, when Walter will be back in town?"

Ethel winced. "I fear I'm to blame for that. While enjoying lunch yesterday at the Newport Casino with Matilda, I became annoyed when Mrs. Wickham suggested to Tillie that Walter didn't deserve the title of catch of the Season considering he couldn't be bothered to enjoy all the festivities the Newport summer has to offer. That's when I may have told Matilda, in an overly loud voice, that Walter was expected back today and that I had every hope his matchmaker was going to present him with a long list of suitable candidates for him to consider."

"That explains why Tillie sought me out yesterday during Mrs. Livingston's dinner, even though I'd been avoiding her because I've concluded she's not a suitable match for Walter, what with her overly competitive and argumentative nature. She was all sweetness and smiles, and even went so far as to insist I join her tomorrow at the Newport Casino for a friendly match of tennis."

Ethel's eyes widened. "Good heavens, dear, you didn't tell her you'd play against her, did you? Surely you recall what happened to Cordelia Lowe and her unfortunate eye after she agreed to what I'm sure she thought was going to be a friendly afternoon on the court."

"I couldn't very well turn down Tillie's invitation when I want to see if she's going to make an attempt to annihilate me while we play, which would definitely take her off my list for Walter." Gwendolyn shrugged. "Besides that, I enjoy a good game of tennis, although I haven't played often. My cousin Catriona is an infrequent player at best, and since I spend most of my time in her company—when I don't feel compelled to take on a temporary position because I need a respite from her—I don't get to practice often."

Ethel frowned. "You're not a paid companion by trade, turned into an assistant matchmaker because of Mrs. Parker's leg?"

"Oh, I'm a paid companion to my cousin, but there's a whole story behind that. As I told your son, I thought it would be relaxing to spend a leisurely summer in Mrs. Parker's employ. However, leisure seems to be nonexistent in Newport, what with the incessant round of frivolities offered every day. But that has nothing to do with this situation, one that may turn contentious if the ladies discover Walter's not at Sea Haven to appreciate their generosity."

"Given the dishes currently swimming in delicate cream sauce, he won't be able to enjoy any of this because it'll spoil before he returns on Friday," Ethel said. "As for the ladies being unhappy, I'm not bothered about that in the least, because *I'm* put out with all of them."

She nodded to a woman with gray hair pulled back in a severe knot and wearing an apron with flour on it. She was rolling out a pie crust on the only surface available in the far corner of the kitchen, the banging of the rolling pin suggesting the woman was in a temper. "Mrs. Boyle is now threatening to leave my employ. She's the best cook I've ever had and has been with me for years."

Mrs. Boyle stopped banging her rolling pin and lifted her head. "Too right I am considering leaving. My pride is damaged, perhaps beyond repair, and all because the summer residents of Newport evidently believe Mr. Townsend has a substandard cook, hence the reason for delivering all these meals to him."

Gwendolyn moved closer to the cook. "We've not been introduced, Mrs. Boyle, but I'm Gwendolyn Brinley, Walter's matchmaker. Allow me to put your mind at ease. I've been observing the young ladies responsible for what is clearly another fiasco, and take my word on this—your abilities in the kitchen have nothing to do with their decision to inundate Sea Haven with meals. This latest instance of shenanigans is merely a result of too many members of the society set longing to add a Townsend to their family tree."

She lifted the lid off a beautiful serving dish that had terrapin soup inside it. After taking a whiff of what was certainly going to be a delicious dish, she returned the lid. "If anything, you should take the delivery of these meals as a sign you'll be able to take the rest of the day off, since obviously you're not going to need to prepare any meals today."

"I can't stop making the pies I was preparing for supper, and the rack of lamb is already basting in the ice chest."

"It would be a shame if a marvelous rack of lamb went to waste," Gwendolyn agreed.

"A crime is more like it," Mrs. Boyle muttered, returning to her pie crust.

"But there's no possibility we can eat all this food," Ethel said. "Even if Walter were here, it's too many dishes, which leaves me with the dilemma of what we should do with it. I hate to chuck it into the refuse pile."

"Terrapin should never be chucked into a refuse pile," Mrs. Boyle said, abandoning her rolling pin again.

"Indeed, but I have no idea how to handle the madness that has swept into Sea Haven," Ethel said before she nodded to Gwendolyn. "That's why I'm relieved you've come to visit. You seem to have a very managing way about you. Any suggestions on how I should dispose of what is truly a feast of magnificent proportions?"

Gwendolyn began wandering around the kitchen, stopping when a thought sprang to mind. She turned to Ethel.

"Dare I hope you're acquainted with Mr. Ward McAllister?"

Ethel arched a brow. "I'm a Knickerbocker, dear, as well as a Townsend."

"I'll take that as a yes, and also take that to mean you're familiar with Mr. McAllister's love of throwing spur-of-the-moment picnics at his Newport residence, Bayside Farm. I believe he's always telling people he's asked to "get up" a picnic several times during the Newport Season, something he apparently relishes doing."

"He does savor entertaining at his farm, although he always makes certain everyone knows what a trial it can be, assigning everyone what dishes to bring for his picnics," Ethel said.

Gwendolyn's lips curved. "Then he'll jump at the chance to not have to worry about that because you'll be supplying all the food."

"Rumor has it Mr. McAllister's staff isn't always pleased about all the extra work his spontaneous picnics involve," Mrs. Boyle said, dusting her hands together. "But I'll volunteer to help set up, as well as bring a few of our maids and footmen to help. It'll be my pleasure because it'll allow me to get my kitchen back and"—she directed a smile to Ethel—"it'll put you in Mr. McAllister's good graces, which may have him offering to assist you with the final details for the ball you're hosting in a few weeks."

"You're hosting a ball?" Gwendolyn asked.

Ethel nodded. "It's a Townsend family tradition to host a ball in Newport. And if Ward McAllister agrees to help me, it'll be one of *the* balls of the Season."

"Then may I suggest you get on your way to speak with Mr. McAllister?" Gwendolyn said. "I overheard him saying yesterday at Bailey's Beach he planned to scour his farm for flowers today and then spend the rest of the morning arranging those flowers for Mrs. Astor, who apparently enjoys it when Ward sends her his arrangements."

"Caroline does appreciate Ward fawning over her, but don't tell him I said that." Ethel settled her gaze on Gwendolyn. "Thank you, Miss Brinley, for your brilliant suggestion. I had a feeling you'd know what to do. Any thoughts on how I should explain why Walter isn't in Newport when I said he was expected today?"

Gwendolyn shot a glance to the window, where weak sunlight was streaming through, and smiled. "Simply tell everyone, if you're asked, he was delayed due to inclement weather, which could have very well been the case if he'd intended on returning today because it didn't stop raining until I was on my way here. With that settled, while you resolve matters with Mr. McAllister, I'm going to spend time with the children."

Curiosity flickered through Ethel's eyes. "Because . . . ?"

Gwendolyn began moseying around the kitchen, lifting a lid on a bowl that had crabcakes nestled inside. "Walter made a valid point on Sunday," she began, returning the lid and moving on to a large tureen that held some type of shrimp soup. "He told me I wasn't putting much effort into his situation, and he was right. I'd allowed myself to become distracted with the concerns of other gentlemen."

She abandoned the soup and turned to Ethel. "That's why

I spent the last few days speaking with as many ladies as I could, running them down in the shops on Bellevue Avenue, sitting beside them at numerous outside cafés, and mingling with them at the evening festivities. The only problem with all that, though, is I'm not discovering very much about these ladies, because all they want me to know is that they'll make excellent mothers, which hasn't exactly been helpful."

"How is that not helpful? Walter's main priority is to provide the children with a mother," Ethel said.

"True, but all the potential candidates are now focusing on that one requirement, trying to convince me their greatest ambition in life is to become mothers. With that said, I've yet to be convinced any of these ladies are qualified to become an instant stepmother, because no one seems to want to expand on their maternal instincts when I question them."

"You've been questioning society ladies about their maternal instincts?"

"How else would I be able to point Walter in the right direction?"

"But they're society. They don't learn maternal matters at any of the finishing schools they've attended."

"Perhaps not, but one would think they'd at least expand on any experience they may have with children. I'm not a mother, but I have younger siblings, and because of that, I'm comfortable dealing with the idiosyncrasies of youth. I imagine most of these ladies have siblings, or at least young cousins, but not once has anyone mentioned that to me. When you add that in with how I haven't been able to get Walter to tell me anything about what he expects in a wife except he would like to rub along nicely with her, I had no choice but to rethink my tactics. That's why I need to speak with the children."

Ethel scratched her nose. "Why do I get the distinct impression you're not happy about Walter's only requirement in a potential wife?"

"Walter should expect more, and I've decided I'm going to find that more for him."

"But Walter and Vivian simply enjoyed a somewhat distant relationship, and neither of them seemed bothered by that in the least." Ethel took a step closer. "And while it's commendable you're hoping to find something more for my son, Walter is not an overly emotional gentleman. He takes after his father, Thomas, in that regard. He's also consumed with business, which means a lady who might hold him in great affection will find herself disappointed with their marriage because Walter won't make himself readily available, especially if he's in the midst of a new investment venture."

"But that might change if he meets a lady he begins to hold in great affection," Gwendolyn countered.

Ethel released a sigh. "I'm not convinced he's capable of that, dear. Walter, again, is exactly like his father. He's quiet, introspective, and doesn't enjoy frivolities much. He's been that way forever. After he became betrothed to Vivian, when I asked him if he was in love with her, he insisted he didn't believe in that type of nonsense. He then went on to tell me he and Vivian had an understanding. She would become one of the most sought-after society matrons because of her marriage to him, and he would get a beautiful wife who wouldn't demand much of his time, and who would be content building up their social status, providing him with an heir, and making use of his fortune however she saw fit."

"That seems like a rather macabre approach to marriage," Gwendolyn said.

"It's how we do things in society. Great affection is rarely seen. Although I have been surprised by the two love matches that have already occurred this season—that between Mr. Higgenson and Mrs. Lanier, and then again with Mr. E. J. Boettcher and Miss Frances Bottleworth." She caught Gwendolyn's eye. "But don't get your hopes up you'll achieve that type of success with Walter. As I said, he's an exact replica of Thomas, and while Thomas and I have been married thirty-four years, we're one of those numerous couples who merely rub along nicely together."

"And you're comfortable with that?"

Ethel shrugged. "I had no romantic expectations when I married him. Thomas was considered quite the catch, and he and I rarely share a cross word between us, although that's probably due to the fact we're rarely in the same city at the same time. He, before you ask, is spending the summer in Scotland, finalizing some sort of wool or sheep deal Walter arranged."

"Your family is investing in sheep?"

"I'm not certain. I don't concern myself with the business aspect of the Townsend family. I do recall Walter mentioning something about high-grade wool he thought would be a sound investment."

"I'll have to introduce him to my mother, because she raises sheep and produces a grade of wool that's becoming much sought after."

Ethel blinked. "Your mother raises sheep?"

"Indeed," Gwendolyn said. "It's been her interest of choice for the past several years. She and my father now have over eight hundred sheep on their farm. Truth be told, Mother was rather put out to learn I was coming to Newport for the summer because she wanted me to help with the last of the shearing for the season."

"You know how to shear sheep?"

Gwendolyn grinned. "When your mother raises sheep for her pet project, yes, you learn how to shear."

Ethel returned the grin. "You're an unconventional woman, Miss Brinley, and perhaps ahead of your time. I don't know many women who would admit to knowing they can shear sheep, or women who don't hesitate to take charge of situations, as can be seen by how you're managing Walter's quest to find a suitable wife." Her grin faded. "But forgive me. I hope I didn't offend you by calling you unconventional. That's not a term most ladies enjoy being labeled."

"No offense taken," Gwendolyn assured her. "I decided when I reached my majority that I wasn't going to embrace the traditional roles expected of women, much to my parents' concern. They thought, given how I've always adored spending time with my younger siblings, I would set my sights on a gentleman and get down to the business of raising a family of my own."

She brushed aside a strand of hair tickling her cheek. "I, however, wanted to explore more of what the world had to offer. An opportunity to do that presented itself when my cousin needed a change of scenery. Becoming her paid companion allowed me to travel extensively while not having the restrictions placed on most young ladies, since I was, in essence, considered the help."

"And your parents didn't object to that?"

"I'm sure they had misgivings, but they also realized my cousin needed me, as well as realized I was being given a chance to chase my dreams. To their credit, they sent me off with their blessings."

Ethel tilted her head. "Have you ever regretted your decision, especially when you must know that women who reach a certain age are usually considered firmly on the shelf with few prospects of ever forming a match?"

"An interesting question and one I'm not certain how to answer, because there were times over the past year when I felt slivers of discontent with my chosen lot in life. That was another reason I accepted Mrs. Parker's offer, believing I'd have time this summer to make a few decisions regarding where I should take my life next."

"You don't appear to have much leisure time at your disposal."

"Too right I don't, especially with Mrs. Parker continuously taking up new gentlemen to sponsor. But speaking of that, allow me to return to the subject of your son. I appreciate your cautioning me against trying to secure him a match steeped in affection, but I'm still going to attempt to accomplish that feat. I was raised in a home with parents who adore each other. Our home was always filled with laughter, and that's something that would benefit Walter's children. I'm hoping my time with them today will help me understand what they'd like in a mother."

"You want to discern their requirements for a new mother?"

Gwendolyn nodded. "Indeed. I've realized their opinions matter the most in this situation. I thought I'd take them on an outing to get to know them better."

"Shall I arrange for the governesses to go with you?"

"That won't be necessary." Gwendolyn smiled. "I'll have no trouble handling your grandchildren. I'm quite proficient with children, and I have no doubt that after spending today with them, we'll be well on our way to becoming fast friends."

Ethel's nose wrinkled. "That's some optimistic thinking, Miss Brinley. And while I hope you're right, don't let your guard down for a second. The twins have outwitted more adults than I care to admit. I'd hate to return home after seeking out Mr. McAllister and discover they've done something dastardly to you, such as lock you in a closet and lose the key."

"I'll consider myself forewarned."

Nineteen

"Can you fix her, Oscar?" Gwendolyn heard Priscilla ask as she reached the nursery doorway, the pathetic note in the little girl's voice prompting Gwendolyn to linger in the hallway instead of walking into the room.

"I can try, Priss, but I've never sewn an arm on before. It might not look pretty when I'm done, but at least Susie will have two arms," Oscar said. "Maybe you should have asked Grandmother Ethel to have one of the maids sew your doll up."

"I did. She just said she'd buy me a new doll. I don't want a new doll. I want my Susie," Priscilla said, her voice quavering ever so slightly.

"That's because Grandmother doesn't know you sleep with Susie every night. You could have told her that."

"She wouldn't understand."

Giving the doorframe a rap, Gwendolyn took a step into the room. "Do you mind if I join you?"

A second later, Priscilla jumped up from her pint-sized chair and barreled across the room, surprising Gwendolyn when she wrapped her little arms around Gwendolyn's legs and gave her a squeeze before she stepped back and beamed a gap-toothed smile at her.

"Miss Brinley, I didn't know you was coming. Oscar's fixing Susie. He's never done any sewing, but Susie's sad about her arm, and Samuel's hiding in the wardrobe cuz he's sad I'm sad, but now that you're here, I'm not feeling as sad anymore, and . . ." Priscilla gulped in a breath of air. "I don't want to see Miss Lowe ever again cuz she was mean to Susie, and Susie doesn't like her now, and I was hoping you'd come by someday so I could tell you that."

Gwendolyn grinned, unable to resist the adorable face peering up at her. Leaning down, she scooped Priscilla into her arms and gave her a hug, not setting her down because Priscilla wrapped her arms around Gwendolyn's neck and leaned her head against her shoulder.

Gwendolyn's heart melted on the spot as she realized the little girl in her arms, who could certainly be a terror at times, just needed what every little girl needed, someone to hug when her rag doll's arm got torn off by a woman who wanted to marry her father.

"I'm sure Miss Lowe didn't mean to rip off Susie's arm. I also imagine she feels quite bad about doing that."

"She didn't say sorry."

Gwendolyn patted Priscilla's back. "I bet she didn't beg your forgiveness because of all that rain. I saw her running toward a carriage lickety-split when the heavens opened and soaked everyone clean to the bone."

Priscilla pulled back, her nose wrinkled. "I didn't feel my bones getting soaked."

"Then you should count yourself fortunate, but if you do encounter Miss Lowe again, I hope you won't try to kick her on behalf of your Susie, even if Susie tells you she wants you to."

Priscilla blinked. "How'd you know Susie asked me to do that?"

"Because my sister Bridget had a doll by the name of Dolly, and every time Bridget did something she knew she shouldn't have done, it was always because Dolly told her to do it."

"Dolly sounds bossy. Sometimes Susie can be bossy too, but I told her no more kicking from me, no matter what she wants. I don't want God to send a lightning bolt after me."

"God's not going to send a bolt of lightning after you, darling. That was simply Oscar teasing you. However, God does expect you to behave, and not simply because you're worried about a lightning strike."

Priscilla's little forehead scrunched. "Will it count if I try to be good but acc . . . i . . . dently be naughty every once in a while?"

"As long as you're trying, and then, if you do something naughty, say you're sorry and really mean it."

"I can do that."

"Then I think you'll be fine with God." Gwendolyn gave Priscilla a squeeze before she set her on her feet and moved to stand next to Oscar, who was sitting at a miniature table, plying a needle and thread to his sister's doll. "Would you like me to take over?"

Oscar's head shot up. "You know how to sew?"

"My mother was a seamstress. She thought it prudent for her children to learn that skill, because one never knows when you'll suffer a wardrobe malfunction."

"What's a malfunction?" Priscilla asked, slipping her hand into Gwendolyn's as she joined them.

"It's when hooks on your frock come apart, or when you trip on your hem and tear the fabric."

Priscilla frowned. "Don't you have a lady's maid to do that fixing for you?"

"I don't, although I make use of my cousin's maid when we travel." Gwendolyn grinned. "It's a bit tricky to button up buttons by yourself when they march down the back of a gown."

As if that made perfect sense, Priscilla nodded before she resumed her seat, taking a moment to consider the work Oscar was doing on her doll. "You're doing a great job, Oscar."

A smile curved Oscar's lip. "That's nice of you to say, Priss, but would you be comfortable letting Miss Brinley give this a go? I'm afraid I'm making Susie's arm look like a scene straight out of that Frankenstein book I've been reading to you and Samuel."

"You're reading them *Frankenstein?*" Gwendolyn asked.

"It was Samuel's request this week, but . . ." Oscar lowered his voice. "I'm not reading the scary parts. Priss wouldn't sleep for a week."

"I heard that," Priscilla said, her expression turning mulish. "And I would too sleep if you read me the scary parts. I'm not a scaredy cat." She turned to Gwendolyn. "The next book is my choice. Oscar's going to read us *Heidi.*"

"I never said I was going to read that," Oscar argued. "You only want to hear the story because it's about an orphan, and as I keep telling you, we're not orphans."

"We don't have a mother," Priscilla said, as if it settled the matter before she looked up at Gwendolyn. "Oscar gets sneaky when he doesn't want to read one of our choices. He thinks *Heidi* will make me sad. That's why he tried to get me to agree to let him read the German *Heidi*, knowing I won't understand most of it."

"I wanted to read it to you in German so you and Samuel can begin learning a second language."

"I don't even know all the English words yet," Priscilla grumbled.

Gwendolyn swallowed a laugh before she arched a brow Oscar's way. "You're fluent in German?"

He shrugged. "It's not a difficult language to learn."

"He knows French too and is learning Latin. Well, until he left school," Samuel said as he wandered out of the closet, lugging a cage Gwendolyn would bet good money held Rat, the extremely troublesome guinea pig. "And he's really good with arithmetic. He taught me and Priss how to count to three hundred, and he's teaching us to add." Samuel set down the cage and rubbed his nose. "He does a better job teaching than our governesses, but Grandmother Ethel says we're getting a tutor soon, so the governesses won't need to worry about teaching us for long."

"Unless Papa gets married and we get shipped off to boarding school," Priscilla said, her lower lip trembling. "I don't want to go away to school. They might not let me take Susie, and she'd be lonely without me."

"Your father hasn't mentioned a thing to me about sending you off to boarding school," Gwendolyn said as she settled herself into one of the miniature chairs, taking the doll Oscar handed her.

"Papa might not want to send us, but a new mother will," Priscilla said. "New mothers send children away cuz they don't like to share."

"Where in the world did you hear that?"

Oscar sat forward. "She overheard one of the maids talking."

"Ah, that explains it." Gwendolyn opened her reticule and began rummaging around in it. "I wouldn't worry you're going to be sent off to school, Priscilla. Your father seems to be a reasonable man. If I actually find him a suitable wife this summer and she suggests such a thing—which I'm certain she won't, because I won't find your father a lady like that—if you tell him you don't want to go to boarding school, I'm sure he'll be more than receptive to simply bringing in a tutor."

She caught Oscar's eye. "Will it offend you if I dismantle your sewing attempts and begin again? White thread will be less noticeable than the black you've used so far."

"I couldn't find any white thread."

"Then it's fortunate I keep a small sewing case in my bag."

She pulled a small silver tin from her bag and took white thread and a sharp needle from it. After snipping away the thread Oscar used with a pair of minuscule scissors, she bent over the doll, making tiny stitches as she began reattaching Susie's arm. "If you're so good with languages and arithmetic, Oscar," she began casually, keeping her attention on her work, "how is it you failed your classes toward the end of last semester?"

"Father told you that?"

"In passing. He mentioned he's considering bringing in a tutor to help you make up the work so you can finish the grade you almost completed. I believe he did that mentioning so I'll be prepared to schedule in time for him to meet with that tutor once he arrives in Newport."

"He won't need to meet with any tutor. I'm not going to make up the work because I'm not going back to school."

"You didn't care for the school?"

"He loves it," Priscilla said, exchanging a look with Samuel before she returned her attention to Gwendolyn, seemingly making a point of not glancing to Oscar. "He only came home cuz he knew me and Samuel didn't have nobody to read us stories at night."

As Gwendolyn's heart gave a bit of a wobble, Oscar narrowed an eye on his sister.

"You weren't supposed to say anything about that, Priss."

Priscilla crossed her arms over her chest. "You told me not to tell Papa. You didn't say anything about me saying something if someone else asked me."

"Because I didn't think anyone would ask about it," Oscar grumbled. "But because you and Sam are both fidgeting, you knew it was meant to be kept a secret from everyone."

"I didn't know it was a secret" was all Priscilla said to that, but given the way she was trying not to smile, it was relatively easy to discern she wasn't exactly being truthful.

Nevertheless, since Oscar obviously didn't care to discuss

the matter further—because he was now pretending to be pre-occupied with looking out the nursery window—Gwendolyn concentrated on stitching on the arm, her mind sifting through the telling information she'd just been served up by a set of precocious twins who seemed to be quite intelligent, like their older brother, who'd clearly failed school on purpose.

After making a knot to secure the thread, Gwendolyn handed the doll back to Priscilla. "There you go. Susie is now almost as good as new. And, since we've gotten her reattached to her arm, what say we get on our way?"

"Where are we going?" Oscar asked.

"I thought we'd go to the beach, but not Bailey's Beach. We'll find a place we can enjoy all by ourselves, build some sandcastles we can then stomp on, collect some shells, and perhaps do a bit of fishing."

"Why would we collect shells?" Samuel asked.

"Because it's an amusing pastime. We can gather up shells and paint faces on them later."

"Why would we do that?" Priscilla asked.

Gwendolyn smiled. "It's fun to see the different faces you can make on a shell. Turns them into something interesting."

"Huh" was all Priscilla said to that as Oscar got to his feet.

"I know a spot not far from here where I fish," he said. "There's a path that leads right to the beach."

"Then that's where we'll go. But first, I need all of you to change into clothing that can get dirty."

"The twins don't have anything like that," Oscar said. "I do, but only because I stash away garments Grandmother wants to send to the ragbag."

Gwendolyn rose from the small chair. "I'm sure there's something in Priscilla's and Samuel's closets that'll work. But speaking of closets"—she plucked a hairpin out of her hair and arched a brow the twins' way—"your grandmother told me the two of you have been known to lock unsuspecting people in wardrobes." She gave the hairpin a wave. "This right here is a most marvelous invention, and one that has far more uses than simply being an object to secure a lady's hair. I'm rather adept at picking locks with pins whenever I find myself, unintentionally of course, locked in a child's closet with the key mysteriously vanishing."

Samuel's eyes grew huge. "You know how to pick locks?"

"Indeed, which means there's no reason for you or your sister to get up to any high jinks, because that type of mischief could very well see you missing our fun adventure today." After sending the twins a wink, Gwendolyn made her way out of the nursery, mutters immediately following in her wake.

"She's a bit scary," Samuel said.

"Some might even consider her terrifying," Oscar added.

"I like her," Priscilla said firmly, which left Gwendolyn smiling as she realized she was having the most fun she'd had since landing in Newport. Which just went to show that sometimes it really was the little things in life that made life worth living—such as learning she'd earned the approval of three children who weren't nearly as naughty as everyone thought them to be.

Twenty

"How are we going to carry everything to the beach?" Priscilla asked, looking at the mountain of pails, shovels, one blanket, and an assortment of fishing gear, including poles, a tackle box, and a pail filled with dirt that contained nightcrawlers Oscar had dug up the day before.

"We can take Bert," Oscar said.

Gwendolyn arched a brow. "Bert?"

"He's our pony. You know, the one Miss, ah, Tilbert gave us," Samuel said.

"She's Miss Tilden," Gwendolyn corrected. "But did you name him Bert because you thought her name was Tilbert?"

"Course not," Samuel said. "His name's Excalibert, but Priss can't say that, so Oscar thought we should just call him Bert."

"I can too say Excali-bart. You're the one sayin' it wrong," Priscilla said. "That means his name should be Bart, not Bert."

"Neither of you is saying it correctly, because it's Excalibur," Oscar argued. "But we're not calling the pony Bur. He'd take that as an insult."

"Too right he might," Gwendolyn said. "But I'm not sure

we should take Bert with us. He is, after all, rumored to be a rather contrary creature."

"Bert's getting better at behaving himself," Oscar argued. "He just needed attention. Now that he's getting that from all of us, he's not contrary at all."

"If Bert gets to go, so should Rat," Samuel said.

Gwendolyn shook her head. "I'm sorry, Samuel, but the beach isn't the place for a guinea pig. If he were to make another escape, there's every possibility we won't be able to catch him again."

"You caught him at the church," Samuel pointed out.

"Which was sheer luck on my part, and I may not get that lucky again."

"But Rat likes to stretch his legs."

"Then perhaps we'll need to consider building him a larger cage. But, darling, taking a guinea pig to the beach isn't taking good care of your pet. He could get too close to the ocean and get swept out to sea. You wouldn't care for that to happen to him, would you?"

"No, but . . ." Samuel stepped closer to Gwendolyn. "Would you really help me make him a new cage?"

"I'm not overly competent with tools, but if we can convince Oscar to assist us, as well as a few of the footmen, we'll be able to build a house Rat will adore."

"He'll like that, so I'll leave him behind."

"An excellent choice."

After gathering up what they were taking to the beach, they made a brief stop in the servants' dining room to tell Miss Wendell and Miss Putman, who were taking their morning coffee break, they could take the rest of the morning off. Their next stop was the kitchen, where they discovered that Mrs. Boyle had already prepared them a picnic lunch.

After thanking Mrs. Boyle for their lunch, Oscar insisted on carrying the picnic basket, which suggested he was in possession of stellar manners when he set his mind to it. A groom was then only too happy to harness Bert to Oscar's pony cart, and once he was done, Gwendolyn handed the reins to Oscar, who led the pony out of the stables.

The twins grumbled a little when she wouldn't let them ride down to the beach, but after explaining she needed to get a feel for Bert's behavior before she'd be comfortable allowing them to ride in the cart, they abandoned their grumbling and took to chasing after the rabbits Gwendolyn pointed out to them.

With the clouds and rain having disappeared, it was a glorious day in Newport. Winding their way down a dirt path that led to a sliver of beach directly behind Sea Haven, they spent their first hour building an entire town of sandcastles, it taking all of five minutes for Samuel and Priscilla to stomp that city into smithereens. The sound of their giggles warmed Gwendolyn far more than the sun streaming over them.

After abandoning the sandcastle building to search for shells, they filled an entire pail before they decided to take a break and enjoy the lunch Mrs. Boyle had provided.

As they finished pieces of chocolate cake dripping with icing, Gwendolyn turned to Oscar. "Ready to tackle some fishing?"

Oscar tilted his head. "Do you really know how to fish?"

"Ah, skepticism at its finest." She tapped a finger against her chin. "I suppose there's nothing left to do now but prove to you I know my way around a fishing pole. Would you care to make a game of it—the winner, of course, being the one who lands the most fish?"

"You aren't going to burst into tears when I catch more fish, are you?"

She waved that aside. "Please. Tears have no business showing up in a fishing competition."

"Good. Then yes, I'll take up your challenge, but be prepared to lose."

After exchanging grins, Gwendolyn nodded to Priscilla and

Samuel, who both had faces smeared with chocolate. "Would the two of you like to fish with us?"

Priscilla shook her head. "Girls don't fish."

"Where did you hear that?"

"One of my old governesses. She told me girls shouldn't like worms."

Gwendolyn pulled out a handkerchief and began wiping icing from Priscilla's face. "Even though there's an excellent chance that particular governess was merely trying to avoid taking you fishing, what you need to understand is this: You're going to be told throughout your life that girls shouldn't do many things. It'll be up to you to decide whether that's true or not. I've been fishing since I was a child. I bait my own hook, and while worms can be slimy, simply being a girl does not mean you're predisposed to squeamishness where worms are concerned.

"With that said, I'm going to encourage you to explore activities throughout your life in whatever way you see fit. If something interests you, give it a try. You may decide you don't care for fishing after experiencing it, but don't neglect to try it simply because you've been told you can't because you're a girl."

She straightened and found that while she'd been cleaning off Priscilla's face, Samuel had stolen up beside her, worry flickering through his eyes.

He dropped his gaze and began tracing a toe through the sand. "I don't like to fish. I think it's mean because the hooks hurt the fish."

Her heart gave another lurch, something it had been doing often during the time she'd spent with the children. She took hold of Samuel's hand. "There's nothing wrong with not liking to fish."

"Boys are supposed to like fishing."

"My brother Duncan doesn't care to fish for exactly the same reason you don't."

"Does he get teased for not liking to fish?"

"Not at all. In fact, he loves animals so much he's currently pursuing what's known as a veterinary degree from Iowa State University."

"What's a veter . . . nary degree?"

"It's a degree a person gets from a university that will allow them to become a doctor to animals, something I imagine you may want to consider when you're older."

"Sam would make a good animal doctor," Oscar said, lugging a pail filled with dirt and worms from the pony cart and sidestepping Bert, who was stretched out in the sand, taking a snooze. "And you only need to tell me, Sam, if anyone teases you. I'll put an end to that."

He nodded to Gwendolyn. "Ready?"

She rolled up her sleeves. "Let the fishing challenge begin."

With Priscilla and Samuel looking on, although Samuel turned his head while Gwendolyn and Oscar baited their hooks, Gwendolyn walked to where the surf was lapping the shore, casting her line into the ocean as Oscar did the same.

Five minutes was all it took for her to feel a tug on her pole, but as she began reeling in her line, her fish made a great escape, leaving her with nothing but an empty hook to show for her efforts.

Oscar sent her a grin, one that held not a shred of sympathy in it, right before his pole began to bow and he was pulled a few feet into the surf.

"I caught a big one," he yelled, struggling to keep a grip on the rod as he worked to reel in whatever he'd caught.

Abandoning her pole as Priscilla and Sam came scampering to join them, Gwendolyn grabbed the back of Oscar's shirt when he was pulled another foot into the ocean, knowing better than to offer to help him reel because, if she'd learned anything about Oscar thus far, it was that he was a capable boy and certainly wouldn't appreciate assistance, not when they were engaged in a friendly fishing competition.

"It's got to be at least thirty pounds," Oscar yelled, as he struggled to pull what did seem to be a massive fish to shore.

A second later, the fish flipped out of the water, but it disappeared beneath the surface before Gwendolyn could ascertain what type of fish it was. Tightening her grip on the back of Oscar's shirt when he was pulled forward another foot, which left them knee-deep in water, Gwendolyn suddenly caught sight of a large shadow from the corner of her eye. Squinting, her heart skipped a beat when she realized what was lurking beneath the surface—and lurking far too close for comfort.

"Children, get back," she called to Priscilla and Samuel, before she snatched the knife she'd tucked into her pocket to use if the fishing lines got tangled and pulled Oscar beside her, brandishing the knife toward Oscar's taut fishing line as the fish broke the water's surface again.

"What are you doing?" Oscar demanded.

"Shark" was all she said, stepping in front of him. Before she could cut the line though, the shark surged out of the water, opening its mouth and showing sharp teeth right before it snapped up the fish flailing about on the end of Oscar's line.

"Let go of the pole, Oscar!" Gwendolyn yelled.

Before Oscar could do that, he stumbled backward, taking his pole with him, which then caused what was left of the fish to go whizzing its way out of the water.

Unfortunately, what was left of the fish was only the head, and given the previous tautness of the line before the shark devoured its snack, the head catapulted though the air, zooming over the shore to land with a splat in front of the horrified gazes of Priscilla and Samuel.

It came as no surprise when shrieking immediately commenced.

Twenty-One

"Walter, wait up."

Turning, Walter found Gideon Abbott striding toward him on the dirt pathway that wound through Bayside Farm, the one the butler had directed him to, telling him it would lead him to Ward McAllister's afternoon picnic.

"When we spoke at the Union Club on Monday, you didn't tell me you were going to be returning to Newport early," Walter said once Gideon reached his side.

Gideon shrugged. "I managed to clear my desk of paperwork and decided it might be amusing to return a few days early, especially when you mentioned you were doing the same. My butler told me about McAllister's picnic. Ward always puts on a good spread, so here I am. I'm surprised to see you here though. You mentioned at the Union Club you wanted to begin spending more time with your children."

Walter started down the path again, Gideon falling into step beside him. "I'm only here because when I arrived at Sea Haven I learned my entire family is here. I figured I'd hardly be able to start vanquishing the guilt regarding the neglect of my children if I didn't hop on my horse and gallop to Ward's event."

Gideon frowned. "As I mentioned after you told me about your guilt, you and I didn't get much attention from our fathers growing up and we turned out alright."

"True, but Oscar's friend, Sherman Kenton, seems to bask in his father's attention, something I believe Oscar envies. To give Mr. Kenton his due, he's obviously realized my son needs a guiding hand in his life and has taken it upon himself to include Oscar in their family activities, such as fishing and learning how to ride a bicycle. I'm ashamed to admit it never crossed my mind to play a larger role in my children's lives after Vivian died. I never realized I was being deficient as a father until Gwendolyn pointed it out to me last Sunday."

"You threw yourself into your work after Vivian died, and no one can blame you for that." Gideon stopped walking. "Her death was an unexpected tragedy, and you needed a diversion from your grief. You found that in your work. It's how many gentlemen deal with sorrow."

"I needed a distraction from my *guilt*," Walter corrected.

Gideon shook his head. "It was not your fault Vivian died in childbirth."

"I should have never listened to her when, after suffering such a difficult birth with Oscar, she insisted on trying to increase our family again."

"Her doctors told her she was perfectly capable of giving birth."

"Except they weren't counting on twins."

Gideon opened his mouth, but before he could voice an argument, Mrs. Wickham rounded a corner ahead of them, stopped walking when her gaze settled on Walter, and began strolling his way. She held out her hand once she reached him, which Walter took, placing a kiss on it as Mrs. Wickham released a titter.

"How wonderful to see you were able to make it back today, Mr. Townsend," she began. "It would have been more wonderful, though, if you'd gotten here this morning when you were expected. If you'd been on time, you'd have seen the remarkable meal my Tillie sent to Sea Haven. Fortunately, your mother arranged with Mr. McAllister to serve that meal here, along with a few other meals delivered to your cottage today—none, of course, as tempting as the courses my Tillie arranged for you."

Mrs. Wickham fluttered her lashes. "Do be sure to try the croquettes de homard in a Blue Willow serving dish. Tillie personally chose that entrée with you in mind." After giving her hand to Gideon to kiss, Mrs. Wickham dipped into a curtsy and glided away, saying something about catching up with them later.

Gideon rubbed a hand over his face. "Any thoughts as to what that conversation was actually about?"

"Except for the idea society ladies have taken leave of their senses? No thoughts at all."

Exchanging grins, they strode down the path again, Walter perfectly content to not resume the conversation he'd been having with Gideon, because his wife's death wasn't a time in his life he was comfortable dwelling on, although it was never out of mind for long.

Rounding a curve in the path, Walter slowed to a stop when Ward McAllister's picnic, complete with at least a hundred guests, came into view.

There was no question Ward had outdone himself yet again.

A five-piece orchestra played beneath a shade tree, directly behind a gleaming wooden floor laid down for dancing.

Guests milled around a recently mowed field, the smell of freshly cut grass lingering in the air as butterflies flitted about and the sound of chirping birds mingled with refined laughter.

Ladies sported their most elaborate and colorful hats, while the gentlemen wore jackets over pristine shirts with paper collars, the heat of the day undoubtedly causing more than a few of them to regret the collars—not that any gentleman would remove a collar to find comfort, Walter included.

"I see Daniel Mizner is still hanging about Newport," Gideon said, nodding to a dark-haired man standing next to a group of gentlemen surrounding a lady whose back was turned. "He made a point to seek me out last weekend, wanting me to invest in one of his harebrained ventures. I politely refused, as I always do, but I got the impression he was going to head back to the city to rustle up other investors. Looks like he changed his mind." Gideon frowned. "Or perhaps, since it's rumored he's always short on funds, he's decided it's time to find himself a wealthy wife, which would explain why he's positioned himself close to Gwendolyn."

Walter's gaze immediately settled on the lady with her back turned. "He'll have a hard time convincing Gwendolyn to take him on. He's an annoying sort, and Gwendolyn doesn't suffer that type of nonsense graciously."

Gideon grinned. "Your matchmaker does seem . . ."

Walter didn't hear whatever else Gideon said, because Gwendolyn took that moment to turn, and the sight of her smiling at something someone had just said left his mind going curiously numb as his gaze traveled over her.

It came as little surprise she was looking very well indeed, dressed in an afternoon gown of ivory, paired with a matching ivory hat that had a simple band of green wrapped around it, holding a notepad in her gloved hand as she continued smiling at . . .

The numbness disappeared in a trice, replaced with annoyance when Walter's gaze settled on a hulking brute of a man with dark red hair, who was standing far too close to Gwendolyn and smiling at her in a manner that suggested the man had taken note of her lovely appearance and was appreciating it to the fullest.

He shot a look to Gideon. "Who's that gentleman with Gwendolyn?"

"Which one?" Gideon asked, squinting in Gwendolyn's direction. "She's got at least twelve gentlemen surrounding her."

"The big one who's looming over her."

Gideon's brow furrowed. "I don't believe I've ever heard that level of animosity in your voice before—which begs the question why you're provoked by a particular gentleman talking to Gwendolyn, who, if you've forgotten, is a matchmaker. I'm relatively certain that's an occupation that requires her to speak frequently with a variety of gentlemen."

Frankly, Gideon's question was deserving of further contemplation because it was quite unlike him to be perilously close to losing his temper. He prided himself on always maintaining his composure, but here he was, clenching his fists and contemplating planting those fists in the face of a man he'd never met before.

It was unquestionably an odd circumstance, just as it had been more than curious to find himself thinking about his matchmaker almost incessantly while he'd been in New York. Images of Gwendolyn had sprung to mind at the oddest of times, such as during a meeting with his banker, once when he'd been enjoying dinner with a business associate, and most concerningly of all, every night while he'd been trying to fall asleep.

It was a troubling circumstance to be sure, because his thoughts had never lingered on a lady, not even when he'd been courting Vivian. That his thoughts now seemed to be doing exactly that, and with a lady who'd given him no indication she found him at all appealing—in fact, he seemed to frequently irritate her—was bewildering to say the least.

"Given you something to ponder, have I?" Gideon asked, pulling Walter from thoughts that were definitely ponder worthy.

"Gwendolyn's merely my matchmaker," he finally said. "But because she's holding the key to my future in her remarkably capable hands, I'm concerned to see her swarmed by so many gentlemen. It won't serve me well if she finds her time divided between gentlemen who may very well be prevailing upon Mrs. Parker to take up their interest in the matrimonial department."

An arch of a dark brow was Gideon's first response to that. "Right. You just continue telling yourself that. But to answer your question about the large gentleman still speaking with the lady you're claiming a bit too strenuously is merely your matchmaker—he's Frank Lambert. He's new money, first generation in fact, but he has an uncanny ability to uncover oil strikes and has amassed quite the fortune over the past ten years. I believe he's well on his way to becoming one of the greatest industrialists in the country."

Walter frowned. "If his fortune's that new, I'm surprised McAllister invited him. Ward's a stickler for the whole three-generational rule to become accepted into society."

"I doubt McAllister has any intention of getting Mr. Lambert accepted into the inner circles. However, quite like he did with the Vanderbilts before Alva Vanderbilt stepped in and forced society to accept them, McAllister has a hard time resisting being surrounded by the wealthiest men in the country. Frank Lambert can certainly be considered one of those."

"Someone needs to take this Frank aside and explain to him that a certain distance is expected to be maintained between a lady and gentleman," Walter said, narrowing his eyes when he noticed Frank leaning closer to whisper in Gwendolyn's ear. His eyes narrowed another fraction when Gwendolyn stopped smiling, quite as if she'd found whatever Frank had whispered troublesome. "That's it. She needs my assistance."

"She won't appreciate your making a scene—words I never imagined I'd ever be saying to you. Besides, Gwendolyn strikes me as a lady capable of seeing after herself."

"I'm feeling a distinct need to have a word with my matchmaker" was all Walter said to that, leaving Gideon behind as he strode into motion. He came to a stop, however, when he spotted Priscilla charging toward him, wearing a pink frock with a matching pink bow in her hair. Surprisingly enough, she was not screaming but smiling as she rushed his way. He leaned down and scooped her into his arms.

"Papa!" she exclaimed. "Why are *you* here?"

After giving Priscilla a kiss on the forehead, he smiled. "Mrs. Boyle told me all of you were attending this picnic. I wanted to see you, so here I am. But why are *you* here?"

"Miss Brinley gave us a task. She wanted to give us something to do to help us forget about the shark."

"What?"

That was all it took for Priscilla to launch into every detail of her morning, telling him in words that rushed out of her mouth how she'd gotten Susie fixed, the house had been buried in food, Mrs. Boyle had been cross but then was happy after Gwendolyn had Ethel strike a deal with some man with a large mustache, but she couldn't remember his name, and then what had happened at the beach. Apparently girls, according to Gwendolyn, were capable of doing things people said they couldn't, like fishing, but Priscilla wasn't keen to go fishing again because Oscar had caught a gigantic fish, but then a shark had jumped out of the water and snatched that fish with very big teeth, which had been responsible for the fish's head soaring through the air and landing directly beside Priscilla and Samuel.

"So we started screaming," Priscilla continued. "And Miss Brinley didn't tell us we had to stop because she was scared about the shark too, cuz it could have eaten one of us. She just picked me and Sam up and raced across the beach, and then Oscar threw everything in the pony cart. Bert, that's what we named our pony, wasn't happy about pulling the cart, but Miss Brinley just snapped her fingers and told him to get going, and he did. Then when we got home, Miss Brinley had Mrs. Boyle make us hot chocolate to calm our nerves, and while we did that calming, she read us a story."

"There really was a shark?"

"Haven't you been listening to me?" Priscilla demanded.

"Yes, there was a shark."

Walter blinked. "I can see why Gwendolyn thought all of your nerves might need calming."

Priscilla nodded. "It worked. And then she told us about this plan she had, and gave us tasks, and then after a small nap we changed our clothes and came here."

"What does she want you to do?" Walter asked.

"We must talk to the ladies who want to talk to us, then tell Miss Brinley if we like any of them, but we're not allowed to be rude if we don't like them. I don't like Miss Lowe cuz she ripped off Susie's arm, but she brought me a new doll today, and I thanked her and even gave her a curtsy."

Priscilla scratched her nose. "Miss Brinley put the doll in the carriage cuz it has a china face and she didn't want me to break it. 'Sides, I brought Susie with me and I don't want her to get mad."

"Where is Susie?" Walter asked.

"She's sitting on Miss Duveen's lap, listening to a story, but you have to put me down cuz Miss Duveen is waiting to finish the story until I get back." Priscilla shook her little head. "I like Miss Duveen, but she loooooooves cats, so you can't marry her, cuz I would be sneezing all the time."

"I'll keep that in mind." Walter set Priscilla down and watched her scramble away, rejoining Adelaide Duveen, who was sitting with Oscar, Sherman Kenton, and Samuel. After Priscilla sat down beside Adelaide and leaned closer so she could see the pictures in the book Adelaide was reading, Walter smiled and returned his attention to Gwendolyn. She was now speaking to Mr. August Ryerson, a gentleman Walter wasn't overly familiar with, but one he'd heard his mother say was a quiet and unassuming sort. He wasn't surprised to find her smiling a genuine smile at August, but her smiling dimmed significantly when Daniel Mizner and Russell Damrosch crowded August out of the way and began trying to monopolize Gwendolyn's attention.

He almost felt sorry for the gentlemen when Gwendolyn crossed her arms over her chest and shook her head. When Russell clearly made the mistake of trying to cajole her into agreeing to whatever he wanted, probably matchmaking advice, she lifted her chin, bobbed a curtsy, and strode away from the gentlemen without another word, faltering for the merest second when she caught sight of Walter, but then she immediately headed his way. The closer she got, the more visible the temper in her eyes became, which left him, curiously enough, smiling.

Twenty-Two

"May I assume you're wanting another word with me because I've done something to irritate you?" Walter asked when Gwendolyn stopped beside him, temper flashing through her green eyes.

"As surprising as this may seem," she began, tucking an errant strand of hair underneath her hat, "I'm not presently annoyed with you because you're not responsible for my plight of being inundated with gentlemen determined to acquire my assistant-matchmaking skills. I'm placing the blame for that squarely at Mrs. Parker's feet."

"So I'm not a gentleman in danger of evoking your temper today?"

"The day is still young, but as of this moment, I'm not irritated with you. In fact, I'm actually delighted to see you've returned early, because I can use you to keep those other bothersome gentlemen at bay." She took his arm and prodded him into motion.

"I saw you speaking to August Ryerson," Walter said as they strolled past a gathering of young ladies who smiled at him but didn't approach, which was a step in the right direction and proved he'd accurately predicted how effective Gwendolyn would be at managing all the feminine attention directed his way. "I find it hard to believe you found him annoying. I've heard he's a pleasant sort."

A sliver of temper faded from her eyes. "August was an exception to the irritating rule today. He's charming and was ever so apologetic about seeking me out. His mother is pressuring him to consider marrying over the next year, and while she's not overly enthusiastic about Mrs. Parker—probably because Mrs. Parker enjoys giving Mrs. Ryerson tips on how to improve August's conversational skills—she's intrigued by the success I've already experienced. August and I were enjoying a pleasant conversation when Mr. Daniel Mizner and Mr. Russell Damrosch very rudely muscled him aside."

"What did they want?"

Gwendolyn grimaced. "I get the feeling Daniel's interested in having me convince Mrs. Parker to sponsor him, but I'm not sure that's a good idea. There's something too earnest about him, but he didn't have an opportunity to speak much because Russell dominated the conversation. Russell wanted me to know he'd take it easy on me tomorrow when I play a friendly game of tennis against him and Tillie Wickham. I use the term *friendly* loosely, because I'm afraid it may turn into a bloodbath, and one where I'm the one covered in blood."

Walter brought them to an immediate stop. "You're playing tennis against Tillie? Did you forget what she did to Cordelia?"

"Considering Cordelia is still sporting bruises around her eye, of course not. But I agreed to the match because I want to see if Tillie's learned her lesson and will at least attempt to play a pleasant game instead of turning it into a battle."

"I thought you'd already decided Tillie wasn't a good candidate for me."

"She's not. But considering Mrs. Parker is taking on more gentlemen to sponsor, Tillie may be well suited to one of them."

Walter rubbed a hand over his face. "Mrs. Parker is taking on additional gentlemen?"

"She was finalizing terms with Mr. Thurman Chandler earlier today. She seems incapable of refusing offers of sparkly baubles, even though she must know she's placing an overly large burden on me."

"One has to wonder what the other matchmakers think of this unusual development this Season," Walter said.

"Most of them, if not all, have decided to abandon this Season and take up again back in New York. Rumor has it Miss Camilla Pierpont left Newport because she's displeased with the antics she's witnessed so far. I can't say I blame her because *ridiculous* doesn't do justice to how this summer is playing out." Gwendolyn blew out a breath. "I'm sure it's only going to get more ludicrous when I get annihilated during the match with Tillie and Russell."

Walter swallowed a laugh. "I doubt you're going to get annihilated, but would you care for me to partner you for that match? I can hold my own on the court."

The barest hint of a smile flickered over Gwendolyn's face. "While that's a very gracious offer, I already have a partner."

"What fearless soul has volunteered for that?"

"August Ryerson. He offered to play with me right after I told Russell I'd not found a partner yet."

"That was brave of August. Russell's a beast on the court."

"Wonderful," Gwendolyn muttered before she lifted her chin. "I'm sure August and I will muddle our way through as best we can. Besides that, it'll give me an opportunity to learn more about him, since I'm going to tell Mrs. Parker she needs to sponsor him."

"You just stated you're becoming overwhelmed with business. Why would you suggest Mrs. Parker take on another gentleman?"

She shrugged. "I might already have a particular lady in mind for August." She fiddled with the brim of her hat. "Besides, I feel I owe Mrs. Parker another sponsorship, because Mrs. Ellsworth has taken Miss Ellsworth back to New York."

Walter blinked. "What?"

"You heard me, and I fear Elizabeth's unexpected departure is my fault. I evidently offended her when, after Elizabeth kept pressuring me to have you spend most of your time with her instead of other ladies, I refused to give in to her demands. She didn't react well to that, and after she lost her temper, which I wasn't expecting because Elizabeth had consistently presented herself as the consummate lady, I may have become . . . annoyed."

"Should I assume matters between you and Elizabeth went downhill from there?"

"Indeed. I'm not one to tolerate condescension, and that's the attitude Elizabeth was taking with me—because of my lowly social status. I didn't hesitate to inform her I wasn't going to have you spend the majority of your time with her because I wasn't convinced she was well suited for you. She didn't seem to hold much interest in your children, *and* she'd apparently been hiding a somewhat volatile temper."

Gwendolyn rolled her eyes. "Mrs. Ellsworth arrived at Mrs. Parker's cottage yesterday, claiming her daughter was extremely distraught over my suggesting Elizabeth lacked maternal instincts—which, to be clear, I did nothing of the sort—and possessed a temper, which I did more than suggest. So they're off to spend the rest of the summer in Saratoga Springs, hoping Elizabeth's unfortunate nerves will have an opportunity to recover before she prepares to take the New York Season by storm."

Walter gave Gwendolyn's arm a pat. "You realize you can't actually be blamed for speaking your mind after Elizabeth turned demanding and condescending, don't you?"

"Of course, but Mrs. Parker is disappointed to have lost

that sponsorship. She relished taking possession of an antique brooch Mrs. Ellsworth promised her if she found Elizabeth an advantageous match." She blew out a breath. "And even though Mrs. Parker can be a trial at times, I've come to believe underneath her slightly greedy nature is a lady who has suffered a disappointing life and finds relief from her disappointment when she adds new pieces to her impressive jewelry collection."

For a long moment Walter merely considered Gwendolyn because, in all honesty, he'd never met a woman quite like her.

She'd been turned into an assistant matchmaker without having any experience to draw upon to help her succeed. And while she was finding some impressive successes, and had done so within a week of the opening of the Newport Season, she still had to have reservations about the position Mrs. Parker had foisted on her. Any other lady of Walter's acquaintance would have been indignant over such a situation, but Gwendolyn didn't seem resentful at all. In fact, she apparently held empathy for her employer, which spoke volumes about the kindness of her heart.

A smile tugged his lips, which, curiously enough, earned him a narrowing of the eyes from Gwendolyn.

"Why are you smiling?"

His smile turned into a grin. "There's no need to sound so suspicious. I do occasionally smile. In this instance, I'm doing so because underneath your sensible and rather terrifying character is a lady possessed of a caring nature and an ability to see the best in some of the most difficult people."

She waved that straight aside. "Well, for heaven's sake, don't tell anyone that. I'm having enough difficulties dissuading ladies and gentlemen from approaching me as it is."

"Your secret is safe with me."

"Thank you," she said, a hint of a smile curving her lips until she glanced to her left, stiffened, and prodded him into motion again.

"We need to keep moving. If we don't, I'll become a target for new requests, especially when you're still smiling—and you're far too appealing when you smile."

Male satisfaction immediately began coursing through his veins. "Appealing?"

She came to an abrupt stop. "I'm sure I meant to say approachable."

He fought a laugh. "Or perhaps you didn't and are now taken aback because you're finding me more on the lines of appealing rather than irritating."

"I'm sure you're mistaken about that, but again, you need to stop smiling. If you haven't noticed, Tillie Wickham is heading our way, probably because you're looking far too *approachable* now. I'd hate for her to suggest I meet her next on an archery field, because that would be far more dangerous than facing her on a tennis court. If you want me to continue as your matchmaker instead of lying about in a hospital room with an arrow sticking out of me, I suggest you summon up a more intimidating expression."

Walter pressed his lips together, then narrowed his eyes— the urge to laugh settling over him again when Tillie suddenly stopped in her tracks. Her gaze settled on his face for a second before she did an about-face and hurried off in the opposite direction.

"Much better," Gwendolyn said, pulling him around guests who were now scooting out of their way. "You may want to keep that particular look settled on me, though, because discouraging Tillie is one thing, given her questionable nature, but we don't want any of the other young ladies to think you're a surly sort."

"But then everyone will believe I'm annoyed with you."

"Given the contentious conversations society has witnessed us exchange, I don't believe anyone would be surprised to discover you're annoyed with me yet again. Frankly, that state might assist me with fending off potential candidates to sponsor, because I've learned you have quite the reputation as a fearsome man of business. If I don't appear frightened of you—what with how I frequently annoy you—that will surely dissuade at least a few gentlemen."

"You have a very odd way of looking at situations," Walter said, his lips twitching, something he tried to put an immediate stop to when Gwendolyn sent him a telling look.

Any sense of lingering amusement disappeared straightaway, though, when he spotted Frank Lambert standing beside Daniel Mizner, who seemed to be talking his ear off even though Frank might not have been listening since his gaze was focused on Gwendolyn. When Frank took a step forward, as if considering approaching Gwendolyn again, Walter stepped ever so casually in front of her, drawing Frank's attention.

For a long moment, they simply considered each other, until Walter gave a curt shake of his head, which left Frank scowling before he finally gave a jerk of his head and returned his attention to Daniel.

Deciding he wasn't in the proper frame of mind to warn off additional gentlemen, Walter steered Gwendolyn across a grassy knoll, not stopping until they were underneath a shade tree well removed from the crowd.

"May I assume you spotted someone you didn't care to speak with, hence putting more distance than I was expecting between us and Mr. McAllister's guests?" Gwendolyn asked.

"Frank Lambert seemed anxious to join you. I noticed him bothering you earlier and thought you might appreciate being taken out of his orbit."

Gwendolyn swatted away a bee. "Bless his heart, Frank does seem determined to procure my services. And even though he seems like a very gregarious sort and has quite the sense of humor, I got the impression he's unaccustomed to being told no. I'm sure he'll track me down at some point to press me on the matter, but I already told him there's nothing I can do for him. Yes, he's a wealthy industrialist, but he's determined to marry into the upper crust, and there's little possibility that will happen because his fortune is too new for him to accomplish that lofty goal."

She rubbed her temple, as if an ache was beginning to form. "But enough about my problems. I've been dying to ask why you've returned to Newport early."

"I was hoping to avoid that question, but will you promise not to gloat if I disclose the reasons behind my return?"

She stopped rubbing her temple. "I rarely gloat."

"I beg to differ. I've seen your expression turning gloat-ish—not that that's even a word—on more than a few occasions."

She grinned. "I shall school my expressions accordingly, as well as any gloating comments I may feel the urge to voice."

The sight of Gwendolyn's grin caused Walter's stomach to clench, something he found beyond puzzling, but he then decided the clenching was most likely a result of what he was going to admit. Drawing in a breath, he caught her gaze. "If you must know, after I returned to the city, I considered some of our conversations and realized you were right in that I was asking too much to expect you to find me a suitable wife when I was rarely going to be in Newport."

Her eyes began to gleam. "Did you just say I was right?"

"And there it is, the gloating expression, which is certain to increase when I admit that, yes, you were right, and not just about the time I wasn't intending to spend in Newport. You were also annoyingly correct when you implied I didn't know my own children—another reason I returned early."

All traces of gloating disappeared in a flash as Gwendolyn laid a hand on his arm. "I'm delighted to hear that, because I've spent some time with your children this week, and they're extraordinary, as well as misunderstood. Contrary to popular belief, they *can* behave when they put an effort into minding their manners."

Walter's brows drew together. "Are you certain we're talking about the same children—my children?"

She laughed. "Indeed. And again, they're adorable when they want to be. They're also highly intelligent and possess a great deal of charm."

"Did you say . . . charm?"

She released another laugh. "Don't sound so surprised. They *can* be charming. Believe me, I've seen it."

"Priscilla told me you've given them a task."

"I've asked them for their thoughts on any ladies they may speak with today."

Walter quirked a brow. "Because?"

"They're the ones who'll be gaining a new mother if you remarry. So I've pointed them in the direction of some of the ladies you'll be squiring around this weekend. They're supposed to give me their opinions on those ladies after we return to Sea Haven later this afternoon."

"I'll be squiring ladies this weekend?"

"Of course. Composing a social itinerary for you is what you've hired me to do. While you were in the city, I drew up a schedule for you, filled with different engagements you'll be attending Friday afternoon until Sunday afternoon. Tomorrow however, being Thursday, you're on your own because I didn't know you'd be returning to Newport early and don't have time to adjust your schedule."

Before Walter could respond to that, Phyllis Duveen wandered into view, caught sight of them, smiled, and strode over to join them. She gave Gwendolyn a kiss on the cheek before holding out her hand to him, which he dutifully lifted to his lips and kissed.

"Mr. Townsend, how delightful to have you back in Newport," Phyllis said after he released her hand. "Have you noticed how my darling Adelaide is currently reading to your children, which suggests she's very good with children, especially when there've been no tantrums thrown throughout the time she's spent with them?"

"I did notice."

Phyllis released a dramatic sigh. "It's unfortunate Priscilla and Oscar don't tolerate cats, because Adelaide would have been a perfect candidate for you, if only she would agree to abandon her herd of cats."

"Something you know isn't going to happen," Gwendolyn said.

"Thank you for dashing any hopes I may have been clinging to, but I'm afraid you're right," Phyllis muttered before she stepped closer to Gwendolyn. "However, Adelaide and her many cats aside, I was actually seeking you out because I need to speak with you about a delicate matter."

"You want me to convince Mrs. Parker to sponsor Adelaide even though Mrs. Parker refused to entertain that idea a few years back?"

Phyllis waved that aside. "Adelaide would have my head if I even suggested such a thing. No, what I need to speak with you about revolves around Mrs. Higgenson. She, my dear, is infuriated with you for encouraging Clarence to ask Mrs. Lanier to marry him. Mrs. Higgenson is not a woman to trifle with, and I'm afraid she has you in her sights—which is why . . . she's invited your grandmother to Newport."

Gwendolyn blinked. "My Grandmother *Brinley*?"

"Indeed."

"Why would she do that?"

"I believe Mrs. Higgenson intends to ruin you, thinking your grandmother—what with how she disowned your father—will give you the cut direct, which will then have everyone in society doing the same."

Walter frowned and caught Gwendolyn's eye. "Forgive me, but I fear I'm at a disadvantage. It almost sounds as if your grandmother travels in society, what with how she evidently can deliver you a cut direct, and that has me questioning exactly what you meant when you told me you weren't an average woman in service."

"It's a long story and now is hardly the time to get into it, but yes, my grandmother is society—Boston society to be exact. We're estranged, but my grandmother values the reputation of the Brinley name above all else. I'm sure Mrs. Higgenson has told her I'm roaming around Newport as an assistant matchmaker, which means I doubt Grandmother Brinley will hesitate to take Mrs. Higgenson up on her invitation to visit."

Walter considered her for a moment. "You don't appear overly disturbed about a future encounter with your grandmother."

Gwendolyn shrugged. "There's little sense in avoiding unpleasantness, because that only prolongs that state. While I'd prefer not to have this specific obstacle placed in my path at this particular moment, a confrontation is probably long overdue. Hopefully, it'll be the last tumultuous circumstance I experience for the rest of the summer, because, frankly, I can't imagine my summer could possibly hold many more unexpected surprises."

Walter opened his mouth, a hundred questions on the tip of his tongue, but before he could voice a single one, the chatter of background voices suddenly disappeared, leaving an odd silence in its wake.

"Is it my imagination, or has everyone stopped speaking?" Phyllis asked before she stood on tiptoe and squinted to where the majority of guests were assembled. "I can't see much from here, but if I'm not mistaken, a new guest just arrived."

"Who do you think it is?" Gwendolyn asked.

"Only one way to find out," Phyllis said, taking hold of Gwendolyn's arm, then snagging hold of Walter's before she pulled them forward.

It didn't take long to make their way to the edge of the crowd, where Gwendolyn stopped without warning right as she drew in a sharp breath.

Walter turned his attention to where she was now staring and discovered a beautiful woman with red hair sauntering toward the guests. Dressed in the first state of fashion, she walked with such confidence it was clear she was a lady accustomed to drawing and holding attention.

She was also a lady who bore a striking resemblance to Gwendolyn.

"I should have known better than to question the chances of something else unexpected being thrust in my direction," Gwendolyn muttered.

"You know that lady?" Walter asked.

Gwendolyn gave a bob of her head. "She's my cousin Catriona Zimmerman. Unfortunately, she possesses a most dramatic nature, as well as the ability to land herself in the midst of shenanigans that would put the antics we've experienced at the hands of society ladies this Season to shame."

Twenty-Three

"I'm still not clear why you're in Newport, Catriona," Gwendolyn said, pausing as she rummaged through one of the trunks Catriona had brought for her. "You told me numerous times you were looking forward to spending the summer in the Berkshires with the Sullivan side of the family because you missed your aunt, my mother, as well as all of your cousins."

Catriona Zimmerman set aside her third cup of coffee for the morning, the numerous cups clearly behind why she kept flittering around the room as Gwendolyn tried to locate one of the tennis ensembles Catriona assured her she'd remembered to pack. "I'm here, as I told you yesterday at that delightful Ward McAllister's picnic—even though I arrived at his picnic uninvited after Mrs. Parker's butler told me where I could find you—because you sent me a telegram. It was marked *Urgent*."

"I thought you'd take that particular word as a sign you needed to ship my things without delay."

Catriona shrugged a delicate shoulder. "I took *urgent* to mean you wanted me here as quickly as possible because you were in need of my assistance."

"Assistance with what?"

"Your matchmaking endeavors," Catriona said, gliding over to a divan upholstered in ivory and gracefully lowering herself onto it. "Matchmaking is not something you've ever done before, whereas I . . . Well, surely you remember when I had a hand in getting that lady in London, I believe her name was Lady Something or Other, engaged to that earl."

"Lady Summerset and the Earl of Stratford were betrothed to each other from birth. You were simply at the ball where they made it official."

"That's merely your side of the story."

"That *was* the story."

Catriona released a sigh. "Why must you always be so argumentative? I'm here to help you."

"If you find me challenging, by all means, return to the Berkshires, where, if you've forgotten, the Sullivans and Brinleys are holidaying. I'm sure you'll find them to be far less argumentative."

"I don't want to return to the Berkshires. Yes, I enjoyed seeing everyone, but the atmosphere there is rather dull. I found myself growing restless, and I missed you. Life is very mundane when you're not around."

Gwendolyn abandoned the trunk and moved to sit beside her cousin. "You know it's never good when you become restless. An admission like that is usually followed by one of your adventures or at the very least getting yourself into mischief. Remember when you grew restless on our trip out West and snuck off to visit a saloon? The next thing I knew you were challenged to a duel after accusing a man of cheating at cards."

"He was cheating."

"That's beside the point. You shouldn't have been in the saloon in the first place, even though you disguised yourself as a man."

Catriona shrugged. "Barnabas taught me how to play poker, and I was afraid my poker skills were growing rusty. And I

201

couldn't very well have breezed into a rowdy saloon wearing a ballgown. That might have caused a riot."

"You did cause a riot after it was revealed you were a lady when that man you accused of being a cheat snatched the hat from your head. You're fortunate I took note of your interest in that saloon earlier and was able to intercede before matters got completely out of hand."

"You do have an odd proclivity for knowing how to ruin my amusements."

"Or keep you alive."

The edges of Catriona's lips quirked. "I suppose there is that."

"Indeed, and while I understand how you may have become restless in the Berkshires, even though you were only there for a few weeks, Newport is not the place for you to find your next amusement."

"Ward McAllister's picnic was rather amusing yesterday, and while you've made it clear that, no matter the extent of my fortune, I won't be accepted by the society set—given we Sullivans are Irish—darling Ward seems to think differently. He told me he'd be honored if I'd dust off my extraordinary vocal cords and sing at a ball he's assisting a Mrs. Dickerman with at the end of the Season. He mentioned I would be the guest of honor."

"You'll be no such thing. You'll merely be the former opera singer everyone will enjoy listening to but won't bother to socialize with after you've completed your songs."

"I definitely haven't missed your quarrelsome nature," Catriona grumbled.

"Another reason why you should return to the Berkshires."

"Did you miss the part where I said I was bored? I'd much rather be here, helping you out."

"The last thing I need is your assistance, because you have to realize you'll be more of a hindrance than a help. Gentlemen become smitten with you at first glance. Besotted gentlemen

202

are not going to endear me to society ladies, especially when many of those ladies will most assuredly be hoping to form attachments to the very gentlemen longing to spend their time in your company."

"Perhaps one of these society gentlemen will become so smitten with me I'll consider marrying again."

"Oh . . . no," Gwendolyn muttered as she rose to her feet. "You've been contemplating getting married again?"

"Well, no, and I'll stop contemplating it now if you'll agree to let me help you with matchmaking."

"Absolutely not. You have to return to the Berkshires."

Catriona tucked a strand of auburn hair behind her ear. "I'm not leaving. I've rented this cottage for the next two months, and I intend to stay here. You would not believe the effort it took for me to find lodgings at such short notice. It was only sheer luck a real estate broker in New York City was able to find me this delightful cottage. At first he told me it's impossible to secure an acceptable place in Newport this late in the Season. The dear man only found success because the Green family unexpectedly quit Newport for some unknown reason, which put this cottage back on the market."

"The Greens hightailed it out of Newport because society refused to grant them entrance into any society events, the embarrassment of that almost causing Mrs. Green, at least according to rumor, to suffer a nervous incident. You're prone to nervous conditions as well, and when you realize society won't embrace you with open arms, you'll undoubtedly descend into one of your despondent states."

"You're more than adept at pulling me out of those states."

"True, but if you've forgotten, I'm not here on holiday. That means I won't have time to coddle you."

Catriona began twirling a strand of her hair. "I distinctly remember you telling me that spending your summer in Newport was going to be a holiday for you."

Tension began building at the base of Gwendolyn's neck. Taking a second to soothe it away, she retook her seat, knowing there was nothing left to do but proceed as delicately as possible with a conversation she could no longer avoid.

"I was hoping to steer clear of this particular topic, Catriona, but it's apparently one we need to discuss, and sooner rather than later, given your arrival in Newport." She reached out and took hold of Catriona's hand. "I'm not certain where to begin, but how about if I start with a question. Have you ever contemplated the explanation I gave you regarding why I was determined to take on a different paid position this summer?"

"*Should* I have considered the matter more closely?"

"Since you made the rash decision to join me, and you also know I don't need to work for a living, yes."

Catriona tapped a finger against her chin for a long moment before her eyes suddenly widened. "Good heavens. It's no wonder you don't want me here. You traveled to Newport without me to find a husband, and you knew if I came with you, you wouldn't be able to devote all your attention to your mission because, well, I can be a handful at times."

The tension in Gwendolyn's neck increased. "That's not it at all, although I won't argue about the handful business. However, how do you think I'd be able to find a husband in Newport when I'm not traveling in society? I'm merely an assistant matchmaker, hardly a position that would have any gentleman clamoring to become known to me."

"Hmmm . . . an excellent point." Catriona bit her lip, tilted her head, and then nodded. "You're obviously hoping to find a Cinderella story, quite like the one your mother found when she met your father."

"You're going to need to explain that a little more sufficiently."

Catriona threw up her hands. "I would think that would be obvious, but since it's apparently not—you're looking for a love like your parents enjoy. That became clear to me when you received more than your fair share of attention from gentlemen as we traveled the world, but you were never taken with any of them, and refused numerous marriage proposals. At first, I was baffled about your disinterest, but then I realized you might have been waiting for them to extend you a special gesture, like the prince presenting Cinderella with her shoe and your father turning his back on society to marry your mother. That right there exactly explains why you're in Newport posing as the help."

"I'm not posing. I am the help."

"That's merely semantics, and you know it. You took up a position for the summer because you're hoping a gentleman will overlook your lowly status as an assistant matchmaker and want you simply for you."

Gwendolyn shoved aside the niggling thought her cousin wasn't entirely off the mark regarding the whole wanting to find a love like her parents enjoyed and forced a smile. "I'm afraid you're mistaken, because I certainly didn't create a convoluted plan to search for a husband this summer. If you've forgotten, I decided years ago I wasn't meant to follow a traditional role and pursue marriage."

"Plans can change, dear. But since that's apparently not the case with you right now, I'm at a loss as to why you took up a paid position here in Newport, unless . . ." Catriona returned her attention to the wallpaper, then sucked in a sharp breath before she narrowed her eyes on Gwendolyn. "You didn't do so because you wanted some time away from *me*, did you?"

It was difficult to know how best to answer. To buy some time while she composed a gentle response, Gwendolyn rose to her feet and wandered over to windows that lent a delightful view of the ocean. She turned a second later and blew out a breath. "I suppose what I should say first is this. We've been constant companions for years, and I wouldn't trade a moment of the time I've spent with you."

It was hardly an encouraging sign when Catriona's mouth dropped open as fire flashed in her eyes. "You sound exactly like one of my old suitors who decided I was far too dramatic. He wanted to part ways with me but did so in a manner I'm sure he was hoping wouldn't have me descending into theatrics."

"I've spent years with you. Your theatrics don't terrify me. But, with that said, you're not entirely wrong because, even though, being cousins as well as best friends, we'll always be close, you must realize we're not meant to travel together forever."

"I don't know why not. We have great fun on our adventures."

"True, but we only embarked on a world tour because you needed to heal from the loss of your Barnabas. I believe we managed to accomplish that to a certain degree, but you're not completely healed, nor will you reach that state until you discover what your next purpose in life is meant to be. You won't discover that if you continue searching out your next frivolity, and you know it."

"But why do I need to find my purpose without you by my side?"

Gwendolyn smiled. "Because I need to find my next purpose as well. I'm twenty-five, and it's time for me to move on to a new phase in my life—although what that phase is, I have no idea just yet. I was hoping to spend the summer pondering exactly that, but clearly, I don't have the time for any contemplation right now."

"You would have had all the time in the world if you'd simply told me you needed some distance from me," Catriona pointed out. "That would have allowed you to enjoy your summer at your leisure because you wouldn't have been holding down a position."

"I wanted to spare your feelings."

A hint of a grin flickered across Catriona's face. "I appreciate that, but now that my feelings are dreadfully hurt, I'm not certain where we take this conversation from here."

Gwendolyn returned the grin. "Your feelings never stay injured for long, but as for where we take matters from here—you need to return to the Berkshires, and I need to hie myself off to the Newport Casino because I have a tennis match to attend."

She wasn't exactly surprised when Catriona's jaw set and she shook her head. "I'm not leaving Newport. I told you, I'm determined to help you with the matchmaking business."

"No."

Catriona abandoned the settee, took a few turns around the room, and then smiled a smile that did not bode well for Gwendolyn. "Fine, since you seem adamant about refusing my help, I'll simply appeal to Mrs. Parker. You told me she has a love of jewelry. As luck would have it, I brought that gorgeous diamond choker we found in Italy. And while it may pain me to part with such a lovely piece, it'll be worth it in the end, especially when I'm certain Mrs. Parker won't hesitate to take it off my hands and give me exactly what I want in exchange for it."

Twenty-Four

If there was one thing Gwendolyn knew quite well, it was how difficult Catriona could become once she turned determined, as well as knew it was next to impossible to get her cousin to change her mind once it was made up.

Before she could get a single argument out of her mouth though, a knock sounded on the parlor door.

Ann, one of Catriona's maids, poked her head into the room, her gaze settling on Gwendolyn. "The Townsend children are here to see you, Miss Brinley. They arrived by pony cart and don't seem to have an adult in attendance."

"Of course they don't," Gwendolyn said, heading for the door and then down the hallway, the heels of her shoes clicking over the highly polished marble floor. Reaching the front entranceway, her lips couldn't help but curve at the sight of Oscar, Samuel, and Priscilla grinning back at her.

"Surprise!" Priscilla shouted before she rushed forward and wrapped her arms around Gwendolyn's skirt. "We brought you a present."

"I'm hoping that present is an adult lurking somewhere out of sight," she said, earning a snort from Oscar.

"Please," he began. "Father wasn't about to let me drive Bert and the twins over here without adult supervision. But he did agree to leave some space between us after I told him no nine-year-old boy wants to chance having his friends see his father treating him like a baby."

"Perfectly understandable," Gwendolyn agreed right as Catriona strolled into view, her appearance causing Priscilla's mouth to drop open.

"Is she a princess?" Priscilla whispered in a voice loud enough for Catriona to hear.

"No, she's my cousin, Mrs. Zimmerman."

"I *could* have been a princess if I'd married this wonderful prince I met in London," Catriona said, moving to stand beside Priscilla. "Gwendolyn nipped that idea right in the bud though, so no princess title for me."

"I nipped it in the bud because the prince was a fortune hunter in possession of a crumbling castle, and besides that, he was a reprobate."

"What's a reprobate?" Samuel asked.

"A man who does not possess the characteristics of a true gentleman, even though he sported the title of prince," Gwendolyn said before she introduced the children to Catriona, finishing up right as Walter stuck his head in the door.

"I hope we're not interrupting," he began, stepping into the entranceway and settling a smile on Gwendolyn, then inclining his head to Catriona, whom he'd met at Mr. McAllister's picnic.

"Miss Brinley was telling us what repro-somethings are, Papa," Priscilla said.

Walter's brow shot up. "Reprobates?"

Priscilla nodded. "That's it. She said they're not gentlemen."

"I was just about to secure Priscilla's promise that she'll keep her distance from such gentlemen in the future," Gwendolyn said, which had Pricilla's nose wrinkling.

"But what if I want to be a princess, but the prince is one of those like your cousin met?"

"Doesn't matter. You'll need to steer clear of such a prince."

Priscilla nibbled on her lip before she finally nodded. "Alright, but I won't be happy about it."

Gwendolyn sent Walter a wink. "You're welcome."

Walter's eyes crinkled. "Given Priscilla's temperament, if she meets a dashing prince when she's older, I highly doubt she'll remember your wise counsel."

"When Priscilla is older, I imagine she'll be incredibly sensible, and she also has two brothers who'll make sure she won't land herself in trouble."

"That's Gwendolyn's role with me," Catriona said, stepping forward and giving Walter her hand, which he dutifully kissed. "She was elected by the family as the keep-Catriona-out-of-trouble-at-all-costs person."

"How's she been doing with that role?"

"I've never landed in jail, so I'd consider her successful."

"But since the children don't need to hear why you've almost landed in jail numerous times," Gwendolyn hurried to say when Catriona opened her mouth again, "allow me to redirect the conversation to that present they mentioned."

"We'll go fetch it," Priscilla said, snagging Oscar by the hand and hauling him through the front door. They returned a moment later, Oscar holding something out of sight behind his back.

"The children picked it out for you, and"—Walter leaned closer to her—"they paid for it with their own allowances."

Warmth immediately coursed through Gwendolyn as she settled a smile on the children. "How thoughtful of you."

"Wait until you see what we got you." Samuel nodded to Oscar, who pulled a long package wrapped in brown paper and tied with twine from behind his back and handed it to her.

Silence settled around the entranceway except for the sound

of paper crumpling as Gwendolyn carefully unwrapped the gift, her vision turning blurry when a tennis racquet was revealed.

"I don't know what to say," she whispered.

"Say you love it," Priscilla said.

Gwendolyn blinked a few times, and when she was certain she wasn't about to turn into a blubbering mess, nodded. "I do love it. In fact, this is the most thoughtful present I've ever been given."

"We didn't want you to go to the Newport Casino without your own racquet," Oscar said. "They have racquets to rent, but they're not very good. Sherman and I rented them once when we went to the casino with his parents but didn't bring our own racquets. We never did that again."

"You play tennis?" Walter asked slowly, earning a rolling of the eyes from Oscar in return.

"Why else would I have rented a racquet with Sherman at the casino? We learned how to play at boarding school last year."

"Sherman goes to your boarding school?"

Gwendolyn wasn't a bit surprised when that earned Walter another rolling of the eyes. "His parents decided to send Sherman to the same school as me because they know we're fast friends."

Walter opened his mouth, but knowing whatever was about to come out of it was not going to be well received by a son who clearly felt his father was severely lacking in the parenting department, Gwendolyn cleared her throat. "Well, I have to say that this is a spectacular present. I will now be able to face my opponents with a renewed sense of confidence."

"It's not a magic racquet, Miss Brinley," Oscar said solemnly. "I've seen your opponents play. It's not going to be pretty, but at least you won't be using a ratty old racquet."

"She'll also be dressed in the first state of tennis fashion, now that I've arrived with Gwendolyn's tennis costumes," Catriona said. "So even if she gets soundly trounced, at least she has a nice racquet and will be appropriately clothed." She checked the dainty watch encircling her wrist, then sent a nod Gwendolyn's way. "You need to get changed and off to the Newport Casino."

"Are you coming with us?" Priscilla asked Catriona. "You could sit beside me and tell me more about princes, the good kind."

Catriona shook her head. "I'm not certain I'd be well-received there, my dear, and the last thing Gwendolyn needs to deal with before taking to the court is a contentious situation. I know she'd rise magnificently to the occasion, because she's never failed to rise to my defense, but if someone were to slight me, the situation could very well turn . . . unpleasant. I'll simply content myself with spending the afternoon reading or perhaps taking a stroll by the sea."

A smile tugged Gwendolyn's lips because, even though her cousin could be incredibly self-centered, she was more astute than most people gave her credit for, as well as considerate at the most surprising of times. Before she could express her appreciation for Catriona's thoughtfulness though, Walter stepped closer to Catriona and inclined his head.

"I've seen Gwendolyn in action when unkindness is directed at anyone, Mrs. Zimmerman. She can be downright terrifying in her defense of those who are placed in vulnerable positions. Nevertheless, there's no need for you to miss the match. It would be an honor if you'd agree to accompany me. No one would have the audacity to slight you while in my company. You'll be treated with the respect you deserve. You have my word on that."

Something warm began flowing through Gwendolyn, increasing when Catriona settled a sparkling smile on Walter, one that had caused gentlemen to fall at her feet for years, but curiously enough, Walter didn't so much as blink.

"What a delightful gentleman you are, Mr. Townsend," Catriona said. "I can hardly refuse such a kind offer." She consulted her watch again. "I'll need a few minutes to change." She nodded to Gwendolyn. "Shall we repair to my room and then meet up with Mr. Townsend in say . . . fifteen minutes?"

"Please, you must call me Walter."

Catriona settled a smile on Walter again. "How gracious of you to offer. You must, of course, call me Catriona."

Walter inclined his head. "And with all that out of the way, the children and I will await the two of you outside."

"Don't forget your new racquet," Priscilla said, scampering to Gwendolyn's side.

"I could never forget that," Gwendolyn said, bending down to kiss Priscilla's upturned face, which left Priscilla grinning before she turned and skipped for the front door.

After giving Samuel a kiss on the cheek as well, which left him red in the face but smiling ever so slightly, Gwendolyn opted to shake Oscar's hand instead of kissing him on the cheek— mostly because he was sporting a look she'd seen often on her brothers' faces, one that clearly said "Do not even think about kissing me."

Smiling as the boys traipsed after their sister, followed by Walter, who told them not to rush, Gwendolyn turned and found Catriona considering her closely, an expression on her face that was usually followed by trouble.

"What?" she asked as Catriona fell into step beside her and they began walking down the hallway.

"He's a very nice gentleman, isn't he," Catriona said, taking hold of Gwendolyn's arm, before she pulled her to a stop.

"Why do I get the distinct feeling you're contemplating something other than the idea Walter is nice?"

Catriona smiled. "How well you know me, cousin dear. And forgive me, because I'm convinced what I'm about to do next is going to annoy you, but after I change, I intend to dig out my diamond choker, since there's a good chance Mrs. Parker will be attending the match as well."

An unpleasant knot began forming in the pit of Gwendolyn's stomach. "Do not say you're going to attempt to convince Mrs. Parker to allow you to dabble in matchmaking, because you're then intending on using that position to match yourself up with Walter."

Catriona released a snort. "Please. Walter Townsend doesn't deserve the likes of me. I possess what can only be described as a dramatic nature. He seems to be one of those gentlemen who needs less drama in his life. But his kind gesture to me lends credence to the notion he's deserving of a spectacular match this Season. I've decided I should return his kindness by assisting you with making that match."

"I don't need your assistance."

Catriona shrugged. "That's your opinion, but I'm not going to abandon my desire to find Walter his perfect bride. In fact, perhaps you and I should look at this as a friendly competition, the winner, of course, being the one who finds success making that match." She batted far too innocent lashes Gwendolyn's way. "In the spirit of fair play though, know that I already have a specific lady in mind for him."

Another pesky knot formed in Gwendolyn's stomach. "Someone you met at the picnic yesterday?"

Catriona rolled her eyes. "I'm hardly going to tell you her name. If you've forgotten, darling, I'm somewhat competitive when I set my mind to it. You're simply going to have to wait and see. You mark my words though—by the end of the Season, I will have had a very large part in finding Walter his new Mrs. Townsend, and it'll be a match that will leave society talking for years."

Twenty-Five

"Thank goodness you were able to locate your tennis gown, Gwendolyn," Adelaide said, joining Gwendolyn as she stepped out of the Newport Casino carrying the racquet the children had given her. "I was worried you'd have to resort to the one I lent you."

"It was in the last trunk I emptied at Catriona's cottage," Gwendolyn said, smoothing down the shortened skirt of her gown, one that didn't boast as much fabric as her other gowns and made playing tennis far more enjoyable since she didn't have to contend with billowing fabric as she ran about a court. "But thank you again for loaning me your tennis dress, even though I wasn't certain how I was going to go about mending the large burn on the back, along with the singed hem."

Adelaide winced. "I had a feeling that would be tricky for you to mend, even with your impressive seamstress skills. And before you ask, I was visiting the Doane family in Bar Harbor this spring. They have a magnificent estate complete with their own lawn court and were hosting a weekend gathering. Anyway, the day was turning chilly, so a footman built a fire in a bricked firepit. I got a touch too close, and the next thing I knew, I was in flames."

Gwendolyn blinked. "What happened?"

"Well, everyone knows you're supposed to drop and roll when you catch fire, but I may have panicked. I started running, and that's when Gideon Abbott tackled me and began rolling me around to smother the flames. Unfortunately, there was a sharp slope beside the firepit. The next thing I knew, Mr. Abbott and I were tumbling down the hill." Adelaide's eyes twinkled. "There just happened to be a pond at the bottom of that hill, so in we splashed, which put out the last of the flames."

"Mr. Abbott sounds like a chivalrous sort."

"Oh, he is. But don't set your sights on him for a potential match for Miss Hannah Howe, the only lady Mrs. Parker is still sponsoring. He's let it be known he's not in the market for a wife, which is why I believe he limits the social engagements he attends." Adelaide leaned closer. "He was at Mr. McAllister's picnic but didn't linger long, probably because he took note of quite a few ladies casting hopeful glances his way. But Mr. Abbott and his reluctance regarding the marriage mart is surely not a matter you should concern yourself with right now."

She nodded to something past the three lawn courts they were standing in front of. "If I were you, I'd be far more worried about playing tennis in front of what is growing into an impressive crowd."

Gwendolyn directed her attention to where Adelaide was nodding and winced. "Surely all of those people aren't here to see my match, are they?"

"Since Tillie reserved the far court, and that's where all the spectators are gathered, I'm afraid they are." Adelaide took hold of Gwendolyn's arm and gave it a soothing rub. "But no need to fret that most of Newport society has shown up today. All the ladies I've spoken with are intending to cheer for you because most of them have been bested by Tillie on the court."

"I have a feeling they're going to be sadly disappointed. I'm an infrequent player, and a mediocre player at best. But . . ."

She narrowed her eyes as her gaze settled on Mrs. Parker, then shifted to the many gentlemen sitting around her. "Honestly, what is that woman thinking?" She turned to Adelaide. "Would you excuse me? I feel a distinct need to have a few words with my employer."

"You don't think she's going to agree to sponsor all those gentlemen surrounding her, do you?"

"That's what I'm going to have a word with her about, along with a few words regarding the latest harebrained idea my cousin's come up with." With that, Gwendolyn headed Mrs. Parker's way, slipping around a fence that separated the court from what was, indeed, far too many onlookers.

"I need a moment of your time," she began as she stopped in front of her employer, forcing a smile when Mr. Frank Lambert, who was sitting on one side of Mrs. Parker—Miss Hannah Howe sitting on the other—sent her a wave of his overly large hand.

"You're looking like a true sportswoman today," Frank boomed in a voice that had more than one society matron sending him looks of disapproval. "I wish you the best of luck, Miss Brinley, and I'm hopeful you and I will have time for a chat after your match."

She narrowed her eyes on him before turning to Mrs. Parker. "We have a few matters to discuss."

Mrs. Parker batted innocent lashes Gwendolyn's way. "If you're hoping I can give you pointers regarding your upcoming match, I'm afraid you're out of luck. Tennis was never my strong suit."

"You know that's not what I want to speak to you about. You're clearly soliciting new business, which we need to discuss—as well as delve into the conversation I'm sure you've already held with my cousin."

"Catriona is a delightful, and very generous, lady," Mrs. Parker said, giving a telling tap to a large reticule sitting on her lap.

"Don't get attached to the choker. You'll be giving it back."

"Perhaps we should find someplace less conspicuous to sort everything out." Mrs. Parker nodded to her footman. "I'd like to repair to that large tree over there, Collin."

As Collin pushed Mrs. Parker into motion, Gwendolyn chanced another glance to Frank Lambert, who sent her a grin before he mouthed the word *rubies* to her. Knowing exactly why he'd done that, she squared her shoulders, pivoted on her heel, and stalked after Mrs. Parker, reaching her just as Collin got her settled and moved a discreet distance away.

"I cannot believe you allowed the lure of rubies to sway you into agreeing to sponsor Mr. Frank Lambert," Gwendolyn began. "May I assume you'll soon be sporting a new ruby bracelet?"

"Not just a bracelet, dear. Frank promised me a ruby bracelet, necklace, and ring. He told me I can pick those out from my jeweler of choice, which is obviously Tiffany."

"You know taking him on is a certain recipe for failure, no matter his generosity to you. It'll be impossible to secure him that alliance he desires with a Knickerbocker family since he's what that set considers *nouveau riche*."

"You shouldn't underestimate your abilities, dear, because I certainly don't. Besides, how could I have possibly refused his far-too-tempting offer?"

"By simply saying 'No.' It's a small word, and one easily spoken." Gwendolyn blew out a breath. "Honestly, Mrs. Parker, I'm beginning to believe you should set up an appointment with Reverend Eberhard at Trinity Church, because you seem to be developing an unquenchable desire for jewelry and are in serious need of some guidance concerning the topic of greed."

Mrs. Parker raised a hand to her throat. "You find me greedy?"

"I don't think that's a question that even needs to be asked. But please tell me you haven't told all those gentlemen who were in your company that we'll find them matches as well."

"I know for certain we won't be sponsoring Daniel Mizner."

"He was only one of several gentlemen sitting near you."

"I can't say for certain we won't sponsor a few of those, and did I mention Mr. Russell Damrosch, your opponent today, sought me out to see if I'd consider taking him on?"

"No, you didn't mention that."

"Well, he did. I may have said yes, but only because . . . I insist you don't call me greedy again, but he wants to give me a diamond snake bracelet and then give me matching earrings to make up for the whole broken leg business."

"Why would you want to wear a snake wrapped around your wrist?"

"Did you miss the part where I said it's made up of diamonds?"

Gwendolyn gave the air a bit of a chop with her racquet, reminding herself that she'd definitely find herself in trouble if she gave in to the impulse to poke Mrs. Parker with it. "Never mind. I'll content myself with the knowledge you didn't take up Daniel Mizner, although now I find myself beyond curious as to why. Did he not offer you the proper amount of diamonds?"

Mrs. Parker's lips thinned. "He didn't offer me anything at all. In fact, he told me I wouldn't be compensated until after vows were exchanged, which left me with the distinct impression Mr. Daniel Mizner is a fortune hunter. It also left me with a feeling the rumors about his being seen often at gambling dens may very well be true."

A discreet clearing of a throat drew Gwendolyn's attention. Turning, she found Mr. August Ryerson standing a few feet away, dressed in tennis whites and looking quite as if he might know what he was about on the tennis court.

"Forgive me for interrupting what appeared to be a rather,

ah, interesting conversation," August began, "but Miss Wickham has arrived. She's not a lady known to possess a patient attitude, so we should probably take our places on the court."

"Indeed," Gwendolyn agreed before she moved closer to Mrs. Parker and lowered her voice. "Do not under any circumstances agree to sponsor anyone else until you and I have an opportunity to finish our discussion."

"We have more to discuss?"

"Too right we do, especially regarding one expensive diamond choker I know you're now in possession of—one that used to belong to my cousin. She will not, if it's in question, be brought on board to help me in the assistant-matchmaker department."

"I think Catriona could add a touch of flair to our endeavors."

"Or burn all future matchmaking possibilities for you to the ground," Gwendolyn said before she moved to join August, leaving Mrs. Parker muttering something about how lovely the choker Catriona had given her was.

"Is everything alright?" August asked as they began walking toward the court.

"Nothing has been alright since I landed in Newport, but it's not anything for you to concern yourself about." Gwendolyn smiled. "We have a match to play, and may I say you're looking very sharp this afternoon, Mr. Ryerson."

He smiled rather sheepishly. "Don't get your hopes up that I'm about to storm the castle, or rather the lawn court, Miss Brinley. Mother had my tailor rush this outfit over to our cottage last night. I'm normally not this well turned out." He leaned closer to her. "Mother heard whispers our match was going to be well attended, and she wanted me looking my best."

"You look downright dashing, but please call me Gwendolyn. We're going off to battle together, so formality seems somewhat ridiculous."

He inclined his head. "And you must call me August, but before we enter into combat, has Mrs. Parker made a decision about sponsoring me?"

"We didn't get that far in our conversation, but I believe I can convince her to take you on."

"Mrs. Parker told my mother she doesn't believe I'm ready to enter the marriage mart yet."

"I don't believe Mrs. Parker's opinion matters regarding your readiness, August. You, and only you, know if you're at the right place in life to marry."

August gave his racquet a twirl. "And to that I say I'm convinced I am. I'm firmly established with the family business, and I now want to turn my attention to courting, if we can possibly find a young lady who wouldn't mind that I'm never the life of any society event."

Gwendolyn gave his arm a pat. "Don't you worry about that. That'll be my job. For now, let's concentrate on making it off the court alive." She slowed her pace when they reached the stands where the spectators were gathered and frowned when she caught sight of Hannah Howe, who was looking quite like a deer in the lantern light, probably because Frank had moved his chair directly beside her.

He was clearly swept up in telling her a story, his large hands gesturing wildly about right as he released a loud guffaw, which had Hannah inching her chair away from him.

"I have no idea what that man is thinking. He should know better than to set his sights on a young lady almost fresh from the schoolroom." Gwendolyn sent a wave Hannah's way. "Miss Howe!" she called. "May I trouble you for a moment? I have a favor to ask."

Hannah was up and out of her seat a blink of an eye later, hurrying her way to join Gwendolyn and August, relief flickering through her eyes.

"I'd be pleased to do any favor for you," Hannah breathed

once she reached Gwendolyn's side. "Especially if it keeps me well removed from Mr. Lambert."

"He does seem to be a gentleman capable of overwhelming a person," Gwendolyn said.

Hannah nodded. "Quite. He was just telling me how he has the means to shower a lady with anything her heart desires, and then asked me if I wouldn't adore living in a castle that he would be only too willing to build for me."

"How did I know subtlety wouldn't be one of his strongest attributes?"

"I don't think Mr. Lambert has a subtle bone in his body," Hannah returned. "Please know he's not a gentleman I'd ever consider as a prospective candidate to marry, if you were thinking along those lines."

"No need to worry about that, Miss Howe. During the exchanges you and I have shared, I've already decided what type of gentleman would appeal to you—someone with a reserved nature but who possesses a romantic and chivalrous heart."

She shot a glance to August, who was gazing at Hannah with something warm in his eyes, although the second he realized Gwendolyn was watching him watch Hannah, he began taking a marked interest in his racquet.

Suppressing a grin, Gwendolyn returned her attention to Hannah. "To spare you more offers of castles, jewels, or who knows what else Mr. Lambert in his eagerness to impress you may offer, I'm going to ask you to join us on the court. We'll need someone to mind the bag I packed with water, towels, and a variety of bandages."

August's eyes widened. "You believe we're going to need bandages?"

"I dearly hope not, but I felt it best to be prepared, just in case."

Twenty-Six

After sending Hannah to fetch her bag from the wagonette she'd driven to the match, Gwendolyn moved with August to where Tillie Wickham and Russell Damrosch were warming up on the lawn court, waving their arms around in circles, Russell going so far as to drop to the court and begin doing pushups.

"I don't think it would be advisable for me to attempt that," August said, wincing as his gaze stayed on Russell. "I might pull something, and then we'd have to forfeit the match."

"Which would definitely be a tragedy," Gwendolyn said as Russell got to his feet and he and Tillie moved to the net. "I think they're ready to begin."

"The sooner we get this over with, the better," August muttered.

"My thoughts exactly."

Trading grins, they walked to join Tillie and Russell, shaking hands all around before Russell's eyes suddenly took to gleaming. "Tillie and I were wondering if the two of you would care to place a wager on the outcome of the match," he said.

"Certainly," August returned without missing a beat. "Especially if you'll take my wager of a dollar that the two of you will soundly trounce us in the end."

Russell frowned. "We were thinking more on the lines of the winners getting to choose a bottle of their favorite Madeira."

Gwendolyn waved that aside. "Absolutely not. The last time you participated in an event with a special Madeira as the coveted prize, Mrs. Parker ended up with a broken leg. Since I'm certain Miss Wickham would prefer to keep her limbs unbroken, what with her being your partner, I'm going to suggest we keep this a friendly match, the winners receiving the satisfaction of a game well played. With that settled, shall we begin? I'm thinking, because I have another engagement later, we should merely play one set of six games."

"You don't want to play the standard three sets?" Russell asked.

Gwendolyn fiddled with the strings of her racquet. "While I would adore nothing more than to play that many games against the two of you, that would eat up the entire afternoon. I'm afraid I don't have the luxury of time. Mrs. Parker keeps adding new responsibilities to my roster, yourself included, Mr. Damrosch. I'm sure you'll want me to get right to your case, so a single set of six games will be best for everyone involved."

"You've asked Mrs. Parker to find you a match?" Tillie asked, swinging her tennis racquet back and forth, although considering she was now swinging it with quite a bit of gusto, it was obvious Tillie was rather annoyed with Russell and his decision to have Mrs. Parker sponsor him.

To Russell's credit, he didn't back away from the swinging racquet as he settled a frown on Tillie. "What choice did I have? Miss Brinley has brought a schedule into play for Walter and has filled that schedule with all the most sought-after ladies, yourself included, which gives Walter a distinct advantage. I wasn't going to sit idly by and allow that to happen. Now I'll be given a schedule as well, which is only fair."

"I believe we're becoming distracted from the game at hand," Gwendolyn said, which earned her a surprisingly sweet smile from Tillie, one that was far too innocent and certainly didn't bode well for her or August.

"Too right you are, Miss Brinley. Shall we take a few practice swings first?" Before Gwendolyn could agree to that, Tillie moved to stand to the right of the center line while Russell moved to the left, each of them pulling tennis balls out of their pockets.

"Did you bring any balls?" August whispered.

"They're in my bag."

"Thank goodness, because with Mother fussing over me before we left for the day, I completely forgot we'd need them."

Thankfully, Hannah took that moment to hurry toward them, carrying Gwendolyn's large bag. After retrieving a few tennis balls and sticking them in the pocket of her tennis skirt, as August stuffed a few balls into his pockets as well, she sent Hannah to the sidelines and lifted her chin.

"Here goes nothing," she said, tapping her racquet against August's racquet as they took up their positions on the court.

"Ready?" Tillie all but chirped.

"Absolutely," Gwendolyn called back, barely having a second to get a firm grip on her racquet before Tillie sent a ball whizzing her way, one she swung at late and missed.

Additional balls followed in quick succession, shot over the net by Tillie, then by Russell. While Gwendolyn managed to hit two of them back and August hit all the balls sent his way—although his rarely landed in bounds—it was clear Tillie and Russell had come for blood.

Stalking up to the net, Gwendolyn narrowed an eye on Tillie. "Forgive me, Miss Wickham, but it's been my experience, when warming up, players are supposed to volley the ball gently back and forth."

Tillie frowned. "That's what I've been doing."

"Me as well," Russell added as they exchanged genuinely bewildered looks between them.

"And isn't this going to be amusing," August murmured behind her.

"Indeed." Gwendolyn summoned up a smile. "I believe all of us are sufficiently warmed up, so what say we get this match underway?"

After losing the choice to serve first to Tillie and Russell, it quickly became apparent she and August were overmatched, because it was a disaster from the start, but not a disaster for Tillie and Russell. They racked up point after point, winning the first three games, although Gwendolyn was satisfied she and August had at least scored a few points against them.

When she and August actually won game number four, Gwendolyn headed to where Hannah was holding glasses of water for them, gulping it down as August did the same.

"You've got them on the run now, Mr. Ryerson," Hannah said, handing August a towel she'd pulled from Gwendolyn's bag.

As he mopped off his face, August's lips quirked. "That's kind of you to say, Miss Howe, but I have the sneaking suspicion they went easy on us that last game."

Hannah frowned. "Why would they do that?"

"They're playing to the crowd." Gwendolyn nodded to where the large gathering of Newport Casino guests had resumed their seats. Most of the guests had taken to standing as Gwendolyn and August had been handed their hats to them for the first three games, only rallying in the fourth because the velocity of Tillie's and Russell's return volleys seemed to have diminished enough to where she and August had been able to not only return the ball but place the ball in bounds, since they'd not had to cower every time a ball came slamming its way over the net.

"Why would they play to the crowd?" Hannah pressed. "Everyone seems to be rooting for the two of you."

August took another swipe at his face. "I'd say they don't want the crowd to be completely sympathetic to us, nor do they want everyone saying they're showing bad sportsmanship by beating Gwendolyn and me into the ground. You mark my words, they won't go easy on us again. I predict the next two games are going to go rapidly, and not in our favor."

Truer words had never been spoken. By the middle of the sixth game, Gwendolyn's hair was soaked with perspiration, she was developing a blister on her right heel, and August's pristine white tennis clothes were streaked with smears of blood, a result of the numerous falls he'd sustained as he'd tried to return Russell's wicked serves, as well as Tillie's.

"Only one point left to win," Tillie called to Russell, who nodded as he bent forward, swinging his racquet to and fro.

A second later, Tillie tossed the ball into the air, bringing her racquet up to meet it and then sending it barreling Gwendolyn's way with so much force it was next to impossible to keep her eye on it. To Gwendolyn's astonishment, she somehow managed to return the serve, although Russell was waiting for the ball at the net.

As if in slow motion, she watched him reach overhead with his racquet and, in an impressive move, smash the ball over the net, directly toward her.

Before she could do more than blink, August was sailing through the air, blocking the ball from hitting her, not with his racquet but with his face.

He went tumbling to the ground a second later, not moving a muscle as Gwendolyn rushed to join him, wincing when she caught sight of a nose gushing blood.

"Good heavens, August," Gwendolyn said. "What were you thinking?"

"I was thinking you wouldn't want to be sporting a black eye like Miss Lowe."

Gwendolyn's lips curved. "And that right there is one of the most chivalrous gestures I've ever seen a gentleman make, and means I'm going to find you the love of your life, no matter if Mrs. Parker wants to take you on or not."

She lifted her head and gestured to Hannah, who was already rummaging around Gwendolyn's large bag. "We need another towel, Hannah, and perhaps some water."

Hannah was by August's side a moment later, dousing the towel in her hand with water before she pressed it ever so gently against August's nose.

"That was the most beautiful defense of a lady I've ever witnessed," Hannah whispered.

August's face turned redder than it already was from his past exertions before he shot a quick glance Gwendolyn's way.

After sending him a wink, Gwendolyn straightened and made her way to where Tillie and Russell were standing by the net, both looking as if they had no idea what to do next.

She held out her hand to Tillie. "What a remarkable show of your skills today, Miss Wickham. It's a shame women don't compete professionally in tennis, because you can hold your own on a court."

"Is August going to be alright?" Tillie whispered.

"He might have a broken nose, but he seems to be in fine spirits." She turned to Russell, who was looking surprisingly contrite.

"Please know I didn't deliberately try to maim you," Russell began. "It was instinctive. But allow me to say I was quite amazed by the backhand you used to return Tillie's serve. You may turn out to be a formidable tennis opponent one day, if you take to practicing, of course."

"Encouraging words indeed coming from you, Mr. Damrosch, but I have to admit the backhand I used was simply a defensive gesture, and it would have been more amazing if I'd hit it hard enough that you wouldn't have been able to return it, which would then have spared August a broken nose."

"I should go speak to him."

As Russell and Tillie hurried around the net to speak to August, who was now sitting up as Hannah continued fussing over him—something they both seemed to be enjoying, which was rather curious since blood was involved—Gwendolyn caught sight of Priscilla and Samuel running across the court. She smiled and kneeled when they reached her, accepting the hug Priscilla gave her and grinning when Samuel gave her an awkward pat on the shoulder.

"You got beat," Priscilla said.

"I can't argue with that."

"But you didn't start crying," Samuel said, as if that were worthy of a badge of honor.

"I would never cry over something as trivial as a game of tennis."

"Everyone was cheering for you," Priscilla proclaimed.

"The cheering might have been why Miss Wickham and Mr. Damrosch really turned up the heat on your last two games," Oscar said, stopping beside Gwendolyn and sending her a grin. "But you did put some impressive effort into staying in the game, Miss Brinley, as did Mr. Ryerson."

"I'm of the belief you actually won the day in the end," Walter said, strolling up to join her. He leaned closer and lowered his voice. "I couldn't help but notice your oh-so-subtle matchmaking efforts before the game. I felt you were wrong when you said Hannah was suited for someone with a romantic, chivalrous nature. But after August saved you from a tennis ball that would have certainly hit its mark, something that left Hannah looking at him in awe, well, it was clear you were quite right."

Gwendolyn glanced to where Hannah and August were now beaming at each other, although it was hard to tell for certain if that's what August was doing, because he had a towel pressed up against his nose, obscuring his face. "Two birds with one stone there," she said as Phyllis Duveen, with Adelaide by her side, hurried up to join them.

Given the worry etched on Phyllis's face, Gwendolyn reached out and took hold of her hand, giving it a squeeze. "There's no need to look so concerned, Phyllis," she began. "I'm not upset we lost. In fact, I'm unbelievably relieved August and I survived the match."

Phyllis's grip tightened on Gwendolyn's hand. "I thought you handled yourself magnificently on the court, dear. You were very gracious and never suggested the match be forfeited, which shows you and August are possessed of great fortitude. The match, however, is not why I've come to speak to you."

"It's not?"

"I'm afraid not." Phyllis blew out a breath, exchanged a worried look with Adelaide, then caught Gwendolyn's eye. "Forgive me for being the bearer of bad news, but I feel it's better to warn you than have you get taken by surprise. Your grandmother, Opal Brinley, is here."

Gwendolyn blinked. "She's already in Newport?"

"Indeed, and worse yet, she's here at the Newport Casino."

Twenty-Seven

Walter immediately exchanged places with Adelaide and took hold of Gwendolyn's arm. "Allow me to escort you home. My driver can pick us up at the entranceway so there'll be no need for you to get near your grandmother."

Gwendolyn's nose shot into the air even as she shook her head. Her refusal of a speedy retreat wasn't exactly a surprise. If he'd learned anything about her, it was that she didn't shy away from contentious situations.

That thought had been reinforced by Catriona as she'd regaled him and the children with stories of what he assumed were her more respectable misadventures, ones that were always rectified by Gwendolyn stepping in and setting matters to rights, no matter what odds she had to face down to do so.

"While that's kind of you to offer, Walter," Gwendolyn began, drawing him from his thoughts, "if you'll recall, I drove myself here using one of Mrs. Parker's horses and a wagonette. We also promised the children the treat of an ice cream, and I have no intention of denying them that treat. However . . ." She glanced at the children and smiled. "Our treats will need to wait for just a bit, because I feel the most compelling urge to have a word with my grandmother."

Priscilla wrinkled her nose. "You don't look like you're going to have a nice word with her, Miss Brinley. Don't you like your grandmother?"

"An interesting question, Priscilla, and one I can't give you an honest answer to, because, frankly, I don't know the woman. But that's a story for another day." She handed her racquet to Oscar. "Would you be so kind as to watch over this for me? It may be best if I don't have a readily accessible weapon on hand for the foreseeable future."

"I thought that's a tennis racquet," Samuel said, peering at the racquet as if he thought it might suddenly turn into a pistol.

"It is indeed a tennis racquet," Gwendolyn returned. " How silly of me to suggest otherwise."

She nodded to Phyllis. "Odd that I need to ask this, but which lady is my grandmother?"

Phyllis began fanning her face with her hand. "I'm not certain I should tell you that because your grandmother is in the company of Mrs. Higgenson. As you've already been apprised, that society matron has it out for you."

"And doesn't that sound exactly like a challenge, so . . . where are they?"

Phyllis gestured to where a gathering of ladies had assembled underneath a shade tree. "Your grandmother is in the green afternoon gown. Mrs. Higgenson is the lady beside her in pink."

"Lovely," Gwendolyn said briskly. "If everyone will excuse me? This won't take long." She stalked into motion, her every step filled with determination.

"You need to go with her," Phyllis said, giving Walter a less than subtle nudge.

"My thoughts exactly."

Walter nodded to Oscar. "You'll watch over the twins until I return?"

"Don't I always?" Oscar asked, an underlying trace of something concerning in his tone.

"Why do I get the distinct impression there's something you're not saying?"

Oscar shrugged. "Maybe there is, maybe there isn't."

Knowing now was hardly the time to discuss the matter further because he had to ascertain Gwendolyn didn't suffer any repercussions from her decision to confront her grandmother, Walter considered Oscar for a moment. "I think it's past time you and I set aside an evening to discuss what's been bothering you of late."

It was less than encouraging when Oscar's only response was a rolling of his eyes. But confident his son could be trusted, as always, to look after the twins, Walter strode after Gwendolyn, catching up with her right as she sailed her way through the throng of ladies gathered around her grandmother, not bothering to stop until she stood a mere foot from the woman.

"Grandmother!" Gwendolyn exclaimed in a downright chirpy voice. "How lovely to see you in Newport, although I wasn't expecting you to get here quite so rapidly. I only recently learned Mrs. Higgenson extended you such a thoughtful invitation. Why, you must have packed your bags the moment you received it and hightailed it to Newport."

Given that Opal Brinley's mouth was now slightly agape, it was evident she'd not been expecting a direct confrontation from her granddaughter, but Gwendolyn didn't stop with her chirpy greeting. No, she moved closer, beaming a smile all the while, then kissed Opal soundly on the cheek, stepping back a moment later.

To Walter's concern, Opal's nose shot into the air, quite like Gwendolyn's had recently done. She then released a sniff and moved to turn her back on her granddaughter, foiled in her attempt to give Gwendolyn the cut direct when Gwendolyn took hold of her grandmother's arm, her smile disappearing as ice settled in her eyes.

"If you think I'm going to allow you to ostracize me, which will encourage others to do the same, you're sadly mistaken," Gwendolyn said, lowering her voice to a whisper. "Know that I won't hesitate to cause a scene, one where our family nastiness will be publicized for everyone to hear. Since your greatest fear is apparently to have even a whisper of scandal attached to the Brinley name, I suggest you paste a smile on your face and nod every now and again as I tell you what's on my mind. You may pretend we're merely enjoying a delightful grandmother and granddaughter reunion."

Ice settled in Mrs. Brinley's eyes as well as she considered Gwendolyn before she gave a slight inclination of her head. "Make it brief."

"I don't deal well with demands," Gwendolyn said before she turned to the crowd of ladies edging closer so they wouldn't miss a word of what was certainly going to be an interesting exchange.

"Ladies, I'm sure you'll understand the need my grandmother and I have for privacy, given how long we've been parted. If you'll excuse us, I hear they're serving some lovely refreshments in the dining room."

It came as little surprise when no one seemed keen to leave what was certainly going to be a gossip-worthy encounter.

Walter cleared his throat and summoned up a smile. "I understand the casino is offering a wonderful lemon sorbet today." He nodded to Phyllis and Adelaide, who'd come to stand beside him. "Would the two of you be so kind as to escort everyone into the casino for their treat, and also be so kind as to request the staff put the cost of the sorbets on my tab?"

Phyllis squared her shoulders. "It would be our pleasure." She gestured to the crowd. "Off we go, and no need to linger to offer Mr. Townsend any word of appreciation for his generosity. All of you may do that after he joins us in the club later."

Even though Phyllis's words were met with frowns and a few grumbles here and there, because she'd taken to looking every inch the formidable society matron she was, everyone turned and headed for the clubhouse, except for Gwendolyn, her grandmother, Mrs. Higgenson, Catriona, who'd stolen up beside him, as well as his mother, who'd surprised Walter by turning up for the match, declaring she was there to lend Gwendolyn her full support.

Evidently, that support was also going to be offered as Gwendolyn faced down her grandmother, although why Ethel had had such a change of heart about his matchmaker, Walter couldn't actually say, but he vowed to get to the bottom of that particular mystery at his earliest convenience.

Once the crowd removed themselves from their vicinity, Gwendolyn returned her attention to her grandmother. "I suppose the first order of business would be an introduction. I'm Gwendolyn, the eldest of your son's six children."

"I know who you are."

Gwendolyn smiled. "Ah, my reputation precedes me." She inclined her head in Mrs. Higgenson's direction. "I'm sure Mrs. Higgenson was eager to apprise you of my role in Newport this Season, just as I'm certain you didn't hesitate to journey here because learning your granddaughter, even one you've never met, is employed as a matchmaker must have irritated you."

Mrs. Brinley's eyes narrowed. "Quite. You've brought disgrace to the Brinley name, although I can't say I'm surprised, given who your mother is."

"You'll leave my mother out of this."

"I most certainly won't. She is, after all, the reason I'm yet again facing censure from society because she hoodwinked my son into marrying her, and then they went off and had you."

"One would think you'd have reconciled yourself with my parents' marriage by now, since it's been over twenty-five years."

"I will never forgive your mother for stealing Pierson away from me, using her beautiful face to do so, one you seem to have inherited. Her desire to elevate her nonexistent social standing caused me to lose Pierson, and yanked him out of a world he adored. I'm certain he's consumed with regret over a choice he should have never made, one that saw him cast from his familiar environment and into a world he didn't know existed."

Gwendolyn's lips thinned. "Father doesn't have a smidgen of regret over marrying my mother. They're still wildly in love, which is occasionally embarrassing for their children, although we grew up in the security of knowing they loved us just as much as they loved each other. There's a certain comfort being raised in a house filled with love."

Opal seemed to swell on the spot. "Love?" she all but spat. "How charming. While you may believe he and Finella are perfectly content with each other, I would bet good money Pierson is harboring a great deal of resentment against her by this time. Because of her, he's had to live a frugal life, one where his own children have no choice but to seek out positions because he's unable to provide for them."

Gwendolyn's eyes flashed with temper. "You're mistaken if you believe I have a job because Father lacks the wherewithal to support me, but my reasoning for taking up my current position is not one I care to discuss with you. What I will discuss, though, is that Father has done exceedingly well for himself. If you're unaware, when you cast him out of the Brinley family, he was in possession of a trust given to him by his paternal grandfather. He used the funds from that trust, along with his flair for financial investments, to increase his fortune."

"I highly doubt that."

"It's true, but if you don't believe me, ask your husband." Gwendolyn's eyes flashed hotter than ever. "My grandfather, although it feels odd to address a man I've never met as such, knows Father doesn't lack for funds. He is also aware that your son began buying up stock in Brinley Railroad Company, anonymously of course, years ago. He eventually bought enough to where he's a substantial stockholder. Grandfather learned who was behind those acquisitions when Father showed up at a board meeting a few years ago."

Opal's face paled ever so slightly. "Frederick's had contact with Pierson?"

"I believe they see each other about four times a year." Gwendolyn leaned closer. "Grandfather hasn't been given the privilege of meeting me or my siblings though, because Father doesn't believe he deserves that honor since Grandfather has consistently stood by and accepted your refusal to welcome my mother into the Brinley family."

"Finella was not, nor will she ever be, of our class."

Gwendolyn inclined her head. "True. She was, after all, merely a seamstress when she met Father, something that didn't bother him because he loves her. He's always claimed he fell in love with her the moment he caught sight of her leaving the dress shop she worked in all those years ago."

A ghost of a smile flickered across Gwendolyn's face. "According to Mother, she tried to dissuade his attentions, because she knew they came from different worlds, but Father was determined to win her over."

"She should have tried harder, but I'm certain she eventually came to the realization Pierson would be the means needed to escape a life of continued employment."

"Mother didn't marry Father because she wanted to stop working. She's still working to this day."

Opal's eyes narrowed. "I thought you said Pierson has done well for himself. That must not be the case if Finella is a seamstress."

Gwendolyn waved that aside. "Mother's not a seamstress,

but she does enjoy dabbling in different ventures. She's currently raising sheep and selling the wool—and is beginning to turn quite the profit."

"My son is married to a sheep farmer?"

"He does enjoy indulging Mother's every whim, which is why he purchased a working farm a few years back. He didn't want Mother to have to limit the number of sheep she wanted to acquire."

"I did not raise my son to live on a sheep farm."

Gwendolyn drew herself up. "Given what I've overheard Father saying about his past, you didn't have much to do with raising your son at all. He was put in the charge of a team of governesses and then sent off to boarding school at the ripe old age of five."

"That's how quality raises their children."

"Then thank goodness Father had the good sense to remove himself from that type of quality." Gwendolyn stepped closer to Opal. "I'm sure you're going to take offense at what I have to say next, but a mother's main job is to love her children unconditionally, protect those children, and to do everything in her power to ascertain her children are happy. By refusing to accept my mother, you were less than successful in the job of making Father happy."

Opal's lips thinned. "Perhaps you're right, but I *was* attempting to protect my son because Finella was not of our station."

"Father believes marrying Mother was the best decision he ever made, even though doing so caused him to become estranged from his immediate family."

Opal's eyes glittered. "Too right it did, since I've not spoken to my son since he married."

"I would hope you regret that, as well as hope you realize you could have simply accepted his decision and graciously admitted defeat."

"Never."

"So pride is more important to you than your son?"

"I never said that."

"You didn't have to." Gwendolyn shook her head. "How sad to discover your pride, as well as your belief in social superiority, is so powerful you've failed to realize what's most important in life—family, love, and acceptance of the choices those we hold dear make."

"She was only a seamstress—not an appropriate choice for my son."

Gwendolyn threw up her hands. "Clearly, there is no reasoning with you. You're determined to hold on to your bitterness, so this is where we say adieu."

She turned to Mrs. Higgenson, who'd not spoken a word but had been scowling at Gwendolyn throughout the entire exchange. "We've never been formally introduced, but I'm Miss Brinley. With that said, I must beg your pardon for what is surely going to be a breach in etiquette, but I want you to understand something that could impact your family forever. If you continue to hold fast to your disapproval over your son, Clarence, choosing to pursue the love of his life, you'll end up exactly like my grandmother—a woman filled with bitterness, as well as a woman who lost her opportunity to share the joy of having her son and his children in her life."

As Mrs. Higgenson's mouth went slack, Gwendolyn turned to Walter. "Would you happen to have anything I can write on?"

As Walter began digging through his pockets, Ethel, who'd been unusually quiet up until that point, stepped to Gwendolyn's side. "I have one of my calling cards you may use, dear."

Ethel handed Gwendolyn one of her cards along with a small pencil before she turned her attention to Opal. "How delightful to see you again, Opal. It's been years, but I simply had to join the conversation because you should know I absolutely adore your delightful granddaughter. She does not deserve your disdain because, contrary to your belief, her intelligence, compassion, no-nonsense attitude, and the way she champions those considered vulnerable bring honor to the Brinley name."

Opal blinked. "I highly doubt you'd find a matchmaker an asset to your family name, Ethel."

"Gwendolyn, whether she's a matchmaker or not, would certainly be an asset to the Townsend name, for too many reasons to count." Ethel caught Opal's eye. "But you don't need to take my word on that. I'm hosting a ball this Season, and I'd be delighted to extend you an invitation. Gwendolyn, of course, will be in attendance, and perhaps you could use the ball to become better acquainted. Since I've also prevailed on Gwendolyn's cousin, the renowned opera singer Catriona Zimmerman, formerly Catriona Sullivan, to come out of retirement and perform at my ball, you'll also be given an opportunity to learn more about Gwendolyn's Sullivan side of the family."

When Opal Brinley took to considering his mother as if she might have taken leave of her senses, Walter chanced a glance to Catriona, who was standing to the right of him. His lips twitched when he took note of the look of astonishment on Catriona's face, something that suggested her singing at the Townsend ball was news to her. Before he could assure her she was under no obligation to come out of retirement, Gwendolyn stopped writing on Ethel's calling card and handed the card to her grandmother.

"This is my parents' direction. If you ever realize what you're missing in life—that being your son, along with his family, I suggest you look them up. I assure you, even though you insulted my mother by refusing to accept her, she will welcome you into our family with open arms." Gwendolyn dipped into a curtsy, causing Opal's eyes to widen ever so slightly. "Perhaps we'll meet again sometime, Grandmother."

For a second Opal merely gazed at her granddaughter. Then she surprised Walter when she inclined her head. "Perhaps we will."

With that, Opal turned on her heel and strode away, Mrs. Higgenson by her side. Before they disappeared around a corner, Walter saw Opal look over her shoulder, a telling gesture, but one Gwendolyn missed because Oscar, Priscilla, and Samuel had run up to join them.

"I kept good care of your racquet, Miss Brinley, but I don't think you would have resorted to using it on your grandmother," Oscar said. "You didn't seem to lose your temper with her much at all." He suddenly extended his arm to her. "I think you should now let me treat you to an ice cream instead of the other way around, and I'd be honored if you'd let me escort you back to your wagonette."

For the briefest of seconds, Walter found himself staring at his son, wondering how Oscar could sound so much older than his nine years, as well as realizing that, somewhere along the way, and through no guidance from Walter, his son was well on his way to becoming a true gentleman.

That realization had a stab of regret shooting through Walter's heart, but before he could dwell on the matter, Gwendolyn dipped into another curtsy before she took Oscar's arm.

"I would be delighted to have you escort me to my wagonette. And, since you're being so chivalrous, perhaps you'd like a go at taking over the reins for me while we seek out some ice cream?"

Oscar grinned as they turned to leave. "I'd like that very much indeed."

Walter's heart gave an odd lurch a second later when Samuel offered his arm to Catriona, who immediately bent to take it, grinning as Samuel, with his face now bright red, hurried after his brother.

"I must say this Season is turning far more interesting than I was expecting," Ethel said, her gaze settled on her grandsons' retreating backs. "I must also note that I've never known a lady to make an impression on society as quickly as Gwendolyn's done." Ethel shook her head. "I find her somewhat intimidating, but truth be told, she's one of the most exceptional ladies I've ever had the pleasure of meeting. It's not just anyone who can take on a society matron like Opal Brinley, live to tell the tale, *and* win the skirmish in the end, something Gwendolyn most assuredly achieved."

"I think Miss Brinley is wonderful," Priscilla said before she held up her arms and grinned when Walter immediately picked her up.

As they strode after everyone, Walter found he couldn't disagree with Priscilla's assessment, nor could he disagree with his mother's belief that Gwendolyn was an exceptional lady, especially when that was exactly what he'd begun to surmise about her as well.

Twenty-Eight

During the week and a half since Gwendolyn's confrontation with her grandmother—something she'd not discussed except to say it had been long overdue—Walter had found himself attending so many society events they'd become a blur. The sheer number lent credence to the notion Gwendolyn hadn't been jesting when she'd told him she was committed to finding him a perfect match.

Unfortunately, even though he barely had time to breathe these days, he'd yet to enjoy anything other than amiable encounters with any of the ladies he spent time with, a situation Gwendolyn claimed was beyond frustrating. Her frustration had then led to her coming up with a new plan—one where she now insisted he dance more than three dances at every ball he attended. She'd also told him, in a tone that brokered no argument, he was going to accompany ladies to Bailey's Beach every day, escort a variety of ladies out and about on afternoon drives, and then join different ladies for dinner during evening events. To top it off, she'd demanded he do all that while maintaining an agreeable attitude.

It had taken a herculean effort to resist telling her that her demands were not leaving him feeling affable in the least, especially when his ridiculously busy schedule left little time to spend with Gwendolyn, except for the hour every day she set aside for them to discuss his agenda.

He found himself looking forward to that hour more than any of the events she arranged for him.

The only time he'd spent with her when they weren't discussing his itinerary was when she'd attended church with him and the children the previous Sunday. To his satisfaction, she'd not invited anyone to join them except Catriona, who'd drawn her fair share of attention when she'd sauntered into Trinity Church looking resplendent in a gown she'd picked up in Paris.

Oddly enough, after his mother had made a point of inviting Catriona to her ball, instead of finding herself ostracized, as so many people did when they attempted to breach the walls of Newport high society, Catriona was now receiving invitations to other society events.

Ethel had mentioned that Gwendolyn appreciated her assistance in making certain Catriona was included in society events because Gwendolyn didn't have a spare moment to devote to entertaining her cousin. Frankly, she barely had a moment to sleep, what with how Mrs. Parker had agreed to sponsor Mr. Russell Damrosch, Mr. Thurman Chandler, and of course, Mr. August Ryerson.

August wasn't a drain on Gwendolyn's time, because he was completely smitten with Miss Hannah Howe, and from what Walter had observed, she was just as smitten with him.

That successful match was exactly why more gentlemen were clamoring to get Mrs. Parker's agreement to sponsor them, and why Gwendolyn now found herself in high demand, the risk of her grandmother threatening to give her the cut direct apparently a distant memory, especially since Opal Brinley had quietly departed Newport mere hours after her confrontation with her granddaughter.

"We weren't expecting you to return until five, Mr. Townsend," Benson, his butler, said as Walter walked through the front door of Sea Haven. "Were you not enjoying the company of . . . Was it Miss Suzette Tilden today, or was your early return due to the storm clouds gathering offshore?"

"Miss Tilden was pleasant enough company," Walter said, handing Benson his hat. "But I overheard Samuel discussing plans to build Rat a new home, and I wasn't willing to forgo assisting him merely to drive down Bellevue Avenue and greet people I'm beginning to see far too often."

"Honestly, Walter," Gwendolyn said, drawing his attention as she glided down the curved staircase, pausing on the last step to settle a frown on him. "Did you not think to invite Suzette to Sea Haven to help with Rat's new home?"

He felt his lips begin to curve, which was rather curious considering she was clearly put out with him. "Of course I asked her, but Suzette declined, mentioning something about needing to return to her cottage early because of the Chandler dinner party tonight."

"Hmmm . . ." was all Gwendolyn said to that, stepping from the staircase and moving his way, her frown turning into a scowl when she stopped in front of him. "But did I hear you tell Benson you had a *pleasant* drive with Suzette?"

"Are you going to launch into another lecture about the word *pleasant* if I admit that's exactly how I felt about my afternoon drive?"

"*Pleasant* is a word one should reserve for when a person enjoys tea with their elderly aunt," Gwendolyn returned. "It is not a term I want to hear time and again when you return from outings I've scheduled for you."

"Pleasant is *not* a bad word."

"It is when you're talking about a potential match. With that said, I believe it's time to take Suzette off your list once and for all."

"Because I merely had a pleasant afternoon with her?"

"No, because you mentioned the children are involved with a project and she didn't leap at the opportunity to help." She blew out a breath. "Dare I hope your morning at Bailey's Beach was more exciting than your drive with Suzette? You met up with . . . I'm afraid I've forgotten."

"I was supposed to meet up with Miss Bowen, a lady I've not spoken with much, but she apparently came down with a cold and sent one of her footmen to tell me she wouldn't be there. That allowed me to spend a very enjoyable morning with my mother and Catriona—an odd couple if there ever was one, but they seem to enjoy each other's company. They were very gracious about letting me join them, even sharing the shade from their umbrella."

To his surprise, Gwendolyn rolled her eyes. "May I assume Catriona spent her time questioning you about a variety of ladies?"

"Not at all. She didn't ask me a single question, although she did impart a variety of opinions she's formed about ladies she's spoken with. She doesn't believe Tillie Wickham would suit me at all because she's convinced that lady would take a militant approach to keeping the children physically active, and she is wary about Suzette because she believes that lady may be flighty." Walter rubbed his chin. "Truth be told, I'm not sure why your cousin was telling me all those tidbits."

"She's in cahoots with Mrs. Parker, and even though they haven't made it official, I believe Catriona now considers herself my assistant, that title bestowed on her by Mrs. Parker after my cousin gave my employer an exquisite diamond choker."

"Catriona's your assistant?"

"Evidently, and consider yourself forewarned—she's determined to have a hand in helping you, and no other gentleman, find the perfect match this Season."

Walter blinked. "Why does she want to do that?"

"It's Catriona. Who knows what goes through that complicated mind of hers? Nevertheless, I believe she decided you're a lovely gentleman who deserves a perfect match, hence her insistence on aiding me, no matter that I told her I didn't want her assistance."

Walter tilted his head. "While it's nice to hear your cousin believes I'm a lovely gentleman, I'm not certain you're right about her only having me in her sights to match up this Season. We encountered Frank Lambert as we were leaving Bailey's Beach, and when we learned he'd been turned away from entering the beach because he wasn't with a member, your cousin didn't hesitate to jump down from my mother's buggy and settle herself on the seat of Frank's impressive phaeton.

"She then informed Frank, who was looking quite starstruck, that Bailey's Beach was overrated and she was going to accompany him to the public Easton Beach instead. She then told my mother not to fret because she was a thirty-year-old widow and was certainly capable of spending an afternoon with a respectable gentleman without needing a chaperone."

Walter smiled. "Obviously not one to reject a fortuitous circumstance that had literally almost landed in his lap, Frank gave a slap of the reins, and off they went before my mother could insist on accompanying them."

"Catriona often travels out and about without a chaperone. But here's hoping Frank can keep Catriona out of trouble, although spending an afternoon at a public beach shouldn't be fraught with too many troublesome situations." Gwendolyn released a sigh. "Enough about my cousin though. We need to return to your troubling situation. Truth be told, I'm at my wit's end with you. We're running out of ladies for you to spend time with."

"You do recall I've found a good handful of my recent companions to be pleasant company, don't you?"

"And I keep telling you that isn't good enough."

Walter's brow furrowed. "Perhaps I'm just not capable of feeling anything other than pleasant toward a person."

"I don't believe that's true" was all she said to that before she turned on her heel and headed for the steps.

Striding after her, he caught up with her on the second-floor landing. "What did you mean by that?"

She shrugged. "You inhabit a world where gentlemen are expected to keep their emotions in check, but everyone is capable of emotional depth. You simply need to take time to explore your feelings." She expelled a breath. "And while I'd be more than happy to assist you with that, we'll have to schedule that in later. I left August Ryerson and Hannah Howe in charge of the children in the nursery. And while children are wonderful substitutes for a chaperone, I agreed to act as Hannah's chaperone after her mother was unable to escort her daughter and August on an afternoon carriage ride."

She smiled. "Poor August has been uncomfortable with all the attention he's receiving after his gallant saving of my face during our tennis match. Frankly, he and Hannah were delighted when I mentioned the children were anxious to get started on Rat's new home, and didn't hesitate to abandon their plans of a carriage ride to come here and assist with the building. I believe Hannah has grown annoyed with all the notice being directed August's way from the feminine set. But she has no need to worry about where his affections lie. The gentleman is clearly besotted. I expect an engagement to be announced soon, but it still wouldn't be wise to leave them unchaperoned for too long. I'm sure they're anxious to steal a few kisses, but I'm not going to allow that to happen on my watch."

"Spoilsport."

She laughed. "Perhaps, but besides watching after Catriona, I've sometimes stood in as chaperone for my sisters. I know the lengths an infatuated couple will go to find a way to be alone."

Heading together up the narrow staircase that led to the

third floor, Walter followed Gwendolyn through the door of the nursery, coming up short when he discovered Oscar and Samuel standing in front of the closet door, Oscar peering through the keyhole.

"Where are August and Hannah?" Gwendolyn asked.

"In the closet," Samuel said.

Gwendolyn's forehead furrowed. "What are they . . . Never mind. I don't believe I need to ask that question."

Oscar raked a hand through his hair, quite like Walter did when he was a little frazzled. "Priss is with them. We thought it would be fun to see if we could lock them in there, and then use the hairpin trick you showed us the other day." He held up a hairpin. "Unfortunately, Samuel and I are finding picking a lock a little tricky."

"Why don't you just use the key?" Walter asked.

"Because Priss took the key in the closet, locked the door from the inside, and then dropped the key. They haven't been able to find it because it's dark in there."

Gwendolyn plucked a hairpin from her hair. "During any other summer, this situation would sound beyond peculiar, but since I've experienced nothing but unusual circumstances since I've been in Newport, I don't find this odd in the least." She headed for the door. "But before someone else stumbles upon the almost isolated couple, and August and Hannah find themselves compelled to announce an engagement sooner than later, allow me to take over the picking of the lock. That will guarantee a speedy return to propriety for our happy couple, and also ensure I don't become known, not as a proficient matchmaker, but as the worst chaperone ever."

Twenty-Nine

"I don't believe anyone would question your chaperoning skills," Walter said as he and Gwendolyn advanced across the room. "It's not as if August and Hannah are actually alone together."

"They're locked in a closet," Gwendolyn argued. "Reputations have been ruined for less."

"True, but it's difficult to suffer irreparable harm when a couple is in the company of a five-year child," Walter pointed out, right as someone began knocking on the other side of the closet door.

"Still haven't found the key," August called. "Priscilla wants everyone to know she's scared of the dark, so if someone could find another key, that would be most appreciated."

"I'll ring for Benson," Walter said, changing direction and moving for the enunciator on the wall by the nursery fireplace.

"Please," Gwendolyn said with a wave of her hairpin. "I'll have the door open before Benson can find another one." Gwendolyn shooed Oscar and Samuel out of the way before she knelt and stuck her hairpin in the lock, giving it a few jiggles as Samuel and Oscar took to peering over her shoulder.

250

"How do you know when it's about to get unlocked?" Oscar asked. "That's what I was having difficulty figuring out."

"You feel it. It'll click and then . . ." Gwendolyn smiled as a click sounded. "There you go." She twisted the knob and pulled the door open, revealing August and Hannah standing remarkably close together, Hannah's hair looking ever so slightly mussed, although that might have been because she was holding Priscilla and his daughter had her arms wrapped tightly around Hannah's neck, her eyes squeezed shut.

"You can open your eyes now, Priscilla," Gwendolyn said, taking Priscilla from Hannah the second his daughter opened her eyes and reached her arms out to Gwendolyn.

Priscilla gave a bit of a shudder. "It was awfully dark in there, Miss Brinley. I lost the key."

"One shouldn't take a key into a dark closet, dear."

"We wanted to practice locking and unlocking. Besides, I didn't trust Oscar and Samuel. They might've decided to lock us in there for fun."

"Probably a wise decision," Gwendolyn said. "But how did you know the closet door could be locked from the inside?"

"Samuel likes to lock himself in there," Oscar said. "One of our footmen put a new lock on that door after Samuel told him he didn't like when the governesses were always scaring him half to death by barging into his special space with no warning."

Walter rubbed a hand over his face, the unwelcome thought striking that he'd had no idea his son liked to lock himself in closets. "Why do you lock yourself in the closet, Samuel?" he asked.

Samuel sent him a look that almost exactly matched the looks of disdain Oscar frequently sent him. "Sometimes Priss is annoying."

"My brothers said the same thing about my sisters," Gwendolyn said before she tousled Samuel's hair and then arched a brow August's way. He was still sporting two magnificently

blackened eyes, but it appeared his physician had been successful with resetting his nose since it wasn't crooked. "I would
think you'd have balked at the idea of allowing yourself to be
locked in a closet with Hannah."

August scratched his battered nose. "I'm sure this does not
speak well of me, but I looked at it as an opportunity I couldn't
pass up."

"I looked at it exactly the same way," Hannah added, her
cheeks decidedly flushed.

Gwendolyn rolled her eyes. "The two of you are going to
have to consider getting married by the end of the Season. At
the rate you're going, you're courting disaster."

"Or true love," August said before he took hold of Hannah's
hand and gave it a kiss.

"Yuck," Samuel muttered before he edged up to Walter.
"Want to see how Rat's cage is coming?"

"Of course," Walter said.

"And it'll get us away from the lovebirds," Oscar muttered.

"I don't see any birds," Priscilla said as Gwendolyn carried
her to the far side of the nursery, where Walter found what
looked like a sandbox on the floor, but with taller sides. Two
pails of green paint waited on the floor, along with a bucket of
sawdust and a bale of hay.

"They're not real birds, Priss," Oscar said. "It just means
August and Hannah are being all lovey with each other, which
means they'll probably get married soon."

After Gwendolyn set Priscilla down, his daughter wrinkled
her nose at Walter. "Are you going to be a lovebird if you find
us a new mother?"

"Ah . . ." was all Walter could think to respond to that, earning a slight twitch of the lips from Gwendolyn.

"Considering your father describes every event he's attended
of late as being merely pleasant," Gwendolyn began, "and because of the reports you and your brothers have given me re-

garding the times you've accompanied your father when he's out and about with the ladies, I think it's safe to say he won't be earning the title of lovebird any time soon."

"The children are still giving you reports?" Walter asked.

"Our task won't be complete until you settle on a particular lady," Oscar said before Gwendolyn could answer. "We haven't really been impressed by any of the ladies she's chosen, but it's not her fault none of the ladies want to have much to do with us. They're far too interested in speaking with you when we go out on excursions."

Gwendolyn blew out a breath. "That does seem to be the crux of my problem, Oscar, and it is something I need to address with your father." She nodded toward the paint cans sitting on the floor. "While I'm doing that, you three may begin to paint Rat's new abode."

After getting the children settled with paintbrushes and telling Samuel he was not to paint anything but the wood of the new cage, Gwendolyn told August and Hannah, who'd finally stopped whispering together, to mind the children for a moment, adding that she'd better not find them in the closet again when she returned.

Leaving the couple looking rather sheepish, she took Walter's arm and tugged him out of the nursery, taking a seat on an upholstered bench in the hallway and patting the spot beside her.

"I fear I'm failing spectacularly with finding you a perfect match, or even an adequate one," she began once he got settled on the bench.

Walter's brows drew together. "Why would you say that? You've set up a schedule for me that has had me escorting practically every eligible lady around Newport."

"But you don't seem to find any of those ladies to be anything other than nice. I wanted to find you someone special. Besides that, the reports the children have given me are less than encouraging. The ladies seem keen to fawn over them at first, but then they lose interest, spending their time in conversation with you and not bothering to speak to the children at all, or pulling you away to join crowds of Newport residents, leaving the children in the care of their governesses."

"Should I not bring the governesses the next time I take the children to Bailey's Beach?"

"No offense, but I'm not certain you're up for socializing and attending to the children at the beach without the support of their governesses, even though, in my humble opinion, Miss Wendell and Miss Putman aren't the most proficient governesses I've ever met. They were seriously delinquent in their duties when they traveled with you and Cordelia Lowe to that local fair."

"I thought we survived the fair quite well. We didn't actually lose the children at any point, although Oscar did go off with his friend, Sherman, and the twins tried to make a break for it when they caught sight of a candy-apple vendor."

"And that candy-apple incident is why I'm now convinced, even though the children told me Cordelia was fairly attentive toward them, she might not be wonderful mother material."

Walter frowned. "Have you ever considered you might be too finicky about the ladies and their attitudes toward the children? I would think their telling you Cordelia was attentive toward them would be a mark in her favor."

"These are your *children* we're talking about, Walter. I cannot be too finicky. They're the ones who will suffer the most if I send you in the wrong direction, and believe me, Cordelia might be the wrong direction. She indulged the twins with three candy apples apiece."

Walter blinked. "Three?"

"Indeed, and being children, the twins ate them."

"I didn't realize that."

Gwendolyn waved that aside. "Samuel told me, after he finished tossing up his accounts, that you were speaking with

Gideon Abbott when Cordelia bought them the apples, Cordelia evidently telling you she'd be fine taking the children around to some games while you spoke with your friend. And while I found it encouraging she'd volunteer to watch over the children, the last thing you need is another woman who'll indulge their every whim."

"I've noticed Mother and Matilda seem to be making an effort to be less indulgent of late, although I'm fairly sure that's a result of their being slightly terrified of you."

"They're not terrified of me, they're merely coming to the realization that their spoiling has led to less than acceptable results," Gwendolyn said. "But returning to Cordelia, I'm not convinced she has the children's best interests at heart. I think she volunteered to watch them merely to impress you but then resorted to plying them with sweets to entertain them instead of joining them in the games the fair offered, which would have been more enjoyable for the twins and would not have seen them suffering sour stomachs."

Walter frowned. "You said Samuel tossed up his accounts?"

"He did, as did Priscilla. I found them in the retiring room with Oscar when I dropped by to see what the children had to say about the fair after a meeting I had with Mr. Russell Damrosch. I was not pleased with the condition I found the twins in."

"If I'd known they were feeling poorly, I wouldn't have sent them home with the governesses while I escorted Cordelia back to her cottage."

She gave his arm a pat. "Since you didn't know Cordelia had overindulged their sweet tooth, you had no way of knowing the twins were soon to fall ill."

Walter pressed two fingers against his forehead, where tension was settling. "Why didn't you mention any of this at the dinner we attended after the fair?"

"Because you were there to spend time getting to know Miss

Harriet Fleischman, a recent arrival in Newport. From what I saw during dinner, you seemed to be appreciating her company."

"She was an enjoyable dinner companion, although she didn't seem to want to discuss anything but the latest fashions, even though I did try, per your suggestion, to speak about current events." He winced. "That didn't go over well, because she doesn't keep abreast of local news."

"Something that's not in her favor, but there was no need to worry you about the children. Ethel and I made an early night of it, and when we returned here, the children were looking much better. I took over for Oscar, who was reading them *Robinson Crusoe*, and the twins fell asleep about an hour later."

"You put the children to bed?"

"Since Ethel and I discovered the governesses sleeping when we returned, yes, I put the twins to bed. But it wasn't a bother. I often put my siblings to bed when I still lived in my parents' house." She smiled. "There is something quite special about tucking a child in for the night."

Warmth immediately spread through Walter, but before he could get a single word of appreciation out of his mouth for Gwendolyn's care of his children, she released a sigh.

"I don't know how to steer you in the right direction at this point. I can't be with you all the time to observe how specific ladies treat the children. And unfortunately, there's not an event planned where all the ladies would be present at the same time as the children, which would allow me an opportunity to compare their mothering skills."

Walter tilted his head. "What about Mother's ball?"

"What about it?"

"I could ask her to modify it, perhaps turn it into a ball where children are welcome to attend. She's been worried everyone will find our ball less than exciting since Mamie Fish held that event where dogs were the guests of honor."

Gwendolyn's eyes began to sparkle. "But that's brilliant, and it will be far more exciting than a dog party. We could bring in a magician and offer pony rides for the children, and offer games like croquet and badminton for the adults. We'll clearly have to modify the dress requirements so the ladies can participate, especially the eligible ones we've had you escorting about. I'm sure Ethel will be agreeable, because it'll make her ball stand out from all the other society events this Season."

"Then it's settled," Walter said, rising to his feet and pulling Gwendolyn up beside him. "I'll speak to Mother later today, but for now, we should probably check on the lovebirds."

"Indeed," Gwendolyn said with a grin, her grin fading when they reentered the room and discovered that in their absence, August's face had been painted with little green hearts on both of his cheeks.

Walter shot a look to Oscar, who rolled his eyes.

"It wasn't us," he said. "Miss Howe did that."

"An unusual flirting technique to be sure," Gwendolyn said.

Miss Howe didn't bat an eye. "I simply couldn't resist."

"Try," Gwendolyn said.

Walter laughed. "I think all of us may need a little fresh air and a diversion from flirting. Which is why it's fortunate a purchase I recently made has been delivered. It's waiting on the front porch."

"What is it, Papa?" Priscilla asked, abandoning her paintbrush as she scampered his way.

"Bicycles. Well, tricycles for you and Samuel, a bicycle for myself, and one for Miss Brinley as well."

Gwendolyn arched a brow. "You bought me a bicycle?"

"How else can you teach me to ride if you don't have a bicycle of your own to show me?"

"I don't know how to ride a bicycle."

"Hmmm . . ." Walter said, rubbing his chin before he nodded to August. "Do you know how to ride?"

"I'm afraid not, but perhaps Hannah does," August said, turning to Hannah.

When they immediately began staring into each other's eyes again, Hannah adding a bit of lash fluttering for good measure, Gwendolyn cleared her throat . . . loudly.

Hannah pulled her attention away from August, her cheeks turned decidedly pink, and then she shook her head. "I don't know how to ride either."

Walter turned to Oscar. "Looks like it'll be up to you to teach us."

Oscar's brows drew together. "You want me to instruct all of you on the finer points of bicycle riding?"

"Indeed. In fact I'm sure you'll be more than up for the task, just as I'm certain you'll relish ordering all of us about."

Oscar scratched his nose. "Might be amusing."

"I imagine it will."

Oscar tilted his head, seemed to consider the possibilities of teaching everyone to ride, then nodded. "Fine. I'll do it. I'll meet everyone outside on the front drive in ten minutes." With that, he strode from the room with a distinct sense of purpose in his step.

Walter watched his son disappear as a feeling of contentment settled over him—one he'd not felt in a very long time, if ever. He couldn't keep from smiling as he helped the twins put the paint and brushes away, his smile widening when Priscilla tugged him out of the nursery, her little hand clasped firmly in his.

As they walked together down the stairwell, he heard Gwendolyn discussing the finer points of bicycle riding with Oscar, who'd rejoined them on the stairs, and in that moment, he realized his sense of contentment was a direct result of her entering his life.

And not that he'd taken an opportunity to truly dwell on a thought that kept flitting to mind, but it was becoming clear that the time he spent in Gwendolyn's company was far more than pleasant, which was quite telling and certainly demanded closer consideration.

Thirty

It had been almost three weeks since Gwendolyn had had her first bicycle lesson, and even though she was currently managing events at the Townsend ball, she kept becoming distracted by a concerning thought that had plagued her relentlessly over the past few days. That thought revolved around the sneaking suspicion she might have broken a cardinal matchmaking rule, because somehow she'd, perhaps, developed feelings, and those of the affectionate type, for Walter.

One minute she'd found him to be the most annoying gentleman she'd ever had the misfortune to meet, but the next she'd found herself looking forward to their slightly contentious exchanges, as well as looking forward to seeing his smile or watching him interact with his children.

He was far too compelling when he smiled, and when he laughed while engaged with the twins or Oscar, her heart—something that never gave her difficulties—seemed to take on a life of its own, lurching about and feeling quite as if it might burst.

It was a very odd predicament to find herself in.

She'd thought about the matter incessantly of late, and her

only conclusion was that her change in feelings had begun when they'd learned to ride bicycles together.

It had been one of the most enjoyable afternoons in recent memory, filled with far too many scrapes to count, because learning to ride a bicycle had been no easy feat. However, even with all the tumbles she'd taken, she'd been unable to do anything but appreciate that time with Walter, helping him push the twins on their new tricycles, and then being ordered around by Oscar, who certainly seemed to delight in his role as boss as he'd gone about the business of teaching four adults how to ride a contraption that seemed to defy gravity.

"Gwendolyn, there you are," Ethel said, walking up to join her, which pulled Gwendolyn from thoughts that were leaving her cheeks decidedly warm. "Ward McAllister is insisting on managing the dancing for me, while also proclaiming this evening an original event if he's ever seen one, what with how we encouraged the guests to bring their children and have arranged activities that allow the children to have their fair share of amusements. With our adult revelers now in good hands, I'm free to assist you with the children, but . . ."

Ethel's gaze settled on Gwendolyn's face. "Are you alright, dear? You're looking flushed."

Gwendolyn flipped open the silk fan Ethel had given to all the ladies at the Townsend ball and began plying it in front of her face. "I'm fine. I've just been running about like mad, attempting to observe the greatest contenders for a match for Walter. They're somewhat tricky to keep track of, given the number of guests."

"Have you noticed any of the ladies showing a particular fondness for the children?"

Gwendolyn stopped fanning herself. "Cordelia Lowe made a point of seeking the children out when she first arrived, bearing lollipops for them, unfortunately. Priscilla and Samuel weren't what I'd call overjoyed when I confiscated their treats the second

Cordelia's back was turned. Oscar, however, was in full agreement with my confiscation, because he recalls the tossing up of the accounts incident after the candy-apple fiasco.

"The twins kept trying to convince me they'd not been that ill, but I'm pleased to report drama didn't commence. Priscilla was looking a little mutinous, and Samuel was eyeing my reticule, where I'd stashed the lollipops, as if he were trying to think of some magic trick the magician you brought in tonight might have taught him to get the treats back. However, after I reminded them they had a task to complete, which meant they didn't have time for stomachaches, they accepted the deprivation of their sweets, and off they went with Oscar."

"They're still giving you reports on all the ladies who speak with them?"

"They are, although their reporting has been slim tonight. Besides Cordelia's giving them treats, the only reports thus far have been that Suzette Tilden patted Priscilla on the head—something she didn't appreciate—and Tillie Wickham tried to impress Samuel by telling him all about a fish her father recently caught, unaware that after the fish-head incident Samuel has an aversion to those."

Gwendolyn smiled. "But no need to look disappointed. I'm sure there'll be a few ladies who rise to the top of possible contenders once we get a rousing game of Annie Over in motion. I've scheduled it to coincide with a lull in the dancing in about fifteen minutes."

"I've never heard of Annie Over," Ethel said.

"It's a delightful game I played often in my youth, and it's not difficult to learn," Gwendolyn said. "Two teams line up with a long table or, in our case, a long hedge between them, and the only game piece necessary is a ball. The team in possession of the ball calls out 'Annie Over' and throws the ball over the hedge. If their opponent catches it, they change sides as quickly as possible. The fun is that the person who catches the ball gets to throw it at an opponent as they switch sides. If that opponent is hit, they're out. The team left standing is the winner."

"That sounds like a marvelous game. I can't wait to watch the children play it," Walter suddenly said from behind her.

Stilling for the briefest of seconds, Gwendolyn forced herself to turn and found Walter smiling back at her. He looked dashing in his formal evening wear, his dark hair falling over his forehead, something that suggested he'd danced every dance she'd scheduled for him thus far. "How was your time with Cordelia?" she asked.

"Pleasant."

She couldn't help herself—she laughed. "Of course it was, and the one you shared with Adelaide?"

"That was downright amusing. Adelaide entertained me with stories about her many cats, but before either of you run off to convince her she should get rid of her little darlings because two of my children can't tolerate them, she told me, and firmly, that while she knows her mother would love nothing more than to see her become a member of the Townsend family, she's convinced we're never meant to be anything other than friends."

He grinned. "From any other lady, I would have taken that as a setdown, but because it was Adelaide, I was completely charmed. But not in a romantic way," he hastened to add.

Ethel shook her head. "I'm ashamed to admit I never realized what a delightful lady Adelaide is until this Season, as well as admit I never noticed how abysmally society ladies treat her. Case in point, the other day at the beach she was the only one to agree to Priscilla's request they build a sandcastle village and then stomp it to smithereens once it was completed."

Ethel's lips twitched. "By the expressions on the other ladies' faces, it was clear they thought Adelaide had taken leave of her senses when she began lumbering about, making monster noises as she demolished castle after castle."

"I'll need the names of those ladies," Gwendolyn said, already pulling her small notepad out of her reticule, which left Walter grinning.

"Tonight probably isn't the time to run them to ground and take them to task," he said.

"I suppose you're right," Gwendolyn muttered, stuffing the notepad back into her reticule before she checked the time on the delicate watch worn over her evening glove. She nodded to Ethel. "We'll revisit the names of those ladies at a later date. For now, I need to get the game of Annie Over organized."

She turned to Walter. "What's next on your schedule?"

Walter reached into his pocket, withdrew the schedule she'd written out for him, and glanced over it. "I have the next thirty minutes free. I'm guessing you gave me a break because there's no dancing while the children play this Annie Over game, but . . ." His lips quirked. "Would you look at that. Even though you gave me the thirty minutes, you made a notation I should use that time to mingle with whatever lady I may find more than pleasant."

"I want you to use your time efficiently tonight."

"Can't say I'm surprised by that," Walter said, tucking his schedule away before he offered her his arm along with a most charming smile. He then offered his other arm to Ethel and escorted them out the door and toward the place where the game of Annie Over was to be played.

As she strolled by his side, Gwendolyn couldn't help wondering if Walter was simply ignoring her notation about his spending his time with someone he found more than pleasant, or if there was some other reason behind his offering her his arm . . . although what that other reason could possibly be, she had not the slightest idea.

Thirty-One

"I can't help but question whether I'm the lady you find to be more than pleasant company, or if Gwendolyn is," Ethel said, which had Walter dragging his attention away from where Gwendolyn was holding Priscilla's hand as she gave Rat, cradled in Samuel's arms, a pat and then said something to Oscar that sent him running off in the direction of a footman.

It was a loaded question if there ever was one, but it didn't need much contemplating, because while he always found his mother's company delightful, spending time with Gwendolyn was far more than pleasant and deserved a much more descriptive word such as . . . remarkable.

She was a captivating mix of temperamental, compassionate, and something he couldn't quite put his finger on but that he suspected was simply Gwendolyn wrapped up in a mesmerizing package. Not that he was going to admit any of that to his mother, or admit that all the ladies he'd been squiring around of late paled in comparison to Gwendolyn.

It was an odd circumstance finding himself all but enthralled with his matchmaker. She'd given him no indication he was anything other than one of the gentlemen Mrs. Parker had agreed to sponsor, but he did think she didn't find him quite as annoying as she used to, which was something, but . . . still.

"I believe I have my answer without you saying a word," Ethel said, giving his arm a squeeze. "I suppose the question of the hour now is what you're going to do next."

He forced a smile. "I'm sure I have no idea what you're talking about."

"And I'm quite certain you do, just as I'm sure you'll be surprised to learn I wouldn't be opposed to . . . Well, perhaps I'm getting ahead of myself." Ethel turned her attention to where Gwendolyn was chatting with Priscilla. "She does have a wonderful way with the children, doesn't she?"

Walter couldn't disagree with that, especially when he watched Gwendolyn whisper something into Priscilla's ear and a second later his daughter was skipping her way over to his mother-in-law. Matilda was standing on the sidelines by herself, a smile on her face, something she'd been sporting often of late. Her smile turned into a grin when Priscilla took hold of her hand and tugged her over to where a crowd was gathering around Gwendolyn.

It wasn't difficult to understand why his mother-in-law had started smiling so much, considering she'd told him a week before that there was something quite delightful about assuming the role of indulgent grandmother, one that didn't require her to intervene when the children misbehaved, because lately they'd been on their best behavior.

The reason for that was, of course, Gwendolyn. She'd managed to get his children's unruliness under control in a no-nonsense fashion, simply pointing out their misdeeds in a gentle and sometimes amusing way.

That she was more than adept at understanding children was reinforced by Catriona, who when she'd encountered him riding his bicycle down Bellevue Avenue with Oscar made a point of telling Walter all about Gwendolyn's love for her five siblings.

"If I may have everyone's attention, please?" Gwendolyn suddenly called out. "We're about to begin a game called Annie Over, but I'd like everyone to know it's not a game simply for the children—any adults wanting to join in are welcome. With that said, we'll need an even number of players on either side of the playing field."

It came as no surprise when Adelaide was the first to take her place on the opposite side of the hedge from where Gwendolyn was standing, joined by Gideon Abbott, who positioned himself next to Adelaide, which was interesting because Gideon wasn't a gentleman who enjoyed participating in society's unusual pastimes.

Russell Damrosch then took up a spot next to Oscar, joined by Tillie Wickham. Frances Bottleworth and E. J. Boettcher took their places next, while Suzette Tilden, accompanied by Thurman Chandler, went to stand beside Samuel, who'd given Rat over for safekeeping to a waiting footman. August and Hannah were the next to join the game, August choosing to stand beside Russell, while Hannah went to stand on the other side of Oscar as a dozen other children scrambled to take their places.

"We still have some open spots," Gwendolyn called, directing her attention to where a few ladies were gathered, crossing her arms over her chest when every lady seemed to make a point of avoiding eye contact with her.

"Shall we?" Ethel said, tugging Walter into motion, then stopping when they encountered Cordelia Lowe lingering on the sidelines. "Care to join us, dear?" she asked.

Cordelia's brow puckered. "No, thank you. I'm clearly not dressed to participate in a children's game. I'm wearing Worth, and Charles Worth never meant for his creations to withstand anything more strenuous than dancing."

Ethel gestured to Gwendolyn. "Miss Brinley is gowned in Worth tonight as well, and she's throwing herself into the spirit of the evening, although she's wearing one of Worth's lawn dresses, something we encouraged ladies to wear on the invitations."

"I took *encourage* to mean *optional*, and I along with numerous other ladies opted to wear ballgowns," Cordelia said coolly. "As for Miss Brinley participating in every game offered, it's not really a surprise, is it, because she's not actually one of us. Frankly, I must admit I'm taken aback she has the wherewithal to afford Worth, but I suppose that's a result of her being related to the Boston Brinleys, or perhaps she borrowed her little frock from her opera-singing cousin. Even so, her wearing Worth doesn't make her acceptable in the eyes of society."

She lifted her chin and nodded to Walter. "I'm suddenly feeling parched, Mr. Townsend. Care to join me in seeking out a glass of cold champagne?"

Manners drilled into him since birth had Walter summoning up a smile. "I'd be delighted to join you, Miss Lowe, but champagne will need to wait until after the game. My children will be disappointed if I sit this one out."

A narrowing of her eyes was Cordelia's only response to that before she pivoted on her heel and marched away.

"And just like that," Walter said as he watched Cordelia's retreating back, "Cordelia is off the list of potential candidates."

Ethel gave his arm a pat. "She did not show herself to advantage just now." Her eyes twinkled. "I have a feeling there'll be many disappointed ladies after tonight, given how many of them aren't clamoring to participate in activities that include children. Add in the notion that numerous ladies seem to have purposefully worn ballgowns to excuse their involvement in the more physical games, and you can bet Gwendolyn will be slashing their names from her list of possible candidates for you by morning."

After trading smiles, Walter and Ethel took their spots near

Priscilla and Matilda. It took Gwendolyn all of three minutes to explain the rules, and then she moved in front of Samuel, handing him the ball and whispering something in his ear. She straightened and moved to a spot beside Walter.

"Are you ready?" she called.

After everyone nodded, Gwendolyn caught Samuel's eye. "Remember what to say, darling."

"Annie Over!" Samuel shouted before he threw the ball over the hedge, directly into Russell Damrosch's hand. Everyone scrambled to run around the hedge, trying to stay clear of Russell, who had the ability to take them out of the game if he hit them with the ball.

A blink of an eye later, Russell took aim at Oscar's friend Sherman. Before Walter could do more than change directions in an attempt to intercept the ball, Adelaide dove in front of Sherman, getting smacked in the head with the ball in the process.

"You're out," Russell called, as Adelaide rubbed her head, sent a glare Russell's way, and handed the ball to Sherman before she marched off the field.

"Mr. Damrosch," Gwendolyn snapped, striding around the hedge and stopping a mere foot from Russell. "What, pray tell, are you thinking? You should hardly be trying to take out the children first, because they're *children*."

"It's a game. They need to learn they can't always win."

Walter wasn't certain, but it sounded as if Gwendolyn told Russell to discontinue with the idiocy before she warned him to behave. She then told him that no, there was no prize being offered to the winner and stalked her way back to her spot beside Walter.

She sent him a rolling of her eyes. "What is wrong with that man, and how in the world does Mrs. Parker expect me to find him a match with that ridiculously competitive attitude he has?"

"Annie Over!" Sherman suddenly called, which had Gwendolyn returning her attention to the game.

Play continued at a wicked pace, both sides dwindling rapidly, although most of the adults were trying to avoid getting the children out. It wasn't until Russell took out Matilda with one expertly thrown ball that things turned a little contentious.

"You took out my grandmother," Oscar said, settling a glare on Russell, who was on his team.

"Someone had to," Russell returned.

"She's old."

"Survival of the fittest" was Russell's response to that as he retook his position and exchanged grins with Tillie Wickham.

"Those two are menaces," Gwendolyn grumbled to Walter. "Did you see Tillie hit your mother with a well-placed toss?"

"I believe Tillie targeted her because you thwarted her desire to take you out of the game and she was annoyed about that. Mother was an easy target because she's not accustomed to running. I agree, though—something needs to be done."

Walter lifted his head and sent a discreet nod to August, who was on the other team and who happened to be holding the ball. He then waited until August threw the ball his way. Snatching it out of the air, Walter was in motion a second later, running directly for Russell and showing that man no mercy as he took aim and let the ball fly. Thankfully, it hit its target and Russell was out of the game.

Priscilla was racing Walter's way a second later, leaping into his arms and placing a sloppy kiss on his cheek. "You did it, Papa. You did it! You got rid of the mean man."

"And avenged Grandmother," Oscar said, dashing past Walter, but not before he sent him a grin.

"I believe you've just become a certified hero in the eyes of your children," Gwendolyn said as he set Priscilla on her feet.

"I merely took care of Russell."

"But in their eyes, you let Russell know that no one can tangle with your family. That's exactly why you've been elevated to the rank of hero—no easy feat. I would encourage you to revel in the moment, because being children, their opinion will change the next time you lay down the law about some misdeed they're certain to believe wasn't a misdeed at all."

Thirty-Two

A most curious feeling flowed through Walter when Gwendolyn gave his arm a pat, then flashed him a grin that left him forgetting where he was for a moment, until someone called "Annie Over" and he was recalled to the idea he was in the middle of a game.

It turned into a battle of epic proportions, one his side eventually lost because Tillie, apparently wanting to avenge Russell's removal from the game, turned more competitive than ever, knocking her teammates out of the way to catch the ball each time it sailed over the hedge—and promptly using it to take out her competition.

After shaking hands, Walter's guests wandered back into the house, the children returning to the activities Gwendolyn had planned for them, the next one being painting seashells. After providing the many governesses in attendance aprons for their miniature guests to wear while painting, Gwendolyn then made certain the children were offered beverages and fresh fruit before she left his mother-in-law in charge.

As the sound of the orchestra preparing for the next dance rang out, Walter and Gwendolyn moved toward the ballroom,

Gwendolyn insisting she needed to make certain Walter's next dance partner was waiting for him—a lady he wasn't hesitant to join because she had scheduled him to dance a second dance with Adelaide—done so, at least according to her, because she didn't want her friend lingering on the sidelines for most of the night. They quickly located Adelaide sitting beside her mother, who for some reason was looking resigned.

"I'm afraid Adelaide won't be able to dance anymore this evening," Phyllis began once Walter stopped in front of them. "She broke the heel of another shoe, and not during the game, which would have been expected."

Adelaide grinned. "I've never been one to do the expected, but before either of you ask, I broke it while I was walking across the lawn. One minute I was strolling along—perhaps even gracefully, but I can't be certain about that—and the next I was stumbling down that incline that leads to the cliffs. If it wasn't for Gideon Abbott, I might have plummeted off the cliff, but because of his timely assistance once again, I merely suffered a broken heel."

"Gideon seems to make himself readily available whenever you're near an incline," Gwendolyn said.

"He does have an uncanny knack for realizing when I'm about to plummet to my death or burst into flames," Adelaide agreed before she leveled a stern look on Gwendolyn. "But don't for a second get that matchmaker mind of yours traveling in the direction I know it longs to travel. Gideon, again, has made it known he's not in the market for a wife, and I'm hardly a lady who would be well suited for a gentleman of the world, something Gideon most certainly is."

She switched her attention to Walter. "With that now firmly out of the way, I'm afraid I'll have to renege on our scheduled dance. I didn't think to bring a spare pair of shoes with me."

Gwendolyn stood on tiptoes and perused the ballroom for a moment. "You should ask Miss Darcy Mortman to join you for the waltz. I haven't learned much about her, but she seems lovely, and rumor has it she's guaranteed to take the New York Season by storm. She's standing next to Mrs. Parker, who given the smile on her face is considering sponsoring her."

"Then Walter shouldn't interrupt them," Phyllis said, before settling a smile on him. "You should dance with Gwendolyn instead."

He didn't hesitate to return the smile. "An excellent idea, Mrs. Duveen."

Gwendolyn's nose wrinkled. "It'll hardly be productive for you to dance with me. I'm your matchmaker. Miss Mortman might turn out to be the lady you find more than pleasant this Season."

"That's some wishful thinking on your part," Walter said. "Besides, I'd much rather enjoy the next dance by not having to worry about engaging in idle chitchat with a lady I don't know."

"And you, Gwendolyn," Phyllis began before Gwendolyn could voice the protest her expression clearly suggested she wanted to voice, "deserve a respite from managing the events of this ball. Consider it a victory lap for helping Ethel host one of the most original events Newport has seen this Season. And that's saying something, considering Mamie Fish hosted a ball for dogs."

To Walter's surprise, after shooting Phyllis a look that held a trace of resignation in it—as if she were quite used to dealing with older ladies determined to have their way and knew which battles to pick and which to abandon—Gwendolyn accepted his arm. A moment later, they were standing in the middle of the ballroom floor, earning more than a few raised eyebrows, and a smile from his mother, which he didn't know how to interpret. Before he could consider that further though, the first note of a waltz rang out, and he and Gwendolyn were off.

He should have known she'd be more than proficient with the steps.

"Had a few dance instructors along the way?" he asked, moving across the floor with her in perfect synchrony.

"Since you were privy to Grandmother Brinley's and my conversation, and I also know Catriona has probably taken the liberty of divulging far too much about me, you're clearly well aware of my background and my circumstances, which are not those of a woman who has to earn a living. So I'm sure you're not actually taken aback to learn I know how to dance," Gwendolyn returned, effortlessly following his lead. "My mother was diligent in making sure her children were provided lessons in decorum, dance instruction, riding lessons, and the list goes on and on. I've always believed her diligence was because she held out hope Father's parents would someday come to their senses and, if they did, would never be able to find their grandchildren lacking in matters of proper decorum."

Gwendolyn followed his turn and smiled. "But enough about me. Did you see the wonderful job Samuel did pulling that rabbit out of the hat when the magician asked him to assist with his act? I was so proud of him. He may very well have a future as a magician."

"A lofty goal indeed," Walter said with a grin, spending the remainder of the waltz discussing the children, enjoying the opportunity to share the things he was learning about them and their many quirks with someone who genuinely cared about them.

Oscar, he'd recently discovered, was far too somber at times and had a way of speaking that made one forget he was only nine years old. He'd yet to explain how he'd come to fail his classes, but one morning at breakfast he'd told Walter he would need to hire on a tutor in the fall, because he wouldn't be going back to his boarding school.

Before Walter had been able to argue with that, Oscar had gotten up from the breakfast table and quit the room, and that's the last time the subject had been broached.

In all honesty, there was something to be said for his son's stubbornness and commitment to his decisions, even if Walter didn't understand why Oscar was so committed to not returning to a school he'd never given any indication he loathed—until he'd failed all of his classes and had gotten up to mischief that was completely out of character for him.

As for the twins, he'd discovered they were complete opposites. Samuel had always been quiet, but what Walter hadn't realized was that his youngest son was thoughtful and kind, possessing a gentle spirit and a love for animals. He also adored his sister, even though Priscilla made a habit of trying to provoke him. But even with Priscilla having the ability to be a pint-sized tyrant, she was a little girl who wanted to seize the day, enjoying different experiences. She would clearly leave a mark on the world in the future, although doing so would probably entail situations that would keep Walter up at night.

It was humbling, coming to terms with the notion he didn't know his own children, as well as knowing he would likely have never drawn closer to them if Gwendolyn hadn't entered his life, and for that, he couldn't thank her enough. Or . . .

"The music's ending," Gwendolyn said, snapping Walter out of his thoughts.

"Forgive me. I fear I was preoccupied," he admitted, as he brought them to a stop in the middle of the floor.

"Children can do that to a parent," she said, her lips curving. "But now, I believe Catriona is due to sing soon, so if you'll excuse me, I need to make certain she's ready. The last time I saw her, she and Frank Lambert were looking over sheet notes." She released a sigh. "I've not had any luck finding anyone willing to dance with Frank this evening, which is why I think he's dogging Catriona's every step. She, at least, seems to enjoy his company and doesn't condescend to him like society is currently doing."

"He's still determined to marry a Knickerbocker?"

"I believe so, even though I've told him numerous times he's not going to find success with that plan. He's stubborn though, which means he's not yet receptive to the idea of looking outside of society for a wife." She dipped into a curtsy. "Make certain to keep on track with your schedule because I'll be expecting an update after I check on my cousin." With that, Gwendolyn strolled away right as his mother joined him.

"She's quite light on her feet," Ethel said, smiling at Gwendolyn's retreating back before she took hold of his arm and prodded him toward the orchestra. "I thought before Catriona sings, we should take a moment to thank the guests for coming."

"By *we*, does that mean you want me to do the honors?" Walter asked.

"Of course. I think you should have the children with you as well. It might remind some of the ladies what one of the main reasons is behind your entering the marriage mart again."

"I imagine Gwendolyn would be in agreement with that suggestion."

"Too right she would," Ethel said, before she told him she'd round up the children and glided away.

Once Oscar, Samuel, and Priscilla had been gathered up and told Walter was going to address the guests before Catriona sang, Oscar pulled the twins aside, telling Walter he needed to have a little talk with his siblings—one Walter hoped centered around encouraging the twins to behave. When the children rejoined him a moment later, Walter stepped in front of the orchestra, waited until silence settled around the ballroom, then presented his guests with a bow.

"On behalf of the Townsend family," he began, "I'd like to welcome you to our annual Newport ball. Next up, you'll be given the privilege of listening to Mrs. Barnabas Zimmerman, simply known as Catriona, of course, to those who saw her perform at the Academy of Music. After that, we'll repair to the dining room, and then there'll be additional dancing and more games for the children." He looked down when Priscilla suddenly tugged on his jacket.

"Oscar wants to say something," Priscilla said.

A sliver of apprehension shot through Walter, but when he glanced to Oscar and caught his eye, Oscar merely sent him a shrug before he stepped forward and bowed to the crowd.

"Good evening," Oscar began as Priscilla and Samuel moved to stand on either side of him. "We're Walter's children, and, according to rumor, my father has reentered society because he believes we need a mother." Oscar grinned as he leaned forward. "I think that's because we can be unruly at times."

Laughter resounded around the room, which Oscar accepted with another grin before he cleared his throat.

"As my father has enjoyed getting to know the young ladies Miss Brinley has arranged for him to meet," Oscar continued, "my siblings and I were given the task by Miss Brinley of telling her our thoughts about the nice ladies who paid attention to us."

Walter's sense of apprehension increased as murmurs began to spread amongst the guests.

Oscar didn't seem to notice as he began wandering back and forth in front of the orchestra. "Miss Brinley thought we should have a say in the final decision about who Father weds, because that lady will become a big part of our lives as well. That's why we decided that tonight we're going to announce the lady we think will be the best option."

Walter stepped to Oscar's side and leaned close to his ear. "This is not the moment for this, son," he said quietly, but before he could usher them into another room to speak privately, Priscilla bounded forward, drawing everyone's attention.

"It's Miss Brinley!" she shouted.

A mere blink of an eye later, chaos mixed with a great deal of hostility erupted through the ballroom—all of it directed toward Gwendolyn, who was standing still as a statue in the middle of the ballroom floor—until she glanced his way. An eternity seemed to pass as her gaze locked with his, but then her eyes narrowed and her lips thinned before she suddenly spun on her heel and stalked out of the ballroom without a backward glance.

Thirty-Three

⚜

"I certainly never expected last night to end in what can only be described as a mutiny enacted by the Four Hundred," Catriona said, causing Gwendolyn to pause in the act of sorting through the trunks one of Mrs. Parker's footmen had dumped off on the front porch of Catriona's rented cottage a few hours earlier.

"I don't know why you'd find their reaction to Priscilla's pronouncement so surprising," Gwendolyn said. "According to Mrs. Parker, as she was in the process of terminating my employment, Newport's social set has decided I'm a conniving, underhanded woman of questionable origins, who purposely steered Walter away from numerous charming ladies in order to snag him myself, going so far as to hoodwink his children into accepting me into their little lives."

"I suppose I'm not actually surprised about society's general consensus, but I was surprised that Mrs. Parker fired you, along with me, in the middle of Walter's drive."

Gwendolyn shook out a skirt a maid had clearly shoved into the trunk with little regard for the silk fabric. "Mrs. Parker's performance was undoubtedly stage worthy, but I understand why she made such a scene, telling me in a very loud voice that I'd fooled her into believing my intentions toward Walter were honorable, when they were nothing of the sort. She's merely attempting to salvage her reputation—something, if you didn't catch it last night, she accused me of trying to destroy, right before she informed me my services would no longer be needed, effective immediately."

"There certainly was no need for her to insist her footman escort us to my carriage after she fired you, as if we were members of the criminal persuasion."

Gwendolyn abandoned the trunk and went to sit beside her cousin on a settee done up in a pale shade of blue. "At least her firing me got us rapidly removed from Sea Haven. Seeing the abject horror on Walter's face after Priscilla's announcement, I certainly didn't care to linger there."

"Perhaps you were mistaken about the look."

"I wasn't. He was clearly shocked and probably a little embarrassed. However, because it's Walter, I was convinced he'd feel obligated to seek me out to discuss the matter. But since I didn't want to endure what would have been a mortifying exchange—one where he'd most assuredly apologize for yet another misunderstanding between us—during my firing, I made a point of telling Mrs. Parker I'd had quite enough of high society and would be thrilled if I never spoke to another member of the Four Hundred again, including Walter."

Catriona frowned. "That certainly explains why Walter didn't show up here last night or this morning."

"I'm confident Mrs. Parker didn't hesitate to tell him what I said, so that's that, and now we simply need to finish packing and catch the ferry back to the city. If you don't mind, though, I'd like to stop by Sea Haven. Not to see Walter, of course, but to say a proper good-bye to the children. They deserve an opportunity to hear my explanation regarding why I can't be their mother. I only hope Walter isn't there, but if he is, I'll bid him a pleasant adieu, and that will be the last time I'll ever have to see him."

Catriona tilted her head. "What would you have done if you'd not seen horror on Walter's face but another emotion instead, such as delight, or perhaps anticipation, as if he'd been thinking along the same lines as his children?"

"That's a moot point because he didn't look delighted—he looked as if he was hoping a large hole would materialize in front of him so he could disappear from sight."

"I doubt that's true," Catriona said before she blew out a breath. "I suppose this is where I need to admit you were right about my matchmaking abilities, since I thought *you* would be Walter's perfect match and actually tried to finagle that match behind your back by telling Walter all sorts of lovely stories about you."

Gwendolyn's lips twitched. "I was wondering why you kept telling him so much about me, but yes, you should abandon any future urges to dabble in matchmaking, as shall I. Frankly, I'm more than ready to put this chapter of my life behind me."

"Our next chapter should include Scotland," Catriona suggested. "I've always wanted to have a pint in a pub and look at gentlemen in kilts."

Gwendolyn took hold of Catriona's hand. "We're not going to Scotland. We've already discussed this. Our days of traveling the world have come to an end. It's past time you stop running and take the rest of the summer to contemplate what *you'd* really like to do with your life. And even though my days as an assistant matchmaker are over, I'm going to give one last piece of matchmaker advice. I think you should consider marrying again. You're still young, and . . . I haven't neglected to notice you seem to appreciate Frank Lambert's company."

To Gwendolyn's surprise, temper flashed through Catriona's eyes. "While I won't deny I may have, every so often, found myself enjoying Frank's company, that's no longer the case."

"Why not?"

"Because he—just before I was about to go out to sing, and before the children made an announcement that disbanded the ball—had the audacity to ask me if I would speak on his behalf to a few of the ladies in attendance last night. He thought they would find him more attractive, even with his being new money, if a worldly woman like myself mentioned, in a way that seemed natural to the conversation, how compelling I found him."

"He didn't."

"He did," Catriona said. "Needless to say, I gave him a piece of my mind, although I never got to finish telling him everything I wanted to say because . . . well, you know, the disaster occurred." She sighed. "If you ask me, gentlemen can sometimes be more trouble than they're worth."

"You always told me Barnabas was trouble, but you adored him."

"I think he was the exception."

"Perhaps he was at that," Gwendolyn admitted before she gave Catriona's arm a rub. "But it's not doing either of us any good bemoaning our sad state right now, because we're beginning to turn rather morose."

Catriona caught Gwendolyn's eye. "I have a feeling your morose state isn't going to disappear anytime soon. I know you were beginning to develop feelings for Walter, and ones of the affectionate sort."

Gwendolyn released a sigh. "You noticed that?"

"We've spent years together, darling. Of course I noticed, and I've also developed a theory regarding the true reason behind your decision to abandon our travels."

"A theory?"

"Indeed, and I hope you won't be annoyed by this, but I'm beginning to believe the unconventional life you've always claimed you want to embrace, isn't the life you're meant to live after all."

"What do you mean?"

Catriona smiled. "You're a woman who is most content when you're around children. Yes, you do possess a bit of wanderlust, and yes, you enjoyed our travels to a certain extent. But even though being an independent woman is something you've always placed great stock in, I believe your true role in life is a conventional one—that being a wife and mother."

"That's about as traditional as a woman can get."

Catriona gave Gwendolyn's hand a pat. "And there's nothing wrong with that. Your mother, even though she was quite like you in her younger days and wanted to pursue a less traditional feminine role, realized after meeting your father that what she truly longed for in life was a husband and children. I think you're exactly like her and will only find true contentment after you discover the man of your dreams and settle down to have your own family with him. That's why I can't help but wonder what you would have done, or what you'd do, if Walter came to his senses and realized you're the match for him."

"I'm not the match for him," Gwendolyn argued. "Walter is a member of the New York Four Hundred, and there are unspoken rules he's committed to following, such as marrying a lady of his social status. And while you may not be off the mark with your theory that what I really want is to take on a conventional role of wife and mother, I've been thinking about what you said to me a few weeks ago—that bit about knowing I want what my parents have—a deep and abiding love that will last for the rest of my days. You were right about that, which means Walter is not my match, because he doesn't love me."

"What if you're wrong?"

"I'm not, because while I'm sure Walter appreciates that his children adore me, he's not like my father. He won't set aside convention to marry a woman outside the Four Hundred. And even on the chance he would, if I've learned nothing else over this summer, I know I don't belong in society. It's too petty and there are too many intrigues. Plus, even though some ladies have abandoned some of their underhanded antics, you know that won't last. Securing an advantageous marriage in society is a high-stakes game, which means ladies will continue to backstab one another while settling smiles on all the gentlemen, acting quite as if they don't have a backstabbing bone in their bodies.

"It's simply not a world I want to inhabit, but Walter is a Knickerbocker. He won't turn his back on society, nor do I believe he'll cut back on the time he spends with his many business interests to be an attentive husband like my father is to my mother."

"Walter cut back on his business to spend more of the summer in Newport," Catriona pointed out.

"True, but that's only because he realized it would be impossible for me to find him a match if he wasn't in town more often."

Catriona rose to her feet and moved to a window that faced the front of the house, opening it to let a light breeze swirl into the room. "But what if you're wrong and Walter actually holds you in great esteem? Shouldn't you at least afford him an audience before you leave Newport to hear if he has anything of worth to say to you?"

"I think I've suffered enough humiliation. As I said, we'll stop by Sea Haven to say good-bye to the children before we leave, and if I encounter Walter, I'll be civil but won't engage in a lengthy conversation with him. We'll then make a discreet exit from Newport because I have no desire to speak with any society members who might be out and about."

Catriona moved aside the curtain, her gaze settling on something outside. "And isn't that unfortunate, because there is an entire parade of carriages making their way up the drive. Given the splendid horses pulling those conveyances, I think society has decided to pay you a call."

Gwendolyn strode to Catriona's side, narrowing her eyes on well-equipped carriages pulled by prime horseflesh trundling up the gravel drive. The elaborate hats some of the ladies were wearing in open buggies obscured their identities, but clearly Catriona was right—the social set had come to call.

"You'll have to tell them I'm not here," Gwendolyn said, twitching the curtain back into place.

"Absolutely not. You've never been a coward, and I'm not about to let you start with that nonsense now."

"So says the lady I once had to rescue from the top of a dresser after you spotted a rat in our Paris townhouse."

"It was at least a foot long, and anyone other than you would have jumped on that dresser with me. That type of fortitude is exactly why we're going to welcome these unexpected guests into this cottage and hear what they have to say."

"We're not giving them tea."

"Fine. I prefer coffee," Catriona said before she sailed out of the receiving room, telling her butler, Gibbons, to see if he could get the trunks stowed away before their unexpected guests arrived.

"Who cares about the trunks?" Gwendolyn asked, hurrying to catch up but stopping for just a second to peer in a hallway mirror, smoothing back a strand of hair that had escaped its pins.

Catriona spun on her heel and marched back to join Gwendolyn. "We will not give any of them the satisfaction of seeing how Mrs. Parker sent your trunks after you as if you were some hired hand she could treat with such disrespect. You're a Brinley, as well as a Sullivan, my darling. Remember that." She leaned closer to the mirror and pinched her cheeks. "We'll receive everyone in the parlor, but only after I have Gibbons leave them lingering about in the receiving room for a good ten minutes or so."

Catriona sent Gwendolyn a wink. "I picked up a few pointers when we were guests of the Prince of Wales. Making people wait always gives one the advantage, and considering we're about to be inundated with people confident in their own superiority, we're going to need all the advantages we can get."

Thirty-Four

It soon became clear that Catriona was in the mood to annoy their unexpected guests, because she made them wait thirty minutes before having Gibbons usher them into the parlor.

Gwendolyn was hard-pressed to resist a laugh when Gibbons opened the parlor door, stepped aside, and one disgruntled person after another marched into the room.

First came Suzette Tilden, followed by Tillie Wickham, Russell Damrosch, Thurman Chandler, Cordelia Lowe, Frank Lambert, and a good dozen ladies Walter had escorted around town. Trailing behind them were Adelaide and her mother. Phyllis immediately bustled over to where Gwendolyn was sitting on a chaise and plopped down beside her, taking hold of her hand.

"I'm here for moral support," she said, not bothering to lower her voice. "As is Adelaide."

"Too right I am," Adelaide said, sitting down on the other side of Gwendolyn, which had Catriona scooting over, although there wasn't much room to scoot since the chaise they were sitting on was built for two.

"How surprising to see all of you here," Gwendolyn began, not bothering to rise to her feet, because she and Catriona had agreed that to remain seated would give them another advantage during what was certainly going to be a contentious exchange.

"I'm sure you are taken aback to find yourself faced with us," Suzette said, stepping to the front of the crowd. "But this isn't a social call. We're here for your notes."

Gwendolyn arched a brow. "Notes?"

"Indeed. Mrs. Parker told us you amassed an entire notepad filled with tasty tidbits, apparently done while you were pretending to go about the business of finding Walter a match, as well as securing matches for the gentlemen present now." Suzette gestured to Russell, Thurman, and even Frank—although she might not have intentionally gestured to Frank since she immediately turned her back on him when he sent her a smile.

"I don't know how any notes I may have taken would benefit any of you," Gwendolyn said.

Tillie stepped up beside Suzette, her nostrils flaring. "We think you might have made a numbered list with ladies you thought would be appropriate candidates for Walter . . . before you decided to snag him for yourself."

"I never made up a numbered list, nor did I try to snag Walter."

"The evidence from last night suggests otherwise," Tillie said with a sniff.

"What evidence?"

"The evidence from the children, of course."

Gwendolyn rose to her feet. "The children were simply being children. Do they care for me? Of course, just as I care for them, but they only came to hold me in affection because I was attentive to them and truly wanted to get to know them better."

"We showed them attention, but you didn't see the little darlings professing they wanted any of us to become their mother," Tillie shot back.

"And calling them 'little darlings' in that snide tone of voice is exactly why you, Miss Wickham, would not have been an ideal candidate for Walter."

As Tillie took to gaping at Gwendolyn, Russell Damrosch stepped forward. "There's no need for rudeness, Miss Brinley."

Gwendolyn tilted her head. "Forgive me, Mr. Damrosch, because I'm sure you'll also accuse me of rudeness for what I'm about to say, but it's something that needs to be said."

She took a second to glance around the room. "I was beginning to hope all of you were taking to heart some of the sermons Reverend Eberhard has delivered this Season. Granted, showering Walter with meals was an odd take on how to love thy neighbor, but I felt it was a step in the right direction. Last week his sermon revolved around the truth of God seeing all of us as equals. It's now evident he was not successful in imparting that lesson, because it's beyond telling how you'd accuse *me* of rudeness, Mr. Damrosch, when you show up at my cousin's cottage, *en masse* no less, and begin hurling unfounded accusations at me, as if it's your right to do so.

"I suppose you, like so many members of society, believe you're not being rude because I'm not considered your equal. I now find myself wondering if that attitude will ever change or if all of you will spend your lives immersed in your quest to obtain the best gilded prize, no matter whom you injure in the process, whether they be a servant, a shopgirl, or one of your own less fashionable society members."

"We didn't come here for a sermon, Miss Brinley," Suzette snapped. "We came for your notes."

"And I'll be more than happy to give those to you, but you're going to be disappointed. My notes aren't what I'd consider organized."

"Did you have matches in the making for any of us you didn't write down before the events of last night?" Suzette shot at her next.

Gwendolyn shrugged. "Of course, and forgive me if this

comes across too bluntly, but if some of you would simply open your eyes, instead of setting your sights on alliances you feel would be the most advantageous, or ones that would see you paired with the shiniest prize of any given Season, you'd see the truth of your perfect matches right in front of you."

Suzette narrowed her eyes. "Do tell."

A most unusual urge to laugh settled over Gwendolyn as she looked around the room, taking in all the scowls settled on her, although Frank Lambert was sending her an encouraging sort of nod, one he immediately discontinued when his gaze drifted to Catriona, who was scowling as well, and directly at him.

Gwendolyn returned her attention to Suzette. "I don't normally respond well to demands, but if I tell you my thoughts, will all of you promise to leave, and without sending more insults my way?"

Suzette shot a glance around the room, where everyone was still scowling, although most people were nodding as well. She turned back to Gwendolyn. "Fine, we'll agree to leave afterward, but no promises about the insults since we don't know what you're going to say."

"Fair enough, and since you seem to be the spokeswoman of this particular gathering, allow me to start with you, Miss Tilden." She caught Suzette's eye. "To be frank, if you're hoping I'm about to tell you I thought you would be a suitable candidate for Walter, I'm not."

"Why not?"

"You gave his children a pony."

Suzette blinked. "The pony was a generous gift. It's ridiculous to think that because of my generosity, I was taken out of the running."

"It was a questionable gift, but that's not the only reason I felt you weren't suitable to marry him. A more important one would be that I never got the impression you wanted to marry Walter."

"He's the catch of the Season."

Gwendolyn resisted the inclination to roll her eyes. "Well, there is that, but Walter's not the only catch this summer." She nodded to Thurman Chandler. "He's considered quite a catch as well."

Suzette's nose wrinkled. "What does Thurman's being a catch have anything to do with me?"

Gwendolyn wrinkled her nose right back at her. "You've ignored what's been right in front of you this whole time, because you, Suzette, and you, Thurman, enjoy each other's company. You grew up together, and while many people grow apart as they age, the two of you seem to have grown closer. That, if you'd take the time to think about it, is telling."

She caught Thurman's eye. "That's what I'd started writing about on the page dedicated to you in my notepad before Mrs. Parker fired me. What the two of you do next is completely up to you, but I suggest you seek out some privacy and discuss the matter more thoroughly."

Suzette's cheeks suddenly turned rather pink as she settled a small smile on Thurman. "I suppose it wouldn't hurt for us to have a private discussion. There's no question we're compatible, but . . . I never considered that might be a precursor to something more than friendship."

Thurman's eyes began to gleam. "I've considered it a time or two but never felt as if you'd want to explore a deeper relationship with me."

"I wouldn't be opposed to doing a little . . . exploring."

In the span of a heartbeat, Thurman was holding fast to Suzette's arm, and together they quit the parlor without another word, although the smiles on their faces were rather telling.

"This is turning into a most riveting morning," Adelaide said, fanning her face. "And good show, Gwendolyn. I think you're exactly right about the two of them."

"Thank you, Adelaide," Gwendolyn said before she looked

around the room and settled her sights on Russell Damrosch, who shot a longing look to the parlor door, seemed to consider bolting out of it, but then squared his shoulders and returned his attention to Gwendolyn.

"I take it I'm next?" he asked.

"Indeed, because you are, after all, another gentleman Mrs. Parker took on and then left me to find you a suitable match. Allow me to apologize in advance for what I'm about to say, because you'll probably find it insulting, given the less than positive attributes I've concluded about your character. But do know I have a reason for pointing them out."

"What negative qualities could you possibly have concluded about me?" Russell demanded.

"You're far too competitive and you lack sensitivity."

"Being competitive is not a deficiency," Russell argued.

"Perhaps not in your opinion, but your heightened competitiveness is the reason I told Mrs. Parker not to sponsor you. And that very nature was evidently aroused when I told you I didn't want to find you a match, which was what clearly led you to offering Mrs. Parker a bauble she couldn't resist."

"But you didn't find me a match," Russell pointed out. "And Mrs. Parker doesn't have your notes, incomplete as they apparently are, so she doesn't know if you encountered a lady who would be a match for me."

Gwendolyn's toe began tapping against the Aubusson carpet. "I *would* have found you a match if I'd not been fired, because I have the perfect candidate in mind for you. With that said, what I'm about to divulge should be considered fulfillment of Mrs. Parker's contract with you."

"I'm listening," Russell began. "Who is she?"

Gwendolyn nodded to Tillie Wickham, who blinked even as her mouth went agape. "Miss Wickham, of course. The two of you are equally overly competitive, that proven when you both seemed to believe it was acceptable to target children while playing Annie Over. And while I could point out other similarities you share, I don't think it would be kind of me to do so, and whenever possible I do try to not ruffle feathers."

She folded her arms over her chest. "I suggest the two of you follow Suzette and Thurman's lead and remove yourself from the parlor to find a secluded place to engage in a chat, or perhaps an arm-wrestling match or something of that nature. The winner could get the prize of deciding when and where you should wed." She waggled her fingers toward the door. "Off you go."

Amusement was swift when Russell glanced at Tillie—who was looking at him as if she were sizing him up against the competition, although there really wasn't any competition to be had in the parlor—took hold of her arm, and strode from the room, Tillie matching his every stride.

"I wish you both the best," Gwendolyn called after them before she turned her attention to the room again. "I have to admit I don't have any ready-made matches for the rest of you, but I'd be more than happy to hash over any grievances you care to level against me."

Fresh amusement swept through her when everyone except Cordelia Lowe, Frank Lambert, and Daniel Mizner, who'd been lurking unnoticed in the back of the room, turned on their heels and bolted out of the parlor.

Thirty-Five

"It's incredibly impressive how you've gotten that whole intimidation business down," Adelaide said, wincing when the fan she was still plying smacked her in the nose. She tossed it aside as Cordelia Lowe stepped front and center.

"With the departure of those ladies who had little hope you took notice of them because they weren't often seen in your company," Cordelia began, "what say we get down to what my role should have been with Walter. May I assume, if you'd not decided to try your hand at stealing him away from the serious contenders, I could have expected to become the next Mrs. Walter Townsend? I was, after all, one of the ladies who spent the most time with him."

She took a step toward Gwendolyn and considered her for a moment. "If you admit I *was* the lady you had in mind for Walter, you could leave Newport with a clear conscience because you would be fulfilling the last of your obligations to Mrs. Parker by securing a match for the final gentleman she agreed to sponsor this Season."

"Mrs. Parker is still representing me," Frank Lambert said, drawing everyone's attention.

Cordelia released what almost sounded like a snort. "Please. You, Mr. Lambert, are the very definition of *nouveau riche*. While you may have an abundance of funds at your disposal, what you need to understand is this—no self-respecting lady of the New York Four Hundred will give you the time of day." She then settled an eye on Daniel Mizner. "And forgive me for my continued bluntness, Mr. Mizner, but I, along with Miss Brinley, I'm sure, do not even understand why you're here."

Daniel scratched his nose. "I have no idea why you're taking that snippy tone with me, Miss Lowe. But to answer your question, I'm here because I'm hopeful that before Miss Brinley departs Newport she can point me in the direction of one of the ladies she spent time with while in Newport." He returned his attention to Gwendolyn. "May I dare hope you have someone in mind for me, someone of high social standing and . . ."

"A substantial fortune?" Cordelia finished for him when Daniel faltered, earning a scowl from Daniel, which she addressed by giving a languid wave of her hand. "There's no reason for feigned outrage, Mr. Mizner. You must know you have little chance of securing an alliance with a member of the upper crust. Everyone is aware you're a habitual gambler, and it's also known you tend to align yourself with questionable business partners. It's no mystery you're in Newport this Season looking for an heiress, probably because your parents have limited your access to their fortune—done, no doubt, because of those questionable characters you mingle with."

"That's enough, Miss Lowe," Gwendolyn said, earning a glare from Cordelia and a small smile from Mr. Mizner.

"Thank you for that, Miss Brinley," Daniel said. "I realized from the moment I met you that you're a remarkable woman, only turning down my request of sponsorship because you obviously realized the difficulty you would face securing me an alliance, what with how ridiculous society ladies have turned out to be, believing rumors without any proof. With that said, can you suggest a lady or two, or perhaps even three, who might not have been privy to these horrid rumors and would give me—a gentleman with the best intentions at heart—a chance at earning their love?"

Gwendolyn resisted a sigh. Given that Daniel had made a point of telling Mrs. Parker she wouldn't be compensated until vows were spoken, she was convinced the rumors were true and Daniel was, indeed, on the lookout for an heiress.

"I'm afraid I have no names to provide you, Mr. Mizner. I made a point of at least beginning to learn about the gentlemen we were sponsoring, and I then took that information to form educated decisions regarding which lady would suit them best. I have no insight into your character, and because of that, I'm afraid I don't know who would suit you."

"What about her?" Daniel said, nodding to Adelaide. "She's been out for at least five Seasons, and I imagine she'd welcome my attention."

"I am sitting right here," Adelaide said, rising to her feet. "And while this may come as a shock to you, Mr. Mizner, I'm not interested in furthering an acquaintance with someone who addresses me as 'her.' We've been introduced before, and to refresh your memory, I'm the lady who unintentionally whacked you with my fan."

When Phyllis rose to her feet as well and settled a glare on Daniel, he swallowed before he returned his attention to Gwendolyn. "Perhaps we could discuss this at a later date, and in a less hostile environment."

"I'm afraid I won't be engaged in matchmaking services from this point forward, Mr. Mizner, but I wish you well in the future," Gwendolyn said.

"How unfortunate, but thank you for the well wishes." Daniel glanced back to Phyllis, who was still glaring at him, and swallowed again. "I suppose all that's left to do now is bid everyone a good afternoon." Sending Gwendolyn an inclination of his head, Daniel headed for the door, paused to remind Frank Lambert they needed to set up an appointment to discuss financial investment opportunities soon, then disappeared a moment later.

"You were right when you refused to sponsor him," Frank said, drawing Gwendolyn's attention. "I didn't get the impression, during the few times we spoke, that he has honorable intentions when it comes to finding a wife."

Gwendolyn arched a brow. "And you do?"

"There's nothing dishonorable about my objectives," Frank returned. "I want to marry well to improve my social station, which will then allow any children I may eventually have to be raised in a world that will accept them. They're certain to be considered outcasts if I don't do exactly that, forced to peer through the glass leading into society and all its advantages, but refused entrance into the upper crust because their father had the audacity to make his money instead of inheriting it."

Gwendolyn took a step closer to Frank. "And while that isn't a dishonorable plan, I'm going to tell you what I mentioned to Walter Townsend numerous times. You need to set your standards higher. You seem to believe that settling for a society lady, who will always consider you beneath her, will set your future children up well in life."

She shook her head. "It will do nothing of the sort, and your children will not thank you for the strife they will certainly grow up in. There's no rule stating a man with wealth must get accepted into society. There is life outside the Four Hundred, and a wonderful life at that. What you need is a lady already in possession of her own fortune, which would allow you to know she's not marrying you for your money but simply for you."

"Where would I find a lady like that?" Frank demanded.

"Honestly, must I spell everything out today?" Gwendolyn jerked her head toward Catriona. "She's right over there."

Catriona glided across the room and settled a frown on Gwendolyn. "I know I mentioned in passing I might consider marrying again, but I didn't mean I was looking to do that anytime soon. Frank and I barely know each other, and more importantly, I'm not overly fond of him at the moment."

"I wasn't suggesting the man drop to one knee and propose to you here and now," Gwendolyn said. "And, yes, you're not currently fond of him, but you didn't hesitate to join him when he was turned away from Bailey's Beach, and you allowed him to keep you company last night before you were set to perform. You never let anyone do that."

"True, but . . ." Catriona narrowed an eye on Frank. "Before Gwendolyn begins listing reasons why she believes you and I will suit, I'm going to point out the main reason she's wrong. You, Frank, are determined to marry a lady who's high in the instep, something I'm certainly not, and that will never change. Besides that, you asked me last night to introduce you to ladies, even going so far as to suggest they'd be impressed because you'd spent time in my company."

Frank rubbed a hand over his face. "I only asked you to introduce me around because you told me you were assisting Gwendolyn with matchmaking. Truth be told, I would have been content to simply remain in your company, but ladies like you don't spend a lot of their time with men like me. I'm rough around the edges, not sophisticated, and don't warrant a second look from beautiful women like you, which is why I had to keep telling myself not to follow you around everywhere, even though I wanted to."

Catriona crossed her arms over her chest. "So what if you're a little rough? You've been able to find success using your intellect and your bare hands if I'm not mistaken. There's nothing shameful about that, and Gwendolyn certainly has the right of it when she says you should set your standards higher."

"I would be only too happy to do exactly that," Frank said quietly, "but you're a standard that's far out of my reach."

Gwendolyn held her breath as Catriona considered Frank for

a long moment before a small smile flickered over her face. "You may be off the mark about that, but since Gwendolyn and I have plans to depart from Newport as soon as possible, perhaps it wouldn't hurt for you and me to repair to the front parlor and discuss what is certainly an unexpected development."

"It would be my honor to escort you to the parlor," Frank said, moving into motion a second later. He took hold of Catriona's hand, pressed a kiss to her knuckles, then extended his arm to her, which she took, and together they strolled from the room.

"I'll say this," Phyllis said from where she'd resumed her spot on the chaise, "if nothing else, my dear Gwendolyn, you're definitely going to be remembered as the most successful matchmaker Newport has ever seen."

"On the contrary," Cordelia countered, drawing Gwendolyn's attention as well as a wince, because she'd almost forgotten Cordelia was still in the room. "If you ask me, Miss Brinley will only be remembered as the notorious woman who, even though she realized I would be the most suited for Walter Townsend, had the audacity to attempt to steal him away from me."

Gwendolyn wrinkled her nose. "For the umpteenth time, I didn't try to steal Walter from anyone—nor, if I may speak bluntly, was I ever convinced you were the lady best suited for him. If you've forgotten, the twins became horribly sick while in your care, and all because you fed them too many sweets."

"I'm sure that happens to children all the time, and it's not as if I forced them to eat all the sweets I gave them."

"They're children, of course they're going to eat all the sweets. They don't know any better. You, on the other hand, should have. And . . ." Gwendolyn shook her head when Cordelia opened her mouth, a protest clearly on the tip of her tongue. "Another mark not in your favor was that, after I told you they'd gotten ill, you didn't take responsibility for their sad plight. You also didn't think to leave the dinner early to check on their welfare. I, however, departed before the sixth course was served, and good thing I did, because the children were still feeling sick and needed someone besides their older brother to tuck them into bed."

"And that right there is exactly why the children were right and that you, Miss Gwendolyn Brinley, would be the best choice to become their mother."

Gwendolyn closed her eyes for the briefest of seconds before she turned, finding Walter standing in the doorway, looking rather disheveled, as well as a touch too appealing. Her gaze settled on his face, and every thought about how appealing he was disappeared when she realized he was smiling at her, quite as if he expected her to be pleased with the declaration he'd just made.

She squared her shoulders and lifted her chin, because she had news for him—she wasn't pleased in the least, in fact, she was what could only be described as infuriated.

Thirty-Six

It was immediately evident to Walter that he might have made a rather large faux pas with his opening remark, because Gwendolyn's eyes were now spewing sparks his way. Before he could make amends though, Cordelia began stalking his way.

"You're *not* serious, are you, Mr. Townsend?" Cordelia demanded, stopping a foot away from him. "You *cannot* believe this woman would make an excellent mother for those adorable children of yours, not when you saw how competent I was with them."

It took a colossal effort to refuse the urge he felt to flee, because the hostile looks he was receiving—not only from Cordelia and Gwendolyn, but also from Adelaide and Phyllis Duveen—were enough to make any man claim a just-remembered appointment and rush out of the room, begging everyone's pardon as he bolted.

He permitted himself the luxury of a sigh instead as he caught Cordelia's eye. "Forgive me, Miss Lowe, because I have enjoyed the time we've spent in each other's company this Season. With that said, it may be best if we're perfectly honest with each other. While I find you to be a pleasant—"

Cordelia held up her hand, cutting him off as her eyes turned icy. "Do not speak another word to me, Mr. Townsend, especially if you're going to use additional words like *pleasant*. Clearly, I've been mistaken about you, and it's now evident we won't suit at all." She dipped into a curtsy. "To be clear, I didn't find your company pleasant in the least."

Lifting her chin, she spun on her heel and stalked for the doorway, disappearing through it a second later, leaving Walter alone with three ladies who immediately settled their attention on him.

"I told you the word *pleasant* was rarely well received," Gwendolyn said before she narrowed her eyes on him. "But pleasantness aside, care to explain what you're doing here."

He gave a tug on a tie that was beginning to feel as if it were strangling him. "I came to speak with you about what happened last night."

"Oh? You mean the humiliating circumstance of my being left to fend for myself after the children, being children, thought they'd found the perfect solution to your quest of a mother for them, and announced to one and all that I was that solution? Or perhaps," Gwendolyn continued before he could respond, "you want to explain your reaction to Oscar's announcement, which was to stand in front of the orchestra and gape at me with an expression of what can only be described as horror on your face."

"I'm sure you're mistaken about that."

Gwendolyn crossed her arms over her chest. "I assure you, I'm not. I was there, watching you, and then, the icing on the cake, after the ballroom erupted with accusations about my character, was that you didn't bother to come to my defense."

Walter took a step toward her, stopping when she settled an ice-filled glare on him. "You must not have seen this, but I was just about to come to your aid when you turned and strode out of the room. I was then waylaid by one irate lady after another, all of whom I'm sure I offended when I cut short their attempted conversations with me. By the time I made it out of Sea Haven, you were gone. Mrs. Parker then informed me you'd told her you wanted nothing to do with members of society, including me. I felt compelled to honor that request, at least until you had an opportunity to get your temper under control."

Given the temper already in her eyes began burning hotter than ever, it was a foregone conclusion he'd been clumsy with his words yet again, because what lady enjoyed being told she needed to, in essence, rein in her temper?

He raked a hand through his hair. "That came out wrong."

"Too right it did. And since I'm not in the proper frame of mind to humor any additional missteps on your part, this is where I'll bid you good-bye."

"I'm not going to leave, because there's much that remains unsettled between us. As I said when I first arrived, although I realize I approached the matter poorly, the children were not off the mark last night. You would, indeed, make a most exceptional mother."

"Of course I would. But speaking of the children . . ." Her face softened ever so slightly. "How are they?"

"They were better this morning, but they were obviously upset last night, as well as bewildered by the reaction of the guests. They were expecting rousing applause and you agreeing that yes, you'd love to become their mother. Instead, they got an unexpected lesson in disappointment."

Gwendolyn blew out a breath. "I'll stop by Sea Haven before I depart Newport later today. I'm not certain what I'll say to them, but tell me what you said and I'll pattern my conversation accordingly."

"We didn't discuss much except that all of us agree you're the best, as well as only, choice to become their mother. I then assured the children I would try to make amends with you for what happened last night. That seemed to calm them, but

Priscilla insisted I stay with them in the nursery last night, and it was incredibly late before they fell asleep. They were then up at the crack of dawn, wanting to come see you, but I told them it would be best to let me speak with you first."

"Dawn was a few hours ago."

"I didn't think it would put me in your good graces if I showed up on your doorstep too early, which is why I ate breakfast with the children first. After they went off with their governesses, I was treated to a long and scathing lecture from my mother. She was so irate she had horses saddled for us, insisting we ride far away from Sea Haven so the children wouldn't hear her shouting. She rode for forty minutes before she finally reined to a stop, then launched into a blistering tirade that centered around what an idiot I am."

Gwendolyn's lips curved. "I would have enjoyed hearing that."

"I'm sure you would have, because Mother is beside herself over what happened last night. She's furious with me for handling the matter, in her words, poorly. She told me in no uncertain terms that my idea to allow you time to regain your temper was foolishness at its best. Given that you were less than delighted to see me upon my arrival here, I believe she was right. I should have braved your temper last night whether you wanted to see me or not."

He raked a hand through his hair again. "I would have been here earlier, but after Mother finished yelling at me, I made the mistake of thinking you'd still be at Mrs. Parker's residence, packing your belongings. It took me a good thirty minutes to get to her house after Mother and I parted ways."

A bit of a snort was Gwendolyn's first response to that. "If you believe I'm going to feel sorry for you because of your detour, you're sadly mistaken, especially when it wasn't a best-laid plan for you to go to Mrs. Parker's in the first place. It's not a usual occurrence, after a member of a lady's staff gets terminated, for them to return to their employer's home and linger about overnight, packing their belongings in a leisurely fashion."

Walter winced. "Mrs. Parker explained, when I arrived at her house an hour ago, that she informed you last night you were no longer welcome in her cottage, and that she'd sent over your belongings this morning."

Gwendolyn smiled a less than pleasant smile. "Had a footman dump my trunks on the front porch before the sun was up." She shook her head. "She must have been very irate, because she sent back the diamond choker Catriona gave to her, claiming she wanted no reminders of me lingering about."

She lifted her chin. "But returning to you, if you're here to convince me I should entertain the idea of becoming a mother to your children, you're wasting your time. There's nothing left for us to discuss." She nodded toward the door. "I'm sure you won't mind seeing yourself out."

Walter refused to budge. "I'm not done. Contrary to what you just stated, we still have much to discuss. I know you adore my children. Besides that, until last night, I was getting the impression you were becoming somewhat fond of me. That makes it difficult to understand why you won't at least consider forming an alliance with me."

It was rather concerning when Gwendolyn seemed to swell on the spot right as Adelaide and Phyllis made a mad rush for the door, saying this was obviously a conversation they shouldn't be privy to before their heels could be heard clattering down the hallway and out of the house.

"You are the last man on the face of this planet I would form an alliance with" were the first words out of Gwendolyn's mouth after Phyllis and Adelaide made their abrupt departure.

Walter ran a hand over his face because, clearly, the conversation was going downhill at an incredibly rapid rate. "But I thought you were beginning to enjoy the time you spent with me."

"I was," Gwendolyn snapped. "However, even though you seem perfectly willing to form an *alliance* with me—which, well, be still my fluttering heart—that isn't something that interests me. I'm certainly not going to entertain the thought of marriage to you knowing that I'm the best solution you've managed to find to provide your children with a mother. Yes, I adore your children, but here's something you should know. Your children—while having a mother would be highly beneficial to their lives—don't actually need a mother brought in. What they need, and have needed for years, Walter, is you—their father."

She began pacing around the room, her color high, stopping in her tracks before she leveled a furious look on him. "Your children are remarkable. The twins are precocious and precious, and all they long for in this moment of their little lives is attention and genuine affection. They don't need more toys or sweets. What they need is love.

"The lack of that from you, difficult as I'm certain this is to hear, is the root cause for their past misbehavior. Oscar realizes that, and he, at only nine years old, has taken it upon himself to ascertain his siblings get the affection they crave. Why else do you think he deliberately failed all his classes and delved into mischief at his school that was certain to get him tossed out, and right before the term ended?"

"He told you that?"

"Priscilla was the one to spill the beans, but apparently Oscar was worried the twins were lonely and no one was reading them stories at night or properly tucking them into bed. He decided to take matters into his unusually capable nine-year-old hands, failed his classes, got expelled from school, and then went about seeing after your children—something that should never be his responsibility, since it's meant to be yours."

A crushing weight settled over Walter.

He'd had no idea what was behind Oscar's failure at school,

but he should have realized something was dreadfully amiss and should have pressed his son to disclose what that something was.

It was little wonder Oscar looked at him with disdain.

Walter opened his mouth, struggled for a response, then realized he had nothing of worth to say because . . . she was right.

He'd been neglectful of his children, burying himself in work after Vivian died. He'd chosen to leave the responsibility of raising his children to the grandmothers, which hadn't been fair to them, as well as to a parade of governesses who didn't always seem to have his children's best interests at heart, but he hadn't even bothered to ask the children their thoughts about any of their many governesses.

"Begging your pardon, Miss Brinley," the butler suddenly said, sticking his head into the room. "Two women have just arrived, saying something about needing to fetch some children."

Before Gwendolyn could do more than frown, Miss Putman and Miss Wendell, Walter's governesses, dashed into the room, looking harried. They skidded to a stop when they spotted him, Miss Putman dashing a hand over a perspiring forehead before her gaze darted around the room.

"They're not here?" she asked as Miss Wendell advanced into the room, looking behind a chaise before she shook her head.

"They don't appear to be."

A sense of unease swept through Walter. "Are you looking for the children?"

"Indeed," Miss Wendell said. "And while this does not speak well of my or Miss Putman's abilities as governesses, your children locked us in a closet, using a missing doll as an excuse to get us in there. We only just managed to escape after the upstairs maid heard us hollering."

"Why would you think the children were here?" Gwendolyn asked, stepping forward.

"Oscar told a groom we'd given them permission to take

their pony cart out to come and have a word with you, Miss Brinley," Miss Putman said, her gaze still darting about the room. "Everyone on staff knows how upset the children are about what happened last night, so the groom didn't question Oscar, merely harnessed Bert to the cart and watched the children trundle up the drive."

Miss Wendell began wringing her hands. "From what we've pieced together, they locked us in mere minutes after Mr. Townsend and his mother rode off the estate, which was some time ago now. But . . . if they're not here, where are they?"

Thirty-Seven

While there had been numerous times when her siblings had gone missing, Gwendolyn was convinced Walter's children hadn't merely gotten distracted by chasing butterflies or wading in a stream they couldn't pass by.

Oscar had made a point of telling the groom where they were heading, and if Gwendolyn knew anything about Oscar, it was that he was the most responsible nine-year-old she'd ever met and would never willingly put his siblings in harm's way.

Given that the children had been gone for a few hours, there was nothing left to conclude except that they'd run into trouble. What type of trouble remained to be seen, but there was a sense of urgency to the situation, which was why she and Walter were now on horseback, traveling down Bellevue Avenue, where society was already assembled.

It didn't take long to get the word out that the children were missing. Carriages filled with the society set soon took off in different directions to join the search, an agreement made that everyone would convene at Sea Haven in two hours to give reports or get additional direction if the children still hadn't been found.

"Where do you suggest we go next?" Gwendolyn asked, turning to Walter after Russell Damrosch and Tillie Wickham told them they'd head off to look at Easton Beach.

Walter rubbed a hand over his face. "They might have thought, like me, you were staying at Mrs. Parker's, not at Catriona's cottage."

"Then we'll check Raven's Roost first." Gwendolyn turned her horse around and settled into a gallop as Walter did the same.

Mrs. Parker was less than pleased to see her, but after learning why they were there, she rang for her butler. When he told them no children had come calling, she called for a footman, telling Gwendolyn she would join in the search. She then voiced what might have been an apology, mentioning it hadn't been well done of her to have Gwendolyn's trunks dumped on Catriona's doorstep early that morning.

Unwilling to waste time discussing what was an inconsequential matter, Gwendolyn strode for the door. But it seemed apologizing was exactly what Mrs. Parker wanted to do, especially when she added that she might have been a little rash with the termination business.

Gwendolyn pretended she didn't hear her, heading for her horse and pulling herself into the saddle before she nodded Walter's way. "If they didn't try here first, they evidently were on their way to Catriona's. Is Bellevue Avenue the fastest way to her cottage from Sea Haven?"

"It is."

She frowned. "Bellevue is the most traveled street in Newport, and Oscar would have wanted to avoid notice. Maybe he decided to take an out-of-the-way route to get to Catriona's." She tilted her head. "I've yet to walk the Cliff Walk, but are there parts where you could drive a pony cart?"

Walter nodded. "Yes, parts, but the path narrows at places. They'd have to take to a road at some point."

"Oscar probably knows that, but if I were him, that's where I'd start. We should return to Sea Haven and puzzle out a route from there."

Once they reached Walter's cottage, they turned their horses toward the Cliff Walk, Gwendolyn scouring the landscape for any sign of a pony cart. When they reached the cliff path, their pace slowed as they steered the horses down it, reaching a spot ten minutes later where the path narrowed to such a degree it would have been impossible for Oscar to get the pony cart through.

Gwendolyn swung from the horse and walked around, stilling when she saw wheeled tracks in the dirt.

"Did you find something?" Walter asked, joining her.

She nodded to the tracks. "Could be from the pony cart."

Walter bent down, studied the tracks, then straightened. "Looks like they decided to head toward the road. Ochre Point Avenue isn't far from here. It would be the easiest road for the children to take to get to Catriona's cottage."

"Then let's try there."

Swinging back into the saddle, Gwendolyn nudged her horse into motion, following Walter, who suddenly kneed his horse to a gallop and raced toward a grove of trees in the distance. Following him, she pulled her horse to an abrupt stop when she caught sight of Bert standing underneath a tree, still harnessed to a pony cart that was, unfortunately, empty.

She was off the horse and by Walter's side a moment later. "Perhaps they're somewhere close," she said. "I'll check through the trees to the right—you go to the left."

Calling the children's names, she made her way through the forest. Her sense of urgency increased when only the sound of the ocean beating against the cliffs answered her calls. Stopping on the edge of the cliff, she forced herself to look over it, relief flowing freely when she didn't spot a single sign of the children.

Turning, she retraced her steps to the pony cart. After giving

Bert a pat, she climbed into the cart, hoping there would be some clue that would tell her what the children were up to—perhaps a picnic basket or . . . Her blood suddenly turned to ice when she spotted Susie lying on the floor.

"What is it?" Walter asked, striding back to join her.

His face turned ashen when she handed him the doll. "Priscilla would never willingly leave Susie behind," he said. "Something's happened to them."

Gwendolyn took hold of his hand. "We won't be of any use to them if we allow ourselves to become distracted by the worst possible outcome. We'll find them—you know we will—but for now, we need to contact the police. Bert will be fine here while we do that, and the police will want to investigate this scene without us disturbing it more than we already have. We'll return to Sea Haven and send a footman to summon the authorities. That way, if the children return, you'll be at home."

Walter managed a nod before he strode to his horse, and a moment later, they were racing back to Sea Haven. Handing the reins to a groomsman, they made their way to the front steps right as Gideon Abbott came striding through the door, looking grim as he hurried to join them.

"I have news," Gideon said once he reached Walter's side.

"The children?" Walter rasped.

"I believe they're unharmed, for now, but we need to speak about this inside, just in case."

"In case what?"

"Someone is watching" was all Gideon said before he headed for the front door, Walter and Gwendolyn following a step behind.

It was not a reassuring sight when Gwendolyn entered the library and discovered Ethel and Matilda huddled together on a settee, both ladies in tears, a sign that something was terribly amiss.

"Ethel received a note about fifteen minutes ago, right before

I arrived," Gideon began as Gwendolyn took a seat between Ethel and Matilda, taking hold of their hands.

"A note?" Walter repeated.

"A ransom note." Gideon picked up a piece of paper from a table and handed it to Walter. "They want a hundred thousand dollars, delivered at midnight to an abandoned boat that sits on the beach not far from Spouting Rock."

Walter glanced over the note and lifted his head. "Whoever wrote this said the children won't be harmed as long as the ransom is paid and we don't contact the police." He caught Gwendolyn's eye. "It's fortunate we didn't go to the police first instead of returning here after we found Bert and the pony cart."

"You found the pony and cart?" Ethel whispered.

"Not far from the Cliff Walk," Walter said. "Priscilla's doll was left behind. That's when we knew something was wrong. We decided to return here and send the police a message, asking them to join us at Sea Haven to begin an investigation."

"It is fortunate you returned to Sea Haven," Gideon said. "I've been involved with a few similar cases, back when I worked for the government. Bringing in the police is something we'll only consider after we discuss options. I'm only sorry I wasn't here when the note arrived because I may have been able to get some useful information from the boy who delivered it."

Walter frowned. "Why are you here?"

"I ran across Tillie Wickham and Russell Damrosch on the far end of Bellevue. After they explained the children were missing, I came directly to Sea Haven, but again, I arrived after the note was delivered. I'll try to track down the boy who delivered it at some point today, after we decide on a plan."

"The only plan is to pay the ransom," Walter said. "I'll visit my bank immediately and withdraw the funds."

"But before you do that, we're going to need to call off the search for the children," Gideon said, taking a seat beside Walter. "Since we know they've been kidnapped, it won't benefit the situation if a society member stumbles on wherever it is the children are being held."

"How are we to call off the search?" Ethel asked. "It seems as if society has rallied around the idea of locating the children. If we tell them the truth, word will spread like wildfire. I can't believe the kidnappers would be happy to learn everyone knows what they've done. They might take their frustrations out on the children."

"They might indeed," Matilda agreed before she dabbed fresh tears from her cheeks with a handkerchief.

"Perhaps we should station footmen at the end of the drive," Gwendolyn said, sitting forward. "They could tell everyone who checks in that the children were found, but that they're now spending private time with Ethel and Matilda, trying to make amends for scaring their grandmothers half to death."

She turned to Walter. "That explanation would also allow you to travel to your bank without arousing suspicion, because everyone will think the children are safe and you're merely going about your usual business."

"Frank and I can stand at the end of the drive," Catriona said, stepping into the room, her hair windswept. "But did I hear correctly? The children aren't lost but have been kidnapped?"

Gwendolyn nodded. "A ransom has been demanded. Walter will be leaving soon to visit his bank to withdraw funds. They've demanded it be delivered at midnight, and we can pray the kidnappers will honor their promise to release the children after the ransom's been paid—which will hopefully see the children returned to Sea Haven not long after that, if they're being held in Newport."

Catriona moved across the room and took a seat across from Gwendolyn. "Since the easiest way to gain access to Newport is by sea, I would bet they are being held close by. I doubt whoever kidnapped them would want to chance trying to smuggle them onto a ferry or private boat, not when the children have a reputation of being capable of causing loud ruckuses on a whim."

"An excellent point," Gwendolyn said. "And because Newport is relatively small, places where someone could stash three children without being noticed are limited. The question of the hour remains where that place is, and how many people are involved with the kidnapping."

"I would think at least two," Gideon said as he began pacing around the room. "One to stay with the children and one to retrieve the ransom."

"Makes sense," Gwendolyn said. "It also makes sense that there's a reason they chose Spouting Rock as the drop-off point." She got up from the settee and moved to the window, looking out for a second before she turned to Walter. "Are there any vacant houses near Spouting Rock?"

"There's a rental agent located on Bellevue I could ask," Walter said. "He supplies agents in New York City with available rentals, as well as listings of cottages for sale."

"That's the type of service I used when I decided to come here," Catriona said. "I was given two available options. The cottage I decided to rent was really the only viable one because it's on a well-traveled street."

"Was the other one more remote?" Gideon asked.

"It was. A cottage called . . . Low Tide." Catriona tapped a finger against her chin. "I don't recall where it was located, only that the agent knew there were no other houses nearby."

"I know where Low Tide is," Walter said. "It's owned by the Charles Perry family. They never gained admittance into Newport society, but they've been unable to sell Low Tide because of its location and the pond that abuts their property is known to attract insects. It's not far from Bailey's Beach—or Spouting Rock, for that matter."

"Then I'll have a look around there, but not until dark," Gideon said.

Walter frowned. "Why look around? I intend to pay the ransom."

"Kidnappings can get messy, so I'm going to stake out Low Tide to see if there's any unusual activity transpiring," Gideon said.

"You'll be doing that as I drop off the ransom?"

"I'll go well before midnight, but again, not until dark. I'll need to get the lay of the land and hopefully discern whether the children are being held there."

"What about the rest of us?" Gwendolyn asked. "What should we be doing tonight?"

Gideon cocked his head to the side. "Do you know how to operate a pistol?"

"Of course."

He smiled. "Can't say I'm surprised about that, but because you can shoot, you should go with Walter when he makes the ransom drop, watch his back."

"What about us?" Catriona asked, nodding to Frank, who'd been lingering in the doorway.

"For now, you and Frank should repair to the end of the drive to tell everyone the children have been found, and you two . . ." Gideon looked to Ethel and Matilda. "You need to make yourselves scarce since you're supposed to be with the children."

He turned to Walter. "While you visit your banker, I'm off to gather supplies for this evening." Gideon rose to his feet. "Then I'll meet you back here to go over how we should handle the delivery of the ransom money and decide exactly what role everyone is going to play."

Frank cleared his throat and stepped forward. "I should accompany Walter to deliver the ransom instead of Gwendolyn. We have no idea if someone will be lying in wait for him, and I'm more capable of stepping in if Walter faces a physical attack.

Besides that, I'm an expert marksman and can watch his back from yards away, staying out of sight. Gwendolyn won't be able to do that with a pistol."

"That definitely sounds safer for Walter," Gwendolyn agreed, "but I'm not going to simply sit at Sea Haven and twiddle my thumbs." She nodded to Gideon. "I'm going with you."

Gideon shook his head. "I don't need anyone to watch my back."

"That's not why I'm going with you." Gwendolyn lifted her chin. "Midnight is forever away from now. The children are most assuredly terrified, and that terror is only going to increase the longer they're held captive. I need to be close if we're fortunate enough to find them. They're going to need someone they can trust, someone who loves them, and they'll need that person as soon as they're found."

She nodded to Walter. "Since you won't be available for that, given that the ransom note specifically states you're to deliver the ransom, I'm going in your stead, and"—she held up her hand when Walter opened his mouth—"it's not up for debate."

Thirty-Eight

———— ❧ ————

"There's definitely someone in the house," Gideon said, dropping to the ground beside Gwendolyn, who was lying in the high grass surrounding Low Tide. "I saw a light moving from the first floor to the second."

Gwendolyn swatted a bug away from her face. "It's frustrating staying out here. I just want to rush in there and get the children to safety."

"An impulse you can't indulge. I believe there's currently only one man in the house, but I might be wrong. We could make the situation worse if we storm in now. Besides, it's past midnight. I would bet good money whoever picks up the ransom will return here soon, or at least send a message to whoever is guarding the children. My hope is they'll then be set free."

"Do you think Walter's alright?"

"I'm fine."

Gwendolyn swallowed a yelp when Walter suddenly joined them, edging down on his stomach beside her. "You just scared me half to death," she whispered. "But did the delivery go alright?"

"It did," Walter said, his face barely visible in the dim light being cast by the moon. "I got there early, waited until exactly midnight, dropped the bag with the money into the boat, then climbed up the cliff, where Frank was hidden, having kept a rifle trained on me the entire time I was gone. Thankfully he wasn't given a reason to shoot anyone, since the man who fetched the ransom didn't slip out of the shadows until I reached the top of the cliff."

"You saw him take the ransom?"

"I did. He didn't linger, merely snatched up the bag and disappeared into the darkness. Frank and I exchanged coats, so if someone were watching they'd mistake him for me. He then rode off on my horse and I ran back to where we'd left his horse and made my way here."

"It shouldn't be long then until something happens," Gideon said, taking a moment to fill Walter in, his voice barely a whisper. He finished right as the distinct sound of horse hooves sounded on the gravel drive leading to Low Tide. "Looks like the kidnapper's returning."

Anticipation, mixed with trepidation, flowed through Gwendolyn as the sound of cantering hooves got closer. The shadowy silhouette of a horse came into view, the man riding the horse reining to a stop in front of the cottage. He swung from the saddle, but before he could do more than take a few steps toward the porch, there was a loud bang, as if the front door had burst open, followed by the sound of pounding feet running down wooden steps.

"Stop right there," the man demanded, rushing toward the house.

"Priscilla, Samuel, run!" Oscar yelled, and that was all it took for Gwendolyn to jump to her feet and rush forward. Walter and Gideon raced ahead of her as she aimed her sight on the two petite shadowy figures running toward her.

"Children! I'm coming," she called, which had the twins increasing their pace.

A mere blink of an eye later, they were in her arms, two small, trembling bodies holding onto her as if they'd never let go.

Hugging them tightly against herself, Gwendolyn turned and ran down the drive, leaving Walter and Gideon to get Oscar to safety, and hopefully make certain that the men responsible for snatching the children would be apprehended, ending the danger to the children once and for all.

❋

"Stay right there, or I swear I'll shoot the boy."

Walter froze on the spot as Gideon did the same, rage coursing through him when he realized the man had grabbed Oscar and was holding him close, the light from the moon glinting off a pistol pressed against his son's head.

His rage increased. "Let him go. You're welcome to the money. We won't hinder your escape. Just release my son and we'll get on our way."

"Hank!" the man called at the top of his lungs, ignoring Walter's plea. "Hank, get out here. Hank!"

"If Hank's the man who's been watching over us," Oscar said in a voice that held not a single tremble in it, "he won't be coming out anytime soon."

"What do you mean?" the man demanded.

"We locked him in the closet," Oscar returned matter-of-factly, an impressive feat since he was currently being held at gunpoint. "Hank's not the brightest of men. When he locked us into the closet earlier, we began trying to pick our way out of it. Thankfully, my sister insists on having numerous hairpins put in her hair every day, because Miss Brinley told her they were useful. Hank didn't know what to make of it when he came to check on us and found us standing in the middle of the room."

Walter frowned. "He discovered you?"

Oscar nodded, but stopped mid-nod because of the pistol

pressed against his head, something that sent Walter's blood boiling. "He did, about ten minutes ago. I was sure we were going to be in big trouble. Samuel gets the credit for fast thinking. He told Hank the closet door hadn't been properly locked because it was broken. Hank didn't believe him, so Samuel told him to see for himself. I couldn't believe my eyes when Hank strolled right into the closet. Samuel slammed the door shut on him, I snatched the key hanging right beside the door, and that was it."

"I'll take that key now," the man still holding Oscar snapped before he began pulling Oscar toward Low Tide. "Hank's boss will involve himself in this matter if Hank isn't set free, and believe me, none of us want to tangle with that man."

Walter stilled. "Who do you and Hank work for?"

"Never you mind about that," the man said before he gave Oscar a shake, who seemed to be intentionally dragging his feet. "Stop it. If you don't give me any trouble, I'll have no issue releasing you, but if you don't cooperate, you'll be sorry."

"I'm just trying to make sure I have the key in my pocket. I may have dropped it when I was running out of the house."

"I'll give you ten seconds to check."

It took Oscar all of three seconds to pull something out of his pocket and then another second before the man holding him started howling, evidently having been stabbed by another one of Priscilla's hairpins.

Walter surged into motion right as Oscar tore free. "Find Gwendolyn and the twins," Walter yelled, which had Oscar flying down the drive, leaving Walter free to sprint after the man now running up the steps and into the house, yelling for Hank at the top of his lungs.

Fury coursed through Walter as he tore through the entranceway, skidded on the marble flooring, righted himself, then charged after the man now heading for a staircase. The faint glow of the moonlight through a stained-glass window made it possible for Walter to keep the man in sight.

He caught up with him before the second-floor landing, grabbed the man's ankle, and gave it a yank, which sent them tumbling down the stairs.

Walter barely noticed the pain when his head cracked against the wrought-iron railing. Giving himself a shake, he pushed to his feet, caught hold of the man who was now staggering down the hallway, and planted his fist in the man's face.

The man crumpled to the marble without a word.

"Impressive," Gideon said from where he stood a few feet away. "I was going to assist you but decided you might want to take the man down on your own."

"You were right."

"Let me go find a light switch, then I'll see about dealing with Hank. Given the pounding upstairs, I have a feeling he's still locked in that closet." Gideon strode away, and the gas sconces on the walls flickered to life a minute later.

While Walter waited for Gideon to return, he drew off his tie, using it to secure the man's hands behind his back. He then yanked off the cap pulled low over the man's face as Gideon rejoined him.

"Would you look at this," he said, gazing at a face he was all too familiar with. "Seems like the rumors about Daniel Mizner's gambling debts were true, because that's the only reason I can think of that would have him resorting to kidnapping."

Daniel took that moment to open his eyes, blinking a few times before he focused his gaze on Walter.

"Care to explain yourself?" Walter asked, keeping his voice measured even though rage had once again begun to smolder.

"I wouldn't think you'd need an explanation. I needed the money, of course. My life was at stake, and everyone knows you're one of the richest men in the country."

"Who was threatening your life?" Gideon demanded.

"I'm up to my neck in losses I suffered at Vernon's Gambling Den."

Gideon frowned. "You gambled at Vernon's? Are you out of your mind? He's one of the most ruthless gambling den owners in the city."

"He was the only one left who'd extend me credit. Unfortunately, I suffered a very large loss at one of his tables a month or so ago." Daniel nodded to Walter. "That's when I approached you and a few other gentlemen about some investment opportunities, but no one seemed keen to shell out any money."

"And that's when you started making plans to abduct my children?" Walter asked.

"Taking the children was a spur-of-the-moment decision, brought about after Vernon sent Hank to Newport." Daniel shuddered. "I owe Vernon ten thousand I lost in a single poker game. Regrettably, my parents have completely cut me off, my father deciding he's not going to bail me out of any debts I incur at the tables. I thought I might find success securing an heiress this summer, but Mrs. Parker refused to sponsor me, and Miss Brinley recently told me she doesn't have any lady in mind for me. I'm in dire straits—specifically, in danger of having my limbs broken—because I can't repay Vernon."

Walter cocked a brow. "The direness of your situation must have increased substantially once Hank showed up in Newport."

"Too right it did. Hank arrived here practically at the break of dawn today. Caught me after I stopped to have coffee at a bakery off Bellevue. He'd apparently been on his way to my cottage, intending to surprise me while I was still asleep, but stopped to get some coffee as well and discovered me sitting there. I soon found myself at pistol point in his carriage and then driven out to the cliffs."

Daniel shuddered again. "I decided Hank might have been given orders to get rid of me instead of merely breaking my legs. But just when he seemed intent on hurling me off a cliff, I spotted the pony cart heading our way, pulled by that cantankerous pony Miss Tilden gave your children. I knew the only way I was going to survive was if we took your children and demanded a ransom. Once I told Hank how much money we could get for their safe return, he didn't hesitate to snatch them. I knew Low Tide was vacant, so that's where we went.

"As I made my way back to town to figure out the details of a plan, I ran into a brigade of society members heading off to speak to Miss Brinley, even though it was too early for social calls." He shrugged. "I steered Hank's carriage to the end of that line, which provided me with a perfect alibi if I found myself in need of one of those."

Walter drew in a breath. "So allow me to see if I'm understanding this correctly—you decided to put the lives of my children at risk in order to spare yours?"

"Your children were never in danger. I knew you'd pay. I planned to give Hank the money, minus a little bit to tide me over, and then we'd set the children free." Daniel caught Walter's eye. "If you think about it, no harm's been done, and Hank's locked away in the closet upstairs. We could say he planned and executed the entire thing, and you could let me go. I am, after all, a member of the New York Four Hundred, and your mother knows my mother. Think of the shame my mother will face if my poor decision comes to light."

"You should have thought about that before you placed your pistol against my son's head, or before having a hand in terrifying my twins, who are, if you don't know, only five years old. For that, you're going to jail—possibly for a very long time."

Thirty-Nine

"Children, we have to stay out of sight," Gwendolyn said, holding fast to Priscilla's and Samuel's hands as Oscar hurried beside her. "There's no telling if there were more than two men involved in your kidnapping."

"There weren't," Oscar said. "It was just the two of them."

"Will Papa be safe?" Priscilla asked, her voice trembling as they stumbled their way through high grass bordering a pond.

Gwendolyn slowed to a stop. "I'm sure he'll be fine, darling. Your father knows how to handle himself in situations."

"He's a businessman," Oscar countered. "I don't think he finds himself handling kidnappers often, if at all."

"True, but Gideon Abbott is with him. From what I've observed, he knows his way around troubling circumstances. And when you add in the fact your father was infuriated with the men who took you, I imagine he and Gideon will soon have those men secured."

"Hank will be easy to catch," Oscar said. "There's no way he can get out of the closet. We shoved a dresser in front of it before we left."

"It was heavy," Samuel added. "Me and Priss had to sit on the floor and push it with our legs."

"How very clever of all of you," Gwendolyn said, right before she heard a carriage rumbling their way. She glanced to Oscar. "Stay with the twins. I'm going to see who that is."

It came as no surprise, when she reached the edge of the road and looked over her shoulder, to see Oscar and the twins following her, although they were sticking to the shadows. Trying to keep to the shadows as well, Gwendolyn watched as the carriage careened into view.

"It's Grandmother Ethel," Oscar said, stealing up beside her and making her jump.

"You're supposed to be watching the twins."

"We're right here," Samuel said.

"Of course you are," Gwendolyn muttered as the carriage drew closer. "Are you certain that's your grandmother?"

"I know what her carriage looks like."

Praying Oscar was right, Gwendolyn drew in a breath and stepped into the road, waving her hands at the fast-approaching carriage, which had the driver, once he spotted her in the lantern light, reining the horses to a rapid stop.

A second later, the carriage door burst open and Ethel and Matilda leapt to the ground, rushed past Gwendolyn, their arms already open, and scooped Samuel and Priscilla close, hugging them tightly.

Ethel finally lifted her head to look Gwendolyn's direction, tears trailing down her cheeks. "You rescued them," she whispered.

"In all fairness to the children," Gwendolyn said, as Oscar stepped to Ethel's side and gave her a hug, "they rescued themselves. But what are you doing here?"

"We're grandmothers," Matilda said, peering over Priscilla's head. "You couldn't have expected us to remain at Sea Haven—not when it's almost one and no one returned to the cottage." She caught Gwendolyn's eye. "We're armed."

Gwendolyn suppressed a shudder when Matilda whipped a

pistol from her pocket, although the gingerly way she held it spoke volumes. "Have you ever shot a pistol before?"

"Of course not, but Ethel and I decided all one needs to do is cock back the trigger, then shoot."

"How about you let me hold that while you and Ethel get the children settled in the carriage?"

"Oh, thank you, dear," Matilda said, not hesitating to pass over the pistol. "I was afraid it might go off in my pocket."

"To which I have nothing to say except thank goodness it didn't."

After tucking the pistol into her pocket—after making sure Matilda hadn't accidentally cocked it, because the night certainly didn't need an accidental shooting—Gwendolyn helped get the twins and Oscar situated between Ethel and Matilda, stilling when the sound of more carriage wheels trundling down the road met their ears.

Before Gwendolyn could move to investigate, Ethel was thrusting another pistol into her hands. "Not certain that monster's loaded, but it might startle someone if you point it *and* Matilda's pistol at whoever's approaching."

"Let's hope it doesn't come to that." Gwendolyn stepped back from the carriage, slammed the door shut, and nodded to Ethel's driver. "Get them back to Sea Haven."

The driver didn't hesitate to snap the reins over the horses' backs, leaving Gwendolyn standing in a cloud of dust as the approaching carriage began to slow.

Cocking the pistol, she stepped to the side of the road and took aim, but lowered it when she realized Frank Lambert was driving the carriage, Catriona riding a horse beside him.

"Where are the children?" Frank demanded, pulling the carriage to a stop the second he caught sight of her. Catriona did the same with the horse.

"They're fine," she returned with a jerk of her head up the road. "They're in that carriage."

"Walter and Gideon?" Catriona asked next.

"I left them at Low Tide after the children came out of the house."

"They may need help" was all Frank said before he slapped the horses with the reins and was off, leaving Gwendolyn and Catriona behind.

"Should we follow him?" Catriona asked.

"No. I think our concern should be the children."

Accepting the hand her cousin held out to her, Gwendolyn swung up behind Catriona and they were off, catching up to Ethel's carriage and staying directly behind it until it pulled up to Sea Haven.

"The grandmothers promised us a special treat for getting snatched," Samuel informed her after jumping out of the carriage, Priscilla right behind him.

"Did they now?" Gwendolyn asked as Priscilla grabbed hold of her hand.

"I don't think you should take the grandmothers to task about indulging us this time," Oscar said quietly, stealing up beside her. "They've suffered quite the fright, and you know it's their habit to offer treats."

"A reasonable suggestion, and I wasn't going to lecture them, not really," Gwendolyn said, earning a rolling of the eyes from Ethel, who'd climbed out of the carriage and moved to stand beside her.

"Of course you were, dear," Ethel said.

"She's very proficient with lecturing," Matilda added as she joined Ethel.

Gwendolyn's lips curved. "I truly wasn't going to lecture you, merely make a recommendation regarding how you might indulge the children this time."

"Avoid additional ponies?" Ethel asked.

"Well, that too, but I was going to suggest you indulge them with the treat of taking them somewhere special, somewhere of their choosing. That way you'll be giving them memories, not simply a new toy that will be appreciated in the moment but forgotten by week's end." Gwendolyn leaned closer and lowered her voice. "You can distract them with suggestions of where they might like to go while we wait for Walter to return."

After they settled into the drawing room—Mrs. Boyle fussing over the children as she served them chicken, potatoes, and a variety of other dishes, clucking that the poor dears were obviously starving since their kidnappers hadn't had the decency to feed them much—Gwendolyn kept an eye on the clock, each tick of it seeming to last a lifetime.

Finally, after an hour had passed, she heard voices in the hallway, and then Walter strode into the room, kneeling as his children flew toward him, all three of them grabbing hold of their father as he kissed each one on the head and pulled them close, seemingly not bothered in the least that his cheeks were streaked with tears.

The sight of those tears struck Gwendolyn straight through the heart, and she realized there and then that, if nothing else had come of her time in Newport, she'd had a part in giving the children exactly what they'd always needed—a father who put their needs before anything else, and a father who probably wouldn't let his children out of his sight for a very long time to come.

Forty

After assuring himself the children were not suffering any ill effects from a day straight out of a nightmare, Walter agreed to allow the twins out of his sight, but only because Ethel and Matilda, in spite of the late hour, wanted to indulge Samuel and Priscilla with a bubble bath, something the twins seemed eager to enjoy.

Smiling as Priscilla skipped out of the room, holding Gwendolyn's hand, Samuel chattering up a storm beside them, Walter put his arm around Oscar's shoulders and pulled him close on the settee, pleased and a bit surprised when his son didn't pull away.

"That was quite the adventure you had today," Walter began.

Oscar bit his lip. "Are we in trouble because we locked the governesses in the closet and took Bert out without permission? I know that was wrong, but the twins shouldn't be in trouble. They just went along with my plan to talk to Miss Brinley. It was a rotten plan, and I'm the one who should be punished. I placed Samuel and Priscilla in grave danger."

Walter gave Oscar a squeeze. "None of you are in trouble,

but you really are going to have to stop locking people in closets, although it did come in handy with Hank."

"But I was careless with the twins," Oscar said. "I think, at the very least, you should insist I spend every hour over the next few weeks with that tutor Miss Brinley told me you were planning to hire this summer. I bet I could make up my grades by the end of summer."

"I wouldn't be opposed to your working with a tutor, but not as a form of punishment." He caught Oscar's eye. "Gwendolyn told me why you failed your classes, and got up to mischief that got you expelled, but before you ask, you're not in trouble for that either. I'm to blame for everything."

Walter raked a hand through his hair. "Right before I learned you and the twins had been abducted, Gwendolyn had much to say to me, and everything she said was true. I've been unforgivably neglectful of you, Priscilla, and Samuel, content to leave you in the care of your grandmothers and hired help after your mother died."

"I don't remember much about Mother anymore," Oscar whispered.

"You were only four when she died, but what you need to remember is that she loved you very much." He blew out a breath. "I'm sorry I haven't spoken often about your mother since she left us. I should have realized you'd be curious about her, and I can tell you all I remember, although I'm beginning to believe I didn't know her nearly as well as I should have, even though I was married to her for a handful of years."

"That's because we're society."

"And perhaps society has it wrong, Oscar. Perhaps we should, as Gwendolyn has told numerous society members, set our bar a little higher when it comes to marriage."

"Did you like Mother?"

Walter smiled. "I *did* like her. She was beautiful, even-tempered, and she loved to dance." He took a moment to allow his thoughts to drift back to his late wife before he finally nodded. "We never exchanged a cross word between us, and we used to enjoy having our morning coffee together as we read the newspaper. She preferred the social section, while I enjoyed the current events. We would then share what we'd read before we bid each other good day and got on with our various activities, mine being work and hers being her social agenda."

"Do you miss her?"

"I do," Walter admitted, realizing in that moment it was nothing less than the truth. He'd spent years burying himself in his business, convincing himself he did so because he felt guilty about Vivian's death, but the truth was he'd done that burying because he'd been grieving but hadn't allowed himself to acknowledge or dwell on that.

"Are you still going to try and find a new wife this Season if Miss Brinley doesn't agree to take up that position?"

"Miss Brinley has been perfectly clear she doesn't want to marry me, Oscar. But to answer your question, no. I thought providing you and your siblings with a new mother was the only solution available to get you in hand, but it wasn't a solution at all. What you and the twins need is simply for me to be a father to you, something I didn't understand, but something I'll never forget again."

He caught Oscar's eye. "I should have been the one to teach you how to ride a bicycle and how to fish, and I should have known that Priscilla and Samuel were lonely at night and wanted someone to tuck them into bed and read them a story. That you, at nine years old, understood what your siblings needed while I, their father, had not the remotest idea they were lacking anything makes me more ashamed than I've ever been in my life."

Oscar gave Walter's knee an unexpected pat. "A lot of fathers in society don't spend time with their children, as well as mothers. Governesses are expected to raise us. Besides, you have the family business to run, and that must take up a lot of time."

"That's kind of you to say, but it doesn't make it right. I've come to realize that my priorities have been misplaced. Business can no longer be my main concern, not when you and the twins are the most precious things in my life."

"You think we're precious?"

The back of Walter's eyes began to burn, and he blinked to keep tears at bay. "That you even have to ask proves I've been an abysmal father, but I intend to make up for that, starting now." He took Oscar's hand, pleased beyond measure when his son didn't pull it away. "I'm going to spend far more time with all of you, until you return to school. I now understand you abandoned it because you had the weight of the world on your remarkably strong yet young shoulders. You won't need to worry about the twins, because they're my responsibility. That means you can go about the business of enjoying your studies, your friends, and everything that goes along with simply being a boy. I'm hoping at some point you'll be able to forgive me, and perhaps come to not dislike me as much."

"I'm nine. I'm supposed to dislike you at times. My friend Sherman occasionally dislikes his father as well, so I think that just comes with the territory of being a boy." Oscar rubbed his nose. "I don't actually dislike you right now."

Walter smiled. "That's reassuring to hear, but what brought that about?"

"Lots of things, but one of them was I heard Hank say they were demanding one hundred thousand dollars for our release. You paid it."

"I would have given them any amount to have you all safely returned to me."

"Huh" was all Oscar said to that before he suddenly nodded. "I wouldn't mind going back to school, but would it be alright if I come home on the weekends? Not every weekend, mind you, because sometimes we have fun activities, but enough to where Priss and Samuel won't miss me."

"Of course, and I can bring the twins to see you as well," Walter said. "Your school is only an hour's drive from the city."

"I'd like that," Oscar said before he rose to his feet right as Gideon strode into the drawing room.

When Gideon shook Oscar's hand and told him how impressed he was with his quick thinking under extreme pressure, Oscar beamed at the man's praise and then excused himself, saying he was off to check on poor Bert, who'd been returned to the stables and was giving the groom sent to fetch him all sorts of trouble.

After Oscar quit the room, confidence in his every step, as if he'd aged a few years in a day, Walter nodded to Benson, his butler, who'd been parked right outside the door ever since Walter returned home. "You'll follow him?" he asked.

Benson inclined his head. "Indeed. But you know he'll realize I'm following him, don't you?"

"After the day we've had, I don't believe he's going to be surprised—or offended, for that matter—that his father isn't going to take his safety for granted. I won't take that safety for granted ever again. Perhaps we'll have to consider sending you off to school with him."

"That might be taking the matter entirely too far, sir, and will certainly offend Master Oscar, because what boy wants a butler dogging his heels?"

As Benson headed out of the room, Gideon settled himself in a chair by the fireplace.

"Anything new to report since we hauled Daniel and Hank into Frank's carriage and took them to jail?" Walter asked.

Gideon leaned forward, placing his hands on his knees. "Daniel immediately sent for his parents, who arrived at the jail with their attorney in tow. Given the direness of Daniel's crimes, the judge, who was summoned from his sleep, refused to grant bond—something that had the Mizners causing quite a scene, but to no avail.

"Hank, unsurprisingly, sent a message off to Vernon's Gambling Den. I imagine Vernon is going to ignore Hank's request for assistance, but I'll make certain of that. After I return to the city, I'll have a word with Vernon and encourage him to distance himself from this situation."

"You're on speaking terms with Vernon?"

"You'd be surprised with whom I'm on speaking terms, but now isn't the time to get into that."

"I doubt we'll ever get into that, Gideon, what with the clandestine nature of whatever it is you actually do."

"True," Gideon said cheerfully. "I *can* tell you that Frank and Catriona seemed to be getting along quite well. I think Gwendolyn may have made a perfect match with them.

"But speaking of Gwendolyn, where is she, or better yet, what are you intending to do about her? She told me earlier you thought the children were right about her making a wonderful mother. From what little else she disclosed, I got the distinct impression the two of you might have exchanged a few . . . words."

"Exchanged would not be accurate since she did most of the talking. Needless to say, she's not receptive to becoming the children's mother, but not because of them—because of me."

"Did you tell her you love her?"

Walter blinked. "Do you think that may have helped my case?"

"If you actually love her, yes, but . . ." Gideon frowned. "*Do* you love her?"

"I haven't really considered the matter. I have been thinking about her often of late, and I get an odd feeling in my stomach when I do that thinking. Truth be told, I've never experienced such a peculiar sensation when I've thought about a lady before, and when you pair that with the notion I find Gwendolyn to be the most exceptional lady I've ever had the pleasure of meeting . . . I might be experiencing love. But I'm hardly an expert on the matter. What do you think?"

Gideon settled into the chair. "I've never been in love, so how would I know? However, I've seen how you watch Gwendolyn, and I'd say you hold her in very high esteem. But only you can decide if that esteem is love."

Walter released a sigh. "I'm afraid I blundered badly with her. I didn't even extend her a proper proposal, merely suggested an alliance between us would be beneficial because of the children and . . . I may have mentioned I thought she'd been becoming fond of me."

Gideon blinked. "A Romeo move if there ever was one."

"I've never claimed to be proficient in the art of romance."

"Good thing, because I don't think I've ever heard a gentleman make such a muddle of a proposal before."

"It was a muddle for the ages," Walter agreed. "The problem is how to proceed from here."

"I suggest you sort through your emotions, my friend. If you come to the realization you're more than fond of Gwendolyn, you'll then need to figure out how best to disclose that revelation to her, and then hope for the best."

Gideon stretched his arms over his head. "While you contemplate love and Gwendolyn and how you might go about making amends with her, I'm going to repair to my cottage. It's been quite the day, and I need to get back to the city tomorrow, so I'm off to find my bed." Gideon stood. "Do have a care if you decide to speak to Gwendolyn about a possible future together. She's incredibly intelligent and may take a declaration of love from you as simply your way of convincing her to marry you so you can provide your children with a mother who certainly would be able to love them."

"I'm not that calculating."

"She doesn't know that, because the two of you haven't known each other long. With that said, Gwendolyn Brinley is a lady I doubt you'll ever be able to forget, so keep that in mind before you say something to her that will see you losing her forever."

"Hardly helpful," Walter muttered as Gideon grinned and strode from the room.

Several minutes later, realizing he might be lingering in the drawing room because he truly didn't know how to proceed with a tricky situation—one that went by the name of Gwendolyn—Walter forced himself off the chaise and made his way to the nursery. He stopped just outside the door as his gaze settled on Gwendolyn, who was sitting on Priscilla's bed, his daughter tucked closely against her while Samuel sat at the foot of the bed, Rat asleep on his lap.

Ethel and Matilda were sitting in chairs pulled up next to the bed, both women watching their grandchildren, who were watching Gwendolyn as she read them a story.

He found himself unable to move as he continued watching her, appreciating the way she told a story, but mostly just appreciating her.

She truly was the most beautiful woman he'd ever seen, even though her hair was straggling from its pins, there was a streak of dirt running across her cheek, and her gown sported more than a few grass stains—probably from the grass she'd been hiding in during the kidnapping disaster.

"And there we have it, a happily ever after," Gwendolyn finally said, kissing the top of Priscilla's head as she closed the book. "And with that happy ending, it's time for you and Samuel to go to bed."

Priscilla tipped back her head. "Will you be here when we wake up?"

For the briefest of seconds, Gwendolyn's eyes clouded and turned suspiciously bright, but then she smiled, although it seemed somewhat strained. "I'm afraid I won't be here, darling. I need to go home."

"You're not going to stay and be our mother?" Priscilla pressed.

Gwendolyn blew out a breath as Ethel and Matilda sat forward in their chairs, their gazes locked on Gwendolyn. "I'm afraid not."

Priscilla's lips began to tremble. "Because we're too naughty?"

"Of course not," Gwendolyn said, cupping Priscilla's chin with her hand. "You and your brothers are perfect just the way you are. It has nothing to do with you."

"You don't like Papa?" Samuel asked.

"That's not it either," Gwendolyn said, smiling ever so slightly. "Your father is a, ah, very nice gentleman."

Priscilla wrinkled her nose. "Then why don't you want to marry him?"

Gwendolyn shot a look to Ethel. "You could help me out here."

"I have no idea how I'd go about that, since I believe you and Walter would suit each other admirably," Ethel said.

"That's hardly helpful," Gwendolyn muttered, turning her attention to Matilda, who released a sigh.

"I'm sorry, dear, but I'm in agreement with Ethel. You are exactly what Walter needs, and exactly what Ethel and I need as well."

Gwendolyn frowned. "Because?"

"You would never deprive us of time with the children," Matilda said, exchanging a glance with Ethel. "We've discussed the matter at length, and one of my reservations about this Season was that Walter might marry a woman who didn't want me, the mother of his late wife, involved in their lives. I know that wouldn't happen with you, which is one of the reasons I want to encourage you to at least consider Walter's proposal."

"He never proposed to me."

Ethel exchanged a look with Matilda. "I had a feeling he might have gone about that poorly."

"Poorly doesn't begin to describe it," Gwendolyn said, before she returned her attention to the twins, who were looking as if they were on the verge of tears. "I don't want either of you to be sad about my not becoming your mother. It doesn't mean I don't love you or that I'm not going to visit you. In fact, I'm going to encourage you to think of me as your Aunt Gwendolyn. You may address any letters you care to send to me at my parents' house—where I'm going to stay for a while—to Aunt Gwendolyn Brinley."

"We'd rather address any letters to Mother," Priscilla whispered.

Gwendolyn rubbed a hand over her face. "I'm clearly not explaining this well, darling, but your father and I do not share a . . . well, special love between us."

"But you said you thought he was nice," Samuel pointed out.

"True, but what the two of you need to understand—and need to remember well into your adult years—is that, when a person is contemplating marriage, love is the most important aspect to consider. Yes, finding someone nice is to be considered as well, but if you're going to spend every day for the rest of your life with someone, I'm of the firm belief mutual love should be involved."

"You don't love Papa?" Priscilla asked.

"That's a question I'm not sure how to answer" was all Gwendolyn said to that, which left Walter feeling all sorts of bewildered.

Before he could contemplate the matter further though, Gwendolyn squared her shoulders, set aside the book, placed another kiss on Priscilla's head, and did the same to Samuel as he settled in his bed.

"It's well past time for the two of you to go to sleep," she said. "And it's time for me to return to my cousin's cottage."

"You won't come by in the morning before you leave Newport?" Ethel asked.

Gwendolyn's lip trembled for the briefest of seconds, quite like Priscilla's had done only moments before, but then she lifted her chin and shook her head. "I think it'll be best for everyone if I simply sail away. But again, I'll visit you all some-day, although probably not in Newport, which seems a bit hos-tile toward me these days." She nodded to Ethel. "Would it be too much to ask you to tell Walter I said good-bye?"

Ethel began blinking rather rapidly. "You don't want to tell him yourself?"

"It's been an exhausting, emotional day, and I don't believe I'm up for another discussion Walter might broach regarding an alliance. I don't belong in society, and your family is firmly entrenched in it. That means it's time for me to go, but I'd be ever so grateful if you would agree to say good-bye to him for me."

Ethel's eyes were brimming with unshed tears as she inclined her head, stepped forward, and gave Gwendolyn a kiss on the cheek. As Gwendolyn went to kiss Matilda, Walter turned and strode into the adjacent room, finding Oscar standing right inside the door, obviously eavesdropping. Putting a finger to his lips, Walter waited until he heard Gwendolyn hurrying down the staircase before he released a sigh.

"Well, that's that, then," he said quietly.

"No, it's not," Oscar argued, moving directly beside Walter. "Miss Brinley seemed distressed about leaving us and didn't want to say good-bye to you in person. That's telling."

"How do you know it's telling? You're nine."

"And old for my years, so you'll simply need to believe me."

"Even if I believe you, it doesn't change the fact Gwendolyn's determined to leave us."

"True, but it can change what you do about her leaving." Oscar shoved up the sleeves of his shirt. "All that's left to do now is come up with a plan, and luckily for you, your children are very good with plans."

Forty-One

"Opal Brinley has sent me yet another letter."

Gwendolyn pushed herself up from the hay bale she'd been lounging on, contemplating her life for the past hour, and settled her attention on her mother, Finella Brinley, who stood in the doorway looking more than amused as she fanned the letter she was holding back and forth in front of her face.

"How many does that make?"

"Twelve," Finella said, walking across the barn and taking a seat beside Gwendolyn. "In this latest letter, she demands I send her the life history of all of my children, complete with a listing of their accomplishments, and then extends all of us an invitation to join her in Boston for Thanksgiving dinner."

Gwendolyn wrinkled her nose. "She wants us to join her for Thanksgiving dinner?"

"Apparently." Finella grinned. "I have no idea what you said to a woman who has been a thorn in my side since I married your father, but good heavens, she does seem determined to turn over a new leaf. I will, of course, compose another long letter in reply, extolling all my children's many accomplishments. Opal does, surprisingly enough, seem to enjoy my responses to her notes, making mention of little tidbits, which suggests she reads them thoroughly." Finella tilted her head. "But again, I'm curious what you said to encourage her to turn over a new leaf."

"I may have told her something to the effect that she was a bitter and, perhaps, miserable woman, those conditions brought about by her ridiculous decision to put her idiotic social responsibilities before her son."

"I don't imagine Opal enjoyed hearing that."

Gwendolyn smiled. "Someone needed to tell her, and if what I said has her rethinking her priorities, then I don't regret speaking my mind. What does Father think about her sending letters?"

"He's relieved, as well as delighted. She is his mother, after all, and while he's been angry with her for years, I know he's missed her." Finella tucked a stray strand of hair that was a shade lighter than Gwendolyn's behind her ear. "I'm sure Thanksgiving will be interesting, but we have more pressing matters to concern ourselves with—such as why you're hiding out in the barn."

"I'm not hiding, merely rethinking my purpose in life."

"Ah, of course you are." Finella gave Gwendolyn's hand a pat. "Have you come to any conclusions?"

"I've been thinking about something Catriona said. And annoying as this is for me to admit, she may be exactly right with her assessment of me."

"Catriona can be unusually astute when she sets her self-centeredness aside. What did she tell you?"

"She believes I'm not an unconventional lady at all, but that I'm actually meant to pursue a more traditional role, complete with a husband and children."

Finella gave Gwendolyn's hand a squeeze. "I could have told you that years ago, darling."

Gwendolyn wrinkled her nose. "Why didn't you?"

"Because all of us have a journey we need to take before

we realize what our true purpose in life is meant to be. You were so determined to be an independent woman, a decision I know you made because you respected that about me before I married your father. Truth be told, I was of the same mindset before your father swept into my life and changed everything I thought I wanted."

"May I assume you've never had any regrets, since it seems you fell in love with Father at first sight?"

"What I felt for your father at first was not love. It was more on the lines of extreme annoyance."

"What?"

"It's true." Finella smoothed out a wrinkle in her skirt. "Pierson was incredibly handsome, of course, but when he saw me walking out of that dress shop and immediately came over to introduce himself, I found him beyond irritating."

"But Father is such a charming sort."

"He was not charming at all when I first met him. He was arrogant."

Gwendolyn blinked. "I find that hard to believe."

"If you'd known him back then, it wouldn't be difficult to imagine at all. Pierson had been brought up to believe himself superior to everyone except other members of the social elite. And even though he was struck by me from the moment he saw me, he clearly believed I should consider it an honor he'd set his sights on me."

Gwendolyn's lips twitched. "I can't imagine you appreciated that."

"I didn't. I led him on a merry chase for a good month before I started to see something in him that he rarely let people see—his true heart. That heart is what finally convinced me he might have potential. I wasn't convinced we should marry though, because I knew it would be a sacrifice for him to marry beneath him—though by then I believed Pierson didn't see me as that.

"It wasn't until I sought out the advice of Reverend Richard

Hunt that I realized a marriage with Pierson might be possible. After I told Reverend Hunt I'd always believed my purpose in life was to open my own shop and subsequently help my family escape the poverty they were living in, he suggested I might be mistaken, and that God could very well have a different purpose for me. He suggested God might have sent Pierson in my direction because, being so far removed from the life he knew, I might very well be his saving grace in the end. I could show him how to live life as it was supposed to be lived—not consumed with the material aspects wealth afforded him but focusing on the possibilities of a life filled with love."

Gwendolyn tilted her head. "Reverend Hunt believed you were Father's saving grace?"

"Perhaps. Or maybe he simply believed God brought me and Pierson together because we complete each other." Finella smiled. "By breaking free of the shackles that kept him bound to convention, Pierson's been able to live a fulfilling life complete with unconditional love, which has allowed me to do the same."

"And while that's a beautiful story, I'm not certain how it relates to my situation."

"It relates to you because your purpose of seeing after Catriona is now in your past. You, being you, couldn't have ignored the pain your cousin was in after her loss of Barnabas, but she's clearly on her way to reembracing life, what with how Frank Lambert has followed her here and they seem to be well on their way to a committed relationship. That means it truly is time for your next adventure—one that, after everything you've told me, might involve Walter. I assume you picked up on the similarities between your relationship with him and what I experienced with your father."

"Except that Father fell head over heels for you from the moment you met, whereas Walter thought I was the most annoying woman he'd ever had the misfortune of encountering."

"Annoyance is occasionally a precursor to love."

343

"In this instance, I believe it was simply annoyance."

Finella smiled. "You're being deliberately stubborn. You told me how much Walter changed during the weeks you spent with him, and I believe you were responsible for those changes."

"He only changed because he realized he'd been missing a great blessing in life—being involved in his children's lives."

"But if you'd not entered his life, he would have probably already settled on one of those young ladies out this Season in Newport and would have handed over the care of his children to that lady, never getting the opportunity to become the father you told me he has the capability to become."

Gwendolyn blew out a breath. "Perhaps, but Walter's capacity to become a wonderful father does not mean he possesses the ability to love me. His mother even made a point of telling me he's not an emotional sort, while also telling me she wasn't certain he's capable of forming a relationship with a lady based on love. I won't settle for anything less in a marriage."

She caught her mother's eye. "You and Father are responsible for that. I want what you have—a partnership. I'll only marry someone I can spend my days laughing with, arguing with occasionally, and then setting aside our arguments to laugh once again."

"From what you've disclosed over the past week, you and Walter experienced that in Newport."

"He doesn't love me, Mother."

"Perhaps Walter simply hasn't realized he loves you. You're an exceptional woman, darling. I'm sure Walter realizes that— just as I'm sure you were the reason he was finding all the ladies you put in front of him merely pleasant."

"I'm convinced he simply found the time we spent together pleasant as well, when I wasn't irritating him. But I won't marry a man who finds my company enjoyable over exhilarating, nor will I marry a man simply because I adore his children."

Finella gave Gwendolyn's hand another squeeze. "Perfectly understandable, but tell me this—do you love him?"

"I'd rather not talk about that."

It was beyond annoying when her mother smiled.

"A revealing remark that suggests you might very well love him, and you're irritated about that because you're not quite certain how you could fall in love with a man who seems to lack emotions. I would bet Walter has more emotions than you realize and is merely deficient with displaying them in public."

"Walter got emotional after he was reunited with the children."

"Well, there you go. He's not emotionless after all."

"It almost made me cry."

Finella arched a brow. "You never cry."

"Indeed, and I won't be crying over him in the future, if that's your next question. The reality is he doesn't love me. He's more interested in providing his children with a mother, something he knows I'd do magnificently. But even though I would be an excellent mother, Walter's not thinking through the repercussions he'll suffer if he marries a woman like me.

"I saw his face when society turned on me after Priscilla announced the children wanted me as their mother. Even though Walter assured me it wasn't horror at all, merely shock at the reaction of the crowd, as well as concern for the children, who were expecting a different outcome, I have no doubt he would find himself shocked and disappointed time and again, because even with his fortune, the social set will never accept me into their exclusive midst.

"Quite frankly, I have no desire to be accepted into their midst after what I witnessed in Newport. Pettiness prevails amongst the socially elite, and I've never been one to sit back and accept that type of attitude from anyone. It would be one confrontation after another, something Walter would certainly grow weary of."

"Pettiness isn't exclusive to society, Gwendolyn, as you very well know. Besides, I'm sure you'd learn to navigate around it somewhat graciously if you found yourself attending society events."

"But society turned its collective back on me at the Townsend ball. As you know from experience, it's rare for anyone not born into inner circles to ever get accepted."

"But unlike my situation, dear," Finella argued, "Walter's mother seems to think you may be exactly right for him, as does his mother-in-law. Their acceptance would make all the difference in the world."

"Perhaps, but I want nothing to do with society."

"I'm not saying you'd need to turn into a Vanderbilt or an Astor, dear. But it wouldn't hurt to mingle every so often with people Walter's known since birth."

"I don't even know why we're talking about this. Walter has clearly reconsidered his situation and realized he may have been mistaken when he proclaimed I'd make a wonderful mother for his children. He hasn't bothered to so much as pen me a letter inquiring about my welfare in the week I've been here. That means there's no need to dwell on any of this because it's a moot point."

"You told me you left on the first ferry, which departed Newport at eight in the morning, mere hours after the children had been rescued. Walter could very well have come to see you at Catriona's cottage, but you were probably long gone."

"It's more likely he came to his senses and realized the last thing he wants in life is me."

Finella opened her mouth, clearly to argue with that, but then closed it when the dogs began barking. She rose from the hay bale and made her way to the barn door. "Are you expecting anyone today?"

"Who would I be expecting? Catriona is here, the rest of the family is still in the Berkshires—which again, you're more than welcome to return to because I wasn't expecting you to rush back here after I sent you a telegram telling you I was coming home."

"I don't know why you'd be surprised I'd return from the Berkshires early. You're my daughter and you'd just been terminated from your position. Of course I was going to rush home because, well, you've never been the type to suffer failure graciously."

"I didn't actually fail as a matchmaker, merely got fired after causing a huge, completely unintentional, ruckus. In all honesty, now that I've had time to think about my unexpected position, I realize I enjoyed it to a certain extent."

"If you really enjoyed matchmaking, you should consider continuing with it. I imagine there are all sorts of matches just waiting for you to arrange during the upcoming winter Season. And taking up residency in New York would put you in Walter's vicinity."

"I swear you're growing more tenacious with age, but I'm not moving to New York to start up a matchmaking business. Even though I may have enjoyed it ever so slightly, I'm not certain the charm of making matches would last long—not when I'd have to navigate through the vindictiveness between ladies. Besides, unless I'd go back to Mrs. Parker, who did let it be known she might have been hasty with terminating my position, society won't allow me through the doors of their exclusive events."

"They would if you married Walter."

Gwendolyn released a snort. "There's that perseverance again. For the last time, I won't be marrying Walter. I left him firmly behind me in Newport, and he's probably even now at the Newport Casino, with Mrs. Parker at his side, discussing potential matches."

"I don't think that's where he is," Finella said, peering through the barn door.

"Why not?"

"Because a man just got out of a carriage parked by the front porch, and . . . Huh, there's one, two . . . three children following him, and . . . two ladies. They look like society to me."

"What?" Gwendolyn dashed to join her mother, her mouth dropping open when she spotted Oscar, Priscilla, and Samuel already playing with the sheepdogs that roamed free on the farm, two of which seemed to be trying to lick Samuel to death. "What in the world are they doing here?"

"Only one way to find out," Finella said, making a beeline through the barn door and heading for the house.

"What are you doing?" Gwendolyn asked, breaking into a run to catch up with her.

"I'm going to greet our guests and introduce myself."

Before Gwendolyn could respond to that, Priscilla's head shot up, she caught sight of Gwendolyn, and then she was racing across the lawn, the ribbons in her hair flying madly about.

"Miss Brinley, Miss Brinley," Priscilla yelled, throwing herself into Gwendolyn's arms as soon as she reached her. "I've missed you. It's been forever."

Allowing herself the luxury of holding the little girl close for a long moment while breathing in the sweet scent of her hair, Gwendolyn kissed the top of Priscilla's head before she set her on the ground. "I've missed you as well, darling. But it hasn't been forever, merely a week."

"Forever," Priscilla said again as Samuel bounded up to join them, the sheepdogs dogging his heels. He gave Gwendolyn a tight hug and stepped back.

"Rat and Bert have decided to be friends," Samuel said in a rush. "Bert even lets Rat ride on his back, but they both miss you and told me to tell you they want you to come back."

"But they don't really talk about that out loud," Priscilla said. "Sam just understands things like that."

"Of course he does," Gwendolyn said, as Oscar walked up

to join them, surprising her when he gave her a hug. "Anything new with you?" she asked him.

Oscar smiled. "I've been fishing a lot with Father and Sherman, but we didn't catch any sharks, which was disappointing. And I've been working with a tutor Father hired. I've almost made up all my work, which hasn't been difficult since I got expelled right at the end of last term. Father's already arranged to have me readmitted to my school come September."

"How wonderful, but what are you doing here?"

"We have a plan we're hoping will have you come back to us," Priscilla said, a statement that left Gwendolyn, for the first time in her life, feeling somewhat wobbly in the knees, because a plan certainly seemed to be something that could very well hold a great deal of potential, although what that potential could possibly be, she wasn't exactly certain.

Forty-Two

꧁꧂

"Honestly, Priss, you weren't supposed to mention anything about our plan," Oscar grumbled, sending his little sister a rolling of his eyes.

Priscilla's lip immediately began to tremble. "Won't it work now that I told?"

Gwendolyn kneeled beside her. "It depends on what that plan is."

"And here is where I take over, children."

Looking up, Gwendolyn discovered Walter standing two feet away, Ethel on one side, Matilda on the other. That he was smiling left her feeling all sorts of peculiar emotions, but before she could sort any of those out, Finella stepped forward.

"I believe Gwendolyn and Walter could use some privacy. I'm Finella Brinley, Gwendolyn's mother, and I would adore showing all of you around the farm."

"You're beautiful," Priscilla breathed, which had Finella grinning as she moved to Priscilla, swept her up in her arms, and sent a wink to Gwendolyn. "I adore these children already." She nodded to Oscar and Samuel. "Would you care to see the tree house Gwendolyn's father built years ago? It's quite the sight, almost on par with the tree house in *Robinson Crusoe*."

Given the grins on the children's faces, and the chorus of "Yes please" that accompanied those grins, it was obvious they were perfectly willing to abandon their father to whatever it was he'd come to say to Gwendolyn.

After Finella sent her another wink, she strolled away with Ethel and Matilda, who sent Gwendolyn winks as well before they began chatting away with her mother, quite as if they'd been friends for years.

"I suppose you're wondering what we're doing here," Walter said.

"Priscilla said you had a plan."

He winced. "Well, yes, but she wasn't supposed to blurt it out like that."

"She's five. It's hard to show restraint at that age."

"Indeed, but her blurting has thrown off how I was going to approach this." He shifted on his feet, the action suggesting he was nervous, something that left her heart beating in a more-than-curious manner. "I'd like to start off by apologizing for the week that's passed since we last spoke. It took me all that time to summon up enough courage to seek you out. I also wanted to run my plan past a few people to make certain I wasn't completely off the mark, because clearly I made a muddle of things after the ball."

"Who did you debate this plan with?"

"Oh, well, the usual suspects, and then a few that will probably surprise you. Gideon and Adelaide were the first to hear my thoughts, but then I decided I should branch out, because those two actually like me and might not have wanted to hurt my tender gentlemanly feelings if my plan was ridiculous."

Gwendolyn resisted a laugh. "Tender gentlemanly feelings?"

"Quite" was all Walter said to that, his lips curving ever so slightly. "I braved the chance of having those feelings shredded when I then sought out Suzette, Tillie, and even Mrs. Parker."

"That was brave of you."

"Indeed. And before I forget, Mrs. Parker urged me to tell you if my plan fails, and miserably at that—her words, not mine—she'd be delighted if you'd forgive her for her brief lapse of sanity when she terminated your position and return to Newport to take up your role again as her assistant matchmaker. She also said, as an added incentive to have you consider her offer, she'll elevate you to *senior* assistant matchmaker come the New York Season."

"How magnanimous of her."

"That's what she believes as well." Walter leaned closer. "She said you have matchmaking in your blood, and once it's in a person's blood, it's impossible to get rid of."

"That almost makes it sound as if I'm doomed to meddle in matters of the heart forever." Gwendolyn's brow furrowed. "Although, since I've recently been wondering how Gideon Abbott feels about cats, Mrs. Parker may not be off the mark when it comes to the whole matchmaker-in-my-blood business. With that said, however, I truly think my matchmaking days are over."

Walter's eyes twinkled. "Probably a good decision, because Gideon is determined to remain a bachelor for the foreseeable future, so any matchmaking you may have had in mind pertaining to him would definitely ruin your run of successful matches."

"And with the threat of imminent failure, I'll definitely leave my matchmaking days behind me."

"Which is wonderful to learn since . . ." He raked a hand through his hair. "I fear I've allowed the conversation to go completely off the rails and I'm in danger of making a disaster of 'the plan' as the children have been referring to it, or as Oscar occasionally calls it—a last-ditch effort to set matters to rights."

She tilted her head. "You composed this plan *with* the children?"

"They insisted on being involved, probably because Oscar

was worried, if I went about it on my own, I'd make a muck of it."

"I don't imagine you make mucks often," she finally said when she realized Walter was looking at her rather expectantly, as if this was a point in the conversation where she needed to respond.

"True, but you seem to be the exception to muck-ness in general." He drew in a breath and released it. "So . . . with all that out of the way, I should probably just delve right into it and hope for the best."

She refused a smile when he took to looking at the sky before he nodded just once and caught her eye.

"I find you to be more than pleasant," he said.

Her heart began beating a rapid tattoo. "Do you?"

He cleared his throat. "Indeed, although I think that was out of order. I believe everyone thought I should tell you something else first."

"Which was . . . ?" she prompted when he began perusing the sky again.

He abandoned the perusing and caught her eye. "You were right once again, about everything."

She blinked. "Everything?"

He took a single step closer to her. "That will take some time to explain, so before I launch into a long list of matters you were right about, is there somewhere we could go where we won't be interrupted? It'll be easier on me if I can get everything out without losing my train of thought."

"You've never struck me as a gentleman who suffers from losing your thoughts."

He smiled. "Oh, I'm not, generally, but you have the uncanny ability to make me lose my train of thought often."

She couldn't resist returning his smile. "The barn has some hay bales we could use. We'll be uninterrupted because the staff are in the fields with the sheep."

"That sounds perfect."

After taking his arm, Gwendolyn walked with Walter toward the barn, her pulse skittering every which way, especially when he kept glancing at her with something warm in his eyes.

What the warmth meant remained to be seen, but it was lending her a sense of anticipation, which was completely unexpected given she'd convinced herself Walter was not meant to ever be a part of her life.

She steered Walter toward the hay bale she'd recently abandoned, and after they got settled her pulse hitched up another notch when he took hold of her hand.

"Where was I?"

"You were at the part where you mentioned I was right—and apparently about everything."

"Adelaide was the one who suggested I open with that. She had a feeling it would capture your attention."

"And capture it you have, so . . . ?"

"I've made the decision to cut back the hours I spend working, something I would have never done if you'd not opened my eyes and forced me to see what my children really need, which is me. I've been horribly deficient with their care, but you made me see how special they are and how much they need me. That's why I've also decided I don't need to marry to provide them with a mother."

Something heavy settled in her stomach. "I . . . see."

He annoyed her when he smiled. "I'm fairly sure you don't, but given the flicker of flames beginning to ignite in your eyes, allow me to finish this quickly before they burst into a bonfire."

"I don't have flames in my eyes."

"Oh, you do. So, returning to your being right about everything, your advice was exactly right when you encouraged me, along with everyone else, to set the bar higher. I've now decided to set my bar on the highest rung, because I don't want to marry a woman I merely rub along nicely with. I want to marry a woman because I know I'll be able to live an extraordinary life with her, filled with laughter and adventure—but more importantly, love."

Her breath caught in her throat. "I . . . see?"

In a blink of an eye, Walter was suddenly kneeling beside her. "There are many more things I know I'm supposed to say to you if I stick to the plan, but I believe I should simply get to the most important part. You, Gwendolyn Brinley, swept into my life and aggravated me to no end, refusing to take me on to find a match, and then grudgingly taking up my case when I bribed Mrs. Parker to do so. You then decided I needed to marry for love and tried so diligently to find me that love. But you were destined for failure, because . . . no lady you introduced to me could ever compare to you."

Tears stung the back of Gwendolyn's eyes, and she found the simple task of taking a breath difficult. Before she could do more than suck in a much-needed gulp of air when she began to turn light-headed, Walter squeezed her hand.

"You gave me my children back and made me see there are so many possibilities in life I never considered. Do I believe you'll make a wonderful mother to my children? Of course, but I don't want to marry you because of that. I want to marry you because you've brought joy into my life, and you've also allowed me to hope that I can spend my life with a woman I don't merely tolerate, but one I can love madly for the rest of my days."

When Walter suddenly stopped talking, Gwendolyn turned and discovered Ethel, Matilda, Oscar, Samuel, Priscilla, and her mother peering around one of the sheep stalls.

"Are you going to be our mother yet?" Priscilla called.

"I'm not quite finished, darling," Walter called back.

"Did you tell her the part where you've raised the bar, done so because you want her, and she's the highest you've ever dared hope for?" Oscar called.

"I believe I said something similar to that."

"What did you say exactly?" Ethel called next.

"I don't remember, but I'm rather busy at the moment. Feel free to stay, but you're going to have to wait with additional comments or suggestions until I'm done."

"What use would suggestions be if you're done?" Matilda asked.

Walter caught Gwendolyn's eye. "I think I'm losing control of this situation."

She smiled. "Then by all means, get on with it."

"My thoughts exactly." He cleared his throat. "To sum up the plan, I want to marry you, Gwendolyn, not because of the children, although—"

"We want you to marry him," Samuel called. "And Rat and Bert want you to marry him too."

"But before you say yes, ask him to buy you a farm just like this one, with a treehouse," Priscilla called next. "We love the treehouse."

"I will buy Gwendolyn whatever she wants, live with her wherever she wants, never attend another society event if that's what she wants . . . but may I *please* finish?" Walter called.

"Well, then stop talking to us and start talking to Gwendolyn," Ethel said.

Walter blew out a breath and leaned closer to Gwendolyn. "I wasn't intending to say all this with an audience present, nor was I expecting them to critique everything that comes out of my mouth. However, if you answer my next question the way I dearly hope you will, I suppose we'll frequently have an audience."

She felt tears sting her eyes again and managed to send Walter a wobbly smile, one he apparently took as a sign of encouragement, because he returned the smile and gave her hand another squeeze.

"Without further ado, and before Priscilla decides to ask for something else, like her own yacht . . ." Walter leaned closer still. "Gwendolyn Brinley, I love you. I don't know exactly when I stopped finding you to be the most annoying woman I'd ever met and started finding you to be the most fascinating, but . . ."

"He's gone off the rails again," Gwendolyn heard Matilda say, which had her lips twitching.

"I'm going to pretend I didn't hear that," Walter muttered. "As I was saying, I find you fascinating, I'm in love with you, and if you possibly return even a smidgen of that love, please put me out of the misery I've been feeling ever since you left Newport. Tell me you hold me in some affection, or at least find me pleasant enough to where you'll agree to marry me."

A single tear fell from her eye. "I find you more than pleasant."

Walter smiled. "You do?"

"I do. I've been rather miserable as well since I left Newport, because I left a large piece of my heart there, and not simply with the children."

He was on his feet and pulling her up beside him a second later. "Are you saying you're in love with me as well?"

"I am, although know that I found you to be incredibly annoying at first, but then, like you, something changed. It may have been when you almost drowned me at Bailey's Beach, although I didn't realize it at the time." She ignored a tear trailing down her cheek. "And then, after I watched you becoming closer with your children, saw that you had the capacity to love them deeply and unconditionally, I knew I was in trouble, especially when I was supposed to be matching you up with the perfect lady during the Newport Season."

He wiped the tear from her cheek and leaned his forehead against hers, locking their gazes. "But you succeeded with your assignment, because you, my darling Gwendolyn, are my perfect match."

Breathing became difficult once again when Walter cupped her face in his hands, leaned forward, and captured her lips with his own, leaving her more breathless than ever.

"They have to get married now, cuz they're kissing," Priscilla said before she giggled, Samuel joining in a second later.

Walter slowly drew away from Gwendolyn, placed a kiss on her forehead, and then caught her eye. "I have a feeling we're soon to be inundated with best wishes and children longing to be part of this happy occasion. Shall we continue this later when we don't have an audience?"

"Absolutely," Gwendolyn said, right as the children scampered to join them, hugging Gwendolyn tightly and leaving her with the sense that she truly and quite unexpectedly had found her purpose in life—and that purpose was to become a wife and mother to a family she adored, where she'd spend her days basking in Walter's love and watching children, who would now become hers, blossom in that love as well.

Named one of the funniest voices in inspirational romance by *Booklist*, **Jen Turano** is a *USA Today* bestselling author, known for penning quirky historical romances set in the Gilded Age. Her books have earned *Publishers Weekly* and *Booklist* starred reviews, top picks from *Romantic Times*, and praise from *Library Journal*. She's been a finalist twice for the RT Reviewers' Choice Awards and had two of her books listed in the top 100 romances of the past decade from *Booklist*. She and her family live outside of Denver, Colorado. Readers can find her on Facebook, Instagram, and Twitter, and at jenturano.com.

Sign Up for Jen's Newsletter

Keep up to date with Jen's news, book releases, and events by signing up for her email list at jenturano.com.

More from Jen Turano

When Arthur Livingston seeks out the agency to find a missing heiress, Eunice Holbrooke realizes her past has finally caught up with her. In order to avoid Arthur and conceal her real identity, Eunice goes undercover on another case. But will the truth she uncovers set her free or place her—and her heart— in peril's way?

To Disguise the Truth • THE BLEECKER STREET INQUIRY AGENCY

You May Also Like . . .

Daphne Beekman is a mystery writer by day, inquiry agent by night. She happily works behind the scenes, staying away from danger. But when Herman Henderson arrives on the doorstep, desperate for someone to investigate numerous attempts on his life, Daphne finds herself in the thick of a case she's determined to solve—and finds her heart in jeopardy as well.

To Write a Wrong by Jen Turano
THE BLEECKER STREET INQUIRY AGENCY
jenturano.com

Gabriella Goodhue thought she'd put her past as a thief behind her . . . until a woman is unjustly accused. But when Nicholas Quinn, a former friend against whom she holds a grudge, catches Gabriella looking for evidence to exonerate her friend, he insists they join forces. But their feelings for each other are tested when danger follows their every step.

To Steal a Heart by Jen Turano
THE BLEECKER STREET INQUIRY AGENCY
jenturano.com

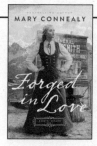

After surviving a brutal stagecoach robbery, Mariah Stover attempts to rebuild her life as she takes over her father's blacksmith business, but the townspeople meet her work with disdain. She is drawn to the new diner owner as he faces similar trials in the town. When danger descends upon them, will they survive to build a life forged in love?

Forged in Love by Mary Connealy
WYOMING SUNRISE #1
maryconnealy.com

BETHANYHOUSE

More from Bethany House

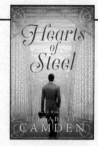

When successful businesswoman Maggie Molinaro offends a corrupt banker, she unwittingly sets off a series of calamities that threaten to destroy her life's work. She teams up with charismatic steel magnate Liam Blackstone, but what begins as a practical alliance soon evolves into a romance between two wounded people determined to beat the odds.

Hearts of Steel by Elizabeth Camden
THE BLACKSTONE LEGACY #3
elizabethcamden.com

Ruth Anniston survived an injury that left her physically scarred. Now, she hides away from curious eyes as a kitchen and dining room supervisor at the El Tovar Hotel. When money begins to disappear from the hotel, she works together with the handsome head chef to save the El Tovar and forge a new path for the future.

A Mark of Grace by Kimberley Woodhouse
SECRETS OF THE CANYON #3
kimberleywoodhouse.com

When Ivy Zimmerman's Mennonite parents are killed in a tragic accident, her way of life is upended. As she grows suspicious that her parents' deaths weren't an accident, she gains courage from her Amish great-grandmother's time in pre-war Germany in 1937. With the inspiration of her great-grandmother, Ivy seeks justice for her parents, her sisters, and herself.

A Brighter Dawn by Leslie Gould
AMISH MEMORIES #1
lesliegould.com

◊ BETHANYHOUSE

More from Bethany House